In a Man's World
Father, Son, Brother, Friend, and Other Roles Men Play

Perry Garfinkel

With a Foreword by
Daniel Goleman,
The New York Times

W9-CDK-227

A MENTOR BOOK

NEW AMERICAN LIBRARY

NEW YORK AND SCARBOROUGH, ONTARIO

Copyright © 1985 by Perry Garfinkel
Foreword copyright © 1985 by New American Library

All rights reserved. A hardcover edition of *In a Man's World* was published
simultaneously by New American Library and The New American Library of
Canada Limited.

Library of Congress Catalog Card Number: 85-63831

Grateful acknowledgment is made to the following for permission to reprint from the
works listed:

The Anatomy of Swearing, copyright © 1967 by Ashley Montagu. Reprinted by permission
of Macmillan Publishing Company.
Big Bad Wolves: Masculinity in the American Film, copyright © 1977 by Joan Mellen.
Reprinted by permission of Random House, Inc.
Diaries 1910-1913, by Franz Kafka, translated by Joseph Kresh, edited by Max Brod,
copyright © 1948, renewed 1975. Reprinted by permission from Shocken Books, Inc.
A Fan's Notes, copyright © 1968 by Frederick Exley. Reprinted by permission of
Random House, Inc.
Fathers, copyright © 1967 by Herbert Gold. Reprinted by permission of Herbert Gold.
Life on the Run, copyright © 1976 by Bill Bradley. Reprinted by permission of Times
Books, a Division of Random House, Inc.
The Male Machine, copyright © 1976 by Mark Feigen Fasteau. Reprinted by permission
of McGraw-Hill, Inc., 1984.
Sherwood Anderson's Memoirs, copyright © 1942, 1969 by Eleanor Anderson. Reprinted
by permission of Harold Ober Associates Inc.
Totem and Taboo: Resemblances Between the Psychic Lives of Savages and Neurotics,
by Sigmund Freud, copyright © 1918 by A.A. Brill, copyright renewed © 1946 by
Gioia B. Bernheim and Edmund R. Brill. Reprinted by permission of E.R. Brill.

SIGNET, SIGNET CLASSIC, MENTOR, ONYX, PLUME, MERIDIAN and NAL BOOKS
are published *in the United States* by New American Library,
1633 Broadway, New York, New York 10019,
in Canada by The New American Library of Canada Limited,
81 Mack Avenue, Scarborough, Ontario M1L 1M8

First Mentor Printing, August, 1986

1 2 3 4 5 6 7 8 9

PRINTED IN THE UNITED STATES OF AMERICA

IN A MAN'S WORLD

PERRY GARFINKEL is a widely published journalist who has worked as an editor at the *Boston Globe Sunday Magazine*, *New Age Journal*, and other publications. His articles on psychology and social trends have appeared in *Psychology Today*, *New York*, *National Geographic*, *Savvy*, and many newspapers. He is the father of Ariana and lives in Oakland, California.

SIGNET and MENTOR Books of Interest

(0451)

To my father, Donald J. Garfinkel

Contents

ACKNOWLEDGMENTS

I would like to thank those people whose efforts helped make this book possible: Sandy Mandel, Ellen Pearlman, Sierra Zephyr, Maria Monroe, and Judy Barule for typing and transcribing at various stages and for their valuable feedback; Suzanne Lipsett of Fairfax, California, for shaping, structuring, "teasing up," and creating an "overarching theme" in the manuscript; Joseph Esposito, for sensitive editorial direction; Daniel Goleman, for his foreword and for bringing this book to the right publisher; Francis Greenburger, of Sanford J. Greenburger Associates, for keeping the faith; and Steve Berman, for planting the seed of the idea in the first place.

I would also like to express my appreciation to those friends who, each in his or her own way, supported me along the way in this effort: Gaeta Bell, Jeremy Berge, Lonny Brown, John Bush, Mirabai Bush, Bill Elliot, Shoshona Frisch, Elliot Kronstein, Michael Levine, Mary McNulty, Richard Nagel, Mudita Ostrin Nisker, Wes Nisker, Peter and Ronni Simon, Mark Weiner, Ed and Arlan Wise, and Cary Wolinsky. And to three ever present women in *my* world: Lillian Garfinkel, Ariana Garfinkel and Iris Gold. And not leastly, to the men who gave of their time and of themselves, whose words and views are represented hereinafter.

Foreword

These are perilous times to be a man in America. There are forces afoot that have changed men's sense of themselves, blurring what once seemed clear-cut modes and models of manhood. John Wayne is dead, and we have not yet picked his stand-in.

In that state of affairs there may lie some new degree of freedom for men willing to seize the opportunity. As the hard-and-fast model of masculinity gives way, it makes room for a greater range of humanness. For as the facades of masculinity crumble we are seeing that behind the strong, rugged silence there lurked thoughts and feelings that men yearned to speak. Men, it seems, have been hemmed in by a web of fears and failings, some self-imposed, others givens of the male condition.

Men are learning to find a new voice. It is not that men have failed to be eloquent—indeed they have dominated the air space around them. Rather, it seems that men—at least American men of this century—have failed to find words for those things that have mattered in their inmost lives. In the world-at-large, men speak freely; in their private lives they fall strangely mute.

Psychologists have known it for years. One of the first to study this silence among men was Sidney Jourard. In the early 1970s, Jourard reported research showing that men, unlike women, simply did not reveal their most intimate fears and hopes, hatreds and joys. They did not disclose their loves and jealousies, envies and infatuations.

Sam Osherson, a clinical psychologist at Harvard Medical School, who specializes in men's problems, calls this "a shroud of silence" that enfolds vast areas of men's experience, their emotional lives in particular.

We have heard about male silence before, in one way or another—often in the complaints of women who feel frustrated and baffled by it. But what is new is research that shows there is a distinct cost—both psychological and medical—to that silence.

For example, James Pennebaker, a psychologist at Southern Methodist University, has done research on the health consequences of confiding. Sharing one's dearest thoughts and most heartfelt concerns, it turns out, is healthy. Dr. Pennebaker has been able to trace a strong relationship between the failure to unburden oneself and poorer health. Troubled silence is a stress in itself; confiding is good for the soul. The bottom line: The male "shroud" of silence is an all-too-apt label.

In the course of writing an article for *The New York Times* on men's problems in the 1980s, I spoke with Dr. Robert E. Gould, a psychiatrist at New York Medical College. One of the key dilemmas for men in this decade, Dr. Gould observed, was their difficulty with emotional intimacy.

"Men are told that in these changing times they should be as emotionally intimate as their wives or lovers," Dr. Gould stated. "But men don't come by intimacy as easily as women do. They've learned since childhood to be adventurous, but not to share their feelings."

Of course men do share much with each other and with the women in their lives. But what we are coming to realize more starkly now is the contour of what men fail to share: their most significant feelings.

"Men's palling around with each other is often a pseudo intimacy," said Dr. Gould.

Shooting the rapids on a raft is not the same as acknowledging how often they are impotent, or don't enjoy sex at all. It's quite difficult for most men to shed their defensive layers and be as intimate as women say they want them to be. A woman may feel hurt when a man doesn't open up to her. But a man just doesn't feel comfortable telling a woman about his weaknesses, or confessing the ambitions he fears he'll never achieve.

The new look at how men hide their feelings is prompted not just by the changing demands of the women in men's lives. There are other forces at work here, both social and economic. Consider some recent statistics, markers of a vast social shift. A nationwide survey done by the University of Michigan found that from 1965 to 1981 there had been a tidal change in the private arrangements of men's lives. Over that period the amount of time women under the age of forty-five spent in housework and child care decreased by 30 percent. Another national survey, by researchers at Ohio State University, found that the amount of time men spent in child care alone had increased since 1967 by 30 percent.

The figures bespeak a significant shift in the interpersonal reality of men in the 1980s, particularly young, married men; they are more involved as fathers—far more in touch and on the scene with their children than were their own fathers back in the 1950s. And as men now look to their past for models of good fathering, many are disappointed. As Joseph Pleck, a director of the Male Role Program at Wellesley College, has observed,

> In the 1950s, the secret was that, emotionally, Dad was not really part of the family. In the 1980s men as fathers are looking back to their childhood for models. Being with their own kids, they suddenly hear a voice they haven't heard in a long time—their father's. They're trying to see the legacy their father left behind them.

Often that legacy is sought when a man enters therapy. What many men discover is that their inability to be open about their feelings with those they care about most has left them isolated. They have wives, children, friends—but keep their true feelings about their lives a secret unto themselves.

The progressive ideals of the "new man" baffle them when it comes to living them out. The sad truth seems to be that most men have not been prepared for what lies in store; the past too often offers too meager emotional resources.

Dr. Osherson, who has conducted research on psychological crises in men's lives as part of a longitudinal study at Harvard Medical School, points out that young men now—particularly those who have become fathers—have a fascination with their own fathers. For many, though, the fascination is tinged with a fear:

> They fear that they will be like their own father, who they may remember as angry, demanding, or isolated. Many men grow up with a loving but distant father who was on the periphery of the family, a hard-working, mysterious, twilight figure. Their wives want them to be more involved as fathers, and they went to, too. But that stirs up conflicts about what it might mean to do so. They fear that they will become like the negative side of their fathers.

The predicament of the male of the 1980s centers on just these issues: Women who no longer will put up with the silent, mysterious man of the past; and a sense of fatherhood as it could be—involved, openly caring, joyous. And with all that, a glimmering among men themselves of what life might be like if only men could break out of the shroud of silence.

Perhaps most important of all for men is that they are able to confront the barriers that have shut them off from each other. For the shroud of silence is at its thickest when men get together with each other. Hearty joviality or philosophical ramblings come easily to men, but too often are weightless, devoid of any sharing of self. Men do not seem to have the capacity to tell each other the real facts of their lives: they shy away from the true talk of fathers and sons, insecurities and sex, fears and career. Instead comes bluster and bluff, women and cars, sports and boasts.

This is not to say that men do not know the occasional soul-bearing talk while driving until dawn across country, or the tear-filled confession to a buddy in some bar of a marriage failed. But these rare moments of openness are lost amid the overwhelming proportion of vapid conversations that men exchange, skirting the surface of troubled waters, but never entering.

And that is a shame.

It is the nature of psychological prisons that one key to freedom is insight into the forces that have shaped their walls. Understanding, in this realm, can itself be liberating. In that sense, Perry Garfinkel has written a manifesto for male liberation. What he sees clearly, and describes ably, is the content and contours of the shroud of silence that too often engulfs men, frustrating the yearning to share freely the thoughts and feelings that truly matter to them with the people about whom they truly care.

In a Man's World offers a well-documented analysis of the psychological and social forces that have made men silent about what matters most to them. What's more, it tells the tale in the words of men themselves—a tale that research on men has begun to corroborate apace. The roots, Garfinkel shows, go back to the most primal relationships men have, as children, with their own fathers, and to the messages—both subtle and overt—they receive as they grow that tell them, in effect, that to seal the heart is to be a man.

The legacy of that lesson from childhood is revealed in the meagerness of what men, once grown, share of their inner lives with others. But although men have been silenced by the early events of their lives, they need not to be bound by them. That, too, is a message of this book, both explicit and implicit. If the great and true wish of men is to live a life more enriched by the rain of feeling, then *In a Man's World* offers an elixir, a dose of insight. And that, after all, is the treatment of choice.

—DANIEL GOLEMAN

Introduction

Man dwells apart, though not alone,
  He walks among his peers unread;
The best of thoughts which he hath known
  For lack of listeners are not said.

                    —Jean Ingelow,
                    Afternoon at the Parsonage

It's no secret that men have had trouble relating to each other ever since Cain killed Abel. The first-born son of Adam slew his younger brother when God chose Abel's offering over his own. Thus was envy born; followed quickly by violence.

The underlying distrust between and among men can be traced as far back as Man's beginnings or as recently as one's own father or son. Men continue to brute or stonewall their way through their male-male interpersonal relationships. They continue to play more and less sophisticated versions of an old sandlot game called King of the Mountain, otherwise known as one-up*man*ship. They continue to try to outperform each other and through their behavior continue to demonstrate— sometimes subtly, sometimes blatantly—the belief that the combative stance is still the order of the day when facing other men.

This dominant competitive theme in men's relationships is clearly the reason that men fear and avoid intimacy with each other. After all, men reason, what fool would open up to one's potential rival? But, finally, what is there to win in what often appears a singularly masculine and a seemingly

1

lifelong competitive event? To win respect? Approval? Acceptance? And from whom? What greater power? What higher authority? And to what end?

All appropriate questions—but all too infrequently asked of men or by men. This competitive credo is accepted as the unspoken, unwritten and mostly unconscious contract that at once binds and divides men.

This book is about power and control, about competition and jealousy, about love, hate, and other repressed, unexpressed emotions. It's about what Freud called "the most primitive organization we know, the association of men." This is a book about how men relate to each other—as fathers and sons, as brothers, as friends, as lovers, as business partners, and tennis partners.

This is, for the most part, unexplored territory on the vastly uncharted continent of masculine psychology—unexplored, and therefore misunderstood. When I told people I was researching and writing a book about how men relate to each other, the usual glib response was, "That's simple; they don't." Of course, it is not that simple. But one fact did become glaringly evident as I began researching and interviewing: It is not a subject about which men often write, think, or talk. And especially, they do not talk about it with each other. It is an issue around which there exists a considerable amount of guilt, hurt, anger, disappointment, and frustration—and it is avoided to such a degree that I began to recognize an element of taboo surrounding it.

Why? What were men hiding? What were they hiding from?

I wrote this book because I was confused about and uncomfortable with my relationships with many men in my life—from my father to men I considered my closest friends. I was unsure why at times I felt alternately at ease and awkward. What I quickly discovered was that I was not alone. While there is a great deal of lip service paid to it, the so-called male bond is one of the great myths of our culture. And we perpetuate it with backslapping and bravado and through the great institutions we have created dedicated to its preservation and proliferation. We speak of our "good ol' boys" networks, we have our sanctum sanctorum, our exclusive men's clubs, and other sacred men-only environments. But what actually goes on between and among us within those contexts—and why?

What man has not found himself at some point in his life in the company of men in such all-male bastions as the Little League, boy's camp, a fraternity, a local gym, the corner bar, the team, or the poker crowd—and felt isolated, alone, and frustrated at not being able to connect with another man on a personal level?

At the same time, almost every man can recall a time among men—celebrating a sports victory, savoring a business coup, reminiscing with college buddies, even fighting wars together—in which a sense of male camaraderie, seemed so strong and so profound that to explain it, even to name it, would diminish its meaning and impact.

Our bonds come through *doing* together; we have not learned about *being* together.

How much men internalize that capacity for and ease with doing together is reflected in the results of an experimental exercise a Boston psychologist told me he observed in his own therapy practice. Working separately with men's and women's groups, he timed how long it took each group of six to form a human pyramid. Inevitably, the men could do it faster than the women. To the psychologist it demonstrated that men are socialized into working teams to a greater degree than women. Implicit in that is some kind of intuitive sense of hierarchy among men. More precisely it is learned behavior, as I show throughout this book.

The underlying questions that insidiously pervade many men's relationships with each other are: "Who's in charge? Who's on top? Who's winning?" The degree to which a man is invested with the answer to that sort of question—the answer to which he invariably hopes is himself—is the measure of the distance he creates between himself and other men.

While the last decade or so has seen the publication of a number of books dealing with issues of men and masculinity—from changing roles, to stages of adult male development, to male sexuality, to women's views of men—I had seen virtually nothing on man-to-man relationships in my fifteen years of writing about psychological trends. Only the scholarly *Men in Groups*, by Canadian anthropologist Lionel Tiger, addressed itself to how men relate to each other. Drawing upon studies of primate behavior and his own speculations about the evolution of society, Tiger (an anthropologist has never been so aptly named) hypothesized that the so-called male bond derives from man's prehistoric background as a member of hunting-and-gathering bands. Tiger admitted from the start that his theory, lacking explicit field research, may be fraught with empirical holes. He confessed: "It was not, and still is not, wholly clear what field research could and should have been done to understand better how males relate to each other and what this means for their communities."

Tiger's omission became my point of departure. Nowhere in *Men in Groups* are there represented the feelings and reflections of the sort of real men that dot the landscapes of our lives—no dentists, no car dealers, no school teachers, no salesmen, no real estate brokers, no artists, no computer programmers.

My style of field research consisted of sitting down and talking with such men. Our discussions were based on, but did not necessarily hold to, a prepared questionnaire that usually served more as a springboard for a dialogue concerning feelings, attitudes, anecdotes and impressions about their relationships with men. (A sample of that questionnaire appears in the Appendix at the end of this book, for those who would like to conduct their own surveys.)

My subjects were chosen in a fashion not unlike the way men establish friendships in their lives—subjectively. I met some through my business associations, others through referrals. Some were men I already knew, men from backgrounds like my own, men from diverse backgrounds, men I considered my friends (though I was brought face to face with the reality of how little I knew *about* the men I claimed to know).

A demographic breakdown of my interviewees would not and should not satisfy the rigorous standards of a data- and strata-conscious sociologist or psychologist. But I did not write this book for them. Anyway, how do you stratify a Hawaiian bellhop, a Maine river guide, and a factory worker from central Massachusetts who had undergone a sex change operation from woman to man? Or a black musician from Brooklyn and the heir to one of the South's great industrial fortunes? How do you put a number on the intensity of emotion in the voice of an Italian construction worker wondering where he "went wrong" with his homosexual son? Or measure the poignance in a man's eye when he talks about the lack of communication between himself and his father?

I interviewed several hundred men, taped and transcribed over a hundred of those interviews to use as primary material. They are men who represent a geographic, cultural, ethnic and economic cross section. But they all have at least one thing in common: They are American men in the 1980s.

I found that race, religion, age, profession, income, or sexual orientation were not so important as the larger group into which all the people I spoke with fit—the family of men. There were men who cautiously expressed themselves on a subject some told me they had never discussed with anyone else—not their wives, girlfriends, lovers, and certainly not other men.

I also found that men's experiences with their fathers, their brothers, friends, and other men are eerily similar. And, too, I found how little of that common experience men communicate to each other. "We are," as one man I interviewed put it, "a fraternity of disenfranchisement."

This book is for anyone who has ever felt disenfranchised from men—whether you are a man or a woman. It is for anyone who has found nearly impenetrable and clearly incomprehensible the bastions of men, and anyone who wants to know what really goes on between and among men.

1

Fathers and Sons: After His Image

And Adam lived an hundred and thirty years, and begat a son in his own likeness, after his image; and called him Seth.

—Genesis 5:1

From the beginning my father always scared me. He's strong and forceful and intimidating. He'd bully us verbally. Me and my brothers all got hit but mostly he'd yell—"GRRR!" You fucking trembled. He called it his "Big Daddy voice." It was scary, believe me, and a lot worse than getting hit. It was constant terror. I always felt scared shitless.

—A thirty-five-year-old chemical engineer from New Hampshire

We—all of us men—are chips off the old blocks. Like father, like son. Like it or not, we are little monkeys mirroring those great apes in our lives, our first and primary male role models—our fathers. From them we learn the good, the bad, and the ugly of how to be men in a man's world.

This initial male-male relationship between father and son is a study in paradoxes and ambivalences, love and hate, bonds and barriers, camaraderie and competition. It contains elements of an age-old struggle for power and control; of deep-seated feelings of inferiority; of emotional inexpressiveness; of reverence, revolt, and ultimately, one hopes, reconciliation.

The father-son relationship is one of great expectations, of belief and trust—and of great disappointment, disbelief, and betrayal. The father is not all he appears at first to be. In fact, as most of the men in my research indicate, the men they wanted to love the most and be closest to—their fathers—were the ones with whom they were least able to feel intimate. The ally is revealed as the rival. The hero has two faces.

Because this first male-male dyad has such a powerful imprinting effect, men look for, come to expect, and—not surprisingly—find traces of patterns established between father and son in their relationships with all men. The father-son relationship is a microcosm and a model of how men relate to each other. As a young man passes through the various masculine training grounds—with brothers, mentors, friends, colleagues, and within all-male bastions—these patterns, and others, are developed and reinforced.

In this developmental process some patterns are altered and transformed. But through the course of this book you will see—as I saw through the course of my interviews and in my reading—that the themes of power, competition, and emotional abandonment are inextricably and unalterably woven into the fabric of men's relationships. The lack of intimacy—or at least the inability to express in words one's close feelings for another man—and the fear of betrayal are also in evidence.

This rather dreary social landscape does not, of course, describe all interactions among all men. Many of my interviewees, my friends, and writers I encountered in my research have had mutually supportive relationships with their fathers and other men in their lives. But it would not be a gross generalization to deduce from this research that for the most part many barriers exist between men—and the building of those barriers begins at home.

It would appear, then, that I paint a bleak picture of man-to-man relationships. For the patterns of behavior I describe here start to be engraved at an early age in a man's life, and have been in evidence since the early ages of mankind. Are fathers and sons meant to be eternal antagonists? Are all men forever to face off in what by now seems

to be a naturally combative stance? Is it indeed realistic to
think that men could—or even should—turn against such a
strong tide? Anyone who is a man in the 1980s or who is
watching men in the 1980s, can bear witness to the fact that
even now some men—fathers, sons, brothers, friends,
colleagues—are breaking down the walls of these timeless
traditions. But, it is also clear that these pathbreakers—or,
more accurately, these barrier-razers—are still in the minority.

For most men life is a long search for reunion with their
lost fathers. Ask Telemachus, whose hunt for his father Ulys-
ses defines what we now call the Homeric Odyssey. Ask
Luke Skywalker, who fought through three episodes of *Star
Wars* to avenge his father's death only to discover that his
arch enemy, Darth Vader, was his father.

One of the most important traditions, pervasive throughout
cultures and around the world, is that of the rites of passage.
Entry into clubs, teams, and manhood itself is marked by
some test of strength and endurance. A man does not simply
take his place among men—he must *earn* it. Because of the
value placed on ritual, men tend to view various stages,
episodes, and events in their lives as rites of passage. For
instance writing this book became a rite of passage for me.

Similarly, I have come to see the stages that men in our
society go through with their fathers as rites of passages—
rites as clearly defined as a Navajo dream fast or a Bar
Mitzvah. In our culture, a son must pass through these phases
of his relationship with his father in order to attain manhood:
reverence, revolt, and reconciliation. All along the way, as I
will show, he picks up vital clues and tools that he will use in
his relationships with the men he meets throughout his life.

REVERENCE

In the first year of his life the infant boy distinguishes between his two parents: one has a softer voice, is always

associated with food, and is almost always present; the other is louder, larger, rarely around at feeding time, or, for that matter, the greater part of the day. Gradually, by a process psychologists call sex-role identification, the boy begins to comprehend: "I'm a male—like my Daddy. When I grow up I'll be a man—just like him."

During those first impressionable years of life, the boy's father is manhood personified. No matter what the father's personal characteristics, the child accepts them and incorporates them into his definition of a man. All other men—in the beginning, at least—are secondary figures compared with this central and primary male role-modeling influence. Just how strong an influence the father is becomes more and more clear the older the son gets. Whether they work to match that model or fight to break free of it, all boys live with the outline of that image in front of them, as if it were a road map to manhood. Even in cases where fathers die or withdraw very early from their sons' lives, those sons feel the stamp of their fathers' personal styles, and struggle either to copy, perfect, and improve on it—or to forever free themselves of it.

Ambiguously, as reverence grows so do hatred and fear; acknowledging the father's centrality is acknowledging his power to dominate. A boy's fear of his father, Freud suggested, has foundations in the Oedipus complex, which boys experience between the ages of about two and five. The complex grows out of the boy's love for his mother and his simultaneous identification with his father. As the child's sexual urges heighten he begins to see his mother as the object of those urges, and he also sees his father as a sexual rival and the object of jealous envy. This creates a new danger for the boy. If he persists in feeling sexually attracted to his mother, he fears being physically harmed in retaliation by his father. Specifically, he fears that his father will cut off his penis, a fear Freud termed "castration anxiety":

> The relation of a boy to his father is, as we say, an "ambivalent" one. In addition to the hate which seeks to get rid of the

father as a rival, a measure of tenderness for him is also
habitually present. The two attitudes of mind combine to
produce identification with the father; the boy wants to be in
his father's place because he admires him and wants to be like
him, and also because he wants to put him out of the way.

So, in a tangle of love and hatred, reverence and fear, the
groundwork is laid, and in a young child's eyes the father
looms larger than life.

THE HERO

The respect born of fear only increases the father's stature.
To a young boy, the father is a giant from whose shoulders
you can see forever. He is all-knowing and all-powerful
and—though he may not realize it himself—one word, one
glance can make a moment to a little boy whose eye is always
glued to his father. There is an exhilaration in a boy's identification with his father. Sons bask under such praises and
phrases as "chip off the old block" and "like father, like
son"—but only if those fathers are positive, present, and
involved role models. Studies of fathers' influence on sons
show that positive identification occurs only where fathers
show sons love and affection.

When they are there to fulfill the role, fathers are not just
men to their sons—they are supermen. In the language of
Freud, fathers are identified with the superego: law, restraint,
industry, severity, aloofness, control and power—qualities
that command awe, respect, and emulation from a son. A
forty-two-year-old business consultant living in New York
told me:

When I was born in 1940, my father was away at war. He
came back a hero, my hero. I remember him wearing tan
summer khakis. He was goddamn impressive. He was
stunning—a striking, handsome man. I was awestruck by
him. Just from the way he held himself you could tell he was

the man with the power. He was the boss, there was no doubt about it. He called all the shots—at work and at home. The house was geared to his schedule, to his temperament, to his wishes—and I wanted to be just like him.

A twenty-eight-year-old Richmond, California, man directly correlated an idyllic picture of his father, the hero, with a sense of power and control:

> I used to go out sailing with him and he would take the tiller. He was very much at home on the water. The boat would be doing all these freaky things and he would be in total control. He'd take pleasure out of setting the thing right. I think he felt at home with me out there. During those times I felt a great deal of closeness to him. Now I notice I feel close with men when we're working on a project together, in a team situation, like I used to feel when I was helping my father on the water.

To be next to his father was to be next to that power and control. To be identified as a father's son—the son of an omnipotent demigod—is to claim some of that power for oneself. And all a son wants at this stage is to be beside his idol. In his autobiographical novel *Fathers*, Herbert Gold captured as few writers have the love, pride, and euphoria at being identified as a father's son:

> Dad tiptoed into my room and rested his hand upon my cheek. I flew straight up out of my dream. . . . He lifted a finger to his mouth. *Shh.* He was wearing pants and an undershirt, needed a shave, grinned and winked at me. He was whispering. "Son, you want to do something?" I was dressed and washed with the speed of one of his best kleptomaniacs. . . . Yes, I wanted to do something. What we did on these occasions of doing something together was to go to the Russian Bath on Sunday morning, before the rest of the family mobilized for breakfast, sneaking down the driveway in the old Peerless before my cousins or brothers could whine about being left out, conspiring against mother and babies, just the two of us men. . . . What a joy to exclude women—my mother and cousins—from the naked and sweating world of the baths! Among the nations of men finally at age 11, I was

my father's son, his eldest, lounging at my ease with a maze
of room devoted to skin pleasure, lung relish, intense getting-
out-the-kinks and dozing and hilarity on rusty chairs. "Looks
just like you, Sam!" "Why shouldn't he? But he'll be taller—
eats American food." And my father, more muscular than the
others, with thick hocks and thick control beneath the pink
salt-bruised flesh, moved in the center of my vision. The
steam room was the sanctum sanctorum. . . . Skinny and
prideful I moved underfoot in the steam room like a drenched
rat, learning the ways of men. . . . In my child's eyes they
were very much alike—swollen sex, hanging gourds, purplish
veins, creased bellies—and to them I was different: a child.
"Sam's kid! Lookit the kid, little Sam, he's learning the
steam room! Sam Gold's boy! You making out, kid, with all
you got in that pinkie of yours?"

Learning the steam room, learning the ways of men, Gold
understood even at that tender age, was afforded by the
power of his father.

To the boy, the father embodies all a man is and could be.
Sociologist Leonard Benson has written:

Boys identify with father not because he is an adult but
because he is a man. They seek rapport with the mature man.
They turn to father because they have been conditioned to
want a validation of their masculinity. The typical father-son
relationship follows a pattern found in relationships between
persons of unequal skills, as between teacher and student or
master and apprentice. Father participates in activities involving motor skills with his son. He serves as an exacting and
insistent coach, acting out masculine patterns of aggressiveness. He drills his son continually, repeatedly calling attention
to his mistakes. Learning male skills involves preparation for
bigger and more serious battles to come. Fathers crack down
on their sons for failure to show signs of progress toward
self-sufficiency.

In a more poetic style this Kwakiutl Indian chant expresses
Benson's meaning:

When I am a man, then shall I be a hunter.
When I am a man, then shall I be a harpoonist.

When I am a man, then shall I be a canoe-builder.
When I am a man, then shall I be a carpenter.
When I am a man, then shall I be an artisan.
Oh father! Ya ha ha ha.

Across cultures and across generations fathers train sons to *do*, to define themselves and to measure their power through the performance of skills. Men are, in Benson's words, "instrumental" while women are "expressive." Girls are "person-centered"; boys are "thing-centered." In a cross-cultural survey Benson cited, fathers were classified as instrumental in forty-eight societies and expressive in eight. Sons work hard to develop skills, to be successful at what they *do*, to live up to their fathers' expectations. It is a lifelong struggle for respect from the man who, in the son's eyes, represents all men. What he slowly learns, though, is that he can never live up to his father's expectations, never totally win that respect, approval, and acceptance. He never seems to be able to *do* whatever it is as well as his father, the fact of which the father does not hesitate to remind his son. In this way, at the hands of his father, a son develops a sense of inferiority, of powerlessness, of not quite measuring up to or doing as much as this model male. This sense of inferiority remains as a shadow upon his relationship with other men. Later I will show how this inferiority complex remains with the son, becoming compounded and more complicated as he interacts with the other men in his life.

For the father, on the other hand, playing the role of the greatest, biggest, best, and sometimes only man in the world is, while certainly an ego trip, often too large a responsibility to bear. With the obligations of work pressing on them, as well as their own conditioning as sons, fathers soon withdraw emotionally and physically from their sons as models and teachers. The sense of abandonment and betrayal by such a father haunts a son and it influences what he comes to expect from all men. A poignant example of abandonment was offered in an interview with James, a thirty-nine-year-old internist at a San Francisco hospital:

I was three, maybe four. This moment—you have to understand how profoundly important this is to me—is the furthest
back I go, my first memory, when I sort of came up from
underwater and took my first breath; when it all crystallized
for the first time: "Here I am, this is me, this is who I am." I
must have done something wrong because my father was
yelling at me and then he said I had to stay in the house while
he and my mother went out. So he locked me in the house
alone and drove away with my mother who, I recall, wasn't
too happy about it but couldn't stop my father. I remember
the moment so clearly—the car, their faces, what they were
wearing and how I felt. I was crying desperately. I was totally
alone—abandoned. And I blamed—still blame—my father for
deserting me. I'll tell you, sometimes I want to go to him and
tell him what a shit he was or just beat him up really bad—but
I don't. And, when I think of it, I don't trust men now
because I never trusted my father after that.

While other men report less traumatic and dramatic demonstrations of father desertion, the loss seems predictable and
the impact on their lives is no less. The pattern, as exempli-
fied by James, is a setup for a letdown. Putting the hero on a
power pedestal only means that the fall will be that much
longer when he disappoints or disappears. Like the child who
learns not to put his hand in the fire after he gets burned,
boys learn the pain of male abandonment from their hero-
fathers. Afterward, they enter relationships with other men
with great trepidation and restraint. No one wants to get
burned twice.

THE OUTSIDER

The aloofness of the hero-father is a universally familiar
notion, woven into the basic organization of societies as
different as Freud's own Jewish upper middle class and the
preliterate community of the Trobriand Islanders. For example, *tomakava* is the name given to fathers in the Trobriand

Islands, in the Velanesian chain east of New Guinea. The word is translated as "stranger" or "outsider." Anthropologist Bronislaw Malinowski wrote about this matrilineal society in *The Father in Primitive Psychology*, first published in 1927. The natives are "quite ignorant of the man's share in the begetting of children," he discovered. These natives "affirm without doubt that the child is of the same substance as its mother, and that between the father and the child there is no bond whatever." In studying this primitive culture whose structure and social order revolve around this obviously biologically unsound notion, Malinowski learned that even though they ascribed no procreative purpose whatever to the man, Trobrianders still regarded the father as "indispensable socially . . . Paternity, unknown in the biological meaning so familiar to us, is yet maintained by a social dogma which declares: 'Every family must have a father; a woman must marry before she may have children; there must be a male to every household.' "

Even in this strong mother-oriented society and without any biological imperative, the Trobrianders understood the importance of the social role of the father in the family.

Why, I had wondered as I read through this material, has it taken our so-called "sophisticated" society—so much beyond primitivism—so long to come to this same understanding? On the same day I had also read the following by John Munder Ross in the *International Journal of Psycho-Analysis (1979):* "Until recently, the father has been a forgotten parent in the psychoanalytic and psychological literature."

One other cultural quirk belies the island people's belief system. Malinowski writes: "Not only is it a household dogma, so to speak, that a child never resembles its mother, any of its brothers or sisters, or any of its maternal kinsmen, but it is extremely bad form and a great offense to hint at any such similarity. To resemble one's father, on the other hand, is a natural, right, and proper thing for a man or woman to do." On this one important point, the matrilineal bond is overshadowed for, Malinowski notes, ''physical resemblance is a very strong emotional tie between two people.''

It was Malinowski's conclusion and conviction that ''the ignorance of paternity is an original feature of primitive psychology, and that in all speculation about the origins of marriage and the evolution of sexual customs we must bear in mind this fundamental ignorance.''

It may sound like an apology or an excuse for the way fathers have—or have not—been with their children. But a form of this ''fundamental ignorance'' echoed through dozens of talks with men who alluded to fathers they never got to know.

''All I wanted to do was be close to the guy but he was aloof, always off over there where I couldn't reach him,'' I was told many times in various words, but always with the same lament in the voice.

'' 'Who are you, Dad?' That was what I always really wanted to ask him,'' one man succinctly put it all. The hero was also a stranger.

In our highly civilized, and strongly patriarchal society, many men might still call their fathers strangers. For them the stranger in the father overwhelms the hero that the boy wishes to see there. The image of the father as an incommunicative and unreachable stranger or outsider recurred throughout my interviews, as it does throughout literature. In his *Memoirs* Sherwood Anderson sketched his father:

> I didn't know what was up and had the queer feeling I was with a stranger. I don't know now whether my father intended it so. I don't think he did. . . . We were there at the edge of the pond. We had come in silence. It was still raining hard and there were flashes of lightning followed by thunder. We were on a grassy bank at the pond's edge, when my father spoke, and in the darkness and rain his voice sounded strange. It was the only time during the evening that he did speak to me. ''Take off your clothes,'' he said and, still filled with wonder, I began to undress. There was a flash of lightning and I saw that he was already naked. And so naked we went

into the pond. He did not speak or explain. Taking my hand he led me down to the pond's edge and pulled me in. It may be that I was too frightened, too full of a feeling of strangeness to speak. . . . Before that night my father had never seemed to pay any attention to me.

It is a powerful image. Shrouded in darkness and silence, our fathers lead us all to the pond of manhood. And their aloofness and silence become their loudest message to us.

Fathers who absent themselves psychologically leave permanent scars on their sons. Those who absent themselves physically as well have considerable effect on the social behavior of their sons. I pondered a pile of sociological surveys that recounted the impact of father absence on sons. Boys whose fathers were absent for various lengths of time from birth to adolescence were less assertive, more dependent, more submissive, and less secure in their masculinity than boys whose fathers were present. Further, recreational directors rated nine- to twelve-year-olds whose fathers had been absent since their fourth year and found them to be more dependent on their peers, less aggressive, and less likely to engage in physical contact games than boys with fathers present. Ten- to thirteen-year-old boys without fathers scored lower on academic tests than classmates with fathers. Boys without fathers had difficulties in self-control. One psychologist speculated that father absence interferes with a boy's development of trust in other people. A team of psychologists observed that rebelliousness against and a rejection of male authority figures were characteristic among father-absent adolescent boys. And sociologist Albert K. Cohen, in *Delinquent Boys: The Culture of the Gang*, defines gang cultures as predominantly male, blaming juvenile delinquency among boys basically on the absence of a male figure in a youngster's life.

Most of these studies were based on data collected from families of military men, of men whose work took them away for long stretches of time, or of men who had truly abandoned their families. But I also found a study that made me realize even sons of so-called present fathers may suffer the same sociological symptoms as father-absent boys. In this study a group of 300 seventh- and eighth-grade boys were asked to keep a careful record of the time they spent alone with their fathers over a two-week period. (Here, I equated time "spent alone" with what I would call quality time—time in which father and son have an opportunity to interact one to one, to feel each other's energies without interference from other family members, to get to know each other and—especially for the father—to make his presence known and to show he cared.) The results: the average time each boy spent alone with his father was seven and a half minutes each week! Thus, as suggested earlier, even father-present boys are father-absent.

Over and over again in literature, research reports, and my own interviews, the hero comes close, then dissolves and disappears. Men come to expect that their male heros—like their first hero—will be elusive, unapproachable, unattainable. But their greatest frustration comes from striving to know the hero who remains the outsider. Some men spend their whole lives searching to fill the void created by their fathers' withdrawal. And, sadly, they get caught in and help create a vicious circle. For while they vainly seek intimacy and warmth from their fathers, they are also learning behaviors from their primary male role models: They quickly learn to return the aloofness they get. They withhold emotions their fathers withheld from them. Through such cycles the barriers between men are perpetuated from one generation to the next, from father to son and from man to man.

John, a twenty-nine-year-old speech therapist from western Massachusetts, strove to evoke an honest and open response from his withdrawn father for most of his years. But the difficulty intensified after John graduated from high school:

> I often sensed something was going on with him but he wouldn't say what it was. I remember going to him as a kid and asking, "Are you mad at me?" I assumed he was pissed off at a certain aspect of me but he wouldn't come across with

it; that's his pattern. I thought I was happy as a kid, and yet there was also always this feeling of insecurity. Yet, I'd have to suppress whatever those feelings were. There was no way to vent them at home, so I put on a front. I wasn't able to confide in him. Once—only once—did I go to him. During this whole time at least my mother would put her cards on the table. She was upset and showed it. With him I felt victimized. I felt he still wasn't coming across and I found I was really hating him for that. That was his ultimate weapon: the turn-off. We'd have arguments that got just to the edge of physical violence—though there was never a question that we'd actually get physical with each other. And even if it did I probably wouldn't have reacted. We'd have fights and I'd say "Fuck you" and leave and feel great about not having to talk to him or deal with him. Later, after I got married and sort of righted myself in his eyes, I remember feeling cheated by my father, cheated of intimacy.

John's father communicated by his silence. His judgments were delivered silently, or indirectly, leaving a lot of room for confusion in a boy's mind. How was John to interpret such silence? That his father had no feelings for him? Or, worse, that the feelings were so awful he could not speak them? That he wasn't worth the time or trouble? Or that his father was an empty man? Much later John realized how he learned to suppress emotions from his father, and that his sense of insecurity was rooted in that confusing silence.

Kim, a thirty-one-year-old graduate school dropout who sells cordwood, described the phantom father in his life:

When I think of my father I see him in a blue woolen winter coat buttoned up, and he has one of those cardboard accordian-style briefcases under his arm, hunched over slightly with a serious inexpressive empty look on his face, standing at the bus stop.

That image of a sullen, silent man locked up in a dark woolen coat hung like a cloud over Kim's life. Similar images appeared throughout the interviews. For these men, fathers are dark and distant strangers who often seem to play a secondary role in their sons' emotional development.

"To be sure," wrote psychiatrist John Munder Ross, "the father is not so constant a presence as mother, but rather he emerges 'off there,' a 'twilight figure' who takes shape mostly in the morning and evening, who is exposed to daylight over weekends and holidays, who may loom mysteriously as a midnight marauder or ogre."

Yet paradoxically, while the father often appears to take a back seat or a shadowy secondary position in the parenting process, he serves as the quintessence of masculinity for the son. The lessons of the man-father are indelibly imprinted on the boy-child. If, as Wordsworth wrote in "My Heart Leaps Up," "the child is father to the man," then it is also true that the father is man to the child. But who is this man and how do we get close to him?

Writers through the ages have expressed an inability to know and communicate with their fathers. John Updike, for example, wrote: "I wanted to speak, to say how I needed him and to beg him not to leave me, but there were no words, no form of words available in the tradition." James Baldwin said: "I have written both too much and too little about this man, whom I did not understand til he was past understanding." And Edmund Wilson stated: "I have always assumed through my college days that my father was as reactionary as I was advanced, and I did not dare discuss my ideas with him; but I had failed, as I realized later, to understand his real point of view."

The conflict between who the father appears to be and who he really is plagues a boy trying to learn how to be a man. Not only does he receive mixed messages, but he suffers supreme disappointment and frustration in investing so much hope and trust—so much love and pride—in a hero who seems, through his silence, to be rejecting the boy.

BECOMING A FATHER

During a workshop I attended at a conference on men and masculinity in northern New Jersey, a group of fifteen men sat in a circle and were asked to complete the sentence, "When I think of my father I feel. . . ." These were some of the responses:

> "Hurt, rejected, half a man."
>
> "A strange distance and confusion about his actual role in my life and a fear that somehow or other I have learned to react in ways he reacts, and I feel trapped by it or him."
>
> "I had such a weak experience with my father that I would like to compensate for it by being good to my children and I've taken that as the most important mission in my life."
>
> "I feel this incredible yearning for love, and such sadness that he's dying. Sometimes I feel very, very empty, the way I'm going to feel alone in the world after he dies."
>
> "Separate, angry, rejected, scared that he'd going to die before I get what I want from him. On rare occasions I feel love."

The men were asked to complete another sentence, "If my father were here I'd say to him. . . ."

> "I'd say what I said the last time I saw him: 'All I ever wanted was to be close to you.' But I fear I'd get the same response."
>
> "I don't know what I'd say to him. I've never been able to approach him and I don't think I could start now."
>
> "I'd say, 'Old man, why don't you cross the street. Why don't you take a risk?' "
>
> " 'Dad, why don't you come out? You seem so bottled up inside and I get hurt by that. I can't reach you and it's frustrating.' "

" 'Dad, I just want to say I love you,' " the last man said crying.

Why is it so difficult for fathers and sons to exchange those three words—words that stick like cement in the throat. If it were to come freely from the heart of the father it would most likely be returned in kind. So, given the fullness of the boy's potential love, what motivates a father's withdrawal from his son?

From the beginning, fatherhood is an awkward role to play. Biology forces men, taught from childhood to be active, into an unfamiliar and uncomfortable, even embarrassing passivity. After planting the seed they take a back seat in the process, watching their wives balloon up. Pregnancy is a woman's journey, a mystery of creation men can never fathom. Men hear about the effects of pregnancy—the nausea, back pains, altered chemistry, altered physiology, altered moods— and they can commiserate, but never experience them. From the start of the process, they feel one step removed. For men—who learn to relate by *doing*, not being or feeling—the predicament is frustrating. "Come, feel your baby," says your wife, and you gently place your hand on her bulging belly. And though you can feel it (him?) move, it remains a theory, a concept, not an actuality. By the time the baby is born the mother has already established a strong relationship with the child based on a physical connection of the last nine months. For the next nine months the father struggles to catch up. His gestation period, when he physically and psychologically adjusts to parenthood, begins the day the baby is born.

For almost nine months after my child was born I was as touchy, moody, and physically depleted as my wife had been during pregnancy. Unknowingly I was participating, I learned later, in a variation of the practice know as *couvade*, a ritual observed throughout ancient and recent times by many cultures and societies to give men some sense of participation in the birth process. The couvade ritual may include taking to bed, simulating labor pains, and symbolically enacting the birth of a child. In the tropical forest cultures of South America, the father of a newborn follows a rigorous diet for a week or so after the birth. Couvade was formerly common in the cultures of the Amazon Basin, Corsica, among various societies of Asia, and, as recently as the early part of this century, among the Basques of France and Spain. Some anthropologists claim that the ceremony is meant to demonstrate the father's sympathy for the pain the mother withstands. They believe the custom actually lightens the pain for the mother. Others interpret the practice as an observance of the mystical relation between the father and the newborn. Some less spiritual psychologists might view couvade as a futile attempt by men to feel as though they too were participating in the birth process. Or, like a child who tries to steal the limelight by showing off, men are trying to rob women of the one power women will always have over men: the power to create life. Sex-role psychologist Joseph Pleck commented on the condition that might explain such a motivation:

> It has been a recurring problem in all cultures to create a social role for men that will give them the social valuation and importance that childbearing gives to women. What is intriguing in this paradox is that while so many different behaviors have been seen as a compensation for or a consequence of men's envy of women's capacity to give birth, there has been so little consideration and encouragement of the most obvious and pro-social way for men to deal with this presumed envy—by taking more direct care of their children.

In his new role as father, the man remains somewhat in the background from the start. Frequently—though he may never have greater expectations—he serves as a general support system for the mother and child, and as an occasional relief parent. In the tradition within which men in our culture are trained—with occasional exceptions—men take the position of provider and supporter. They create the frame and the context for the picture; and mothers, women and children are the content, the picture in the frame. This conclusion was brought home for me on a personal level as I leafed through a family album not long ago. In it I found photographs of my mother, my sister, and myself in the mountains, by lakes, at beaches, on back porches and front steps. I found only three photos in the whole album of my father, and only one of me pictured alone with him. My father, like most fathers, was always taking the pictures—telling us where to stand, when to smile. His sincere desire to have a ''picture for posterity'' effectively took him outside the family circle. And it left me to rely on vague fleeting memories to outline my phantom father.

We look into the mirror that our fathers could be, but the reflection is foggy. I found this especially ironic—and pathetic— in light of why many fathers say they want sons in the first place: as a mirror of themselves. It may sound egotistical and, some may add, sexist, but ask a man for the truth and he will likely sound like Charlie, who had himself become the father of a boy five weeks before I talked with him:

> Sure I wanted a boy. Why? Part of it was ego, a matter of keeping the family blood flowing. A lot of the stuff I want to teach, I want to teach to a boy. It's not that I couldn't teach a girl, it's just that a boy. . . . A lot of feelings I have toward a child have to do with passing on experience. I've read a little about ancestor worship; you go back and you go back and you go back until finally you're back at God. But—and I've never really crystallized this before in my mind—but the link is between men. The passer is male. When my wife was pregnant I prayed, ''God, embody yourself in my child, come forth in the kid.'' And part of wanting a male child was the feeling that God incarnates in the role of a teacher most often as a male. I don't want to sound sexist but it's just some kind of feeling that men have this special role to fill.

It *did* sound sexist, but that was his point. The lineage comes through the male, he was saying. The passing of experience, wisdom, knowledge, and skills was part of a tradition singularly male. I could hear feminists around the world recoiling with indignation and yet there was a part of me that agreed with Charlie. The lesson of the importance of the lineage of men begins with the father.

CIRCUMCISION

Once the father has his son, it is no exaggeration to say that his first act is to put his mark on the boy, physically and permanently. The act of cutting off the penis is ritualized in cultures all over the world in the performance of circumcision, the surgical removal of the foreskin. In my overview of the father-son relationship, circumcision is the necessary endurance test that is part of this first rite of passage into manhood. And it seems appropriate that the man we revere is the man we must first learn to fear—that our protector-hero is the enemy-outsider against whom we have to protect ourselves.

History's first circumcision was performed on Abraham and all the males in Abraham's house. Later the covenant of circumcision was established with Abraham's son Isaac as a symbolic demonstration of obeisance to God the Father. The degree to which later generations in our own culture have taken over the legacy is illustrated by the fact that, according to a *New York Times* report, male circumcision in 1976 was the most common surgical procedure in the United States. Over the years, anthropologists, medical scientists, and psychoanalysts have offered a variety of reasons for the continued widespread use of an operation for which the American Pediatric Society in 1975 concluded "there are no valid medical indications." Hygienic explanations do not hold up. Circumcision does not control what was termed "masturbatory insanity," one of the original rationales (which was developed ironically long after the operation was already in wide practice). Nor does it prevent cancer, a theory put forward in the 1930s. It does not increase or effect sexual sensitivity. And aesthetic preferences remain, as always, in the eye of the beholder.

Some suggest that circumcision represents a boy's willingness to bow to the power of his father, though in no culture do boys circumcise themselves or even ask to be circumcised. In most societies boys are forcibly subjected to the ceremony when they are too young to understand consciously the meaning of father-power or masculinity. No matter what the age of the boy at circumcision, from infancy to adolescence, the operation marks his first rite of passage into manhood, and a painful one at that. In one of the most explicit examples of this, boys in the Transkei region of South Africa stand up immediately after the circumcision is performed, beat their chests and shout in their tribal language, "I am a man!"

Though pediatricians may argue the point, the explanation that circumcision in our culture is a reenactment of a primitive ritual is propounded convincingly by psychologist Karen Ericksen Paige and her husband Jeffrey Paige. After a four-year world-wide study of 114 tribal societies to understand the functions of circumcision, the Paiges found that the 23 cultures that practice the genital surgery share a common political structure: "They are composed of what we call strong fraternal-interest groups, related males who are united to pursue common political objectives." In these cultures, they continued:

> The common pattern is for a village elder or chief to command a reluctant father to have his son circumcised. Evidence like this persuaded us that male circumcisions are a public demonstration by fathers to elder kinsmen of their loyalty to the fraternal-interest group. The greatest sign of loyalty is to entrust one's son's reproductive ability to someone else, and it is precisely because the ritual involves this risk that it is such a powerful emotional symbol.

Nigerian fathers laugh nervously during the ceremony, telling the circumciser: "Easy, easy, many women will weep if you err."

Research shows that babies and little boys do not quickly forget the attack on the source of their masculine power. Circumcised baby boys show greater increases in heart rate in response to sounds than do girls and uncircumcised boys. After circumcision, another study showed, male babies change their sleep patterns, staying awake for longer periods of time than they did before the operation. Circumcised male babies cry more and sleep less than females and are harder to console when they get irritable.

Whether or not the circumcision is performed by the father, a son justifiably associates the act with his father, who, in fact, was responsible for authorizing it as a show of his "loyalty to the fraternal-interest group"—be it the body of religious elders, the body of medical elders, or the body of family elders, *all* bodies of men.

"I think it was a kind of commitment my father wanted from me," said a circumcised man who knew nothing about Freud or covenants or rituals or research. "I think it changed my attitude toward authority. *They can get me.* I now feel cowed by what happened to me. And I think any aggression I feel is a kind of reaction or compensation for it."

This son, and all others, learned that the passage to manhood will be a painful test of his power. And he realizes, first subconsciously and then later much more consciously, that the man responsible is his father. This first wound inflicted by the father runs deep in the son. But, even in this, "ambivalence" pervades the father-son experience; for the son has two reactions to being made to withstand the test. He hates his father for being made to suffer the humiliation and pain of the attack, but he also loves his father and is indebted to him for initiating him into the fraternity of men to which his father belongs. This ambivalence—of love and hate, of gratitude and revenge—ripples through the interactions of fathers and sons throughout their lives. It resonates in this letter from Franz Kafka to his father:

> For me you took on the enigmatic quality that all tyrants have whose rights are based on their person and not on reason. I was, after all, weighed down by your mere physical presence. There I was, skinny, weakly, slight; you, strong, tall, broad. I felt a miserable specimen, and what's more, not only in your eyes but in the eyes of the whole world, for you were for me the measure of all things. You were . . . completely tied to the business, scarcely able to be with me once a day, and therefore made all the more profound an impression on me,

never really leveling out into the flatness of habit. What was always incomprehensible to me was your total lack of feeling for the suffering and shame you could inflict on me with your words and judgments. It was as though you had no notion of your power. How terrible for me was, for instance, that: "I'll tear you apart like a fish." It was also terrible when you ran around the table, shouting, grabbing at one, obviously not really trying to grab, yet pretending to, and Mother (in the end) had to rescue one, as it seemed. Once again one had, so it seemed to the child, remained alive through your mercy and bore one's life hence forth as an undeserved gift from you.

To such a sensibility, circumcision is very clearly just one of a series of physical humiliations that endlessly reasserts and reinforces the father's power over the son.

WHAT FATHERS TEACH THEIR SONS

Through the considerable ambivalences and mixed messages, fathers do pass along to their sons a number of important lessons on how to exist in a man's world. Many such lessons are transmitted nonverbally, and it is clear that sons pick them up simply by imitating their fathers' behaviors. First and foremost, these lessons have to do with power.

By the time children reach kindergarten, teachers are observing a strong relationship between a boy's sense of masculinity and the degree to which he perceives his father as making family decisions. Third- and fourth-grade boys who show more so-called "feminine" traits reported having fathers who take a relatively passive role in setting limits on the boys. By adolescence, according to another study, boys whose fathers set limits scored higher on masculinity interest tests than boys whose fathers did not set limits. And male college students who described themselves as strongly masculine on adjective checklists rated their fathers as high on limit setting and competence.

Boys learn that limit setting and decision making are two demonstrations of power and control. Achievement and accomplishment, which can be seen as by-products of power and control, are two other demonstrations of masculinity a boy learns from his father. If a father is a high achiever, chances are good the son will be too. One study of seventh- and eighth-grade males showed that sons of men who held jobs demanding entrepreneurial responsibility scored much higher on achievement motivation tests than boys whose fathers had no such responsibility at work. Fathers of high-achieving boys are often competent men willing to take a back seat while their sons are performing—"beckoning from ahead rather than pushing from behind," as one researcher put it. This quality presumably also helps a boy develop a sense of self-reliance.

In short, sons learn about power from their fathers by example—and they learn that fathers have it but sons do not. This is demonstrated time and again from the beginning of the relationship. Dad is bigger and stronger. He controls the flow of money and Mom. The house schedule revolves around his comings and goings (mostly his goings). He knows everything and there is no way to argue with him, no way to compete, no way to keep up, no way to *do* as well as he does.

As I interviewed more and more men I began to see that most of us spend lifetimes trying to make up—to them and to other men—for feeling less than a man among men. Elliot, a thirty-one-year-old dentist, described a scene too familiar to most men:

> I used to go down to the basement with my father to work with him on his carpentry in the evenings. I wanted to learn, so he'd cut a sheet of plywood, draw a line and give me a handsaw. I'd try but go off the line a little or jam the saw, and my father would fix it a couple of times but then he'd finally just grab the saw from me and do it himself. Same with the nail and hammer. I'd hit and miss. He'd put up with this for a certain amount of time. Then he'd finally say, "Go upstairs, I

want to get this done.'' I'd just disappear because I didn't **want** to be around his critical energy anymore.

Our fathers are our first male oppressors. As soon as we can, we turn around and oppress the next man down the line.

Elliot continued:

Recently, a friend asked me to show him how to build something because now I'm a pretty good carpenter. So I showed him and then he tried. Every time he made a mistake I grabbed the hammer from him. He hated it. ''Can't you just show me how to do it?'' he said, just like I used to say to my father. Then I saw it so clearly: ''Here I am, my father revisited. I *am* my father.''

In this way fathers teach sons that they are inferior to themselves. They leave their sons with a feeling that they are not as good as—not as much of a ''man'' as—this man who stands at first for all men. In Chapter 6 we shall see this sense of insecurity and feeling of inferiority a male feels in terms of other men played out in male-male peer relationships.

Another lesson, taught by its absence, relates to emotional expressiveness among men. A psychologist at the University of Pennsylvania found that in intimacy workshops more than half of the male participants reported that they do not remember their fathers hugging them, especially after they were somewhat older. Typically, interviewees told me they had seen their fathers cry once or twice in their lives, usually at weddings and funerals. Said one man, ''I have a very emotional response to seeing my father cry. It makes *me* want to cry. But it also made me feel closer to him, to see he had a vulnerable side. I've felt he's always been cut off from himself emotionally.''

Some boys, deprived of any kind of emotional expressiveness from their fathers, welcomed even negative reactions rather than nothing at all. Gay Talese, in *Thy Neighbor's Wife*, described this scene from the life of a man who became something of a role model to a lot of men:

Although Hugh Hefner's father, a competent swimmer, had tried to help his son overcome the fear [of swimming], young Hefner stubbornly refused, and one day his father became so frustrated and angry that he hit him. It was a rare and welcome display of emotion from his father, a remote, repressed man who seldom revealed his feelings to his family and spent most of his time working quietly as an accountant in a large Chicago firm.

Through their silences, and even through such rages as Hefner's father permitted himself, fathers transmit another fundamental lesson: self-reliance. By example, emotional aloofness is shown to be the hallmark of manliness, leaving excessive friendliness, as will be shown in Chapters 6 and 7, to be viewed with suspicion if not disgust.

What, then, of the famous man-to-man or heart-to-heart talks reputed to take place between father and son? In reality, such intimate and emotional father-son encounters are few and far between. Men report that the two most common occasions that precipitate such tête-à-têtes are when a son announces he plans to marry and when a son announces he plans to divorce. Often, these supposed dialogues quickly turn into monologues, dissertations by the father on how the son should live his life—in short, demonstrations of superiority in an ongoing power struggle. George, a magazine editor whose father was a newspaper editor, recalled for me such an exchange and the effect it had on his life:

When my father wanted to have what he called "a talk" with me, he would call me down to have lunch at his favorite restaurant. It was an event, like a command performance. Except they were never dialogues. They were opportunities for him to expound on life and letters and other things of import—like marrying the wrong woman. He came right to the point: "I think that girl is absolutely wrong for you. I have strong negative feelings about her." "Well, Dad," I said, "I'm sorry you don't agree." And that was about it—except that it had an incredible impact on me. Years later, after my marriage had ended in shambles, I went back to him just before he died. "Do you remember that luncheon, Dad?"

I started. "I remember it vividly. It had a reverse effect on me, you know. I wanted to prove you were wrong even though I sensed what you were saying might have been true. Well, I just wanted to tell you that you were right." I had built up to this moment a long time, but somehow I don't think my father understood what it meant to me. He made light of it and said something like, "Well, that's life. It's silly to talk about it now."

"Talking about it" is not what real-life fathers do with their sons, contrary to the cozy scenes in such television shows as *Father Knows Best*, *Leave It to Beaver*, and *My Three Sons*.

REVOLT

"The law for father and son and mother and daughter is not the law of love: it is the law of revolution, of emancipation, of final supersession of the old and worn-out by the young and capable. I tell you, the first duty of manhood and womanhood is a Declaration of Independence; the man who pleads his father's authority is no man," wrote George Bernard Shaw in *Man and Superman*.

The magazine editor's story contains allusions to the inevitable next stage of the father-son relationship—revolt. To assert his own power, George had to go against his father—even while he knew somewhere deep down that his father was right. Sons who begin identifying so strongly with their fathers soon must do all within their own power to define themselves in their own terms. Eventually sons understand that the first men to guide their way along the path to manhood are also the first men to block it. Rejecting and passing one's father becomes the next rite of passage into manhood. George's father left George with an especially weighty cross of identification to bear. George carries the same name as his father, just as his father had borne the same name as his grandfather:

My father was always Big George, and I was Little George. And that was crucial. I was Georgie. That was the burden one had to bear having the same name, of being the little member, junior, of being in constant competition. My father was Pacific Editor of *Yank*. There's no doubt about it—ever since that time I wanted to be what he was. If not a newspaperman I wanted to be a journalist of some sort. There seemed to be an uncanny inevitability to it. It was so much a part of me from the beginning. And I wanted to prove to him I could do what he did. My first job was for UPI in San Francisco. I'd call for the police chief and say, "This is George E—" and I'd get right through. The chief would come on and I'd say, "This is George Junior." "Oh, you must be George's kid," he'd say and I'd cringe. "Yeah," I'd say and then I'd have to listen to five minutes of "your old man and I go way back together." "I know chief," I'd interrupt, "but what about the matter of the. . . ." But I could never break through. I wasn't being treated like a professional. I wasn't accepted for myself. I was somebody's kid, somebody's namesake.

In order to prove himself different and, he hoped, better than his father, George adopted a personal style diametrically opposite his father's. "I did everything I could to discourage the notion that I was a chip off the old block. My father had a reputation for being a hard-nosed feisty editor. Nothing could have pleased me more than to hear people talking about me: 'That's George's kid? But he's such a nice fellow.' " That's also why George married a woman of whom his father did not approve, why he moved 3000 miles away, and why he was drawn to magazines. "I chose magazines because they have more depth and dimension than newspapers. And I think that's the major difference between my father and me."

For many sons, unlike George, the struggle with the father is unsuccessful. As historian Ben Johnson wrote in *Timber*, "Greatness of name in the father ofttimes overwhelms the son: they stand too near one another. The shadow kills the growth." Such, perhaps, was the case with a writer I interviewed (who preferred to remain anonymous) whose father was a famous writer:

> I was about sixteen when I decided I wanted to be a writer. One of the strongest reasons was because I had no understanding of myself—mainly because I had no understanding of my father. I had no sense of intimacy with him. I became a writer to find out what this man was involved with, to understand his terms of reality so I could connect them with mine.

This man had jumped into the most intense fire of competition: He entered the same arena as his father and was going to try to outdo his father at what the other did best. I found this to be a common pattern among the men I interviewed. Men who join their fathers' businesses, who get involved in the same sports as their fathers, who adopt lifestyles similar to their fathers are all trying to beat their fathers at their own game. Following in their fathers' footsteps or taking the path of least resistance, sons eventually strive to pass their fathers on the path. Sons who do—and almost all try—are merely putting into practice that for which their fathers had trained them.

Fired by revenge for the humiliation of circumcision, the pain of abandonment, and the various other childhood wounds, and fueled now by a growing confidence in his own strengthening body and ideas, son eventually confronts father in order to claim his own territory and establish his own identity in the world. He separates from his father to be able to stand on his own ground. The actual confrontation—many men specifically recall one pivotal scene—usually occurs when a boy is about fifteen or sixteen. Richard, a twenty-five-year-old graduate student, described his scene:

> I was 16. I had taken a theology course in school that focused on civil rights. I started reading things like *The Autobiography of Malcolm X* and *Manchild in the Promised Land*. It felt like scales were falling from my eyes. I grew up in South Carolina with all that kind of stuff—separate drinking fountains for blacks and whites. The night I'm thinking of, my father and I

sat up late after everyone else had gone to bed. It was a rare occasion and we talked late into the night. We must have been drinking a little too. I don't know how we got onto it, but we started talking about racial issues. We talked an incredibly long time and we finally got to a point where we both had reached positions on which we were unwilling to compromise. I felt there was no difference between blacks and whites, and he felt blacks were inferior. So there we were, crystallized into two opposite positions. We had been through all the intellectual arguments and we still disagreed. I remember thinking, "I'm here and he's there. I have my own opinion." It was a definite break and it felt great. It gave me ground to stand on that wasn't my father's.

Some men report much more violent confrontational breaks with their fathers during their revolt years. In literature this confrontation is often resolved either symbolically or literally with the death of the father at the hands of the son. Sons killing fathers or sons having fathers killed is a theme that runs through some of the greatest and most enduring literature of the world: *Oedipus Rex, Hamlet,* and *The Brothers Karamazov.* This is not surprising since, as Freud also noted, "parricide is the principal and primal crime of humanity as well as of the individual." He traces the very roots of religion— and "the most primitive organization we know, the associations of men"—to a ceremonial slaying and eating of a totem, or animal, which, he asserts, is a symbolic substitute for the father. In Freud's psycho- and pseudo-historical setting for the primal father-son struggle, a band of brothers who had been driven away by "a violent, jealous father who keeps all the females for himself" set out together to slay the father. Explained Freud:

This violent primal father had surely been the envied and feared model for each of the brothers. Now they accomplished their identification with him by devouring him and each acquired a part of his strength. The totem feast, which is perhaps mankind's first celebration, would be the repetition and commemoration of this memorable, criminal act with which so many things began—social organizations, moral restrictions and religion.

In the end, the brothers Freud described found that they could not have what they wanted: "No one could or was allowed to attain the father's perfection of power, which was the thing they all sought."

As seemingly obtuse as Freud's theories sometimes are to the man or woman on the street, John Munder Ross pointed out,

> The truth of Freud's notions about fathers is undeniable. At some level and in some measure sons did then and do now hate their fathers, do wish to take their place, notwithstanding their love and filial duty. And however beneficent and well-meaning they may be, fathers in their turn must nonetheless discipline and deny their sons the full enjoyment of their pleasures and ambitions; for such are the requirements of childhood and the obligations of paternity. What Freud presented was inevitable, the dynamic dualism of a son's grateful affection for a father nurturant and giving, and the enraged, defiant son's battle against a depriving and constraining overlord.

There is no breakdown of statistics in the FBI's Unified Crime Report that shows how many homicides involve sons killing fathers, or fathers killing sons. The Criminal Justice Research Center in Albany, New York, one of the largest repositories of data on crimes, refers inquiries to more general studies on domestic violence, where details on father and son murders remain hidden. In the overall pattern of homicides, figures on murders involving fathers and sons probably constitute a very small percentage. The fact is, sons act out the death wish on their fathers in other ways. One is for the son to withhold his own love and intimacy, as his father had done to him. I believe that this results in as many love-starved sons as love-starved fathers.

Another possible version of symbolic patricide is vasectomy, an operation by which a son puts an end to his father's lifeline into the future. I talked to one man whose son had the operation and with whom the father had had an intensely competitive relationship. "I took it personally," the man said. "He deprived me of grandchildren. I saw it as his way of getting back at me. He was saying, 'I don't want to do to a son what you did to me.' " So ends the grandfather's dream of immortality. He feels his own death and blames his son.

The most common version of this symbolic patricide is the son's rejection of his father as the model of masculinity. By adopting a different personality, a different style of dress or lifestyle, by changing speech patterns, hand gestures, and everything else about himself that reminds him of his father, a son commits psychological patricide. He kills the father in himself by trying to exorcise his father's influence from himself. "It's a way of saying, 'Fuck you, Dad,' " as one man put it. By refusing to let any part of his father live on in himself, the son effectively kills the father within.

All this is part of the revolt stage. The irony here, inherent in many aspects of the father-son relationship, is that psychological patricide is a form of psychological suicide. By cutting himself off from and killing the father within, by denying that the father ever had a powerful influence in determining his own personality, the son suffocates and kills a very important part of himself. As I have shown, the father does in fact play a very significant part in the formation of his son's development of self-view. A son's failure to acknowledge that role can be a significant barrier to his self-knowledge and to his growth and development into a fully mature man. Not until he comes to understand that point can he ever hope to resolve his differences with his father, and with other men.

RECONCILIATION

If the motto of the revolt stage is "No pain, no gain," then for this final stage it might be, "What goes around comes around." For finally, a son comes to terms with his father and with those traces of his father that he finds in himself.

"In spite of everything," Freud wrote, "the identification with the father finally makes a permanent place for itself in the ego. We give it the name super-ego and ascribe to it, the inheritor of the paternal influence, the most important of functions."

The Russian novelist Ivan Turgenev made the same point in *Fathers and Sons*, first published in 1861 amid a storm of controversy and contradiction that persists to this day. The novel tells the story of generations in conflict, of the old giving way to the new. In the end, the hero, Yevgeny Bazarov, the idealistic rebel and symbol of change and "renunciation," dies of blood poisoning. His easily influenced friend Arkady Kirsanov marries and becomes a "zealous proprietor"—like his father. Turgenev seems to be saying that attempts to revolt against the father are all in vain. Somehow, no matter how much a son changes, he retains a considerable part of that man with whom he first identified.

Turgenev told a story that all of us know; if we have not lived it ourselves, we have heard it a hundred times. My interviews resounded with descriptions of sons' struggles to gain independence from their fathers only eventually to step into their fathers' shoes. Consider the account of the New Jersey building contractor who ten years earlier had been a wiry, free-thinking, social reformer. This was the man who never wanted to settle down, who once shouted at his father, "Take your life and shove it." He now works for his father, embraces his father's goals and lifestyle, owns his own suburban split-level, has a pot belly, a wife, and a son for whom he wants to do everything his father did for him. Or consider the son of the wealthy industrialist, a Harvard graduate who turned his back on the family fortune to become a student of Zen meditation and a writer of short stories, who gave up the opportunity for unimaginable comfort to live in a modestly furnished, rented cottage—and who then returned to take over the family finances.

And, finally, there is Ken, whose story reflects a reidentification with his father plus almost every other theme I have mentioned so far, from reverence to revolt to reconciliation:

> I had a lot of respect for my father. He's a self-made man. He started out with a pushcart in Brooklyn, went into the vending machine business, then managed a motel in Palm Springs, bought out the franchise and now makes probably $100,000 a year. Plus he invests in land, stocks, speculations—overall he does pretty well. I remember it was a big thrill to go with him Saturday filling the coffee machines. We got along well working together. I felt like I was really helpful. It was also one of the few times I got to do something alone with him. He worked a lot and I didn't see him too much. The heart-to-heart talks? Hardly ever. I recall one—when I split up with Kate. Only once did I ever see him express any real deep tender emotion, when he cried at my older brother's wedding. It was just after both his parents had died. It was the first time I had seen him let go in 20 years. With his sons, he was into corporal punishment. We knew when we did things wrong and we expected to get whipped. His philosophy to us: "Succeed! Work hard." When I turned sixteen I stopped seeing my father as God. There was a power struggle. He was clinging to it but I saw the inevitability of change. I sort of lost respect for him from then on. Everything became an issue: my lifestyle, my dress, the length of my hair, my friends, when I could use the car. Once he said I could never use the car again. So I went out and bought my own with my own money. I got one of my teachers to sign the papers because I was too young. I brought the car home and said to my father, "Keep your goddamned car, I got my own!" He flipped out. I had usurped his power.

Ken rebelled for years against his father's middle class morality: He dropped out of the mainstream culture that his father represented, dropped out of college, lived on a farm in New England with Kate (whom he never married), wrote an unsuccessful novel, started a restaurant that failed, started a maple syrup business but left it, had a son (who was never circumcised, "which is still a big issue with my parents," said Ken), left Kate, moved to Los Angeles to try writing screenplays but never sold one, waited on tables in a hamburger joint, took a real estate course, married "a nice girl" (his parents' description), and is now buying and selling houses and condominiums with an eye on some Palm Springs properties.

After rejecting his father's model adamantly for many years Ken now sees the irony of his turnaround:

> I guess I *am* like him, in terms of my goals and my energy and my self-motivation. I have always been a big achiever—or tried to be. It's in my nature. All my life I've wanted to come up with a scheme that would make me rich quick. I guess I got that from him. I now have a lot of respect for him. Does he respect me? I don't know. I wonder. I think he's beginning to. My father measures respect in dollars. If I were making double what I am now, he'd respect me twice as much.

For many men the struggle to come into their own and out from under the shadow of their fathers takes a turn when they first father their own children. (If the child is a boy, says grandpa, that much the better.) For one thing the burden is now off the son to carry on the family name; it is now shifted to the grandson. For the new father there is now a sense that he must "act like a man" because he is being watched as a role model. And he develops a new appreciation for what his own father had to do. Ken's son Amos clearly served that function:

> He was their first grandchild. Also I began to see it from the other side of the coin. To see what it's like to be a parent, to see your flesh and blood and have dreams for him. I couldn't totally excuse my father for a lot of his actions but I understood him a lot more.

Ken, and many of the other men I interviewed, hoped they could be somewhat different as models to their sons from those their fathers had been to them. Their attitude was: "I want to do everything for my son that my father did for me—but more." But breaking the chain of events that set a son up to be just like his father is not easy, though sons may try. "I'm a liberated version of my father," Ken told me:

> I'm not restricted in my doctrines. He's locked in his ways. I'm flexible. He never was. With my son I try to be a lot more emotionally expressive. We have a lot of heart-to-heart talks. I want him to accomplish whatever it is he wants to do. I want to participate in things with him but at the same time help him develop a strong sense of self.

Interestingly, much as Ken and others insist that their approach to their sons is distinctly their own, echoes of their fathers' goals resounded through many of the interviews. Men want their sons to be "self-made" and independent; it is not surprising sons become accomplishment-oriented and emotionally inexpressive.

DEATH OF THE FATHER: THE FINAL RITE

By first confronting his own father and then becoming a father himself, the son comes ever closer to becoming his own man. But, as a forty-year-old investor from Washington, D.C., put it, "You always feel like a boy next to your father, no matter how old you are." Until, that is, the final rite of passage in the filial relationship: the death of the father.

"What's been your biggest disappointment in life?" forty-three-year-old country and western singer-songwriter Merle Haggard was asked.

"The death of my father," he replied without hesitation. "It happened more than 30 years ago, but a day doesn't go by that I don't think about him."

"Who have your biggest heroes been?" he was asked.

"My father, of course."

I was talking with a literary agent in New York who had taken over his father's business shortly after his father died.

"Did you feel a lot of grief when your father died?" I asked.

"No," he said, "in fact it felt like an enormous weight was lifted off my back. It was like a semi-religious experience. I felt free for the first time, even though I loved him very much and I felt very close to him."

Freud cites the death of the father as the most important event in a man's life—significantly, not the father's *life* but his *death*. When Freud's own father died, he wrote, "I felt as if I had been torn up by the roots." Not long after that he initiated his self-analysis and began to develop his theory of the Oedipus complex.

Some men respond with anger at their fathers for once again abandoning them—this time by dying. Others respond with guilt caused by the realization of the repressed death wish. Still others respond with fear, a fear of now being alone in the world without a father to fall back on. Regardless of their emotional reactions, most men I interviewed expressed the feeling that with their fathers' death they had now finally attained the full stature of a man, if only out of necessity. Now that they no longer had their fathers looking down on them, these men felt that they were nobody's "junior" anymore.

The father's death is the final reconciliation with the one who both guided the way to and blocked the way to manhood. With that break comes a feeling of freedom, but with that freedom comes a new responsibility: Now the son must step into the role of family elder, or patriarch. He must accept the power for which he has strived all these years. He must show that he can fill his father's shoes. He must sit at the head of the table now, carve the Thanksgiving turkey, and lead the family in prayer with the same authority that his father did. It is a role for which he has practiced his whole life, and yet it comes awkwardly.

The bereaved son experiences a reconciliation with his father, and an acceptance of those traits he had worked so hard during his father's life to negate and deny. I interviewed a man from Los Angeles who was twenty-one years old when his father died:

After he died I became very much like him. I was aware that he had gone but that he lived on through me. He existed in me. And whatever he had passed to me I would carry forward. In our family I'm the oldest son so I immediately took over. I grew up instantly the day I found out he died. I stopped being a kid and started being a man. Losing him was the biggest change in my life. It was the first time I began to sense my own mortality. Until then I think I believed life worked out fairly, that you reach some sort of sense of accomplishment, happiness, whatever. . . . And then my father died—unhappy, unfulfilled, he didn't get a chance to finish what he had started—and it sort of came as a shock to me. I still haven't gotten over it ten years later.

Without reconciliation fathers remain outsiders. With it, sons complete the cycle of manhood and the circle that brings them back to themselves. Until they come to know the man they revered and modeled themselves after, they will never know themselves. Even reconciling with the idea of the man after he is dead is better than remaining forever at arm's length from one's father, one's primary male hero.

Through these stages or rites—from reverence to revolt to reconciliation—a boy discovers the stranger in the hero, the opponent in the supporter, and at each passage he generalizes lessons learned from one man to all men. If he has learned well—about the importance of power, achievement, competition, and emotional inexpressiveness—he will enter relationships with other men with great caution and distrust.

2

Grandfathers and Mentors: Bridges to the Outside World

"I expected to be coached by men
after the images of my heroes.
Men, Ladies and Gentlemen, who one
could depend on, look up to, believe
in. I wanted what I had coming."

—Mark Medoff,
"The Locker Room Kid,"
Esquire, October 1975

Fathers—absent or present—are not enough. Nor should they be. Throughout their lives men pick up valuable pointers from other men about the basics of the masculine connection, about how men act with each other. A boy needs and gets messages from elsewhere about the mysteries of masculinity; and while each new man in his life may add new depth and breadth to his understanding of himself in relation to other men, he also begins to recognize familiar lessons learned at his father's feet. These are lessons about power and control, the male hierarchy, and closeness and distance between men.

As a boy begins to look around in his life for other male role models, he finds two men—his grandfather and his mentor—who contribute in significant ways to his development. In his grandfather, and later in his mentor, he finds two men whose partial appeal is that they are devoid of the emotional entanglement and competitiveness that arises with his father—at least at first.

GRANDFATHERS: THE SOFT SPOT

If we have learned anything, it is that the source of male power and empowerment comes down to us from the father. The man above him—the father's father—must, we can only assume, have manifold power. We are pulled to grandfathers as a connection to our male lineage, and as a key to understanding our fathers and ourselves. They are drawn to grandsons as perhaps their final opportunity to assure the continuation of their names or at least their wisdom. In grandfathers we see our past. In grandsons we see our future. The link between the two was explained in a gripping fashion in a dream told to me by a thirty-two-year-old Boston attorney:

> In the dream my grandfather had just died. We were at the funeral, except my grandfather was still alive; I guess it was that state before the soul is supposed to leave the body. Anyway, he was dressed in a white tuxedo sitting in a white wheelchair, surrounded by white walls and clouds. My father was pushing the wheelchair and I was walking next to it at my grandfather's arm; we were dressed in white tuxedoes too. My grandfather directed my father to a door and into a room that looked like the basement of my grandfather's house. My father used to haul winter storm windows up from there for my grandfather when Grandpa got too old to do it himself. He told my father to start bringing the windows upstairs. Then my grandfather turned to me—and I'm not sure here whether he actually said it or told me with his eyes—but the message was clearly, "You're the one." It was a strong image and a strong message. I was the inheritor of the family chalice, the family name; he was passing the family reputation down to me. I felt my father was bypassed.

Memories of grandfathers frequently came up in interviews as the soft spot in their man-to-man relationships. This, I realized, was quite possibly one of the very few men in a man's world with whom you were practically guaranteed to be free of power struggles, competitiveness, and ego-clash. Why? The difference in generations accounts for a relative lack of

assumptions and expectations of what constitutes success in
the world—two factors that engender conflict between father
and son, as demonstrated in excerpts from interviews in
Chapter 1. Lower expectations produce higher satisfaction;
they allow for emotional interchange but with a lot less static.

Also contributing to the relative emotional neutrality of the
grandson-grandfather bond is the old man's power position in
the world at large at a time when the boy is growing up and
watching him intently. While the boy's father struggles to
define and maintain his power/position at work, the grandfather may well be into the power years of his life—those 50s
and 60s in which he is part of the command generation—in
which he has clearly established his domain. But apart from
his position in the outside world, his unquestioned role as the
elder male in the family hierarchy may be enough to assure
his superior position, both to himself and his grandson, rendering
competition out of the question.

On the other hand, when the grandfather is "past his prime,"
retired, physically weak, and viewed by the rest of the family
as a dependent figure, the boy may feel no threat of being
overpowered and may be, therefore, much freer to open his
heart, fears, and hopes to his grandfather.

So though the boy may be drawn to the grandfather's
power, it is exactly the lack of competition for power that
makes this such a rewarding conflict-free relationship. For
both people it is distance that affords closeness.

This distance/closeness theme was reinforced in the two
most commonly recalled images that surfaced when I asked
men to tell me about their grandfathers. In both, the grandfather appears as a less-than-real, remote figure.

One view came in romantic sepia tones and diffused lighting, in an oval cameo, blurry at the edges. Here was the man
with the largest, most inviting lap in the world, with all the
time in the world. A warm man full of deep laughs, deep
personal contentment, and always those deep sparkling eyes
gazing adoringly at us. Clearly out of focus, it was the vision
of a man so loved, so idolized, that I suspected these young

boys never really got to know the man in a clear objective light. He remained a distant and distorted image—his own kind of stranger.

The other picture of the grandfather was quite different but no less distant. In cold, dark lighting we now see a dour, grumpy man with a long gray beard, speaking perhaps in a foreign language—a man who smelled funny, and never seemed to be paying full attention to us. He was the tyrannical patriarch whom everyone feared. When this man turned his attention to us—for however briefly—a shiver went up our spines. He too was a stranger.

Here again—as we learned from our fathers—we find built-in distance and separateness in one of our closets male-male relationships. With all its richness and warmth, the grandfather-grandson relationship brands us with that message. In later chapters we see how this lesson gets retaught and relearned. Nonetheless, a deep longing for closeness that all humans share draws men to each other, urges them to break down those barriers.

Closeness to one's grandfather also holds out the hope of closeness to one's father—though, ironically, sometimes the man who may attempt to block that hoped for connection is the father himself. These are the first words of Herbert Gold's *Fathers*:

> My father has never spoken his father's name. "He hit me for whistling like a peasant, he brought home a carp for the holiday, he took me to the rabbi, but I didn't want to go." *He* did this or that. What my father has left me of my grandfather is a silent old man with a long white beard, a horse, a cart, a cow, a mud-and-log house—an old country grandfather fixed in my mind like the memory of a painting. That's not enough, of course. This stylization of images does not satisfy the craving for history. I must tempt out the truth.

A father's attempt to thwart his son's knowledge of the grandfather may reflect the father's own unresolved anger, pain and frustration with *his* father. Boys watching their fathers for clues as to how to relate both to father and all men pay careful attention to the interaction of grandfather and father. What they may find is a mirror of what they're encountering themselves. These observations were offered by two men from what appear to be diametrically opposite backgrounds, one an upper-class older white Anglo-Saxon Protestant (WASP), the other a working-class black man of twenty-two. First the WASP:

> By the time I came along things were pretty hostile between Dad and his father. One reason was that Grandfather was financially dependent on my father. And my grandfather was a man of tremendous pride. And my father also resented some of my grandfather's earlier successes that my father never lived up to even though their roles were reversed by the time I can remember. My father and grandfather were up against it most of the time they were together. My father and his argued a lot.

Now the young black:

> I think grandaddy had a real wicked temper but only with his sons, not his grandsons. I guess I figured my father must have done something bad to warrant my grandaddy's anger, because all the rest of the time with us he was so gentle. But I sensed my father and his had their own thing going, and I sensed myself as very much on the outside of it.

Feeling ostracized from the interaction of father and grandfather only adds more confusion and a sense of inferiority—a feeling of being the outsider—in the shadow of ''grown-up men.'' But, as Gold also implies, a boy craves to understand himself through understanding his own history—and in most cases that understanding comes through the lineage of men in his family—so he pushes through father to reach grandfather. Even when the grandfather has been long gone when the boy arrives, his craving is so strong he will find out about the man—if not from his own father, then from other relatives, (usually the women). Charles, a twenty-two-year-old computer programmer from western Massachusetts, told me about his grandfathers:

I never knew either of my grandfathers. One died when I was three, the other at four. In the last couple of years I've started to hear more about my father's father. I hear it all from my grandmother. My father never talks about him. You can't ask him or he gets evasive. They didn't have a relationship, as far as I could tell. I don't think he had much contact with his father except in what they always referred to as "projects." Like the time my grandfather bought a ton of grain and didn't know what to do with it, so my father started a chicken farm to get rid of it. And it's the same with me and my father. My only contact with him has been over these "projects," when I was building something with him. My grandfather was apparently the source of a lot of energy in our family. His philosophy was, "Don't just stand there—do something, even if it's wrong." He built a boat in the basement and then had to pull down part of the house to get it out. There's a story about my grandfather coming into the shoe factory he owned one winter day and telling the workers huddled around the hot steam pipes, "Get to work, you get warm that way." Knowing these stories bolsters a lot of fantasies I have about being the third in a line of driven men, men who get things done, who accomplish tasks quickly.

There was a swelling sense of pride in this young man's voice as he related these cherished family tales about his grandfather, a significantly different voice than when he talked about his father. It made me realize how much our grandfathers can mean to us—especially in light of disappointments with a father. Into them we can pour all the love we may have had trouble giving to our own fathers. They are our fathers once removed.

A fifty-five-year-old banking investor from San Francisco looked to his grandfather for an image when he rejected his father as one:

With my father I developed an attitude of I-don't-give-a-damn-what-he-thinks, mainly because he never approved of anything I did anyway. I think my father meant well but he suffered from being the son of a well known vaudeville song-and-dance man when vaudeville was in its heyday. He performed in Europe and Japan and all over the world. I never knew him but my aunts told me stories about him. He had a powerful presence, I was told; he was elegant and arrogant. On his death bed, in his 90s, he propped himself up on his bed deciding in what pecking order the relatives could come in and visit him. He was probably a horrible person to know but a remarkably self-assured son-of-a-bitch, from what I could gather.

It was clear after sitting with this gentleman two hours that he had followed in his grandfather's footsteps. He was a short, stocky, self-assured son-of-a-bitch who savored army stories in which he put superior officers to shame. His employees, I was told before I left his office, called him Napoleon.

OTHER GRANDFATHERS

There are some men whose grandfathers made more than brief appearances, or came in dreams or retold stories. In the last century and early in this one, men left their families for months or years for jobs that would make them enough money to send for the rest of their families or retire early back to their homeland. The education of the man's young son, left at home with his mother, fell to the grandfather. I was told of such a relationship by a sixty-three-year-old Greek restaurauteur living in New York City. I asked him, "What was the most important thing your father gave you?" "My grandfather," he answered. He explained:

I didn't spend much time with my father because people at that time, in that area of the world [Greece], migrated or went to sea, or wherever there was work. Sometimes I wouldn't see him for a few years. It was kind of strange. Since my mother was rather young and busy raising the family, it was my grandfather who really brought me up. He had the time, he had the interest and he knew so much. I was in awe of him, held him in the highest regard. I remember how people from different villages would come to talk to him, seeking advice. My grandfather would take me for walks and inject me with his philosophy of life. He talked about religion and war and Greek history. I admired him so much.

When I asked this man what he learned from his grandfather, he emphasized three points. The first was discipline. The second was what he called "worldly wisdom—he gave me a sense of the scope of the world, and what I had to know to be in it." And the third was the importance of lineage: "Our family structure is based on patriarchy. Everything is spelled out quite precisely. I understood that anything my grandfather told me came from the same source as my father."

Another kind of relationship between grandfather and grandson emerged through the interviews—a type of bridging relationship that helps the son who is revolting against his father nonetheless maintain contact with the men in his family. The young man, usually in his early or mid-twenties, is looking for a friend and approaches his grandfather for solace, camaraderie, conversation, and intimacy, and as a means of staying in touch with his own lineage. The grandfather, somewhat more dependent, himself lonely with his children preoccupied making a living and his own peers slowly dying off, appreciates an "ear." A thirty-six-year-old Los Angeles school administrator, Craig, described such a relationship:

My grandfather's 87 years old. I wasn't that close to him when I was a kid. He was your basic immigrant who killed himself working. He started with nothing and built up a pretty successful business. I really have a great deal of respect for him for that. Our closeness started about six or seven years ago, just after my grandmother died. I used to walk him to the dentist and he and I would walk and talk. It was beautiful. He talked about his childhood. He was so generous with his feelings, in a way that I couldn't be. And I was so responsive to that. I started to feel so open to him. We became very close, a deep friendship—without any regard for the older-younger thing or the fact that he was supposed to be my superior. He never moralized like my father. I couldn't share with him many of my contemporary experiences but we maintained a good level on lots of things and personal issues. I just spoke with him the other day on the phone for 45 minutes. It was heaven. I feel very lucky to have contacted him again.

"He never moralized like my father." Here is a key to the grandfather's role in a young boy's life—he can reminisce with, love, and *enjoy* the boy without feeling, as the father does, the need to create a fledgling man who reflects well on himself as masculine standard bearer. Through the old man the boy tastes the freedom to relate to a grown man on his own terms while still remaining anchored safely to the family.

Soon, though, the growing boy is impelled outward. As he matures he comes to acknowledge the need for a guide, or more accurately a bridge, out of the family and into the world of men. Crucial though their influences may be, neither fathers nor grandfathers can suppply all of what a boy needs to feel fully equipped in a man's world.

MENTORS: BRIDGING THE GAP

Young boys eventually begin to look outside the family circle for other male role models—especially if they have been disappointed by fathers they could not depend on, look up to, or believe in. In this new turn outward, boys are looking primarily for training and development in specific skills; reinforcement, approval, and acceptance as individuals; and entree into the world of grown-up men. These desires were echoed by men I interviewed, with comments like these:

> "What I needed was someone who'd show me the ropes."
> "I was looking for a man I could talk to, who *listened* to me, who appreciated me for who I am and what I could become."
> "I wanted someone who would take me under his wing."

Enter the mentor. He is a man who fills in those gaps in a young man's education by teaching him the nuts and bolts of a chosen field of interest; by encouraging and simply paying attention to an apprentice's development; and by serving as a stepping stone to the next level to which the younger man aspires. Such men pass through a boy's or man's life as teachers, coaches, or instructors; as mechanics, grocers, or the guy down the street; as supervisors, department heads, or bosses.

The mentor is usually a half generation older, from eight to fifteen years—too old to suggest competitive peership and not old enough to invite comparisons to one's father. He is a transitional figure, embodying equal parts peer and parent and serving as a bridge between them for the protegé. A man's mentor is almost always male, according to my research and that of others, a fact that reconfirms to me men's belief that power (in this case skills, knowledge, and access) comes through a male hierarchy.

Most relationships with mentors are encounters that may last several years. A mentor may be someone a man meets only briefly but who leaves a lasting impression. Or he may be someone he never meets but who remains an inspirational male model to emulate (sports heroes, for example, or movie or rock stars, writers, politicians, war heroes). And then there is the actual teacher with whom a man interacts for a number of years.

Throughout history and across cultures, mentors have held a highly regarded place in a man's world. The Japanese might call him *sensei* or "the person born before," or "older"; it is one of the highest forms of address that can be bestowed on a person in that culture. In the Hindu tradition he is a *guru*, "venerable one." The Latin word *mentor* means "advisor" or "wise man." In Greek mythology, Mentor was a trusted friend, a consultant to Odysseus, and later a guide to Odysseus's son Telemachus.

Plato expressed the strong emotional bond a protegé feels for his mentor as he sat beside Socrates, who was about to take the poison hemlock:

And we waited, talking and thinking of the greatness of our sorrow; he was like a father of whom we were being bereaved, and we were about to pass the rest of our lives as orphans. Hitherto most of us had been able to control our sorrow but we could no longer forbear and in spite of myself my own tears were flowing fast (so that I covered my face and wept over myself) for certainly I was not weeping over him, but at the thought of my own calamity in having lost such a companion.

Though the relationship of Socrates and Plato became a model for almost all mentors thereafter, scholars say one would have to hunt and peck through volumes of Plato's writings for passages revealing the nature of that relationship. In fact, almost no one analyzed the mentor-protegé relationship until 1978 when Yale psychologist Daniel Levinson stumbled onto it in the course of researching his book *The Seasons of a Man's Life*. Looking at the stages of adult male development, he called the relationship with a mentor "one of the most complex, and developmentally important a man can have in early adulthood."

Yet, as important as mentors appear to be, surprisingly few men in my study or Levinson's could identify actual men in their lives whom they would describe as mentors. Most recite the names of heroes from history or film: from John F. Kennedy, to John Wayne. Why do male figures like these loom larger in men's lives than real-life people? Are there so few men worth emulating? Despite their own understanding of the need to find such mentors, are men simply afraid of seeking out and making contact with potential mentors?

One explanation may be that men define the mentor in such idealistic and heroic terms that finding *any* man who could live up to the expectations in the first place would be difficult. Levinson described the "functions" of a mentor this way:

He may act as a teacher to enhance the young man's skills and intellectual development. Serving as a sponsor, he may use his influence to facilitate the young man's entry and advancement. He may be a host and guide, welcoming the initiate into a new occupational social world and acquainting him with its values, customs, resources and cast of characters. Through his own virtues, achievements and way of living, the mentor may be an exemplar that the protegé can admire and seek to emulate. He may provide counsel and moral support in times of stress.

Observe first that Levinson applies a *functional* index to the definition, making it seem like a list of accomplishments one checks off. Also note the order in which he lists them, with skills first and emotional support last, and even that only "in time of stress."

Another clue to the reason for a relative scarcity of real-live mentors came out in my interviews. Men responded to questions about mentors with descriptions of what they referred to as "heroes" and "father figures." The repetition of these terms forced a comparison to our father/heroes. Were these so-called "father figures" based on real father models or mythical archetypes? If men are looking for mentors who resemble their fathers—or their ideas of what their fathers should be—it would be reasonable to expect them to have trouble relating to the outsiders they actually encountered, given the proscriptions against intimate father-son interaction. In the search for "fatherly" mentors, men are inevitably bound to come face to face as protegés with the same issues, patterns, and stages they encountered as sons.

In cases where the mentor-protegé relationships are established, men often hope to gain companionships free of the emotional complexities they found with their fathers or sons. In fact, the emotions in this relationship run very high, setting up the familiar reverence and revolt stages as seen between father and son. Reconciliation is often less noticeable simply because the relationship is so short-lived. Here is a closer look at the stages.

Reverence

A mentor earns much of the reverence he is paid by a younger man simply by demonstrating a belief in the latter's skills and abilities. The mentor sees promise in the protegé and often gives a vote of confidence just when the young man is trying to prove himself to his own father.

A Maine potter, age thirty-five, told me about his "male hero":

> His name was Bill Foster, an older guy, my father's age. I grew up down the street from him in suburban Rochester, New York. I had worked for him since I was young. I cut his lawn, painted his house. He started building a houseboat in his backyard and I helped him on that. And I loved him; he was a wonderful guy. I guess he was the closest thing for me to a "good guy" father figure: My own father used to scare the shit out of me—when he wasn't working. But Bill—he related to me as a person. We'd talk for long periods while he worked; he'd tell me stories about when he was a kid. It was very important for me to see other males acting like regular people. He was a warm kind of guy—and it was through him that I knew such a feeling was possible between men.

Without all the complexities, Oedipal and otherwise, inherent in the father-son relationship—a matter of being *too* close, too emotionally involved and egotistically invested—the young man can share his hopes and dreams, his fears and insecurities with the mentor without fear of reproval and rejection. The young and the older man usually share an interest in a subject, a sport, a car or machine; they have a common language in its jargon and technicalities. Here is a universe in which the two can interact, where the standards are objective and the criteria for excellence mutually understood—as contrasted directly with the domain of a father and son.

Growing up in a working class district of Pittsburgh, a forty-four-year-old man recalled treasured friendships with older men who took the time his father could not:

After school I would go to the local bus garage. And I met a guy there, Hugh McDonald, and he taught me all about how to deal with machinery. Every day I used to go help him fix the buses. It went on for years from the time I was seven. He'd expect me to come and I really enjoyed going there, seeing how excited he was to see me. He'd give me a cup of tea. . . . I was thinking recently that my "male learning" came from men like that, passing figures, rather than my father. There was another guy who ran a little two-acre farm nearby and every weekend for four or five years I'd go hang out with him. I'd help him tend the cows and sheep and plow the fields and plant vegetables. So during the week I'd be with one guy and on weekends with the other. More than anybody else, these two guys taught me the skills of being alive in the world. I learned about mechanics and I learned about the earth—powerful elemental tools.

Where a father is likely to challenge his son's chosen interests, weighing them for value against his own or against his own aspirations for the boy, the mentor accepts the boy's interest as a given, sharing what he knows and even justifying the boy's interest by holding it himself.

Revolt

Slowly things begin to turn. Just as in the father-son relationship, the young man who had felt respect, admiration, commonality, gratitude, and even love for—and from—his mentor now reaches a point in his growth where he needs once again to declare his independence, as he did with his father. He needs to assert his position and authority—to be autonomous. Now he feels hemmed in by the mentor: patronized, unappreciated, and resentful. He views his mentor's ideology and methodology as old-fashioned, uninventive, and unbending. Having attained some stature of his own in the world into which he was ushered by the older man, the protegé sees the limits of the mentor—and he sees something for himself beyond his mentor. He begins to feel that in the world of grown-up men his mentor is not such a big deal after all. And in order to become a big deal himself he must put his mentor behind him. Of this phase Levinson wrote:

> The mentor he formerly loved and admired is now experienced as destructively critical and demanding, or as seeking to make one over in his own image rather than fostering one's individuality and independence. The mentor who only yesterday was regarded as an enabling teacher and friend has become a tyrannic father and smothering mother. The mentor, for his part, finds the young man inexplicably touchy, unreceptive to even the best counsel, irrationally rebellious and ungrateful. By the time they are through, there is generally some validity in each one's criticism of the other.

The break is often bitter and hostile. But it is essential for the young man if he is ever to feel fully empowered. The mentor as well grieves at losing a special relationship. It is a tribute to the intensity of the relationship that it takes a while for feelings to settle. After the break, the two may never see each other again or they may establish a much cooler and cordial working relationship.

Reconciliation

Once the protegé feels that his power is his own and that he is recognized for it, he can usually acknowledge freely the important role the mentor played in his life. As time heals wounds, each is more able to understand the effect of their meeting and their influence on the other. Whether they reconcile their differences with each other in spoken words or not (though, true to most man-to-man relationships, they probably will not) the protegé will reconcile with his mentor in one of the most important ways—by making the mentor a more intrinsic part of himself, his philosophy, and his style, by incorporating into himself aspects of the older man he admires and even some of those he does not. Just as the son who later realizes he *has* followed in his father's footsteps or picked up his father's values, attitudes, and even physical mannerisms, so too does the young man come to terms with the imprint of his mentor on himself. Nonetheless it may take a lifetime for some men to acknowledge the influence of their mentors—if they even can claim to have found one.

THE MENTORS OF
AN AMERICAN BUSINESSMAN

The majority of the mentor-protegé relationships I heard about occurred in the business context. That stands to reason. Rising through the ranks of any business, a man has a number of opportunities to apprentice himself to a mentor. Organizations are structured hierarchically, and getting to the top is the aim. A man in middle management finds a superior at the executive management level from whom he can learn the ropes and who might later help promote him. Each teacher is a rung on a ladder by which the young man hoists himself to the top. At each step he picks up more valuable information about how men relate to each other and to the world at large.

No interviewee demonstrated the case better than Bill Rudd, the fifty-two-year-old president of a successful New York investment and real estate firm, who supplied me with an explicit account of the series of mentors who schooled him in the ways of the business world. Rudd worked his way from the bottom up, from mail room to management. Along the way he apprenticed himself to men who seemed to care about him for himself (he would believe the contrary later), men who guided him toward productivity and upward mobility. From these men he also learned the pitfalls in a man's world—distrust and emotional inexpressiveness. Rudd traces his interest in business to the influence—or lack thereof—of his father.

"Your father taught you how to be a businessman?" I asked.

Oh, no. In fact I haven't got a single memory of anything my father ever told me, not one conversation. I'm sure we did things together, but for some reason I just go blank when I try to think about that. The biggest favor my father ever did for me, though, was to leave me this image of himself as a big businessman. He died when I was young, before he had a chance to really teach me anything. I was completely at sea except for this idea I had of him being affluent and grandiose, all of which was negated by my family years later.

Rudd felt cheated by the early death of his father and he took it out on all figures of authority for a while. He was kicked out of four all-boys schools for disciplinary problems.

My first mentor, I would say, was a guidance counselor at a vocational school I was at. He was important because through him I learned a man could show care and concern for me without overpowering me. He also showed me I was playing this game—me against the authorities—as a reaction to my father's death. I resented all authority because, I figured, what did it get you? They all abandon you in the end—like my father—just at a time when you need them the most.

When school ended, so did their relationship. Rudd felt let down again, but he came away, nevertheless, with a desire to become a psychologist, based on the model of this guidance counselor. After a stint in the U.S. Army, however, Rudd ended up in business school and then got a job in the mail room of an advertising agency, where he met his next mentor, Max.

He was my boss. This man opened my eyes to the whole world of business. Through the work I was doing for him I slowly came to understand the workings of the entire hierarchical structure of American business. Also he was a meticulous person about everything he did. He taught me how to organize my time, how to use it, how to set priorities. He gave me an image I've lived with ever since of how a business person functions within himself and, at the same time, within the business structure. I was particularly fortunate because he was a production manager—responsible for producing things. So I was immediately impressed by the imperatives—deadlines for tonight, deadlines for tomorrow, think ahead, think ahead.

The lesson was do, do, do. Produce, perform, meet a deadline. Above all, understand the hierarchy and learn to work within it; maintain the appropriate outer form.

"And what about your personal relationship with this man?" I asked. After a long pause he answered:

I don't really know. I don't know. There wasn't much of one. There was another man in the department who I also thought of as a surrogate father type. With him I had a warmer relationship. He was more concerned with me; he *cared*. If I didn't look well he'd worry about my health. And he had this impenetrable calm. You could run into his office and shout, "The building's on fire," and he'd say, "Call me when it gets two doors down, I just want to finish this layout."

While Rudd did appreciate this man's more human side, he also took to heart the lesson of emotional restraint in the face of work. After another long pause he added:

But even with him there was no great personal relationship. I'm wondering if I had that kind of intimacy with any of the people who taught me what I know. They all helped me fill myself professionally but not personally.

The next guy, Bill, was considerably older than me. He refined me. He's the one that taught me how to dress, that it's better to be thinner, that you carry a handkerchief and use it. He taught me grooming and bought me a hairbrush I still use today. He took a personal interest in my appearance but, I realized later, it was more for his business than for me. He taught me how to modulate my voice. From him I also learned how to listen and be more responsive.

All these were tools to improve profit margin, not interpersonal relationship. Rudd received more training and outer armament. But by this point in his career, he was able to return something to his mentor:

I learned a lot from him but I was also helping him grow and eventually became a partner. I came in and took an old established business with a good name and a fine product but no promotion and I doubled his business two or three years in a row.

"And how did he show you his personal appreciation?" I asked.

"See, it was a work relationship, again. He showed his appreciation by increasing my salary. He was proud of me—I could tell by the way he introduced me—but it was never spoken between us." By now Rudd had learned to control the urge toward emotional expressiveness.

Rudd's education as an American businessman was capped by his last mentor, from whom he learned perhaps the most important lesson about trusting men—even mentors:

This man was head of an even larger corporation, which had bought out the company I was with. He was definitely a powerful father figure to me. He taught me how to wheel and deal, how to be hard. That was what I ultimately learned from him. I had trusted him and found out he was trying to screw me on a contract. I went into his office one day with a tape recorder strapped to my leg and made him repeat all the terms of our agreement. When the showdown came, I produced the tape. He taught me sometimes you really have to play rough.

In playing rough with his mentor, he graduated into autonomy as he was trained to live it: seek out the advantage and do not let your feelings get in the way.

BEING A MENTOR

It would appear that most of the value of the mentor-protegé relationship is gained by the protegé. What is in it for the older man?

My interviews and the literature suggest that being a mentor is as important a developmental stage as *having* a mentor.

To step into the mentor role is to acknowledge a man has accumulated enough knowledge, skill, and expertise to graduate from student to teacher. That in itself is enough reward for many men continuously yearning to be looked up to by other men, after being looked down upon for many years.

Men in their twenties and thirties become mentors to younger men but it is not until they reach their forties that their full potential is realized. A mentor of forty would be passing through a phase of adult maturation Levinson termed the "mid-life transition." Beginning as a man leaves his early adulthood behind and enters his middle adulthood (forty to sixty) this transition is marked by awareness of physical decline, career solidification, family stabilization, and generally greater responsibility as an adult. A man's relationship with his parents changes; roles reverse. His children, if he has them, are becoming independent. Psychoanalyst Erik Erikson identified an important aspect of middle adulthood as the concern for the nurturance of future generations. He termed this natural inclination to assume responsibility for the education and indoctrination of the next line of adults as "generativity." A man acts on this drive as a father, Cub Scout leader, teacher, supervisor, or mentor.

For a man of this age, finding a protegé to whom he can transmit knowledge can be a deeply satisfying way to fulfill the urge toward generativity. The mentor's own meaning is justified by the new knowledge that part of himself will be projected into the future via the younger man.

At the same time it makes him feel connected to the future, the mentor role connects a man with his own youth, which he sees quickly fading. Contact with young men—working with them, planning, directing, socializing—recharges the middle-aged man's own youthful energies and reminds him of the continuity of the life process as he comes to terms with the inevitability of his own death.

But there is a negative side as well. Being a mentor can be an awkward and heavy burden to carry. I learned this first hand on a visit I paid to an editor who had been an important professional and personal influence in my life. When I started out as a freelance writer he had given me several key assignments for major magazines that helped both my career and my self-confidence. More than that, though, I admired the humanistic touch he retained while wielding power and ideas in a big way. In the library of his Princeton, New Jersey, home I finally got up the courage to declare my debt, respect, and thanks.

The first thing I learned, as I tripped over my own words, was how difficult it was to take the leap into feelings. His response did not help matters. He quickly deflected the compliment and my awkward expression of gratitude:

> Mentor? That always troubles me as a way to be thinking about relationships. Ultimately, it's the language I dislike. It implies dominance by one over the other. I don't know of a mentor-protegé situation in which both aren't gaining something. It's not a one-way thing. There has to be a fundamental exchange going on.

He seemed to have jumped so quickly from the personal to the general that the emotion of the moment I had built myself up for was lost.

"What I wanted to say to you was that I really appreciate our friendship beyond all that," I said.

"So do I," he said and then went on:

> I know it doesn't work unless there's a parity. I benefitted as much from the things you've written as you have, in a purely commercial sense. I needed somebody to do a story that nobody else could do and you did it. Part of my stock in trade is to be able to have access to writers like you. That's what editors get paid for. So the books are balanced at the end of the day in those terms.

This all sounded hard-boiled and out of character from a man with whom I had had long talks about magazines and human nature. But what I realized was that in all that time we had never broached the subject about our feelings for each other. They were understood. There was mutual admiration and respect, personally and professionally. When it came to talking about it, however, my mentor became curiously impersonal.

"Does it make you uncomfortable knowing that you're such a strong role model for me?" I finally asked.

"Well, it does bother me," he admitted. "I get scared of it. Am I deserving of it? I wonder. But I don't take it seriously. I know you won't be blinded; you see my weaknesses and flaws. If I do take on 'protegés' they are usually of the sort that I know are too independent to buy my model entirely."

It took me a long time to realize that in giving vent to my feelings for him I had stepped outside the bounds of our structured relationship into the never-never-land of feelings. That was all that was needed to make him close up and back off—just as he was undoubtedly trained to do by his father and perhaps his own mentor as well.

TWO CLASSIC MENTORS

Most of us, sadly, miss out on having mentors or being mentors. We must rely on the stories of others. Perhaps that is why we revel in the legacies of some of the great mentors of history: Gandhi, Vince Lombardi, Buckminster Fuller, Gurdjieff, Linus Pauling and many others all served as mentors to young men who saw them as teachers.

Two famous mentor-protegé relationships were richly documented in letters: those of editor Maxwell Perkins and writer Thomas Wolfe; and psychoanalysts Sigmund Freud and Carl Jung. The results of these two intense relationships produced words and ideas that changed their fields. Of interest in both cases are the dramatic stages of devotional reverence followed by painful revolts, and, at the end, token reconciliations. Also evident are themes cited earlier: the important function the mentor serves by believing in the protegé, and the difficulty expressing emotions relating to the interpersonal relationship. It is also interesting to note that much of the so-called personal interaction that took place between these men occurred not face to face—indeed a threatening position for most men attempting to say how they feel about each other—but through the safer distance that the medium of letter-writing affords.

MAXWELL PERKINS/THOMAS WOLFE

In publishing, the name of Maxwell Perkins is synonymous with model editor and model mentor. In his thirty-six-year career with Charles Scribner's Sons, "Max" guided the careers and development of such writing talents as Ring Lardner, Erskine Caldwell, Taylor Caldwell, James Jones, Van Wyck Brooks, Marjorie Kinnan Rawlings, and others. The simple reason that so many writers considered him their mentor lay in his philosophy of dealing with writers. He coddled, prodded, supported, encouraged, and in all other ways appeared to believe in his writers. But to three who were to become America's foremost writers—F. Scott Fitzgerald, Ernest Hemingway, and Thomas Wolfe—Perkins transcended the role of "editor of genius" to serve as mentor, not just as an influential editorial advisor but as an inspirational older male figure.

One can read many of the qualities of the mentor relationship in the Perkins-Fitzgerald and Perkins-Hemingway matchups, but in the Perkins-Wolfe pairing we see the full-blown manifestations—both positive and negative—of the mentor-protegé bond. The relationship begins with reverential admiration and appreciation, turns into a struggle for power and control, and ends on a sad note of reconciliation just before Wolfe's death. At the start, hearing his book had been accepted by Perkins for publication, Wolfe echoes every young man's desire for recognition:

"I can't tell you how good your letter has made me feel," he wrote to Perkins. "Your words of praise have filled me with hope, and are worth more than their weight in diamonds to me.'' In his first correspondence he described for all men what he wants from a mentor: ''I want the direct criticism and advice of an older and more critical person.''

Wolfe revealed in a letter after their first meeting how important Perkins's praise was toward alleviating his self-doubt: ''I was so moved and touched to think that someone at length had thought enough of my work to sweat over it in this way that I almost wept. It was the first time, so far as I can remember, that anyone had concretely suggested to me that anything I had written was worth as much as fifteen cents.''

Working with an unwieldy manuscript the way no editor in publishing had before, Perkins helped Wolfe shape and produce *Look Homeward, Angel*. With its publication Perkins became recognized for what any good editor and any good mentor knows is his purpose and his reward. ''Without that other genius—Max—the world would never have heard of Tom Wolfe,'' a literary commentator said at the time. The compliment would become a double-edged sword later in the relationship.

Wolfe's reverence for Perkins continued to grow. Here, in one letter of affection, he linked his own success with finding a mentor:

> One year ago I had little hope for my work, and I did not know you. What has happened since may seem to be only a modest success to many people; but to me it is touched with strangeness and wonder. It is a miracle. I can no longer think of the time I wrote *Look Homeward, Angel*, but rather think of the time when you worked upon it. . . . You have done what I had ceased to believe one person could do for another— you have created liberty and hope for me. Young men sometimes believe in the existence of heroic figures stronger and wiser than themselves, to whom they can turn for an answer to all their vexation and grief. . . . You are for me such a figure: You are one of the rocks to which my life is anchored.

Characteristically humble, Perkins returned the compliment and the appreciation. ''I'm mightly glad you feel as you do—except for a sense of not deserving it,'' he wrote back, and then makes the point that the mentor gets back as much as he gives: "I hope anyway that there could be no serious thought of obligation between us but, as a matter of convenience of speech, I would point out that even if you really owed me a great deal, it would be cancelled by what I owe you."

The two men would walk the streets of New York at night, talking mostly about work, publishing, ideas for books and stories. It was on one of those walks that Perkins mentioned he "had always thought a grand story could be written about a boy who had never seen his father, his father having left when he was a baby—and of how this boy set out to find his father and went through a series of adventures . . . and finally did find him in some odd situation." Wolfe picked up on this theme—appropriately suggested by his own father figure—and wrote for the next four years on the subject of a man's quest for his father. That book became *Of Time and the River*.

It is no coincidence, I believe, that Wolfe initiated the first stages of his revolt and break from Perkins while trying to complete *Of Time and the River*. In order to come to final terms with one's father—and one's father figure—a man must move very far away from him.

"We create the figure of our father and we create the figure of our enemy," Wolfe wrote Perkins in a letter he never sent. The implication is that they are one and the same figure, and that both are merely a creation of our minds. Wolfe was caught in a struggle with himself, with the two sides of himself, the boy and the emerging man, the son and the father; and with the feelings, even against his strongest inclination and need, that he must shed this father figure in order to find himself.

But his need for support against his own self-doubt won out the first round of his revolt. He still wanted Perkins's approval. Working hard in London, he wrote Perkins: "I am a brave man, and I like myself for what I did here and I hope you like me too for I honor and respect you and I believe you can help me save myself. . . . I turn to you because I feel health and sanity and fortitude in you.''

But when Perkins urged Wolfe to hurry up and finish, applying some patronly pressure, Wolfe pulled away even further. "The only standard I will compete against now is in me: if I can't reach it, I'll quit. . . . What I do now must be for myself."

Perkins understood well the role he played in his protegé's life. In an article he published years later, he wrote:

> I, who thought Tom a man of genius, and loved him too, and could not bear to see him fail, was almost as desperate as he, so much there was to do. But the truth is that if I did him a real service—and in this I did—it was in keeping him from losing his belief in himself by believing in him. What he needed most was comradeship and understanding in a long crisis, and those things I could give him then.

The big break came after the publication of *Of Time and the River*. The reviews were favorable, for the most part, except in suggesting that Wolfe could not have written the book without Perkins' help. As soon as Wolfe realized that he was to be accepted for his accomplishments only if his mentor's participation was acknowledged as well, he was compelled to end the association so he could affirm his place as a full-grown man among men. Things became volatile between the two, with Wolfe pulling away and Perkins trying to appease him. The deterioration of their relationship accelerated. Wolfe himself understood the process, at least on some level. Writing later in his novel *You Can't Go Home Again*, Wolfe's protagonist George Webber says to his editor: "For I was lost and was looking for someone older and wiser to show me the way, and I found you, and you took the place of my father who had died. . . . The road now leads off in a direction contrary to your intent."

And so it did with Wolfe. It was then that Wolfe declared his complete autonomy from Perkins by severing his contractual agreement with Scribner's. Perkins was hurt, confused, and distressed. Officially he "faithfully and honorably discharged all obligations" of Wolfe to the publishing house; personally he again failed to express his deeper feelings. In a letter after Wolfe's declaration of independence he wrote:

> I can't express certain kinds of feelings very comfortably, but you must realize what my feelings are toward you. . . . You seem to think I have tried to control you. I only did that when you asked my help and then I did the best I could do. It all seems very confusing to me, but whatever the result I hope you don't mean it to keep us from seeing each other, or that you won't come to our house.

Wolfe would have none of it now. After a sticky legal settlement over a suit charged against Wolfe, in which Perkins suggested he pay just to end the case, Wolfe shot back at Perkins:

> Are you—the man I trusted and reverenced above all else in the world—trying, for some mad reason I cannot even guess, to destroy me? Don't you want me to go on? Don't you want me to write another book? Don't you hope for my life—my growth—the fulfillment of my talent? My health is well-nigh wrecked—worry, grief, and disillusionment has almost destroyed my talent—is *this* what you wanted? And why?

Wolfe's own insecurity at not being accepted as a separate entity from his mentor was motivating his need to disassociate from him. He began work on another book but he would not discuss it with Perkins "for fear that . . . it may be killed at its inception by cold caution, by indifference, by the growing apprehension and dogmatism of your own conservatism. Tell me," he continued in a letter, "what there is in the life around us on which we both agree; we don't agree in politics, we don't agree on economics, we are in entire disagreement on the present system of life around us, the way people live, the changes that should be made."

The break hurt Perkins terribly but he kept his feelings to himself. For the most part he never struck back, realizing the break was inevitable, staying inside the bounds of his mentor role. After hearing that Wolfe had signed with another publisher, Perkins wrote, ''I can easily imagine a biography of Tom written 20 years from now that would ascribe this action to his instinctive and manly determination to free all his bonds and stand up alone.''

Throughout a breakup that was intensely emotional (though consciously subdued as much as it could be), Wolfe made several gestures at reconciliation, and paid tribute to Perkins, for he could not entirely let go of this man he sincerely loved and admired. In one letter he concluded:

> This letter is a sad farewell but I hope it is for both of us a new beginning. . . . I am your friend, Max, and that is why I wrote this letter. . . . I am your friend and want you to be mine—please take this last line as being what I wanted to say the whole way through. I am your friend and always will be, I think.

In the last months of Wolfe's life—tragically cut short at thirty-eight by a brain tumor—Wolfe finally broke through his negative feelings about Perkins. From a hospital bed in Seattle, after a particularly close bout with death, Wolfe scribbled a letter to Perkins:

> I've made a long voyage and been to a strange country, and I've seen the dark man very close; and I don't think I was too much afraid of him, but so much of mortality still clings to me—Whatever happens I had this ''hunch'' and wanted to write you and tell you, no matter what happens or has happened, I shall always think of you and feel about you the way it was that 4th of July 3 years ago, when you met me at the boat, and we went on top of the building and all the strangeness and the glory and the power of life and of the city were below.
>
> Yours always,
> Tom

SIGMUND FREUD/CARL JUNG

The competition for power, the lack of personal exchange about intimate feelings, the great need for approval and confidence—all dynamics seen in the father-son relationship—are clear in the relationship of Sigmund Freud, known as the "father" of psychoanalysis, and Carl Jung, Freud's leading disciple. Though the two men saw each other in person but a few times during a seven-year period, they maintained close contact through letters. *The Freud-Jung Letters* is a collection of 360 letters written from 1906 to 1913. This correspondence is "the record of a friendship, a spiritual father-son relationship between two unique and ultimately irreconcilable talents," according to the book's editor, William McGuire. Though there are pages and pages of letters exploring the evolving theories and practices of this new field of research and practice, only here and there—and sometimes only between the lines—do these two lift the professional veils to focus on the interpersonal relationship between them. When they do, one of the things they reveal is that their relationship was at least as important as their exchange of ideas. For students of psychiatry, this relationship carries special meaning as well; these were, after all, the founding father and the heir-apparent of psychoanalysis.

In the first stage of their interaction, the reverence and respect they exhibit is mutual. Each had the effect of building the other's confidence, though for different reasons.

"You have inspired me with confidence for the future," Freud wrote to Jung after the young man had written to the older telling him how much he admired his theories and wanted to be his student. "I now realize that I am as replaceable as everyone else and that I could hope for no one better than yourself . . . to continue and complete my work."

"I only fear that you overestimate me and my powers," Jung wrote back, confessing his lack of self-confidence, especially in the shadow of his hero.

Freud understated the point when he wrote Jung: "I hope you will gain the recognition you desire and deserve . . . it means a great deal to me too." Finding an able second in Jung ensured Freud's own desire to gain recognition.

In the early years of their relationship Jung continued to put Freud on the hero's pedestal. "My veneration for you has something of the character of a 'religious' crush." Ironically, the issue of religion and its place in analysis would eventually cause their schism.

At one point in their correspondence, Jung suggested a form by which they continue their interpersonal liaison: "Let me enjoy your friendship not as one between equals but as that of father and son. This distance appears to me fitting and natural. It strikes a note that would prevent misunderstanding and enable two hard-headed people to exist, alongside one another in an easy unrestrained relationship."

Distance? Prevent misunderstanding? Unrestrained? Surely this student of psychoanalysis was not inviting them into what they both knew was the briar patch of human relationships.

Inevitably their friendship began to turn. Differences began to surface. Jung wanted to explore parapsychology and precognition; Freud rejected these pursuits as nonsense. One evening, while they talked together in one of their few personal encounters, a loud noise sounded in a bookcase. At once, Jung predicted it would happen again—and it did. But Freud would have none of his friend's claim to psychic power. "That evening freed me inwardly from the oppressive sense of your paternal authority," Jung wrote. Freud replied that he indulged in Jung's interest in what he called the "spook complex" with the interest "one accords a charming delusion in which one does not participate oneself."

New differences arose around such theories as incest and libido. Jung's letters began to contain a tension: He chomped at the bit of theoretic discovery while Freud tried to tame his impatience. Freud wrote back to Jung: "Rest easy dear son Alexander, I will leave you more to conquer than I myself have managed." The reference to Alexander is an allusion to the ancient lineage of mentors and their protegés—from Socrates to Plato to Aristotle to Alexander the Great. Jung, however, would not be satisfied with Freud's leftovers, and he invoked these lines from Nietzsche's *Zarathustra*: "One repays a teacher badly if one remains only a pupil. And why, then, should you not pluck at my laurels? Now I bid you lose me and find yourselves; and only when you have all denied me will I return to you."

If only every mentor had that enlightened attitude. Now, in order to find himself, Jung had to revolt fully from his mentor. He realized "how different I am from you—enough to effect a radical change in my whole attitude." He felt Freud "underestimates my work by a very wide margin." He lashed out at Freud, suggesting, "Look at your bit of neurosis— but you could not submit to analysis, 'without losing your authority.' " Later he added this critical appraisal:

> Your technique of treating your pupils like patients is a blunder. You produce either slavish sons or impudent puppies. . . . You remain on top, as the father, sitting pretty. . . . If ever you should rid yourself entirely of your complexes and stop playing father to your sons and instead of continuously aiming at their weak spots took a good look at your own for a change, then I will mend my ways and at one stroke uproot the vice of being of two minds about you.

At first Freud, emotionally tongue-tied, could only muster a brief, terse reply. Then he wrote again: "I propose we abandon our personal relation entirely. I shall lose nothing by it for my own emotional tie with you has long been a thin thread—the lingering effects of past disappointments—take your full freedom." He added, "We are agreed a man should subordinate his personal feelings to the general interest of his branch of endeavor."

Following that there are only stilted letters back and forth. Jung eventually resigned from the editorship of the publication of the psychoanalytic society Freud started with Jung's help. Then Jung resigned the presidency of the organization.

Freud barely mentioned Jung's name after that while Jung, though crediting Freud as his teacher and founder of the field of psychoanalysis, never contacted his mentor again. Their eventual reconciliation was only an obligatory payment of obeisance to each other.

Whether one's mentor is Freud or Freddie the Fireman, the importance of his contribution to a young man's development is the same. He serves as a bridge from the inner circle of the family to the wide-open outside world. He supplies the polishing phase of the young man's training, one in which objective criteria, not the father's subjective standards, are made explicit, and then applied. In a sense, when a young man has found a mentor, learned from him what he can, and then surpassed him, he is truly a man for better or worse. No longer merely a son, a grandson, a student, or protegé, the young man has earned his autonomy as a full-fledged man in a man's world: the embodiment of a special culture transmitted to him by now-receding figures of fathers, grandfathers, and mentors.

Nonetheless, there is one role a man plays forever in his life, and it is one that apparently changes very little over the course of development: He'll always be a brother.

3

The World of Brothers:
Cain and Abel in the Land of Nod

I think there's always been a level of competition
between my younger brother Kevin and me. I think
he's felt that way because I was stronger and bigger
and taller. I'm a lawyer now, and I think he still feels
prodded on to compete against me professionally. He
decided to go to medical school, I'm convinced, just
to one-up me. When we were younger I used to beat
the hell out of him all the time. I'd go up to him
and say, "Do you want to wrestle?" and he'd say,
"No," and I would say, "Too bad," and pull him to
the ground. We fought constantly.

> —Dan, forty-one

We were very close, my brothers and me. We did a
lot of things together. We created our own little
world—of illusions, games, sports. We published little
magazines. We designed futuristic cars. But the
most important thing I learned from having two
brothers is what I call the "male-oriented approach."
That there is always a clearly defined pecking
order, based on age, athletic ability, and intelligence.
You learn how to take first place, second place,
and third place and you learn very quickly where
you'll usually fall in. Men are definitely competitive,
and brothers more so. I felt as though I performed
well among my brothers, that this *is* a man's world
and that I was strong in it.

> —Alan, twenty-eight

The legacy of brothers—in literature, myth, psychological
study, and real life—is marked by the competition for power
as well as the failure to communicate on personal matters. As

in relationships between fathers and sons, the bond between brothers is made complex by fervent loyalty and fierce rivalry, closeness and distance, camaraderie and competition.

In general, all sibling relationships contain such characteristics. Dr. Jane Pfouts, associate professor of social work at the University of North Carolina, has written:

> When people speak of their siblings, they speak of ambivalence, of solidarity and rivalry, of the desire to be equal and yet differentiated. The sibling world is a fateful world, for it is here that children first learn the costs and rewards of interacting with peers and it is here that permanent adult roles have their beginnings. It is also a primitive world of naked emotions, cruelty, betrayal and Machiavellian deceit.

I contend that if those are the traits of male-female sibling relationships, we can assume two males—trained in competition and rivalry—will double the effect. Is it not surprising, then, that the brother bond has been an adversary one for so long? Remember Cain and Abel? Only four chapters into the Old Testament and we have the young society's first murder: fratricide. Cain slew Abel out of jealousy of their father's— their Heavenly Father's—favor. And the punishment for that murder: "If you till the soil it shall no longer yield its strength to you. You shall become a ceaseless wanderer of earth. . . . And Cain left the presence of the Lord and settled in the land of Nod, east of Eden."

Fitting the crime, the punishment is harsh: Cain's strength (power) is taken away and he is rejected by his father, abandoned, and banned to the Land of Nod. And then there was Isaac, tricked into giving the blessing intended for his oldest son Esau to his younger son Jacob. The blessing:

> May God give you
> Of the dew of heaven and the fat of the earth,
> Abundance of new grain and wine.
> Let people serve you,
> And nations bow to you;
> Be master over your brothers,

And let your mother's son bow to you.
Cursed be they who curse you,
Blessed they who bless you.

It is indeed a blessing to covet: a blessing of wealth (power),
of supremacy (power), of mastery over his brothers (power).
When Esau learned that his brother had gained the blessing he
"wept aloud." Isaac spoke these words to Esau: "By your
sword you shall live and you shall serve your brother." But
Isaac also promised his son revenge: "But when you grow
restive, you shall break his yoke from your neck."

Esau's own vow: "Let but the mourning period of my father
come, and I will kill my brother."

A generation later the sons of Jacob, now known as Israel,
rose up against a favored youngest brother: "Now Israel
loved Joseph best of all his sons, for he was the child of his
old age. . . . And when his brothers saw their father loved
him more than any of his brothers, they hated him so that
they could not speak a friendly word with him." Later they
plotted his death but sold him off as a slave instead.

The stories of the Bible can be taken in many ways—as
true historical events, embellished truths, parables, folklore,
or even fanciful nursery rhyme—but in any case the massive
impact they have had on our culture, attitudes, values, and
behavior is undeniable. What the biblical stories tell us is that
brothers vie for the affection, attention, and approval of their
parents and that a definite hierarchy exists among brothers,
determined most often by order of birth. These conclusions
were reconfirmed a couple of thousand years later by the
modern literature of psychological research on siblings.

Brothers base their attitudes and behaviors in terms of each
other on comparative abilities and accomplishments, on a
hierarchical ranking according to what they *do* and how well
they do it.

Two psychologists found that manual workers are more
satisfied occupationally when they perceive their occupational
positions as better than those of their brothers, while the least
satisfied are those whose occupational levels are lower than

their brothers'. Bert Adams, in *Kinship in an Urban Setting*, has written:

> Siblings are in fact the comparative reference group *par excellence*, being among one's effective kin from birth or soon thereafter, and being social givens, unlike friends. We are now prepared to suggest that middle-class values, and personal comparisons and identifications in terms of them, are central to the relations between siblings in our urban, industrial society. To be more explicit, a young adult is more likely to feel close to, and possible identify with, his sibling if the sibling is middle-class than if he is working class.

If the brothers are "occupationally disparate"—that is, if one winds up in a professional job and the other in a blue-collar job—they are unlikely to feel close to one another. Adams explained. "In this case it appears that occupation is too salient as a measure of personal success or failure to allow the working-class male to be subjectively close to his middle-class brother. To do otherwise would be to admit within the family his own occupational shortcoming."

In other words, their relationship is determined by what they *do*, not what they say. These occupationally disparate brothers, Adams noted, "are the most likely of any category of sibling—male or female—to assert that they have little in common, or little basis for a close relationship."

Of the men I interviewed, Joe and Harry best exemplify this finding. Their case is made all the more interesting by the fact that they are thirty-two-year-old twins. Said Harry, the older twin by half an hour:

> I'm a social scientist. Joe's a welder. We live a half hour from each other but we rarely get together. Ever since we were kids I used to boss him around. That little half hour difference was enough to make me feel like the older brother. I dominated him. I'm the same way now. I definitely let him know how I feel. I'll get mad if he tells me something he screwed up at work. When we were kids we fought a lot too. Especially after report cards would come out; I clearly was smarter than him. He resented it and felt frustrated because

there wasn't much he could do about it. Our parents have always tried to treat us equally but there were subtle ways they gave me more attention and encouragement to achieve. One birthday I got an expensive set of science books; Joe got a football. Or they'd take me out to dinner when I made the honor roll. Now when we see each other at family gatherings it's awkward. We have all this shared family history but we also feel like we have nothing in common. We never confide in each other—mostly because he'd never come to me for help or admit something's not going right for him.

University of North Carolina's Dr. Pfouts's was one of the few psychological studies I found concentrating exclusively on brother-brother interactions. In the 1972 study, fifty pairs (no more than four years apart between the ages of five and fourteen) were classified into groups on the basis of scores on personality and IQ tests.

The study found that when two brothers were both gifted and their scores were nearly equal on IQ and personality tests, their relationship was ambivalent and highly competitive in the academic, athletic, and social realms. When one brother scored in the gifted range and the other at least fifteen points lower, the more able brother was ambivalent toward his less able brother and the less able was quite hostile toward the other. When both brothers were equal in intelligence but one was better adjusted socially, the well-adjusted brother was ambivalent, but the maladjusted brother was hostile toward the other. When one brother was both gifted intellectually and scored high on personality tests and his brother scored low in both areas, the able, well-adjusted brother was ambivalent and the deficient brother was hostile.

Here again we see the emphasis on competitive performance as a basis for emotional feelings—not only in the dyad of brothers but in the psychological community designing the studies. This study suggests that the healthiest emotional environment is between brothers of equal competitive level. My own research bore that out.

I interviewed another pair of twins, Steve and Mike, who

were matched in almost every category. Academically they scored within points of each other on their college entrance exams; they graduated among the top ten in their class; they both went to the same law school, were both class officers in college and were equally popular and equally competitive in sports. That made them feel better about each other. Said Mike,

> I know I would have felt bad if I did much worse than Steve. But I also wouldn't have liked to do better either, though it'd be better than doing worse. When I found out our high school class rank was the same, I thought that was good. When we got our law board scores back I did really well and thought, "Oh God, poor Steve," but when he told me he did the same, I was able to feel great.

Steve commented on the same subject:

> I certainly would have felt better to do better than him than worse, but at the same time when I found out I did well on something I was relieved when he did as well. I didn't like the feeling of doing better either. When we took the bar exam, I passed. At first Mike's name wasn't on the pass list due to an administrative oversight. I felt terrible. But he did pass. There was something comfortable about being even. It obviated the need for competition. If I heard someone say we were the same athletically, that was very satisfying to hear; I preferred hearing that than hearing I was better.

However, the need for competition was not obviated, as Steve purports. It was, rather, precisely because they were equal on competitive achievement that they felt comfortable *being* competitive. Later, examining men's friendships, I observed a similar phenomenon. Men who felt equal competitively enjoyed the competition and the friendship that much more, as elaborated in Chapter 6.

For Steve and Mike, as for other brothers, being equal created another problem: how to establish a separate identity. Steve addressed the issue:

Because of my brother I was never the only person. I was never separated from him for any substantial amount of time until I was nineteen or twenty. I was never alone. We played together, went to school together. I don't have a sense of what it's like to get up in the morning and not have someone there to play with. Even now I don't visit friends a lot, don't talk about my feelings as much as I imagine other people do because I never felt the need to do that with my brother. I'm aware of what he's thinking. I know he's thinking the same things that part of my subconscious are thinking because of shared history, genes, etcetera. By college we were associating with different kinds of people and it really felt wonderful to be taken into someone else's confidence in a way that separated me as an individual.

Said Mike:

Sometimes we're frighteningly similar. Basically we're more alike than not. We share a certain sense of humor. We say the same things at the same time. I think as the years went on we had to create differences. He's more audacious. I'm slightly conservative. I always felt embarrassed about the fact that we chose the same schools, the same professions and live in the same city. But the kinds of women we went out with were always different.

Asserting their differences became the issue of these brothers who were so much alike. For others who cannot compete on equal footing, the difference can be a sore spot forcing a face-off.

The dilemma of two brothers competing on unequal ground is violently protrayed in *True West*, a starkly straightforward play by Sam Shepard, whose works reflect the masculine tendency toward action and physical senses more than intellectualization and expressiveness. *True West*'s protagonists are two brothers: Lee, the older desert drifter who envies the younger, Austin, a successful screenwriter. Lee ends up selling an idea based on the ''true west'' while Austin's version is rejected as being too unrealistic. Lee, whose envy and hostility toward his brother are clear, gloats over his victory, until Austin, in a last desperate attempt to preserve his own sense of worth, tries to strangle Lee to death. In the closing scene the two square off, "keeping a distance between them." A single coyote is heard in the distance and as "the lights fade softly into moonlight, the figures of the brothers now appear to be caught in a vast desert-like landscape, they are very still but watchful for the next move."

The stage directions are bleak and, granted, it is only a play, but the same scene is acted out every day on the business stage.

I talked with a man who runs a successful construction company together with his brother. How did they manage, I wondered, to work together without running into the brick wall of all this male/brother rivalry? He said:

> It's two things. What it comes down to is: Business comes first in our relationship. Personal feelings and emotions are secondary or nonexistent. In fact my brother and I aren't that compatible. A lot of what he does pisses me off. We've got different value systems. I'm more into the work and the responsibility. He likes the money but doesn't want to have to work for it. But we don't discuss any of this. We actually don't have intimate talks about anything, especially about ourselves and least of all about the business. So that's part of it. The other thing is, well, I'm older so I give the orders. That's our understanding and we never even verbally agreed on *that*; it's just been that way since we were kids. I told him what to do and he did it.

"Since we were kids." Many people assume that that childhood competitiveness dissipates in adulthood, but the evidence contradicts that notion. In a paper presented to the American Psychological Association in 1980, University of Cincinnati psychologists Helgola Ross and Joel Milgram made a strong case for the persistence of rivalry into adulthood. (Again, this research does not apply exclusively to brothers, but we can make some deductions about men from it.) Of sixty-five subjects aged twenty-five to ninety-three, from a

midwestern community, 71 percent said they had been rivalrous with a brother or sister. Of those, 36 percent claimed to
have overcome the feelings but 45 percent admitted the feelings were still alive. Half said the rivalrous attitudes were
precipitated by parents favoring one sibling over another.
And, they added, when competition continued into adulthood, it was fueled by the continuation of parental favoritism.

One problem these researchers identified as contributing to
the difficulty sorting out these rivalries—even into adulthood—
was that most siblings rarely talked about their rivalry, as the
working brother quoted earlier indicates. Successful siblings
often did not even know their achievements were causing
envy, and siblings who felt inferior did not want to say so. As
Ross and Milgram stated, "admitting sibling rivalry may be
experienced as equivalent to admitting maladjustment. To
reveal feelings of rivalry to a brother or sister who is perceived as having the upper hand increases one's vulnerability
in an already unsafe situation."

These comments, viewed in the light of the competitiveness that dominates male-male relations, help to explain why
rivalry among brothers begins at a very early age and continues well into adulthood. In fact, as brothers get older and are
ever more deeply indoctrinated by their fathers and mentors
into the world of men, it should be no surprise that competition between brothers grows more intense. Both research by
psychologists and comments by men I interviewed bear out
this expectation. Bert Adams observed in *Kinship in an Urban Setting* that grown men report less closeness and contact
with brothers than women do with sisters, even when differences of geographical proximity are taken into account. And I
was startled by the comments of a fifty-eight-year-old man
who began talking about his sixty-year-old brother as though
the two of them were still adolescents:

> My brother lives in Chicago. I'm in Boston. He never comes
> to see me. I always have to visit him. This was the first time I
> had seen him in about three years; I combined the visit with a
> business trip. On the first day together we decided to play a

round of golf—like we did when we were kids. Well, right away he reverted to this big brother stuff—telling me which club to use, how to play the ball, what I was doing wrong. It was as though we were ten and twelve again, and playing older brother/younger brother. And don't you know I fell right into the same role. Defending myself, trying to outdo him. The rest of that week with him was—as far as I was concerned—very remote. I don't know how he felt. We never discussed it.

The younger brother is a car dealer; his brother the owner of a retail business. Both are successful at their work and respected in their worlds. And yet, with each other, they are reduced to two boy-brothers vying for control, for superiority. And as in other interviews with men—whether fathers and sons, mentors or brothers—they both exhibit an inability to talk about their situation with each other and resolve their differences.

WHEN BROTHERS BOND

Where, then, is that highly touted brotherly love, that spirit of brotherhood, that he-ain't-heavy-he's-my-brother sensibility? Or is the brother bond just one more of those male-male relationships that holds out the promise of more than it delivers—and therefore conditions men to expect little or nothing from men in their lives? The answer is yes and no. Yes, our culture pays a lot of lip service to the notion of brotherhood, but brothers as supportive men on whom men can depend is not necessarily substantiated by the research or the anecdotes of men I interviewed. No, on the other hand, because a very strong bond does exist between many brothers that is potentially one of the strongest, most positive dyads in a man's world.

Aside from the older brother/younger brother tug-of-war, the competition for father's attention and blessings, and the rivalry in adulthood, brothers are there for each other the way few men are. One element contributing to the strength of the bond is the sheer amount of time spent together. Another element is the biological connection. Still another factor, no doubt, is some version of Freud's somewhat overdramatic notion of the brother horde banding together to kill the father. In *Totem and Taboo* he envisioned this scenario:

> One day the expelled brothers joined forces, slew and ate the father, and thus put an end to the father horde. Together they dared and accomplished what would have remained impossible for them singly. Perhaps some advance in culture, like the use of a new weapon, had given them the feeling of superiority. Of course, these cannabilistic savages ate their victim. This violent primal father had surely been the envied and feared model for each of the brothers. Now they accomplished their identification with him by devouring him and each acquired a part of his strength. The totem feast, which is perhaps mankind's first celebration, would be the repetition and commemoration of this memorable, criminal act with which so many things began, social organizations, moral restrictions and religion.

Later, Freud added: "In thus ensuring each other's lives the brothers express the fact that no one of them is to be treated by the other as they all treated the father. They preclude a repetition of the fate of the father."

This does not necessarily mean brothers go around plotting to kill their fathers. They can, however, gain a power together over their father they couldn't individually. And, in so doing, break through barriers between themselves. And they can "kill" their father in other ways, as a twenty-two-year-old named Carl explained in less psychoanalytic terms:

> On almost every level I can think of, my brother Rich and I were as different as day and night. He's dark-featured; I'm light. He's introverted. I'm an extrovert. He reads a lot and is a good student. I like sports and hate homework. But we had one thing in common: We both hated our father. It seemed to us like he played us off each other. "Why can't you get better

grades, like your brother Rich," he'd chide me. "Hit the ball, klutz," he'd embarrass Rich. We used to plot little ways of screwing him up. Like leaving his lawn mower out in the rain to rust. Or making a mess of the den just before his poker gang would come over—and then disappear for the night. We used to complain about him to each other and it really brought us together. Now we're closer than ever, we can respect and even admire each other's differences.

Whether killing, in a symbolic sense, or working or even wrestling, brothers bond—like most men bond—by doing things together.

The transcendant power of the brother bond is most dramatically demonstrated in times of stress: When a brother has a drinking or drug problem, when a brother's marriage falls apart, when he is breaking up with a woman, when he has lost his job, when serious illness befalls a brother. In this regard brothers are like men in other kinds of relationships with men: They come to each other's aid in times of crisis, and sometimes only at those times. This account by a thirty-seven-year-old Los Angeles sales representative reminded me of experiences sons related in terms of their fathers:

When my brother and I were young we were inseparable. We fought, yes, but it was like puppies. It was playful. It would pass in a second and then we'd be off on our next adventure or a project like building a tree house. Years later we had a falling out. His lifestyle changed, and I didn't like it. He was married but having affairs and flaunting them. His business scene was questionable; I wondered whether he was selling drugs. But I never asked, that was his business. Then he started acting very wierd—moody, irresponsible—and I knew it must be drugs or pills. His wife left him. He had no money. He was a wreck. Even though I had lost all respect for him, he had no one to turn to so I asked him to move in with me. I mean, *this was my brother*. I couldn't bear to see this guy I grew up with—my flesh and blood—just fall to pieces. It was like when he bled, I bled. I covered his expenses, spent long evenings just talking with him—crying, laughing, reminiscing—got him to go to a therapist and basically get his act back together. I never knew I could be there for anybody the way I was there for my brother.

I had heard stories from sons about having so-called "man-to-man" talks with their fathers in similar times of crisis: when they were either getting divorced, getting married, or going through career crisis and transition. Only when pushed to the edge, it seemed, would men come to each other's side, open up, and reveal their vulnerabilities and needs. It appeared the same way with brothers.

BIRTH ORDER AND
THE QUALITY OF BROTHERHOOD

"My relationship with my older brother and my two younger brothers was always strained," began Steve, a thirty-eight-year-old small-press publisher from San Francisco:

We were all very competitive. Michael, the oldest, would come home from school and take out his defeats on me. I worshipped him anyway, though. My mother was aware of the little jealousies between us; my father was basically unsupportive. I think generally I'm still kind of terrified of anyone who I picture as an older brother. Nowadays Michael and I don't communicate on what you'd call an intimate level. We joke a little but I feel like I'm playing charades around him. It's not like there's a lot of contact. I came to the realization that while I don't necessarily fear him anymore, I still associate my lack of confidence to always coming in second to him. I still look to other men to fulfill successful role models for me—and I'm still unfulfilled. One summer I came home from a madly romantic affair with a young lady, feeling much older, and I remember specifically thinking, "Now Michael will accept me"—which he didn't. I have another brother 20 months younger than me. With him it was a classic case of some guy coming along and almost literally taking the nipple away from me. I still get anxious today when people are serving food; I always think I'm not going to get my portion.

Recent studies suggest that birth order is an important factor in reinforcing the rivalry of siblings. University of Michigan social psychologist Hazel Markus reported in the June 1981 *Psychology Today*: "Firstborns develop particular ideas and expectations about power, leadership and responsibility; about what is socially acceptable and about the importance of friendships and relationships with other people. These ideas are likely to be markedly different from those that develop in later-borns."

Recall Little George, from Chapter 1, who always felt himself to be in competition with his father, who strove all his life to outdo his father or to be as different from him as he could. George took the brunt of the pressure from his father, saving his brother Frank from feeling it. Younger by four years, and now a sales manager for a radio station, Frank told me what it was like to be "Number Two Son" in his family:

> My father and I had a very comfortable relationship. I got to be the spoiled brat of the family; in fact I got away with murder. He didn't have all the expectations of me that he had of George. I didn't fight against my father the way George did, and I didn't feel the need to establish my own identity from him. I went through a healthy rebellion stage, but for the most part I admired the tough-guy image of my father and even tried to emulate it. It's the best reputation you can have in this business. I never wanted to write so I felt out of competition on that count. That was left to George. When my brother and his wife decided not to have children, my father tried to pressure me into naming my first son after him. But I felt that was George's responsibility—not mine. But my father was pleased it was a boy anyway, to continue the family name.

George was a buffer between Frank and their father. He was also a buffer between Frank and the world:

> When I was just entering high school, George was graduating. When I was entering college, George was just graduating. George knew the ropes and ushered me into each of these scenes. I relied on him a lot. It was nice being known as

George's younger brother. It gave me access and credibility. I got friendly with his friends, who were always older, and that made me feel special—accepted by the big guys. I joined the same fraternity he belonged to. Even today some people by mistake call me George, and I like it.

George was a model to whom I looked for how to act. When our mother died we were at camp together. I remember being driven home from camp that night and watching George to see how I should be responding emotionally.

At some point, though, it became important for Frank to differentiate himsef from his brother. I asked him how he did that. He recalled:

I've been watching a lot of old family movies lately. Most of them show George and me wrestling. That was our thing, to argue, fight. I always took it as fun but there was also something very serious about it to me. I remember specifically when I was twelve and he was sixteen and we both realized after one fight that George no longer had the physical edge. I was the better athlete and that became my thing. George was the thinker; I was the jock.

Psychologists have given birth-order effects some careful attention. In a study at the National Institute of Mental Health, researchers observed thirty-two first-born and second-born siblings when each was three months old. They found that parents spent less time with their second-borns than with their first-borns in social, affectionate, and care-giving interaction. Stanford University's Eleanor Maccoby and her colleagues at the Stanford Longitudinal Project watched mother-child behaviors, noting instances of positive, negative and neutral bids for mother's attention, as well as instances of mother's warmth, praise, pressure to complete tasks, and verbal and physical attempts to prohibit their children from doing something. The results showed mothers to be more restrictive of their first-borns than their second-borns. The reason for this may be that parents become less anxious about their skills as parents after the first child is born and allow second-borns more freedom. The effect, studies show, suggest that later-borns appear to be less anxious and less controlling. And, according to a study by psychologists Norman Miller and Geoffrey Maruyama at the University of Southern California, later-borns seem to have another advantage: greater popularity than first-borns. Later-borns were more likely to be chosen as people to play with or sit by in class than were first-borns or only children. Psychologist Markus's explanation: "Later-borns see themselves as *powerless* [italics mine] and as occupying subordinate roles. They seldom have a direct pipeline to those in *control* [italics mine] of the family organization and must therefore learn to work with and around other family members to achieve their goals."

On the downside, however, later-borns were found to have less pride in themselves than first-borns. Never the sole focus of their parents' attention, later-borns were less likely to think that people held them in high regard and therefore their self-esteem rated lower in studies by University of Cincinnati students. In addition, later-borns find it difficult to assert their independence since they had not only parents but older siblings as well to treat them as dependent and in need of help.

Among first-borns, the most reliable and best-known findings in birth-order research repeatedly suggest they are the achievers—and often the overachievers. First-borns are also leaders, taking initiative and assuming responsibility. They tend to see themselves as in charge—taking over whether others need it or not, which may account for their relative unpopularity. Because they are older siblings, they tend to act as though anyone else is a younger sibling needing direction.

One younger brother I know named Darryl, who was about to travel from Maine to California to visit his older brother Raymond in order to "straighten out some things," talked to me about how Raymond always kept him (Darryl) under his thumb:

> When we used to wrestle he'd sit on my chest. It wasn't puppy play; I'd have trouble breathing and he wouldn't get off me. Then it changed because I became a much better athlete

and physically stronger than him. So he started abusing me mentally because he was smarter. Until last summer he'd call me ''Dummy.'' He eventually apologized in a roundabout way but not until after he had barraged me with a total attack on me: ''What are you going to do with your life? What are you doing about poverty in America?'' On and on without letting me get a word in edgewise.

That's part of why I'm going to see him, because what he's doing to me is actual violence. In a way I don't know if I have the strength to do this—to go to him—but I really love Raymond. I simply want to say, ''Look, I've been coming to you my whole life. When are you going to start coming to me? When are you going to show me you love me?'' What he does is use mind games to pull it right out from under you. After all these years he's still an unknown to me. That's part of his intrigue, and his power. He sucks you in with his mystery, his coolness and aloofness. Raymond always lets me know he's doing something I'm not. We'll talk on the phone and he presents himself through the things he's *doing*. ''I'm writing. I'm building a cabinet. I'm studying art.'' But he never reveals what's behind it—his feelings about it. And he never, never says, ''I love you. I care about you.''

Darryl's frustrations were clear. But unlike so many other men he was willing to break set by expressing his true feelings to and for his brother. He himself recognized the strength he would need to ovecome the barrier of inexpressiveness—and suffer possible rejection, or worse, indifference—simply to say ''I love you'' to his brother. It was one of the most poignant interviews I conducted and it brought home the difficulty all men have of saying those three words to each other—even under the most heartrending circumstances.

As an aside to the discussion here, I would note that throughout the interviews in this chapter are statements by men about the lack of communication between brothers—especially when the talks relate to feelings about each other. This is not inconsistent with what surfaced in earlier chapters and what will reappear in later chapters. But there are times, as many men assert, when talk is superfluous, when words pollute a simple shared moment. While interviewing brothers, I was told about such a moment by a brother:

> My brother and I often spent long periods of time together in absolute silence. And there still seems to be a kind of communication that goes on within it. I don't feel like it's lost or wasted time when we're together like that. One time we were both in law school, living in the same city, and not seeing each other much so we decided to have lunch together. We went to his apartment and made tuna fish sandwiches and we sat in total silence for half an hour munching and chomping and grunting. And when we were all done he said to me, "We'll have to do this more often." We both became totally hysterical laughing. It struck us that here we were and nothing was going on in terms of interpersonal communication—and yet just being together was enough.

BROTHERS PLAYING MENTOR

One element that can strengthen the bond between brothers, yet that derives from birth order, might be considered an adaptation of Erikson's generativity theory. An older brother can serve as mentor to his younger brother, ushering his same-sex sib into the world of men even as he himself is just figuring it out. Just having someone—even a "kid brother" —under him has its own attractions. But further, from the generativity point of view, playing mentor provides the opportunity to learn on the job, so to speak: how to pass knowledge down to generations (even if that future "generation" is only a year behind). Of course the other side of mentoring is inherent in the role: There is always the threat of the younger brother surpassing the older in achievement. And too, as psychologists Ross and Milgram noted as well, the young person runs the risk of having his brother-mentor criticize his accomplishments rather than praise them, suffering yet another setback as a man among men.

While the older brother plays mentor, the younger watches

him for messages as to how to relate to other men, and, as in the father-son relation, moves from reverence to revolt to reconciliation. First he idolizes his brother, playing monkey-see-monkey-do. He feels flattered to be accepted into his older brother's group of friends. During this phase he appreciates being the student.

At some point, however, the younger brother revolts in order to begin defining himself as an individual. The turning point comes when the younger brother can finally overpower his older sib physically; or when he finds an area in which he excels and his brother does not. That point might come, as we have seen, when the younger brother becomes successful in a career.

Having finally confirmed for himself that he is not living in the shadow of his brother, the younger brother can reapproach his brother on more equal footing (though the evidence in this chapter shows how difficult it is to maintain this new stance). For the most part, the brother bond prevails and reconciliation is accomplished. The biblical Joseph finally forgave his brothers for their mistreatment of him, but not until he was in a very secure position of power in Egypt. Even Esau as a grown man forgave Jacob. When Jacob knew they would meet again he feared Esau's revenge and hid his family. But Esau met his brother with outstretched arms.

Often, reconciliation between brothers (and all siblings) is precipitated by the witnessing of the aging or illness or death of a parent. The loss of a parent can prompt siblings to pull together as a way of strengthening their own family bond. Whether Freud's theory of the brother horde killing the father totem is valid or not, brothers whose father is dying may be brought closer together by their shared guilt over the love-hate ambivalence both may have felt for him over the years.

Still, even where a new closeness is forged by a family crisis it is clouded by ambivalences. Purdue University developmental psychologist Victor Cicirelli conducted a twelve-year study of sibling relationships. Though the bulk of what he found was that siblings remain important to each other into old age, sometimes becoming more important with time, he also discovered that siblings' negative feelings toward each other surface when their parents become more dependent or seriously ill. Typically the younger will expect the older to take care of the parent, while the older will resent the younger for passing the responsibility. Conversely, some sibs compete to do the most for the dependent parent, with the younger or less-favored child viewing the parent's need of help as an opportunity to win a lifelong family contest. Finally, after the death of a parent, sibs may jockey for position of leadership as they move into the roles of family elders.

Societal changes are making reconciliation between brothers a greater imperative than ever before. Michael Kahn suggested as one of the main theses of *The Sibling Bond* that "siblings are becoming more and more dependent upon one another in contemporary families because of the attrition in family size. If you have only one sibling, that one becomes enormously important." Divorce, one-parent homes, two working parents, and the fact that a transient culture splits up nuclear families geographically all underscore the need for siblings to maintain contact with each other.

The bridge to the land of Nod is not long. Bound by blood, bonded by their maleness and all that "time in" together, brothers could very well be the model of what we idealistically call brotherly love—except for all those barriers on the bridge.

For, as we have seen, brother teaches brother what father teaches son, what mentor teaches protegé, what man teaches man. And that is that rivalry rules. He who comes in first—who is born first, scores higher, earns more—is better. Like an endless game of one-up*man*ship from cradle to coffin. The lessons of competition and emotional inexpressiveness come through the brother bond as well. In short, it is a relationship full of the same ambiguities and ambivalences as all male-male connections.

And yet the pull is there. The love between men—between and among brothers of blood and otherwise—compels them to cross that bridge. By now, though, they have learned to proceed with caution.

4

Beyond Brothers:
Men's Clubs

> Our strongest descriptions of relations between men
> are analogies to kinship, as when an older benefactor
> is described as "like a father," or two inseparables
> as "like brothers." When human relations have
> meaning to men, we judge them to be at least akin
> to kinship.
>
> —Wilson Carey McWilliams,
> *The Idea of Fraternity*
> *in America*

In his in-depth analysis of American history and political
thought, McWilliams continued: "Kinship does more than
describe group feelings. It introduces men to hierarchy, authority and command." The central theme of life in a man's
world could not be expressed more succinctly. McWilliams's
massive work is based on what he calls "the long-cherished
ideal of the past: fraternity, a relation of affection founded on
shared values and goals."

"Of all the terms of kinship, none has had so enduring an
appeal and so firm a place in political symbolism as fraternity." And yet, he pointed out, "of all human relationships
. . . fraternity is the most premised on imperfection, the most
fraught with ambiguity, the least subject to guidance by fixed
rules, the most dependent on choice."

The dilemma is even those groups that proclaim universal
brotherhood face the problem that men fall short of the ideal.
In other words, real men do not measure up.

Moreover, he explained, the definition contains seeds of its
own destruction. Adhering to the hierarchical structure of

such organizations means a man must suppress disagreement for the sake of order, which only "produces self-contempt in the suppressing individual . . . and to hide disagreement is to draw lines of superiority and inferiority between the self and the other."

Members of the Kiwanis, the Masons, the Knights of Columbus, the Rotary, Sigma Alpha Mu, Tau Delta Phi, Phi Beta Kappa and the Wednesday night bowling league might argue adamantly against such an analysis. Their organizations, they would say, are the very affirmation of the definition of fraternal: brotherliness. But such a defiant single-mindedness fails to account for the two-sided nature of brothers' relationships as confirmed in the preceding chapter. Associates who call themselves brothers step into an obstacle course full of hierarchy, authority, and command. They also take on the ambiguity, ambivalence, power struggle, and competitive stance that are the hallmarks of the blood-brother bond.

Nonetheless, men join clubs.

As a man moves through his life, he becomes a member of many men's clubs, organizations, and fraternities. They exist in all social strata—from the Harvard Club to the Harlem playground. Each has its own rituals, its own rites of passage, its own rules and hierarchy. Men join these clubs or groups, I believe, for two reasons. One is, as stated in the dictionary definition, to pursue a "common purpose or interest." For men oriented as "doers," that is important. They can focus on the object or task at hand rather than on their interpersonal relationship. Oddly, though, the other reason men join men's clubs and organizations is the direct opposite of "doing." It might be called "being," in a world where men need an excuse simply to be together. Lacking the ability to create interpersonal relationships with men in the world of men at large—with their fathers or sons, their mentors or heroes, or their brothers—men seek the formalized and sanctioned structure that at least promises a degree of more intimate contact.

In practice—on the surface—that need is fulfilled. But only to a degree. What men learn about how to relate to other men from belonging to clubs and fraternities appears to be closer to McWilliams's assertions than simply relaxing and hanging out with the boys.

BIG MAN ON CAMPUS

After the Boy's Clubs, the YMCA, the Cub Scouts and Boy Scouts, and high school leadership clubs, men have the opportunity to get a major lesson in the context of college fraternities. Here—amid the rushing and mixers and hazing and raiding and chugging, the sometimes physically abusive and almost always humiliating initiation rites, the selectivity and exclusivity—young college men are trained, armored, and prepared to take their places in a man's world.

Most people think that fraternity life as depicted in the highly popular 1978 film *Animal House* was grossly exaggerated. Consider, however, what happened that same year at Dartmouth College (the alma mater of Chris Miller, Alpha Delta Phi 1960–1964, co-author of the screenplay for *Animal House*). A Dartmouth English professor had proposed the abolition of fraternities on campus after a woman, on leave from a mental institution, was found to be the object of various sexual acts performed by several brothers of a particular fraternity. The woman was, in brotherly tradition, passed on to another house and another. By the end of the evening light bulbs and fire extinguishers had been introduced as props in the act. All of this was verified. The professor was charging that the fraternity system perpetuated, among other unacceptable qualities, racial stereotyping, uncivilized and destructive behavior, theft and vandalism, anti-intellectualism, excessive drug and alcohol use, and sexism.

I missed out on such fun and games when I was in college. I was turned down by the fraternity I wanted to join. It was one of those great traumatic rejections that mark a turning point in one's life. Being ostracized from a select body of men put me outside, made me feel less of a man, and finally put me back into and onto myself. It turned out, as those things do, to be the best thing that could have happened to me: I was left to my own devices to create a personal identity.

Years later, while working on this book, I ran into a friend named Robert who did pledge the frat that had rejected me. I was, needless to say, quite curious as to what the experience taught him. Now a corporate lawyer living in New York, Robert spoke of "a positive experience." But the experience seems to have had more to do with management training than establishing deeper and more intimate relationships with his fraternity "brothers." For those people who took advantage of it, Robert said,

> it was an opportunity to learn management skills and take leadership roles. You had to make sure there was enough money to buy food and run the house. There was a sense of belongong that was nice, although I haven't maintained much contact with anybody. If you would have told me back then that's how it would work out I would have been surprised. The fraternity was too big for it to be anything but a superficial grouping. I don't think the fraternity fostered closer relationships. The important thing was belonging to a desirable group rather than being a faceless freshman in a dorm, without a car. I couldn't wait to get my fraternity jacket. It meant a lot of status. But in terms of relationships . . . ? I got to learn about people from seeing how to deal with a group. *That* was useful. But as far as having enriching, good strong relationships you'd have forever, that obviously was not the case.

Robert's fraternity education focused on how to control men, how to lead them, how to "manage" them—and very little on how to exchange feelings with them. Even the exalted hazing—a symbolic rite of passage repeated in so many cultures—left him cold. He continued:

> There was another guy in the house named Robert too. He was a racist and selfish and I didn't like him at all. One time

we pledges raided the other brothers with shaving cream and we got in a big water fight. We were all rolling around on the floor and they poured flour and sticky stuff in our hair. At one point they made me and Robert roll around arm-in-arm and you know, for a while after that there was a certain closeness between us that came out of sharing that demeaning experience. Let's say I disliked him a little less. But having a common enemy did bring our class together. Though we were artificially motivated, it worked to a degree. But it was superficial—it didn't last long. I guess I had false expectations. I wanted it to be different. Rolling around on a floor together doesn't make you friends for life.

The same kind of experience was reported by a man who belonged to another kind of fraternity—the exclusive men's club. In fact, Ken, an old guard editor at one of New York's highly respected publishing houses, belongs to four men's clubs in New York—the Century Association, the Coffee House, the Dutch Treat, and the Player's Club. It seemed like a lot of clubs. Actually, he told me, it is for business contacts and intellectual stimulation that he belongs:

I would never belong to four clubs at my own expense, but it turns out that clubs are very useful for professional people. I take writers there for business lunches. It's exhilarating to go in and sit down and end up talking with a British publisher working on an exciting project, or the president of a college or a film executive. It's a place to meet important people and exchange ideas. I suppose there must be an emotional life at clubs, I guess maybe men talk about intimate things late at night at the club bar over lots of drinks. For myself, I don't ever remember unburdening myself about my problems to another man at the clubs or listening to anyone do the same. I feel I wouldn't go in there and pour my soul out to another man unless I knew him very, very well. And even after all these years, there's no one there I feel that close to.

These sort of private clubs—as well as other fraternal organizations—do bring men together. But for what? Better business contacts, training in leadership, simply the feeling of belonging. To the men perpetually fighting the feeling of being an "outsider," less than worthy of membership in the club of grown-up men, that last reason is paramount. The primacy of that need is reflected by the fact that men put such a high price on belonging. Membership—acceptance in a man's world—must come at a cost.

INITIATION RITES

Attaining manhood is a test one passes . . . or fails. All societies of men require potential members to go through some sort of trial or initiation rite to separate the men from the boys, as it were. They are a reminder that there is a ruling class of men who accept or reject us as their equals. The lesson hits us hard: There are insiders and outsiders. Such rites span the dramatic—God demanding Abraham sacrifice his son—to the pragmatic—a member measuring the strength of an initiate's handshake. In between, cultures have incorporated such ordeals as depilations, head-biting, evulsion of teeth, sprinkling with human blood, immersion in dust or filth, heavy flogging, scarification, smoking and burning, circumcision, and subincision.

In almost all cases they require that the potential member demonstrate his subordination, functioning to ensure the maintenance of a line of command—a hierarchy and a "lower-archy." These rites are a ritualized paying of obeisance to authority. They are also an enactment of the graduation from boyhood to manhood. As such, they are not unlike the rites of passage that become a standard part of all men's relationships with each other. Fathers and sons, mentors and protegés, brother and brother—all contain aspects of dominance and submission, all reach a turning point in which one betters the other. Initiation rites act out that psychological break with authority. In turn, however, we become servants to yet another authority.

Consider also the trials initiates go through to prove their courage, worthiness, status, and willingness to submit to the senior men in the group.

In ancient Greece young men of sixteen or seventeen were admitted to the city-state with full voting rights only after they had sworn allegiance to the religion of the city.

Boys among the North American Plains Indians, upon reaching puberty, are sent out to spend some days fasting on a mountain and receive a vision from some spirit. In the American subarctic culture, Kaska Indian boys approaching adolescence are sent into the forest alone to seek a vision, inspired by "dreaming of animals in a lonely place."

Among the Masai of eastern Africa, boys twelve to sixteen years old are circumcised and after that left in seclusion for four days, followed by a period during which they are dressed in female attire, and their heads shaved. Finally they are admitted to adulthood and allowed to become warriors.

Aboriginal Australian boys' initiation includes piercing of nasal septum, tooth pulling, hair removal, scarring, playing with fire, and circumcision and a blood rite.

The Yurupary Indians of the northwest Amazon region in the South American tropical forest induct their boys into the secret society of mature males. They are shown the sacred trumpets and the masks representing ancestral spirits. They are subjected to violent whipping, which they must tolerate in silence. Among the Ge of central Brazil, rites span a ten-year period beginning at age ten, including three years in isolation from the community.

Most rites involve enduring physical pain or some other expression as a demonstration of respect for the elder men, be they religious leaders or company presidents. They also include periods of isolation—and here we see more of the ambiguous message behind such men's organizations. For, to be a full-fledged man one must know isolation—psychologically and physically. We must know how to make it on our own; we must be self-sufficient. And yet, initiation rites require a man to humble himself and defer to the group. He must give up his individuality for the group ethos. Thus the messages men learn from the rites are themselves "fraught with ambiguity."

In *Men in Groups*, anthropologist Lionel Tiger refers to initiations as "part of the male-male 'courtship' pattern tied to the tendency of males to seek status among other males, to form groups with them, and to value highly the corporate 'presentation-of-self' to the community at large." Courtship is an interesting word, given the fear of homosexual tendencies that is conspicuous in pairs of men or groups of secret societies (discussed in depth in Chapter 7). It is significant that so many fraternity initiation rites, for instance, involve partial or complete nudity and have definite homoerotic overtones. In one, for example, pledges stand naked in front of an open fire in which branding irons are conspicuously heating. The pledges are blindfolded, told they will be branded, the branding irons are drawn from the fire and plunged, with a hiss, into a cold bucket of water as cold irons are jabbed against the buttocks of the candidates. Another fraternity strips pledges and ties bricks to their penises. Blindfolded, the pledges are told to throw the bricks without knowing the strings have been cut. At Cornell University it was reported that one fraternity made pledges bring five-inch nails and a bottle of petroleum jelly to the initiation ceremony. They are made to strip, articulate various vows and then bend over. Behind them stand senior members of the fraternity. The room is darkened and the pledges extend their hands back to the seniors to receive the nail presumably to insert into their anuses. Instead a can of beer is placed into their hands, the lights go on and they party the night away.

One interviewee echoed the memories of such rites, but from a different social context altogether: He told of a club in junior high school that did not appear on the official school agenda of extracurricular activities. It was called the SSSS— Sam's Secret Sex Society:

> We met once a week at Sam's house after school before his mother came home from work. Membership requirements?

You had to have a penis and be curious about how it worked. We were about twelve or thirteen and just finding out all the potentialities of our bodies. Sam's father was a fisherman so he'd bring his father's tackle box up to his bedroom. First we'd time how long it took to get a hard-on. Then we'd see how strong they were by hanging fishing weights on them. Each event was worth a certain number of points. The guy who accumulated the most points made Grand Master and we had to do things for him, like finish his homework or shine his shoes. The club finally got disbanded when a teacher intercepted a note in class announcing the next meeting.

Acting out sexual submissiveness to another man is the ultimate demonstration of servitude and powerlessness in a culture that sees homosexuals as "unmanly."

THE POWER OF SECRET SOCIETIES

People fear what they do not know and cower to those who do know. Secrecy ensures an insider and an outsider. It assures the authority of those at the top and it defies the authority of society at large. Secrecy is power, which is the rationale behind the existence of secret societies.

Lionel Tiger commented:

Secret societies . . . are the consequence of an effort of individuals—usually and mainly men—to create the social conditions for exercising their gregarious propensities, the expression of which may be (or may be seen to be) inhibited by their community. . . . Secrecy protects members from detection by authorities . . . and may also disguise the weakness or strength or the nature of members' activities. What is striking is that when a secret society operates within a culture from which (almost by defintion) it seeks to dissociate itself, power-holders in that culture and other persons generally react to the society with great antipathy. The secret band is defined as a hostile group, potentially antipathetic to constituted authority in its unwillingness to yield to open authority and expose its workings. . . . The function of secrecy is . . . to create a line of demarcation between those who know the secret and those who do not.

Tiger's biological-anthropological explanation of the male bond as a result of our early hunter-warrior training fails to give enough attention to the psychology of relationships between individual men. But in this analysis of secret societies he touches on several key issues I have identified in terms of male-male psychodynamics—namely power and authority; "in" groups and outcasts (hierarchy); and a fear of sharing weaknesses and vulnerabilities. However, those opening remarks shed light on an aspect of men's inter-relationships I had observed in another context. Tiger's implication is that men join secret societies to do what society at large inhibits: that is, the exercising of "gregarious propensities" man to man. In other words, we are so well trained by fathers and other men in our lives to inhibit expression for one another that, if we want to do so, we must retreat out of sight of a society that teaches us it is taboo. But the desire to do so appears so strong that we do form secret societies despite all that training—though the reality turns out to be less fulfilling than the ideal.

Moreover, as I saw, our male friendships may be considered a secret society of two, quite possibly for the same reason. In interviews men told me that they had special friendships based on a shared sense of secrecy. In these relationships, both men saw the outside world with the same skewed view. They shared a sense of the absurdity of life. They both had the same feeling of isolation and alienation from society. When they were younger they created imaginary worlds of dragons and pirates and space odysseys. When they were older they confided in their disdain for a superior or a spouse, or a secret desire for a certain woman.

However, as discussed in Chapter 6, even in the intimate relationships between two men, there remains an inability to express those deepest feelings of affection.

Hanging over all this, of course, is the taboo of homosexuality. Societies and individuals who suffer from homophobia—the fear of homosexuality—are immediately suspicious of men who congregate secretively. *What are they hiding?* Homophobia clearly inhibits men in pairs or in groups from expressing their "gregarious propensities," as Chapter 7 elaborates.

THE SEARCH CONTINUES

Whether it is secret or public, highbrow or low, intellectually or athletically oriented, the men's club serves as a retreat for men from the society of men-at-large, a society in which they have come to expect to be inferior, ignored, and unnurtured. They join groups to differentiate themselves from the sea of men "out there," to create (however illusionary) an air of exclusivity and superiority. Once inside, however, they are faced with similar struggles and competitions for power and control. Will they be accepted and promoted within the hierarchy of the club? Or will they become one of the mass of men among the rank and file of the organization? And from among the members, will a friend emerge with whom one can share feelings, weaknesses and vulnerabilities, hopes and fears?

Finally, a man comes away from his men's club and fraternity experiences with mixed feelings. His need to belong is fulfilled but his need for closeness to men may not be. Appointed as a member—accepted by a higher body of men—he is, nonetheless, disappointed by what he gets besides the basic training in masculine skills with which by now he is very familiar. For, at this point in his life, he understands too well the importance of being on top of the heap, of performing (doing) at peak and of maintaining the "strong silent" stance emotionally. He is also reminded of the ambivalence and ambiguity of relationships with men. He is fed, in part, by the camaraderie of the group but he is starving for the one true friend in whom he can confide. And, like the salmon who swims against the tide, he moves upstream in search of such a friend.

Mentors We Never Meet: Reflections of Men in the Media's Eye

I love a man who can best me.
—Errol Flynn

All the while that we pass through basic rites with the real men in our lives, we are more subtly—though no less importantly—taught and influenced by men we never actually get to meet. These are the male figures we see on the silver screen, in advertisements, books, and magazines. These are the unreal men the media make, whom we watch almost every day of our lives, who become more real to us by virtue of their pervasive presence. Everywhere we turn we are bombarded with images of how men should relate to each other, how they should behave.

This was brought home for me in interviews with men who cited personal heroes and mentors such as John Wayne and Robert DeNiro instead of real men in their lives. In a society in which actual mentors are few and far between, in an age when the mythological figures that once inspired and guided us are fading from memory, men have come to rely on such media heroes. The Marlboro Man and John Wayne—these are our modern-day archetypes. Ancient figures such as Prometheus and Parsifal have given way to newer ones, to television's fast-flashing, constantly-dissolving, discardable images of the likes of Howdy Doody, Mighty Mouse, Popeye, Superman, Batman, Captain Kangaroo, Soupy Sales, Buck Rogers, Sky King, Mr. Rogers, Mr. Wizard, and Mr. Magoo.

What they tell us is consistent with what we learn from the

other men around us. The message of the media man can be summed up in six points:

Winning—whether it is a gun duel or a top corporate position—is everything. Accomplishment is all.

In order to win, a man must be ready to resort to violent or otherwise aggressive behavior.

Because the rise to the top can be so brutal emotionally a man must hide his pain behind a wall of silence and inexpressiveness.

Maintaining that wall of silence requires an independent stance.

Living up to the model of the Media Man, like living up to expectations of fathers, mentors, and older brothers, is practically impossible—which only reinforces a man's inferiority in the shadow of other men.

The image of masculinity is ambiguous, out-of-focus, elusive, and evasive. The outer form is emphasized over the inner.

Those are the messages that get flashed between the lines and behind the images. Witness how they work.

PAPER-THIN HEROES

Take the classic Marlboro Man, the billboard dream man. A more virile male image could not have been created—with his broad shoulders, deep-set eyes, strong jaw, always pictured alone, a million miles from civilization, or so it seems. A man with a mission. A difficult man to match. The advertiser would have us believe we too could become this way by smoking a particular brand of cigarette, but the more important message we get is that this man's man is handsome, strong, powerful, active—and alone.

Magazine ads in such men's publications as *GQ* and *Esquire* suggest that men should want to be on top. "He's wearing something that makes him different from every other man,'' the fragrance maker declares.

''You're at the height of your powers, when nothing is too much and everything is just enough,'' encourages another.

''Panatella separates,'' claims a cigar ad. ''You'll stand out from the herd without getting fleeced.''

''Winners pick a winner,'' boasts a camera promotion.

The worst offenders are liquor companies. ''Because you enjoy going first-class,'' the scotch maker makes it seem as though his product is a reward for placing first. ''When you make it with Myers's, you've made it . . . a rum that means you've come up in the world,'' claims another. And all the classic Dewar's Profiles, studies of men of great achievement. Even the ballpoint penmaker would like you to believe his product is a recognition of your ''mark of distinction.''

The standards they all set are high, often unattainable. But the man who cannot reach those heights can at least learn how to look the part—if not from his actual mentor, then from the media. Even here, though, the pickings are slim. ''Every change in men's fashion is seen as a revolution because so little happens,'' six-time Coty Award-winner Ralph Lauren has said. His comment suggests that men are left to search very scrupulously for clues.

In the late 1970s, responding to the paucity of direction for men in fashion, a number of large format paperback guides to grooming for men were published to cast some light on the subject for men in the dark. Trouble was, they either confounded men more or made them feel more inferior. *Looking Good* by Charles Hix (Wallaby, 1977) and *The Ultimate Man* by Henry Post (Berkeley, 1978), two perfect examples, are the kinds of books that make a man never want to look in the mirror again. Their pages are filled with pictures of those male models who appear to have been manufactured in some factory in Detroit, designed to intimidate the rest of us, with their chiselled features, clear complexions, slim builds. And while these authors offer tips on how to take care of our drooping bodies, our wrinkling skin, our thinning hair, how to mix and match accessories, how to affect the "rough man" look and the "classic man" look, neither Hix nor Post can actually identify what it is they are trying to create. Wrote Post:

> The Ultimate Man is the guy you and I have wanted to be ever since we first realized that each of us would grow up to become men. But what kind of men would we be? Would we be like the man we admired? Would we have what he had—great looks, style, and sex appeal? The Ultimate Man was a dream, a vision of youth that seemed far away from the reality of our mirrors.

Hix tried defining the ideal man:

> What is "the look?" I make my living with words, but I'll be damned if I can describe it. The closest I can come is to say that it's looking put-together, with equal portions of good health and self-confidence yet without looking vain. No, that's not it. It's standing out in a crowd of men by being a better example of what every man in that crowd would look like if he had the same raw material. That isn't right either. Is it making the most of what you've got? Yup. It's how you've always wanted to look and secretly felt that you could if you tried. You can. Try.

They made fashion and grooming a competitive event. "You can. Try." They emphasized aspiring to an unattainable dream; on those outer qualities of looks, style, and sex appeal; on standing out in a crowd and being better. Granted, the situation may be far worse for women. Trying to live up to the impossible models paraded before them on the glossy pages of women's magazines, women all but surrender in defeat or become compulsive dieters or frenetic fashion freaks. Or else they completely reject the model. The competition is no less keen than it is for men but, unlike men, most women are very definite, well-versed, and expressive about what the current look is and how to attain it. It is much more part of their vernacular than men's. Hix was so ill-at-ease with expressing it verbally he was reduced to clichés. Finally he gave up. In the end, he suggested, each man must find his own answer, leaving men once again without a model to follow. Henry Post agreed: "In the end it's you—and you alone—who make the difference. . . . Be yourself. Make your style you. From that point on it becomes all too personal, all too elusive to pin down."

By now men have become accustomed to an image that appears elusive as soon as it approaches "personal."

Why look so good? To impress other men, but of course. The point was underscored by Bill Blass, the three-time Coty winner and one of America's best-known designers:

> The way you look creates the first impression. A man's wardrobe will help him get a better job or help him feel good about himself socially. There are three reasons to dress well—to give yourself pleasure, to advance yourself professionally, and to make yourself more attractive and sexually desirable. You travel around and you see how bad it is in corporations, for example, where you can't one-up your superiors. And in many companies the man's clothes have to follow in the style of the boss's clothes.

Even the way a man dresses, then, must follow the top-down mentality as prescribed.

THE GLOSSY MAN

In the mid-1970s magazines rekindled a romance with men that flared up for a while but then smoldered into the same old smoke cloud of confusion and illusion and scarce few clues as to how men can, should, or do relate to each other.

In 1975, *Rolling Stone* may have been the first national periodical to focus an entire issue on men. "Men on the Ropes" was the cover line but editorially *Rolling Stone* was at loose ends. Michael Roger, in his introduction, wrote:

> Men—to rephrase the fellow who may have inadvertently started the whole tangle in the first place—"What do they want?" Beats us, frankly, even though we've spent the better

part of a year thinking about it . . . and the longer we thought about it the murkier the whole subject became. And as the discussion deepened, the block began to look increasingly sinister: What dark secret were we, in fact, trying to hide?

Most of the articles in that issue reflect the subject that seemed then (as now) to be threatening men: sex. Included in that issue is a long excerpt from boxer Muhammed Ali's autobiography, *The Greatest: My Own Story* in which, at one point, St. Louis trainer Reverend Williams compared Ali to a dinosaur: "Everybody's got buddies, I know. But not dinosaurs. The dinosaur's different. He's got his own satellites. His own crowd. Dinosaurs go it alone."

If men were teetering on the ropes, unsure of *who* and *how* they were, a 1977 survey of 28,000 conducted by *Psychology Today* magazine did not make much more social-scientific sense of the changing image of the male. "The macho frontiersman is well on his way out as the model of the perfect American man," the magazine's researchers concluded. "But he isn't gone yet, and men have more trouble defining the new male than women have."

During that same period *Esquire* returned from a general interest magazine to a men's magazine. It did not take long, however, for *Esquire* to demonstrate that it would follow an old lead rather than forge a new one. By 1978 it was proclaiming "The Year of the Lusty Woman: It's All Right to Be a Sex Object Again." Two years later it was heralding the return of "the hard-line culture" and the demise of the "age of vulnerability and self-absorption." In this new/old sensibility, "tough-guyism came into vogue. We began to wonder how we'd do in a fistfight in a bar. We began to admire—not just appreciate but *admire*—the John Wayne ethic and principled brawling." The election of Ronald Reagan, the magazine noted, was a clear indication that this was the direction men were taking.

BOOKED UP

And then there were the books, which started trickling out in 1975 and grew into a deluge by the end of the decade. Warren Farrell's *The Liberated Man*, Marc Feigen Fasteau's *The Male Machine*, and Herb Goldberg's *The Hazards of Being Male* became must reading for any man looking for a new model to follow. The first was basically written in reaction to the liberated women's movement. The two others, as their titles imply, point out the down side of male behavior.

In *The Male Machine*, Fasteau stated:

> The male machine is a special kind of being, different from women, children and men who don't measure up. He is functional, designed mainly for work. He is programmed to tackle jobs, override obstacles, attack problems, overcome difficulties, and always seize the offensive. He will take on any task that can be presented to him in a competitive framework, and his most important positive reinforcement is victory. He has armor plating which is virtually impregnable. His circuits are never scrambled or overrun by irrelevant personal signals. He dominates and outperforms his fellows, although without excessive flashing of lights or clashing of gears. His relationship with other male machines is one of respect but not intimacy; it is difficult for him to connect his internal circuits to those of others. In fact, his internal circuitry is something of a mystery to him and is maintained primarily by humans of the opposite sex.

The only problem is, as Fasteau admitted by the end of the book, as he had at the beginning, "from Daniel Boone to our mobile corporation executives to our most dedicated scientists, our success myths . . . are about an individual (virtually always a man) who by his lonely independent efforts raises himself above and away from his fellow man and accomplishes great things, preferably of the kind that can serve as a monument to himself."

His conclusions lead men back to where they started. His hopes for the new man of the future fly in the face of his analysis of the man of the past and present.

Other books tried to help men out of confusion, studies like *Male Sexuality, Beyond the Male Myth, What You (Still) Don't Know About Male Sexuality, The Phallic Mystique, Sexual Solutions, Men in Love,* and others.

All in all, however, the print medium reflected back to men a model that was at best fuzzy at the edges, and reassured them that a man has to stay on top, he must hide most of his emotions, he will remain alienated and separated, he is inferior to most other men, and that how he actually should act with other men was unclear.

HOLLYWOOD HEROES

There is no shortage of models for men in the medium that has most pervaded our lives since its beginnings in the early part of this century. Film, and especially American film, has given us the Hollywood heroes, the bigger-than-life characters who loom over us on the silver screen, casting great shadows of self-doubt on us by their very magnitude.

"Hollywood knows well that men cannot live by the models of masculinity it proffers," wrote Joan Mellen in *Big Bad Wolves: Masculinity in the American Film:*

> Never intending that men actually attempt to model themselves on such heroes, it offers fulfillment to the audience through figures capable of feats of power and control inaccessible to mere mortals. Such heroic images afford men and women vicarious release while rendering them small and timid by comparison. They wish they could *know* such men; they have no illusions about resembling them. An abiding malaise results in the male, victimized by this comparison of himself and the physical splendor of the hero with whom he has so passionately identified. The vicarious discharge in the dark of his daily frustrations carries with it an unavowed threat of emasculation because he must re-enter the world feeling even less adequate—the opposite of what the movies seem to promise. . . . When we leave the theater, catharsis behind us,

we are left with nothing so much as an overwhelming sense of our own inadequacy. In seeming to entertain us, movies in a very real sense have exacerbated our pain.

The William S. Harts and Tom Mixes, the Gary Coopers and John Waynes, the Errol Flynns and Marlon Brandos, the James Deans, Paul Newmans, Clint Eastwoods, the Richard Geres, Sylvester Stallones and Robert DeNiros—these are powerful men in control of themselves and of others. They are men of authority, men of action. They *do* now, think (maybe) later. They are loners, strong and silent. They are competitive, always out to prove themselves better, stronger, faster, smarter, sexier than other men. They are aggressive and violent when they have to be.

These film heroes, these inspirational mentors—like our fathers and other mentors—seem to undermine men's self-confidence even as they purport to bolster it. Besides being left with the feeling of inadequacy, men are also left with a feeling of disappointment and a kind of abandonment after seeing that even their film heroes fall in behind an established hierarchy. As Mellen put it:

> American films have not only sought to render men powerless by projecting male images of fearsome strength and competence. They have also proposed consistently over the years that the real man is not a rebel but a conformist who supports God and country, right or wrong. The heroes who exhibit the most power stand for the status quo, even as they suggest that physical action unencumbered by effeminate introspection is what characterizes the real man. Thus, in the most profound sense, the bold exterior of these men on screen conceals the fact that the films actually foster a sense of passivity by suggesting that such men are never rebels but can always be trusted to acquiesce in the established order.

Further disappointment comes when we discover that when we look behind the big silver screen the stars in whom we had invested a great deal of belief are not, in fact, who they appeared to be. Plastic surgery and cosmetics do wonders. Clark Gable had his ears pinned back. Gable and James Dean wore false teeth. Alan Ladd, a short man, had to stand on boxes while being filmed. People are often surprised to learn how short Richard Gere and Sylvester Stallone are in reality. Errol Flynn had a bobbed nose. Marion Michael Morrison was considered too effeminate a name for the persona they had in mind for a certain actor so he changed it to John Wayne. Wayne and Henry Fonda wore toupees. George Raft wore elevator shoes. Brando wore a corset to conceal his bulk. And so on.

And while the view of his exterior gets blown up, propped up, and otherwise altered, the view of his interior is basically concealed altogether. ''Strong silent type'' is the phrase we apply to men who display this trait—both film stars and our idealizations of the romantic men of power in real life. As Mellen explains:

> . . . The silence of the male hero in American films dates from *The Virginian*—ironically enough, from the beginnings of the sound film itself. Its origins was the frontier code in accordance with which companions on a cattle drive would not ask too many questions or inquire into each other's past. . . . On the cattle runs the true cowboy was supposed to eschew complaining, bragging or lying. He was judged by how silently he could endure the rigors of his life. His solace had to come, not from what were considered weak-minded confessions of uncertainty, regret or fear, but from inner strength, self-confidence and pride in tasks well done. To talk too much would violate this code and demean his mission.

William S. Hart, the first great American hero of the Western film and after whom many other male movie stars molded themselves, revealed in his autobiography, *My Life East and West*, that he, like many of our male movie stars, bought the full cloth of the goods he was selling: ''The bigness of the West makes men quiet; they seldom talk unless they have something to say. The altitude clarifies their brains and gives them nerves of steel.'' Hart also impressed on his male audience the importance of taking first place. ''I would go through hell on three pints of water before I would acknowledge defeat,'' he said of the heroes he played. His credo: "One of the most dangerous things in life is to lose your courage. If you can keep your fighting spirit, you always have a chance. The very fact of keeping an undaunted front may cause the other side to weaken. If your courage goes, you are whipped—your enemy and the world soon know it."

With few exceptions, Hart's model endured over the decades—through the gangster movies of the 1930s (James Cagney, Paul Muni, and Edward G. Robinson, whose Scarface advised, "Do it first, do it yourself, and keep on doing it"); through the 1940s war films (Cary Grant and Humphrey Bogart, whose credo in *Casablanca* was "I stick my neck out for nobody"); through the dark films of the 1950s (James Dean and Marlon Brando, whose Stanley Kowalski in *Streetcar Named Desire* proclaimed, "Every man's a king and I'm king here"); through the 1960s dominated by Sean Connery (whose ultimately superficial James Bond hid behind a facade of superhuman feats and womanizing); and into the 1970s and 1980s which brought us full circle with the popularity of Clint Eastwood's Dirty Harry character.

Demonstrating the degree to which Eastwood had been accepted as the quintessential male role model on the screen, the epitome of masculinity, in 1983 an annual poll of thousands of owners of American movie theaters put Eastwood at the top of box-office attractions. It was his sixteenth appearance since 1968 among the top ten—more than any other living star (only John Wayne and Cary Cooper had more times on the list).

His return to the top spot was thanks to his year-end hit *Sudden Impact* which starred Inspector Harry Callahan, the consummate man of few words. Harry's .357 Magnum, one of the most obvious phallic symbols in American cinema, said it all. His beady, icy blue eyes—almost always hidden behind a pair of dark sunglasses—saw it all. Eastwood's "Dirty Harry" was the Zen cop, alienated, nihilistic, aggressive and destructive, emotionally repressed and nonexpressive. His suit was always dirty and wrinkled, as though to worry about his outer appearance would be to descend into feminine vanity. He traveled alone—no partner, no wife, no woman.

"The kind of thing I do is glorify competence," Eastwood has said of the roles he plays.

"Do things someone else's way and you take your life in your hands," said Harry in *Magnum Force*.

Writes author Mellen of Eastwood: "With consummate inexpressiveness he assumes the role of superman, immune to either the praise or the gratitude of others, living by his own code in a world where men like himself have long since become obsolete."

And then there were the highly touted "buddy movies" of the 1970s which were purported to glorify male friendship. We saw, among others, Robert Redford and Paul Newman in *Butch Cassidy and the Sundance Kid* and later *The Sting*, Dustin Hoffman and Jon Voight in *Midnight Cowboy*, then Voight and Burt Reynolds in *Deliverance*, Elliot Gould, Donald Sutherland et al in *M*A*S*H*, and Art Garfunkel and Jack Nicholson in *Carnal Knowledge*.

Of course these were not the first films to revolve around friendship between men. *What Price Glory* (1926) depicted two professional soldiers during World War I, comrades on the battlefield and off as well as friendly rivals for the same woman. In the same year *Beau Geste* also exalted male camaraderie. The opening title proclaims: "Love of man for woman waxes and wanes. Love of brother for brother is steadfast as the stars."

Throughout the years that followed, American films showed men in pairs: the cowboy and his sidekick (John Wayne and Walter Brennan, the Lone Ranger and Tonto, Roy Rogers and Pat Brady, Hopalong Cassidy and Gabby Hayes; the gangster and his partner (epitomized by Edward G. Robinson and Douglas Fairbanks Jr. in *Little Caesar*); and the comedy teams (Martin and Lewis, Laurel and Hardy, Abbott and Costello). Most of these pair-ups exemplify a kind of dominant-submissive friendship in which one clearly holds sway over the other, a pattern of friendship I examine further in Chapter 6.

But if these films cast men's relationships as competitive, imbalanced, or nonexistent, the so-called buddy movies of the last decade were potentially the herald of a more enlightened, more sympathetic, more positive model of how men could relate to each other. What they showed, however, was a male bond based not on mutual appreciation and affection, but on a collaborative escape from an increasingly hostile environment and an utter rejection of women. The message behind these movies was that men are better off with each other than with the opposite sex. Finally, though, these films end with the destruction or defeat of a men-only society.

In *Butch Cassidy and the Sundance Kid*, Katharine Ross, as Redford's girlfriend, is all but ignored by the twosome and the pair is left to die a bloody death alone with each other. (To illustrate, again, how these male actors embrace the parts they play, Paul Newman's real-life wife Joanne Woodward was quoted as saying, "When those men get together, forget opening your mouth if you happen to be female. Bob and Paul really do have a chemistry. Someday, Paul and Bob will run off together. And I'll be left behind with Lola Redford.")

The only female lead in *M*A*S*H* is a woman derogatorily named "Hot Lips" Houlihan, played by Sally Kellerman. She is meant to be unattractive sexually and dumb enough to take Army regulations seriously. The film ends with a metaphorical football game, player after player hauled off on stretchers, reminding us that the context of *M*A*S*H* is war, a men's "game" in which no one ends up better off.

In *Midnight Cowboy* women are excluded except to be hustled by the male prostitute Joe Buck (Voigt), who finds true caring in his crippled new-found friend Ratso (Hoffman), who finally dies in Joe's arms on a bus en route to Florida's warm sun.

And in *Carnal Knowledge*, one of the most seering of this genre of films, though the plot follows both Nicholson's and Garfunkel's episodes with a number of women, their friendship is the enduring relationship. In the last scene Nicholson is pathetically and impotently alone with a female prostitute who precisely follows his sexual fantasy instructions, while

Garfunkel couples off with a young hippie he deludes himself into believing holds the "secret" of love.

THE NEW ANTI-HERO

Finally, after three-quarters of a century of cinema, there emerged in the late 1970s a new American film hero whose very attraction was that he was not a hero. This was the fallible male, the underdog, singularly ordinary. He was sensitive, vulnerable, tender. He was John Travolta, Jon Voigt, Richard Dreyfuss; he was the "new" Burt Reynolds or the ever self-effacing Woody Allen; he was Dustin Hoffman and Dudley Moore.

These were men who did not necessarily have the classic handsome looks or the intimidatingly perfect bodies and if they did we could admire them without insecurity because the heroes themselves seemed to take their looks for granted, or were insecure about them themselves. They did not present the macho all-powerful front of former film heroes. They were not aggressive. In fact, they were so laid-back, one female film reviewer defined this new hero as "masculinity declawed." Winning was not everything; breaking even was considered good enough to these guys. The reviewer described this new hero:

> We can see the new male image in contrast to the mature, dependable, rock-like heroes of the Fifties, who reeked of integrity and were unbudgeable in their *strong silence* [my italics]. The Original Sensitives—Montgomery Clift, Brando, James Dean—began the revolution. All were somehow brutalized, ravished beyond repair, poetic in their pain; no question about it, they had feelings. They would not qualify as New Heroes, however, because they were too unstable. The new hero is not crazy; it is extremely important that he be good at *relating* to people. . . . In recent films, masculinity is felled in a variety of ways. It is deglamorized, brought down to size, put in its place, left in the dust. The New American Hero

avoids the cliches and prerequisites of the male. He is non-threatening.

He was young, like Travolta, or looked it, like Gere, or appeared it, like the shortish Moore. He had not yet found his place in the world, did not have all the answers, and was the first to admit it. His career was not paramount. Travolta was a clerk in a paint store in *Saturday Night Fever*. Dreyfuss was an out-of-work actor in *The Goodbye Girl*. His power was questionable. For all his physical front, Sylvester Stallone as *Rocky* was totally unsure of his prowess. And Woody Allen, no matter what movies he writes, directs, and stars in, is the eternal self-doubting klutz.

Cool he is not. In contrast to the men he had grown used to seeing on the big screen, a man could watch these portrayals and not cower with twinges of inferiority. Rather than a moralizing bigger-than-life father figure, he saw the reflection of a man with whom he could identify his own inadequacies, weaknesses, and other hang-ups.

Many male actors made the transition from tough guy to softie—Al Pacino had gone from the heavy in *The Godfather* to a homosexual in *Dog Day Afternoon*, Robert Redford from the gun-toting *Butch Cassidy and the Sundance Kid* to the more sensitive introspective *Electric Horseman*, Paul Newman from *Hud* to *The Verdict*, and Burt Reynolds, who turned from good ol' boy pictures like *W.W. and the Dixie Dance-kings* and *Smokey and the Bandit* to *Starting Over* and *The End*.

Of this new type of character Reynolds told an interviewer:

> People are tired of getting screwed by everything and everybody, and in my pictures, I like to play this character who's not quite all there, who steps down from his truck and scrapes the manure off his boots and who's always fighting for his dignity. He's anti-establishment, he's funny and he's somebody to cheer for—a hero.

As for himself, he said: "I mean, I go into the crapper, too, and it doesn't come out in a little plastic bag once a month. And I actually get sick and I cry at movies and I sometimes have trouble breathing."

TOMORROW'S MEDIA MEN

Along with the new film heroes there came the new film-makers—not Spielberg and Coppola and others of that ilk, but the young independent documentary filmmakers who took a very close look at the issues of male identity and how men relate to each other. Josh Hanig and Will Roberts produced *Men's Lives* in 1975 on a shoestring budget and within three years it was an underground hit among men looking for new roles to play. The documentary traces the male growing-up process from boy scout camp to factory. "What choices are open to men growing up in America?" the narrator asks after showing a collage of images that we all grew up with, which dramatize male priority and prowess: Superman of the comic strips, Tarzan beating his chest, Walt Frazier the basketball superstar, a growling Broderick Crawford bragging in a western about who is fastest on the draw, Charles Atlas *after*, and the ever-masculine John Wayne in a war film. Interviews with typical men from Dayton, Ohio, show a high-school football player exclaiming, "I like to kill. I like to kill opponents," and a young boy who cherishes his car because girls "think it gives you strength to handle a car like that." In other interviews young men proclaim "without competition, there's nothing," and "a man needs to be in control." And with each utterance you can hear echoes of all the decades of masculine training that has come from films, fathers, and other male figures. Filmmakers Hanig and Roberts, in the narrative, share their discovery that most men see themselves as inadequate, especially in the shadow of the supermen they see projected on the screen. Men in *Men's Lives* admit they can never let other men know them well for fear of appearing weak, unable, and vulnerable. The film leaves one with the sense that competitiveness and aggressiveness pervade our

society, especially the society of men, and that survival—
emotional and economic—depends on developing such tendencies.

Behind the scenes of the making of the film, Josh Hanig
found the same was true. "Making the film was an emotional
and gut-level experience," Hanig told me several years after
the film had gained a solid reputation. He was twenty-seven
at the time and planning to move from San Francisco to Los
Angeles to pursue his career more ambitiously. He said:

> We had never made a film so we were in the process of
> learning filmmaking, of trying to sort out a very complicated
> issue, and of trying to make a working relationship. Will had
> one child and another one on the way. We felt we had bitten
> off something that was much too big for us. I was living with
> a woman and here she was pointing out the classic contradic-
> tions: I was off working all the time and not putting any
> energy into our relationship. But I felt obsessed to finish the
> film. We felt tremendous pressure. And both Will and I are
> strong-willed men, so there was a lot of competition between
> us that we had to deal with. We fought a lot. We cried a lot.
> Sometimes it was just the responsibility and the fear of fail-
> ure. We were sure it was going to be a lousy film. In fact
> most of the time we worked on it we were afraid that it was
> going to be bad and that we would be in debt and have
> nothing to show for it. And our personal lives were falling by
> the wayside.

His reflections on his self-doubt sounded much like the
same inferiorities men spoke about in his film, and the same I
had heard men speak about in countless interviews. And his
making work a priority over a relationship also mirrored a lot
of social training. When I asked him what he learned about
how men relate to each other from making the film, he
replied:

> I think it's much more complex than I used to think. I see
> some good things that I didn't used to see. Camaraderie, for
> instance. Men come together over seemingly artificial situ-
> ations—mostly sports, or drinking in bars, or in business
> relations—but at least it brings men closer. It makes them

able to talk about what it is they're going through but for the most part it *is* true: men are frightened to death of intimacy. They're scared, they don't know how to deal with it. They've never been trained to deal with it. They're cut off from it. Male rage seems to be the most common, most honest form of emotional expression for men. And we live in a great deal of confusion about who to direct that rage toward.

One of the people whom Hanig admitted he himself had felt anger toward was his own father:

I felt he never really taught me the well-kept secret. The secret of how to be a real man in the world. I felt like I never quite had it down the way other guys did. It can be very hard for me to talk to him. Last time I was home we got into a big fight. He saw a new film I was working on and had a lot of criticism. And the way he expressed his criticism was very unsupportive; it hurt my feelings. I got angry and told him he was my father, not just any old person, and he had a responsibility to respond to me with some dignity. That opened a big door. We started talking about our relationship and my inability to feel close to him sometimes. I feel *very* close to him at times but can't express it. I told him I thought we avoided each other, were afraid of each other, competitive with each other. It was hard for him to hear, but he agreed to much of what I said. It could have been a much better talk but it was the first of its kind for us and a big breakthrough.

That talk was Hanig's first step toward a reconciliation with his father, as his film was one of the first attempts of that medium to truly come to terms with its effect on how men relate to themselves and to each other.

6

Male Friendship:
No Man's Land

If one would have a friend, one must be willing to
wage war for him: and in order to wage war, one
must be capable of being an enemy. . . . In one's
friend, one shall find one's best enemy.
          —*The Philosophy of Nietzsche*

Every single one of my male friendships is tainted
with some kind of competition: "Where do I stand in
terms of that guy."
          —Tim, thirty-one

MY DINNER WITH DENNIS

I had not seen Dennis for seven years. We had grown up in
the same neighborhood, played basketball, baseball, or football every day after school, played music together, gone to
countless parties, movies, sports events. We were what you
call friends. We hung out a lot. We "rapped," as I recall, but I
could not tell you how he really felt about things—about his
bossy father, about the pressure of "being a man," about
anything of emotional significance. After high school we
went our separate ways. Since I had last seen him he had
been through a tumultuous marriage and a vindictive divorce,
moved from the suburbs to the city, transferred from a small
firm to a major corporation. Ostensibly, we were getting
together to talk about our friendship as part of my research.
  Our first two hours together were awkward. We talked

about our work, about the upcoming election, our travels. Had he seen so-and-so? Had I heard from whats-his-face? Dead end. In the cab on the way to dinner we said almost nothing. I wondered: Is the evening going to be a total loss? Do we have anything in common anymore? In traffic I mumbled about the atrocities one must put up with to live in the city. He told me his parents had moved from our old neighborhood. An elegant dinner consumed and distracted our attention. We ordered, admired the decor, and discussed the food and the clientele around us. It was not until we were sipping our coffee that we got to talking about anything that resembled how we *felt* about ourselves, our lives, and what we had gone through in the last couple of years.

"So how goes the battle?" I tried.

"It goes."

"It goes how?"

"It goes hard. Up and down. Now that the divorce is final I feel like I'm finally recovered from a long case of the grippe."

"You mind me asking?"

"No, it's o.k."

"So . . . what happened with you and her?"

"I don't know. Things just. . . ." His voice trailed off. I waited.

"What? Things just what?"

"Things just . . ." he started and looked up from his empty coffee cup, searching my eyes for a sign of betrayal. Was I still his trusted friend? "Things just broke down. She was too demanding, too selfish. She wanted me to be available for her when she wanted me, but she wanted her space too. I started to feel like a yo-yo. And then. . . ." He stopped, looked away, looked back at me. I could almost hear his interior thought: *Can I trust him?*

"I was having sexual problems."

So he told me about his sexual problems and then I told him about my sexual problems and then our sexual problems did not seem like such a problem anymore. It was a moment of disarmament; the barriers dropped. We went back to his apartment, now talking about everything. He played a couple of songs he had written. It was like old times again.

That encounter—replete with its disappointments and its fulfillments—is a pretty good example of the cautious approach two men take toward each other in establishing contact. Step-freeze, step-freeze seems to sum it up and generally at each freeze point men are sizing each other up. *How will I compare to him? Can I trust him?*

Behind the bear hugs of camaraderie, men seem to be holding each other at arm's length. They keep a safe distance—a buffer zone—between themselves and other men. This safe space is quite literally a *no man's land*, an emotional twilight zone few men appear to be willing to navigate.

And who can blame us for assuming an avoidance stance after an initiation into man-to-man relationships such as we have had? After all, what had come of trusting fathers, mentors, brothers? Betrayal. Disappointment. Distrust. Unrequited love. Men enter into friendships with men well-trained in the disciplines of masculinity. We should not be surprised, then, that the issues of power and competition, one-upmanship, and a failure to communicate feelings verbally for each other permeate men's interrelationships.

Nor should we be surprised, therefore, that so many men report so few "best friends."

"Who's your best male friend?" I asked in interviews. Repeatedly I'd get unfulfilling answers:

"I have none; I'm a loner."

"I had a close friend from my old neighborhood but we haven't talked in a long time."

"I have a number of acquaintances but none who I'd call a best friend."

"That's not in my context."

"I see it as a continuum. My best friend last year is not my best friend this year, and will not be my best friend next year."

So unconditioned were many men to the arena of male friendship that they would answer as though they had not heard the question:

"My wife."

"My girlfriend."

The replies seemed contorted and evasive until I was confronted with the complexity of the issue when the tables were turned on me. Who was *my* best friend? I was hard put to name the single man in whom I truly confided. There were several, spread over time and place. Or there were none at the moment. And too, I could not be sure that my current "best friend" also considered me his best friend, and that seemed important if not relevant.

Daniel Levinson in *The Seasons of A Man's Life*, wrote: "In our interviews, friendship was largely noticeable by its absence. . . . Most men do not have an intimate male friend of the kind that they recall fondly from boyhood or youth."

Still, men do establish friendly relationships with other men. The desire for male contact is a pull men cannot ignore. We are each other's mirrors, each other's source of energy, each other's touchstones to an elusive and evolving male reality.

But how *do* men relate to each other? And why do women ask me that question more frequently than men—and why are they always too quick with their own answer: "They don't." And why are men, presumably closer to the truth of it, much slower with and less sure about their responses?

At least part of the quality of—and appeal of—men's friendships includes, I have learned, their enigmatic nature. Men grope for descriptions of what makes a particular friendship unique or special.

"We just click."

"He's a nice guy."

"Whenever we see each other—no matter how much time has gone by—there's this sort of golden chord that we strike together."

None of it seemed to satisfy. All of it indicated men's ambiguity, ambivalence, and lack of clarity about their relationships with all men.

Part of the dilemma of men's friendships—as in other male-male dyads—is the discrepancy between real and ideal. Men have high expectations of men friends. They expect loyalty, someone who will stand behind them to the bitter end. A friend who would lend any amount of money, provide a place to stay for any length of time, drive any distance in an emergency. A friend who would lend an ear, listen to one's problems when no one else will.

In reality, that mythical friend more than likely did not and does not exist—or he may have at one point but, as I heard so often, time passed and so did the friendship.

But through the interviews there emerged some answers to questions such as:

> How and by what criteria do men choose friends?
> When do men go to each other?
> What do men do with each other?
> How do they communicate? What do they talk about?
> What types of friendships are there?
> How do the issues of power and competition effect men's friendships?

Social science studies tell us that male friendships are formed in the playgrounds and continue down the corporate corridors, from nursery school to nursing home. From the start, research shows, the relationships that boys develop with other boys differ substantially from those girls have with girls. When asked to represent "best friends" of one's own sex in a play construction task, boys put greater spatial distance between figures standing for themselves and their best friends than do girls. Also, boys show less stability in their best friendships than girls. Psychologists Elizabeth Douvan and Joseph Adelson found male-male friendships among adolescents less intimate than those among young women. Paren-

tal expectations also play into the picture: One study found
that parents expected young boys to be less involved in
personal relationships than girls.

As adults, Sidney Jourard pointed out in *The Transparent
Self*, males generally disclose less about themselves to other
men than women do to women. Sociologist Alan Booth
compared men's and women's friendship patterns and observed that while men report a greater number of friendships
than do women, men's friendships are described as less close
and spontaneous. Constraints imposed on men's friendships
by society and the family inhibit intimacy. Thus, men's
friendships tend more toward sociability than intimacy. There
is even evidence that men see simply *wanting* relationships
with men as a negative quality. Men rated high in the motiva-
tional syndrome known as "need for affiliation" are judged
by other men as being dependent and needing approval—
qualities they consider unappealing.

To put it in context, psychologists Douvan and Adelson
had this to say about adult friendship in general:

> To a disquieting degree, the adult friendship is no more than a
> mutual flight from boredom—a pact against isolation, with an
> amendment against intimacy. Those things which are crucial
> to personal integration, such as a person's history, values or
> work are studiously excluded from the interaction.

This description accurately portrays the male-male interaction. In my own case, I was embarrassed at how little personal history I knew of interviewees whom I already considered
close personal friends. "What was your father like? What
was your relationship with him like?" These seem now like
such basic questions to ask a man if you want to get to know
him or understand him better. But I asked it so infrequently.
Did I not care enough to probe that deeply? Or did I understand that the question had the power to let loose a flood of
deep, dark emotional undercurrents? When we do ask personal history—"Where'd you grow up?" "Where'd you go

to school?'' ''How do you like your job?''—it is with the unspoken agreement that we will not break the code against intimacy. We will not show too much of ourselves.

MISERY LOOKING FOR COMPANY

The pact against isolation, I found, had far greater pull in bonding two men than I had realized. For, as my own research and analysis shows, the ultimate irony of social relationships among men is that what brings them together is what keeps them apart, separated and alienated from each other. That is, many men say that their closest friends are those with whom they share "a sense of being outlaws," alienated from the mainstream of society. Isolated themselves, through training and practice, they identify with those who also feel isolated. The bond is that they feel no bond. I came to think of this dichotomous rallying point for many men as the camaraderie of alienation. Here's how some of the men I interviewed expressed it.

A thirty-seven-year-old lawyer from suburban Boston said:

> A lot of times when I feel alienated from life I seek out male friends rather than female. Men, more than women, understand it better. We talk about existential things, not necessarily our personal problems but the absurdity of life. Tolerance is important. My friends will still accept me if I don't fit into the social norm. With my best friend I see a little bit of the thief in him and I respect that.

A thirty-three-year-old anthropologist from Washington, D.C. told me:

> I felt the closest rapport with guys who explored the outer limits of the culture, the edge of hipness. They were always older and countercultural. Hegel on their bookshelves, Modigliani on the walls, Coltrane on the turntable, coffee and a bag of pot on the kitchen table.

A forty-one-year-old real estate broker from Los Angeles put it this way:

> My best friend is kind of broody and moody. He's kind of out there psychologically. We have a similar outlook on life: it's ridiculous. Like, it doesn't make sense. We see a lot of non sequiturs. Our favorite expression when we see one of these non sequiturs is, "No meaning." Often we'll even say it at the same time.

We can trace that feeling of alienation to experiences men have with their fathers or their fraternity brothers, and we can celebrate and revel in it and each other, affirming that *our connection is our disconnection*. It is shaky and vulnerable ground, for it admits to a great weakness. But men who dare to cross the turf find a reward: Misery loves company.

"I don't let myself get depressed very often," a man in his late twenties told me, "but when I do I either want to be alone or I want to be with a man friend. It's the drown-your-sorrows effect. I think it's easier with a man than with a woman because when it comes to sorrows I think men understand that alone and abandoned feeling better."

"It's commiserating together about how hard it is to be in the world—how hard it is to be a man," a thirty-four-year-old musician attempted to explain. "We get down together. We sing the blues together."

Men gather at bars to cry in their proverbial beers, to drown their sorrows in the company of a male friend who *understands*—or at least claims to. We are accomplices to a plot over which, we feel at times, we have little or no control—at work, with women, with our own decaying bodies and minds. Men pair up to become partners in crime—outlaws, thieves, aliens—seeking solace from the storm of solitude and disappointment, the frustration and disempowerment they feel at the hands of other men. These are the secret societies-of-two that I alluded to in Chapter 4. By forming these pairs, men can at once deny complicity in a system that oppresses them *and* affirm complicity in a friendship that allows them to subvert that system.

MAN TALK

How all this gets expressed in a man's world—in a world where the verbalization of such feelings has been neither modeled nor encouraged—is another matter altogether. I was at a café in San Francisco's North Beach, sitting next to two men who had embraced robustly upon meeting and then, after bright talk about recent activities, moved on to this dialogue:

"So how are you *really?*"

"O.K.—as good as can be expected. You?"

"Same, I know what you mean."

"Yeah."

"Yeah . . ."

"Yeah . . . it's heavy . . ."

"It *is* heavy."

"It's not easy . . ."

"I know what you mean: it never is."

"But, hey, no pain, no gain."

"Pain's good for you."

"That's what they say . . ."

"So what else is new?"

Somewhere in that exchange, these two expressed financial pressure, physical ailment, marital trouble, and general fatigue and depression—maybe. But what they mostly expressed, unaccustomed as they were to putting feelings into words, is that they were not alone in their pain—a pain born of isolation, insulation, and alienation. You could call what they were conveying sympathy, pity, or self-pity, but to me the word that best defines how men relate to each other is empathy: "understanding so intimate that the feelings, thoughts, and motives of one are readily comprehended by another." Empathy lets men off the hook of actually having to *say* anything. We can empathize our way through a variety of communications and miscommunication—and never have to talk about it.

A twenty-six-year-old radio disc jockey named Mark, living in Providence, Rhode Island, explained why he does not necessarily need words to express emotions with friends:

> I have maybe four close men friends. But we just don't discuss emotions. We've had so many experiences together we don't have to say anything. There's such a beauty in that. If you've been through a heavy experience with a man friend, watched him go through it or vice versa, you've seen each other at your worst and best but it's not spoken. I don't want to talk about it. I treasure that. With my wife and her girlfriends, the first thing they ask is, "How's your relationship with Mark?" With my male friends it's nothing like that. It's more of talking about whatever business is at hand. With friends I'd rather be *doing something*—that defines it all. I think doing something with men replaces love-making with them. If you like me and I like you and we know how much we're into it, that's exquisite. Words sometimes just pollute pure experience. That's why I could have a friend for ten years and only twice get down to the kinds of emotional sharing that women get down to in casual phone calls. But still, men know what's important. I know this guy would stand up for me, put up money for me, even maybe jeopardize his life for me.

My question remained whether men can "readily comprehend" others' feelings and thoughts without ever verbally expressing them? Wouldn't that shroud of silence create too much room for confusion, miscommunication and misunderstanding?

Actions speak louder than words, men learn from their fathers. "I don't care what you do," my father frequently reminded me. "You can dig ditches *but* dig the best goddamned ditches in the world." Men *do*. Some of the strongest bonds are formed between men who do things together. Whether it is sports or business or war or meeting for drinks at the corner tavern, men feel more comfortable *being* with each other when there is a clearly defined context of *doing*. And *doing* eliminates the need for talking.

On several occasions after interviews of an hour or two, men's wives would join us, astonished. "Why, I think that's the longest Earl has talked to anyone about his feelings since I've known him,'' one woman said following a session in New Jersey. In Bolinas, California, a photographer's wife came into the living room saying, "I was just out in the kitchen thinking how strange it is that there are two men out there talking about their feelings—and one of them is *my* husband. I could see women doing this—but men? I know it sounds like a cliché, but around here the main topic of conversation between men is cars.''

Was it just a cliché? A regional phenomenon? Or a metaphor for the mechanical kinds of things men talk about? What *do* men talk about if not their feelings? What is this so-called "man talk?" And how about those highly touted "man-to-man" talks?

As I interviewed more and more men, I found that those not used to talking about their feelings, but longing for contact with men, focus on something over there—not on what is between them (i.e., their relationship, which goes unmentioned). The object of shared attention—cars, stereos, sports equipment, sports events, business deals—becomes a Matter of Great Meaning. Men can get animated and excited about the subject without having to get personal. We can express personal opinions about this make of car or that sports team, even partake in heated debate about which is worse or better—giving it all the facade of passionate involvement— without ever venturing a *real* personal feeling.

Man talk, now that is serious stuff. No women allowed. Man to man. These are usually the kinds of talks that come up in times of crisis. When the situation becomes so stressful that men are forced to finally "deal with it.''

"Harry, it's about that money I owe you?''

"Carl, your wife and I are having an affair.''

"Bill, my girlfriend just left me.''

"Stan, I just lost my job.''

"Bob, you're the only person I can turn to with this problem.''

"Steve, I had a little accident with your car.''

We break the news. We share the hurt. Bottom line. These are the situations men recounted to me when I asked them when they had had a man-to-man talk with another man.

Help. I need help. I need a friend. This is the real stuff of life when men call a cease-fire, declare a neutral zone, drop their defenses and cross the no man's land. Because they had had so few—most can remember only one or two and those only in such critical times as impending divorce or impending marriage—they said they were very awkward scenes. Men were not sure exactly how to act. They tended to overdramatize, get *very* serious. Furrowed, earnest brows—like they had seen on *Father Knows Best*. A sympathetic arm—briefly— around the other guy's shoulder. A commiseratory—but fleeting—glance. These gestures are intended with sincerity and I do not mean to imply that they are insincerely meant. But men are so unfamiliar with—and, therefore, so uncomfortable in—these situations that they act them out in a stiff and stilted fashion that could be read as superficial obligation.

Here's the way a twenty-seven-year-old carpenter named Paul described a man-to-man talk he had with one of his closest friends:

> Warren and I had known each other five years. We'd worked together, socialized with our wives together, confided in each other. I had told him about an affair I'd had with a woman named Ginny while I was married. Later both Warren and I split up with our wives and he fell in love with Ginny. I ended up living near the two of them and one time, when Warren was going to be away on a trip, he came to me to talk about what he called "skeletons in our closet." It turned out he still didn't trust me—he was afraid I was going to steal Ginny when he left. I assured him I wasn't that kind of guy. We both felt relieved and I thought it brought us much closer together. But when I got up and walked over to him to embrace him as a sign of solidarity, he sort of slid away. His gesture—that is, his failure to return my gesture—made me realize he really didn't trust me and that until I proved to him he could trust me, it would all be just words to him.

"Man to man" implies that two men meet on equal ground, as equals—which is probably why these talks occur so rarely. And why they are so uncomfortable as well. Dropping the barriers, admitting mistakes, weaknesses, frailties—and "fuck-ups"—means one or the other or both men must give up some power. And that is never easy for men. That also may explain why, though men like to talk about their latest sexual conquests, they do not talk about sex in a serious vein to each other, as Bernie Zilbergeld found in his study, *Male Sexuality:*

> Men are extremely secretive about their sexuality. They may joke about sex, talk a lot about this or that woman's character-istics and how they'd like to get her in bed, and make many allusions to their sexual prowess, but, other than these bits of bravado, most men simply don't talk about sex to anyone. One of the cornerstones of the masculine stereotype in our society is that a man has no doubts, questions, or confusion about sex, and that a real man knows how to have good sex and does so frequently. For a man to ask a question about sex, thereby revealing ignorance, or to express concern, or to admit to a problem is to risk being thought something less than a man. Almost every man tends to think that all other men are having a better time sexually than he has. . . . This reinforces his idea that it's best to keep his mouth shut.

Given that, one wonders why the subject men talk most about is women. Men are either bragging about their latest "conquests" or complaining about the one who broke their heart. They are praising the ground women walk on or pro-claiming them instruments of a demonic force. They are bemoaning the fact that they are married, or bemoaning the fact that they are not. They are admitting their confusion about women (not sex, mind you) or claiming their superior understanding of them. Either way, by making women "the other," they can draw closer together.

TALKING DIRTY

Mantalk frequently refers to a particular manner in which men talk when they are alone. It is also called talking dirty and it is how men break the law, how they affirm that they are outlaws. This Australian "rigmarole" shows, perhaps in excess, how men manipulate language:

> I was walking along on this fucking fine morning, fucking sun fucking shining away, little country fucking lane, and I meets up with this fucking girl. Fucking lovely she was, so we gets into fucking conversation and I takes her over a fucking gate into a fucking field and we had sexual intercourse.

Talking dirty is the secret male language. It goes along with foxholes, locker rooms, campgrounds, and playgrounds:

> "Heeeeeeyyyy muuuuthaaafuuuuckaaaa!!!"
> "How the fuck are ya?"
> "Fucking-A right!"

That is the extreme. There are modified versions for businessmen and other civilized sorts:

> "If you don't deliver by Friday, *God damn it*, you don't get paid."
> "The *hell* I don't."
> "Hey, kiss my *ass*, buddy."
> "Up yours, *sonofabitch*."

There is something crude, brutish, and mannish about "cursing like a sailor." It is a verbal beating of one's fists on one's chest. *I am tough. No sissy here.* You can often tell which man is feeling a little unsure of his masculinity by how frequently he spices his language with so-called dirty words. Young boys quickly learn that swear words are the passwords that gain them entry into the big boys' club.

Curse words are often the substitutes for the emotional content men otherwise fail to express to each other. Ashley

Montagu dissects man's propensity for profanity in *The Anatomy of Swearing*:

> Almost everyone appears to have recognized the function of swearing—namely, an effective means of permitting the escape of excess steam. It is especially appropriate for the grown individual, the man who knows that even though the pain be sufficient and the occasion great enough to cause him to weep, he cannot do so because he has learned to consider such conduct unmanly. In a man to whom swearing has become an ingrained habit, it may become psychologically as well as physiologically very much more satisfying than either weeping or laughter.

Men whose verbal expressiveness has been either thwarted or underdeveloped build up a lot of frustration—"excess steam"—which finds a vent in swearing. Notice sometime how the incidence of profanity increases when men gather. In such situations, I have come to recognize each swear word as a buzz word for men's inability *really* to talk to each other.

COMPETITION: THE COMMON GROUND

Though there may not be a "best friend," there are all kinds of men friends: work friends, sports friends, poker friends, neighborhood bar friends, hobby friends, childhood friends, wives' friends. Each fulfills a different need. Each need only goes so far and no further toward intimacy. A man may tell his bowling buddy how tough work is, but not that his job is threatened. He may tell a drinking friend about the possible pink slip but not that he feels humiliated by it. He will tell that to an old childhood friend, but probably not even to him will he admit how much being jobless would emasculate him.

But—to the man, as we say—all these friendships have at least one thing in common: competition. The need for one man to know he is better than another is rooted deep in male-male psychology. It can be traced, as we have seen, to relationships with fathers. It is reconfirmed, as succeeding chapters have demonstrated, as we move through relationships in a man's world.

From the start, from the initial handshake, the meeting of two men is a face-off, a measuring against one another. One woman I know compared an introduction of two men to two dogs circling around and sniffing at each other. As these images suggest, the competition begins with physical comparison. Bigger, of course, is better.

Society seems to predicate masculine success potential on height. We look up to six-footers—figuratively and literally. Short men will always be boys—or do a lot of Napoleonic toe-lifting to compensate for their lack of inches. Men who are looked up to have the psychological advantage. They also have the economic advantage, according to studies. They get ahead, so to speak. An investment banker with Merrill Lynch White Weld Capital Markets Group, working in conjunction with a labor economist, once correlated income with height in a sample of 17,000 Army Air Corps cadets. Of this group, 10,000 reported their salaries after twelve years, and 5,000 after twenty-five years. They concluded that those six feet or over made approximately 8 percent more money annually than those five-foot-six or shorter.

A marketing professor at Eastern Michigan University asked 140 sales recruiters whom they would choose between two equally qualified candidates—one who was six-foot-one or one who was five-foot-five. Seventy-two percent said they would opt for the taller man. In researching his book, *The Height of Your Life*, Ralph Keyes interviewed the head of the country's largest employment agency for accountants and financial officers, who admitted that tall men have an easier time finding jobs because "they fulfill an image, they look the part." A former IBM director of corporate information told Keyes that tall men were given preference for visible positions, such as salesman and corporate officer. "They wanted salesmen to look domineering, aggressive," Keyes reported. "Tallness was part of that."

Very tall men pay a price, however, for being head and shoulders above other men. They have to act the part: They must live *up* to the restrained, mature, aloof role of a full-grown man. They must always represent their stature—without unduly wielding the power that comes with it. As a result, they are much more emotionally strait-jacketed than men of normal or short height.

"I always tried to be one of the guys but never was—mentally or physically," a very large man told me. "I had one or two close friends for a short time but then they'd leave me. I intimidated them, they said." On the other hand, short people can "act out" boyish immaturity as much as they like. To claim their power and assert themselves, they have to be feisty. Eternal boys, at least in the eyes of others, they feel freer to be as emotionally outrageous as they want. The manliness inherent in the tall man's bearing does not have the same hold on the shorter, "boyish" man.

A five-foot-four media coordinator living in New York City analyzed life as a short person:

I've found that because I am short, I appear nonthreatening. My friends seem more comfortable letting go with me. I also notice men feel freer to be physical with me. Not sexual—but physical. Recently I was going through a depression and a rather tall male friend of mine gave me a very warm embrace. I think he could do that because he felt a certain relaxation because I was a little guy, almost like a child, not another adult male with whom there might be all kinds of question marks regarding homosexuality. I'm always amused at my own outspokenness with tall people. I'll say, "Shut up or I'll knock you across the room." Kind of mock threat language which people never take seriously because physically I couldn't do it but it enables me to express hostility. I can get it off my chest and never worry about being attacked because men won't beat up on a little guy; it doesn't look good. I don't think I have a Napoleonic complex but I guess I have a sort of control thing, a manipulative thing. I use my height disadvantage to my advantage. I give orders and I think people follow them because they don't feel threatened or competitive with me precisely because of my height. I've also found people like to show me off. In certain social contexts friends will bring up topics they know I'm expert in, and they are proud to see me pontificate—which is something they might not do for someone who was four inches taller. People enjoy seeing and hearing me put down rough tough-guy types. Maybe because everyone sides with an underdog and that's what a short guy often feels like.

Physical stature is only the start. As we grow older social stature becomes even more important. Our personal possessions bear a price tag other men quickly estimate in terms of their own possessions; what we can afford indicates who is doing better. If a picture is worth a thousand words, then things—objects—become the novellas by which men reveal themselves to each other; and, conversely, by which they judge each other. A man's clothes or his tennis racket speak for the man himself. A high-priced cigar, lit at the appropriate moment, can say as much for a man as a high-level communiqué. When the Boston Celtic's former coach Red Auerbach ceremoniously lit up a big one, he was saying, "The game's over, boys, and I've won again."

Men invest their possessions with great personal meaning, with masculine identity. This concept can be taken to seemingly ludicrous extremes. Take the razor, for instance. Gillette, Wilkinson, Schick, and Bic fight tooth and nail—or more correctly, whisker and follicle—for control of the $450-million razor blade market, hyping not just shaving but the instrument itself as a reflection of masculinity. In an article for *Esquire* mazagine (February 1980) Chris Welles wrote:

> Though shaving may now require less skill and involve less danger than it once did, most men still want the razor they use to reflect their belief that shaving remains serious business. They regard their razor as an important personal tool, a kind of extension of self, like an expensive pen, cigarette lighter, attaché case or golf club set. Gillette has labored hard, with success, to maintain the razor's masculine look, heft, and feel as well as its status as an item of personal identification worthy of, for instance, a Christmas gift.

And, to move in for an even closer look, beards and moustaches have always been more to men than so many facial hairs. At various times and places in history, a man's beard was the embodiment of his honor. Pulling another man's beard was tantamount to the ultimate insult, answerable only at gunpoint. It seems obvious that men associate beards with masculinity—if only because women cannot grow them. That also makes shaving a singularly male morning ritual, and one more male bond. But another aspect of beards and moustaches makes them attractive to men: They hide the face, they conceal the vulnerable upper lip and chin, they make the man less naked, less available. They are a built-in male mask. Besides, they make him look older and wiser, reinforcing the importance of a hierarchy based on age. They say, "I'm wise, I'm manly," and "Don't get too close."

But the competition can be simply for control of a situation—for instance, in conversation. Domination of a conversation between and among men is a kind of competitive game, in which being recognized as the ultimate authority in the group is the object. As much as men do not like to talk about their personal feelings, they love to talk about themselves—their accomplishments, what they know, who they know. They will hold forth on seemingly any topic, even when they do not know the answers or what they are talking about. Conversation with these sorts of men become contests for control in which there are no rules of usual etiquette. One man will start talking before the last man has finished—and usually in a louder voice. This, one can well imagine, escalates rapidly into loud talk-bouts. A woman friend and I had dinner one night with two other couples—all involved in fields related to my research for this book. Later it took a woman—my friend—to draw my attention to the fact that all three of us men attempted to dominate the conversation in booming voices of authority, interrupting each other. I recalled a well-known study that showed men use the word "but" more frequently than women (who use "and" more), implying men are more argumentative while women are additive. "But" is a conversational crossed sword of the male trained in competition. "And" is the supportive link of the nurturing female conditioned to cooperate.

MAKING SPORT OF SPORTS

Deception is crucial to success; and to young men who have learned early and painfully that life is a battle for survival, basketball is one of the few games in which the weapon of deception is a legitimate rule and not the source of trouble.

—Jeff Greenfield,
"The Black and White Truth About Basketball," *Esquire*

One of the socially acceptable ways that men vent this competitive urge has traditionally been through athletic competition. Sports is the Great Contest for men. If you can hit the long ball, you are immediately promoted among the ranks of men. By grade school we have already psyched each other out, scouted each other's athletic potential. This is dramatically illustrated on the playgrounds every time boys choose up sides. There is nothing so humiliating as always being one of the last chosen. It burns lifelong scars into some men's memories.

Men choose their friends by how well matched they are athletically. Two boys or two men enjoy the head-to-head combat/competition, especially when they know they each have a fair chance of winning an equal number of times. But what happens when one excels too often? Predictably, the other drops out. I was astounded at how frequently this pattern repeated itself among the men I interviewed. The testimony of a twenty-eight-year-old Long Island chemist and an avid "jock" is typical:

Stanley was my best friend in grammar school. He was good athletically. We were sports companions. I remember hours and hours of football, baseball, basketball—playing, watching on television, even trading the cards that came with the bubble gum. He was a year older and later, by high school, he was a better basketball player, the star of the team. I idolized him—though I'd never let him know that even today. But when he got a lot better than me, that created a separation. I just couldn't keep up with him. But with all my friends, when I think about it, sports was an important touch point.

To let the fact that one beat another at a sport be cause for ending a relationship between two people would rarely occur to women, I am assured by women. For men, though, it is surprisingly important. Once that friend knows our weak spot, we feel too vulnerable to expose ourselves to him again. To me it echoed lessons learned earlier at fathers' feet, where coming in second was a regular event. Rather than chance placing second again, men prefer to drop out of the contest altogether even though it may mean forfeiting a valuable friendship.

If we think the competition on the playgrounds is intense, it's unimaginable in professional sports. Maintaining friendships in that arena is nearly impossible. Bob Woolf, one of the leading sports attorneys in the country (his clients—and friends—have included, among many others, John Havlicek, Jim Plunkett, Larry Bird and Carl Yastrzemski), told me:

Most athletes—despite the size of their bodies—are kids. Kids in very big bodies. Every athlete has been catered to since he was in seventh grade. "You're the greatest, a hero," they're told. But it's an illusion because when they get into the professional environment they find out all the other guys have been told the same thing. Every day they face so much competition. So much insecurity. I know a lot of guys who sit on the bench screaming, "Get a hit, baby," but hoping the guy strikes out, or gets an injury or traded. Friendships in professional sports are a dangerous thing. Next thing you know your roommate—a person in whom you may have confided insecurities, weaknesses and deep dark secrets—is traded and now he's supposed to be, and eventually really does become, your enemy.

I watch their careers develop. A lot can cope with the fame and money and flamboyant living. Then some develop this attitude: "I have proved myself as an athlete but I have to prove myself in other areas." Off court they're all still vying against each other for their manhood.

In *Life on the Run,* one of the few readable sports autobiographies actually written by the star, former New York Knick basketball star (and later Senator) Bill Bradley elaborated on the topic of competition, in this case between himself and teammate Cazzie Russell, both vying for a starting forward position:

I came to view our competition as a sad but necessary aspect of professional basketball. . . . However much Cazzie and I respected each other, every game and every practice became a battle to show [Coach Red] Holzman that one of us was better than the other. Our head-to-head competition drained me of much emotional energy, for I was never sure that I would win. . . . Above all, I could never relax. I felt tension the moment I stepped onto the court. . . . Each of us looked for any kind of edge. . . . Even off the court, the anger and aggressive drive spilled over and prevented closeness. The tension between us never became bitter or hostile. . . . I think we understood each other and possessed a mutual respect more basic than words could convey. I finally realized that Cazzie and I were pawns in a larger game, like corporate executives apparently competing for promotion but most directly benefitting the corporation that established the arena for competition. Many fans saw the familiar signs of their own work situations in our competition; their interest in part derived from the anxieties generated in their own lives and projected onto us.

The Princeton graduate and Rhodes Scholar's insights on the vicarious competitive thrill fans get from spectator sports are astute indeed. For those of us disinclined to participate in sports or disqualified from high-level competition—but who still have been instilled with the competitive urge—spectator sports is a socially acceptable safety valve and another rallying point for men.

No one summed up the psyche of a spectating athlete better than Frederick Exley in *A Fan's Notes:*

> Why did football bring me so to life? I can't say precisely. Part of it was my feeling that football was an island of directness in a world of circumspection. In football a man was asked to do a difficult and brutal job, and he either did it or got out. There is nothing rhetorical or vague about it; I chose to believe that it was not unlike the jobs which all men, in some sunnier past, had been called upon to do. It smacked of something old, something traditional, something unclouded by leger-demain and subterfuge. It had that kind of power over me, drawing me back with the force of something known, scarcely remembered, elusive as integrity—perhaps it was no more than the force of a forgotten childhood. Whatever it was, I gave myself up to the Giants utterly. The recompense I gained was the feeling of being alive.

For men who have had to kill off or suppress their emotions for and against men in so many other ways, sports *is* a lifesaver. Men who have first been trained to compete, and then have had to thwart and frustrate their need for competition, can experience the thrill of victory and the agony of defeat vicariously in the neutral zone of their living rooms or in the bleachers, without ever having to put their own egos on the line. A man can invest his favorite team or superstar with all the lost, hoped for, and gained glory he could not savor for himself. Men can sit in the stands or around a television set in the den cheering, clapping, slapping each other on the back, punching each other in the arms as though they themselves had won.

Even in discussing and watching sports, we assume a combative stance. I have seen men with blood in their eyes while debating whether a ball landed in or out, whether the Yankees would win the pennant, or whether one man or another could win at pool, darts, running, swimming, or any other sport. These are the men to whom ERA will always be the measure of a pitcher's worth, not a constitutional amendment guaranteeing women's rights. How well informed a man is—about standings, statistics, college prospects, rookies to watch, sports history and records, capacities of stadiums and the percentage of beef in the hot dogs sold there—becomes itself a competition.

EDGING OUT THE COMPETITIVE EDGE

What is the common denominator of all men's friendships? Texts like McWilliams's *The Idea of Fraternity in America* suggest that it might be a quality he terms "value homophily." Which is to say that men like men with the same interests and standard of judgment. They like men who are like themselves— their mirror images. Men with common interests can *do* and enjoy the same things together. They pick friends with the same (hopefully high) standard of judgment to confirm and reaffirm their own (hopefully high) rank among men.

McWilliams's analysis is accurate—as far as it goes. In my own examination of man-to-man relationships, however, the deeper I probed the more I recognized that the primary fact of life in a man's world is competition. It stood to reason, then, that the true common denominator of men's friendships is competition. Value homophily is just a nice way of putting it. We measure our own worth—and each other's—by the friends we keep. If my friends are richer, more handsome, more hip, and better athletes than yours, I am better than you. In the ideal, we conceive of our friendships with men as nonthreatening, noncompetitive oases in a desert of solitude. But men are so well indoctrinated to competition in all their other male training grounds that the urge to one-up each other is seemingly irrevocable. As I studied power dynamics of the various kinds of relationships men described, I discovered the way in which men sidestep what can frequently become down-and-dirty and potentially humiliating competitions for supremacy. Rather than enter into friendships in which competition will be an issue, they enter into friendships in which competition will not be an issue. And yet, power, control, and competition remain the determining factors. Let me explain.

Two types of friendships emerged from my interviews that exemplify this. I call them the Star and the Nerd, and the Fifty-Fifty Friendship. The first pair, in which one is dominant and the other subservient, escape a fierce face-off for authority because one clearly already has the power. There is literally no contest; both know who is in charge. At the same time, as we shall see, both profit from such a mutuality, both gain from the alliance. The Fifty-Fifty Friendship, on the other hand, can skirt the competition for power and control because both win an equal amount of times. Their equalness means neither has the clear advantage over the other. Neither feels overpowered. And yet both can continue to compete head-to-head, each victory negating the last defeat.

Such a friendship, as we shall see, promises a healthy venting of competitiveness without threatening one's ego.

THE STAR AND THE NERD

Surely you have noticed every hero has his sidekick. Don Quixote had his Sancho Panza, Johnny Carson his Ed McMahon, Dean Martin his Jerry Lewis, Batman his Robin. Elementary school teachers frequently notice boys at the top of the class—academically, athletically, socially—befriending boys at the other end of the competitive scale. What is in it for either of them? Where is the "value homophily" in such a pair-up? If it is true that men seek their mirror image—or the image they aspire to—what is the star who picks a nerd for a friend saying about himself? And why would a nerd, who knows he is only going to look that much worse next to someone that much better than himself, set himself up for such a humiliation?

In such relationships, where the lines of power are so clearly drawn, a great deal of pressure is taken off both parties to perform according to the other's expectations.

What each gains is appreciation for being valued for qualities that have been thwarted and unrecognized by other men. The star can act like a nerd without losing stature. And the nerd can, simply by association with the star, gain a little glitter for himself.

Moreover, it *is* lonely at the top. Everyone else is too intimidated to try to get too close to the star. The Big Man on Campus tends to have lots of acquaintances but few true friends in whom he can confide his own weaknesses; with others there is too much image to protect. With a friend he outclasses, that would never be a danger. So the star lifts the self-profile of the nerd and the nerd allows the star to get down off the precarious pedestal on which he lives.

Two of my interviewees, Paul and Ken, whom I spoke to separately, serve as great examples. They were next-door neighbors in grade school. More than proximity, however, brought them together; in the first place there was the need to escape the oppressive atmosphere each felt in his own home.

Paul was the weaker, less popular of the two. Thin and frail, with braces and big ears, an effeminate gait and speech, he was the youngest of four children and the only son. His father had been bedridden since Paul was five (and died by the time Paul was twelve).

His home was full of warmth and family sing-alongs around the piano but the intensity of being surrounded by so much female energy had a suffocating effect on Paul. What he wanted was contact with a male and even the "big brother" his mother hired did not suffice.

Ken, on the other hand, was handsome, athletic, an academic achiever, the guy with whom everybody—boys and girls—wanted to be friends. At home, though, he lived in a stifled environment. His father was forty-seven when Ken, an only child, was born; his most vivid memory of his father was of a man "hunched over with a serious kind of inexpressive look on his face and passive toward me." His mother was the predominant person in his life. The house was sterile; it left a feeling of being in a void. Ken never felt comfortable there. He describes his parents' marriage in similar images: "emotionally paralyzed, sterile." In our interview he continued:

It was creepy in my house, which is why I always went to Paul's house every afternoon of my life. With Paul it was like having a twin brother. What Paul and I shared was a great deal of inventiveness. We were really funny together. Alone together, we were somewhere else—just whacky, crazy, zany. We spent a lot of time making up games and ways of communicating. We'd build offices in the backyards and invent phone systems and interplanetary television shows. We made up operas, radio shows—wrote and put them on just for each other.

Paul remembered the early days of their relationship:

The only thing I had over him was that my family was richer. But he was stronger, much more physical, more attractive to the girls and a better student. You see, Ken was very popular, so if he came over to play with me, that was a plus for me. Others would think, "If he likes Paul, then Paul must be o.k." To get him to come over I'd bribe him with candy. Or I'd tell him I'd hidden presents in my house and if he found them he could keep them. I bought his friendship. I worshipped him. He was my hero. And when we were alone he would open up like with nobody else. We'd stay up all night making up stories and really get out there. But then sometimes in school he'd be mean to me, and he had this sadistic streak in him. It was complicated between us. I think there was a tremendous animosity in him and he wanted to get back at me. For what? My family setting? Our money? My creativity? Yet he loved me. We were buddies.

Ken countered:

Yes, I was an aggressive kid but that's not to be confused with being mean to Paul. There was no vindictiveness on my part. I think I was that way because things were so repressed in my house. What Paul saw in me that most others didn't was my wit and humor. I may have been all the things Paul says but I didn't have that many friends who would call me up and say, "Hey, come on over." Paul was always calling me up. He had a very low self-profile. Sometimes I would be in a bad mood and look at him and call him a "scrawny kid, a little shit," things like that. But we never fought. No, my

power over Paul was not physical. I dominated him emotionally. The way I would use my power was to threaten not to
play with him. I held myself back. I'd threaten him with
social extinction—which was worse than punching him but no
less destructive. He had this thing where he desperately needed
me almost every day and often I needed him too. There was a
balance, though some of the reasons for our needs were
different.

Behind the seeming lopsidedness of their relationship, there
was indeed a balance. Each gave and received something
very valuable. The degree to which the friendship depended
on the lopsided power balance is illustrated by what eventually became of these two after the scales were tipped several
years later.

They went to different high schools and as Ken became
more and more popular with girls and more successful in
athletics, he pulled away from Paul. "I started to think,
'Yeah, Paul is different, weird. I'm mature, sexy. He's not,
so forget him. Fuck his little shows and enterprises.' All I
wanted to do was play baseball, which he didn't like to do,
and play with girls—who didn't like him." Boys trying to be
men put aside their childish playthings and Ken pushed Paul
into the background of his life.

Paul went off to college in Boston, Ken to New York. It
was not until the year after they graduated that they saw each
other again. Ken had tired of life in New York; nothing was
happening. He went to visit Paul who was now involved with
a group of exciting and innovative media personalities. Ken
was impressed with the new power of his old friend, and
moved to Boston, assuming he would quickly become the
kingpin in Paul's circle, and Paul's life. But it was now Ken
who had to make overtures to Paul. Neither felt comfortable
dealing with each other on an equal basis. They fought. None
of the lightness was there. Said Ken: "I had my own reputation to save, my old authority to reclaim. And he had a new
reputation to live up to."

They remained friends through those years, and for many
more, but the tight camaraderie—the feeling that they could

really confide in each other—was gone. And without it, the friendship faded.

Paul best summed up the history of their friendship:

> Ken was great for me. And I was great for him. I used him and he used me but we never felt as though we were taking advantage of each other. There were ways in which I had the power and there were ways in which he had it. From the outside it appeared as though he had it, but from the inside we both knew there were times I had it. Even when I let him walk all over me, there was a sense in which I was in control because at least I had his undivided attention. *I* was the one he wanted to walk over. I think one of the reasons we're not as close now as we might be is that that power structure doesn't exist. The tables turned in a sense and when we tried to play our old roles they didn't exactly work. And now that I appear to have more power, it's hard for him to assume this new role. It's too bad because I still love the guy.

It *is* too bad. Too bad that a shift in power could destroy a friendship, but in their case—as in others—the friendship was based on the fact that power was not an issue. When it entered into the picture, the friendship could not last.

THE FIFTY-FIFTY FRIENDSHIP

The Fifty-Fifty Friendship occurs between men of approximately equal achievement. Their relationship is charged with competitiveness, and it remains healthy and inspiring as long as each man has the opportunity to come out on top from time to time. This sort of relationship can be highly volatile and even destructive, but it can also be a powerful vehicle by which the participants work out their man-to-man issues and their personal issues as well. The difference lies in talking. Two men who can discuss the pros and cons of their friendship can achieve mutual respect and friendship that transcends competition.

The Fifty-Fifty Friendship is worth fighting for.

Both thirty-two, both dark curly-haired Jews from Brooklyn, both dentists, both sons of dominating mothers and absent or passive fathers, both of equal height and build and equal athletic and academic ability, Evan and Jon are a matched pair.

Theirs is a friendship that could be built on rivalry and competition, an endless keeping count of every win and loss. But as potentially competitive as it could be, this relationship is one of the closest and mutually supportive among all the men I know and interviewed. What is their secret? They "work it out," as they put it. They let very little slip by—inconsistencies, betrayals, nonsupport—without drawing it to the other's attention. In sports it is called keeping the defense honest, or calling a foul when you see one. In the vernacular, it is called "calling him on his stuff." In this way, no matter how competitive they are with each other, neither man is allowed to get too far ahead.

Jon told me:

Evan and I met in dental school. I was drawn to him at first because he was a sort of anti-establishment comrade, one of a handful of dental students who stood up against the dental education system and institution. But we never got to know each other until we met at a party given by a mutual friend. Actually, our girlfriends met first and they introduced us to each other. I don't know if we ever would have gotten as close as we did if it wasn't for our girlfriends. We were forced to spend a lot of time together because of them. And frankly, at first I liked Evan's girlfriend more than I liked Evan. Evan and I certainly had a lot in common, but Evan kept saying he felt this "resistance" from me. I remember the first of our "work-outs." We were walking through a park with our girlfriends. They had lagged behind, and Evan and I were talking about our future plans. In the middle of the conversation he said, "Jon, I really get the feeling you don't like me." "That's not true," I shot back and tried to change the subject. But every now and then he'd come back again, checking this feeling with me. I wasn't used to a man pursuing feelings; I felt pushed and wanted to retreat. I can get very cold. I just disappear emotionally. Withdrawal—that's my power number. Evan wouldn't let me. Somehow I can listen to Evan. With anyone else I'd say, "Leave me alone." I trust Evan because I know we're on equal footing. He gets me to admit that my resistance isn't to him but to most men, and that when he really pushes me I can trace it back to my father.

My relationships with other men are quite different. For instance my friend Richard and I—we're living in the same house now—we don't have conflicts. Maybe we brush it under the rug. I don't make a lot of demands of him and he doesn't make them of me. I never feel like I am disappointed in or disappointing him. I never feel guilty with him. If I have pain I don't expect him to make me feel better.

Though Jon described himself as "totally caught up in power," he said he doesn't have many conflicts with his men friends:

The only person who I have real blow-out fights with is Evan. He's very good to fight with. He doesn't run away. He will take an attack and make sense out of it. I'd run away but he's taught me a lot in that regard. If I confront him with something he stays with it until we get to the other side. I see him doing that and I figure, "Jesus, it's better to work it through." I become more willing to accept my part in the dispute. I realize by the end of my sessions with Evan that I could have been more sensitive, that there was some middle ground between us. I've never had another person I could do that with. He has an incredible amount of guts to pursue a question like "Why don't you like me?" And that's why I like him. I have tremendous respect for him for that.

It all seemed so simple. When they talked, they worked it out—all the defensiveness, all the competitiveness, all the barriers dropped away.

In Fifty-Fifty Friendships like that between Jon and Evan—in which one's best friend could indeed be one's worst enemy— men who are willing to brave it across those barriers against verbalizing their feelings find that they can detonate the potentially explosive bomb of competitiveness.

Working it out may cause sparks, smoke, even fire, but

those men who stay in there and fight it out, if necessary, find their friendships are deeper, more meaningful and longer lasting. Tell him he is ripping you off. Tell him he is screwing up his life. Show him you care enough and you will have a friend for life.

And yet talking—about feelings, about fears, about issues of conflict within the friendship itself—appears to be the hardest thing in the world in a man's world. Everything a man has learned from men and about men through the various training grounds we are discussing in this book encourages him to keep his lips sealed. From his father to his film heroes, the message has been that a man's strength is his silence. That approach is also necessary in a competitive environment where what you say might be criticized, put down, or otherwise held against you. Fearing such response certainly would lead a man to believe that what you *do not* say to men will not hurt you.

Besides, men figure, why bother investing all that emotion in a relationship that will probably end the same way all their other man-to-man experiences have ended—in abandonment, betrayal, or simply lack of fulfillment? Anyway, men have been conditioned to believe, women are the ones in whom you are supposed to invest your emotions.

That kind of thinking, of course, leaves too many men alone and lonely when they begin to look around at—or for—men friends.

THE BENIGN FRIENDSHIP

To be sure, most friendships between men appear to float along pleasantly—if passionlessly—without such verbal workouts. They weather time, distance, and differences. There seems to be a tacit agreement not to disagree, not to call each other on their stuff. Some of these friendships go back to college, high school, grade school, even kindergarten. When men told me about such friendships, I asked what held them together. What kept the fire of friendship ignited? Their answers invariably begged questions:

"Why have you remained friends for so long?" I would ask.

"Because we've been friends for so long," they would reply.

Longevity, they were saying, was the basis of the friendship. The bond of a shared history created a loyalty to a friendship that might very well be all but nonexistent in substance in the present. This benign friendship, I learned, was the predominant type between and among men. Men in these friendships, I also discovered in interviews, appear to give little conscious thought to and verbal expression of the what and the why of a bond they claim is important enough in their lives to maintain and continue.

Donald and Stan, for example, both nearly forty, seem as different as two men can be. Donald is outgoing; Stan is reclusive. Donald is a doer, a carpenter. Stan is a thinker, an investment analyst. Donald is stocky of build, like a running back, with an open face; he is likeable, engaging, sometimes overbearing. Stan, tall and thin, aloof and impenetrable, hides behind thick, dark eyebrows and a handlebar moustache. Unlikely as it seems, they have been friends since high school, bridging gaps of time, philosophy, and personal style. They now live in neighboring towns.

I wanted to know what made the friendship of Donald and Stan tick. Where was their common ground? What attracted them to each other? How did they make the friendship last? Their answers—or at least their attempts at answers—came out over a weekend of talking, first with Donald and then with Donald and Stan together. The clearest conclusion is that they are unclear about such issues. The saddest is that their cloudiness is typical of the men I interviewed when it came to examining their friendships with men.

It was Donald's wife, Kathy, who first posed the most vivid image of these two men's friendship. She told me that Donald and Stan are like two old villagers who meet every day at the same time at the town water well. Whether they want to meet or not is no longer relevant; meeting at the well is so much a part of their daily ritual that they could not imagine life without it.

Donald immediately objected to the depiction: "That's not an accurate description. It's not just habitual. I have feeling for him. There's something deeper. I truly care about Stan's welfare, that he's doing okay."

I hoped Stan would have a better reply when I asked him, "Why are you and Donald friends after so long?"

Stan curled the end of his moustache, thinking. His eyes narrowed to a slit.

"Time," he finally answered:

> I think it's time. Durability. Donald and I met when we were eleven years old at camp. There was no particular relationship formed but we met. Then we met again—ninth-grade home-room. Again, there was no relationship of any significance until the last semester of high school. Even then, though, our relationship was neutral. We saw each other on a daily basis—with no particular relationship.

These two simply cannot identify what holds them together. What they finally agree on is that they can not agree on how and what they feel for each other. And that they rarely even think about it. Despite this resistance to exploring the origins and dynamics of the friendship, Donald and Stan's is a friendship, like many men's, that continues and endures almost in spite of itself. Their loyalty is to the longevity of the bond, not really to each other. The way it continues is for them to refrain from venturing across those boundaries that protect their privacy (read vulnerability). Maintaining the distance—respecting the difference, not making waves—inhibits depth, I suspect. And for many men, this sort of friendship works. It gives them what they want: male companionship without confrontation. Nobody calls anybody on his stuff. It is safe but not challenging. And, in my estimation, not very rewarding.

If I could sum up and tie up this chapter in two words they would be *trust* and *respect*. These are the qualities men cite most frequently when they talk about what they look for in men friends.

In a competitive environment, there are few men you can trust. That lesson has been repeatedly brought home for men in the various training grounds we have been discussing. You can never fully trust—never totally confide in—a man who has been conditioned to see you as someone he must surpass to prove his own supremacy. How can you trust a man who distrusts you? It is a vicious circle only some men are able to break.

And why do we place such high value on respect? Because it comes so dearly from our fathers. In the eyes of every man we meet, we look for the approval and acceptance we tried—most of us vainly—to gain from the first and primary male role model in our lives.

When we do find a man we trust and respect and, perhaps more importantly, who trusts and respects us, it is a welcome relief—like coming home. In that relationship we have an opportunity to reconcile and resolve issues that plague fathers and sons and brothers—in fact, all man-to-man relationships. We should develop such friendships and we should cherish such friends. They are rare men indeed and, moreover, they may be the keymasters to the gate that leads to self-discovery.

Homophobia:
The Unspoken Barrier

"The seemingly shameful homoerotic feelings that
sank from awareness are always ready to resurface.
The discomfort that would be associated with their
reemergence into awareness acts as an efficient
guardian of sexist training. The secret shame of these
hidden feelings is the dragon at the gateway of full
self-awareness."

—Don Clark, Ph.D.,
Loving Someone Gay

Textbooks define homophobia as "the dread of being in close
quarters with homosexuals or, in the case of homosexuals
themselves, self-loathing." The double issue of homosexuality and the fear of homosexuality have gone unmentioned so
far in this book, as they remain unspoken in a man's world
except in the form of taunts and bad jokes. Spoken or unspoken, heard or unheard, visible or invisible, homosexuality
lurks insidiously behind many encounters, threatening heterosexual men and forcing them into emotional and physical
straitjackets. Homophobia accounts for one of the major barriers inhibiting closer and more intimate relationships between men.

Homosexuality is the dark pool of masculinity, a mirror
most heterosexuals and some homosexuals would rather avoid
looking into too deeply. The fear of it—in others, in
themselves—makes men think twice about touching each other
with any more tenderness than that displayed in beefy bearhugs
or quick pats on the shoulder. It makes men avert their eyes

from a stare held too long. It inhibits them from expressing love for other men on the chance that it will be "taken in the wrong way," as the men I have interviewed put it.

Likewise, men have been conditioned and trained not to expect gestures of intimacy from men. When a physical gesture is offered, therefore, we are suspicious of its origins and motives. That kind of paranoia leads us to believe that, especially in situations where he has nothing to gain economically or socially, a man who reaches out to us *must* want something. But what? Sexual favor is the answer that springs to a mind conditioned in such a way.

Behind such suspicion lies dread. On the face of it, the dread appears to be of "the others" on whom the training did not take. Studies have shown that lower species of animals and children demonstrate a basic dread of anything or anyone they perceive as different from themselves. This man squeezing my shoulder just a bit too tenderly, staring into my eyes with too much affection—could he be a deviant, loathed, feared, or misunderstood by the majority of society?

To me the reason is simple: Behind the fear of being propositioned, of finding oneself in an awkward situation, or even of discovering an insistent anticipatory pleasure that calls into question one's own sexual preferences—behind it all stands a basic fear of the unknown. Few phenomena so widespread as homosexuality have remained so poorly understood by the majority. Men both in my interviews and in some of the social-science research covered here confirm that a distorted view of the gay world is the norm among heterosexual men. But when men reach across this gap of information, they discover human beings—men—on the other side, men who are not that much different from themselves. Once they do break through the myth of differentness that separates straights from gays, the heterosexual man seeking to be honest with himself has a new fear to contend with: not the fear of difference, but the fear of similarity.

"EVERYBODY'S GOT A STORY . . ."

A gay friend of mine asked, not half-joking, how I could write about homosexuality without having "sampled the fare." My field research did not include going to gay baths or submitting myself to a hands-on homosexual encounter. But long before writing this book I had had ample opportunity to examine my own so-called homosexual "tendencies" and my attitudes toward homosexuality in incidents I have come to learn are typical of most growing men.

"Garfinkel, your ass wiggles like a girl's," the sixth-grade class bully shouted down the hall at me, in ten seconds affecting a years-long self-consciousness regarding at least my gait. And then there was the exploratory encounter with the kid down the street which I never admitted to another soul until I began interviewing men for this book. In college, when my roommate came out of the closet and told me about "his scene," as he used to call it, I felt as though I had been slapped out of a heterosexual naiveté. I went deep inside to ask myself why I was attracted to a man who was gay and why he was attracted to me. His deepest fear at that time, he told me later, was that if he told me he was gay he would probably lose me as a friend. He remains my friend, however.

Still later, travelling with a five-man jazz band, I felt a love of men and male companionship—a quality of communication unrivaled by contact with women. The ease of the feeling, the completeness of the rapport, made me wonder further about where one (and specifically this one) draws the line between loving a man and making love to a man. But when one of the fellow musicians suggested we physically consummate our mutual love and appreciation, I withdrew. I knew if it had been a woman I would not have hesitated. I had to ask myself again why I could feel love for another man but not want to express it physically.

As Kinsey documented in studies long ago, most men have at least one early "experiment" with sexual activity with another male. Further, Kinsey and his co-authors wrote in 1948 that 30 percent of the adult men in the United States have at one time or another been brought to orgasm as a result of oral genital stimulation by another man. Whatever private meaning such encounters have for those who remain heterosexual, it is safe to say that—as mine did—they remain tightly locked away: secrets, dangerous memories, threats to one's own not always stable sexual identity. For despite the confusion homosexuality engenders, what remains clear is the potency of the taboo surrounding such activities. This chapter looks at those taboos, where they come from, and how they inhibit men from forming closer relationships.

WHO HATES GAYS—AND WHY

Let me state my thesis clearly right from the start: I contend that homophobia is a learned stance built into the training that most boys receive early in their lives. That is, homophobia is typical of all men in our society—gay or straight. It is built into our culture, reinforcing traditional masculine attributes by teaching that men who do not compete and who need intimacy and emotional support from other men are at best weak, at worst (when emotional intimacy leads to physical intimacy) sick and sickening sociopaths to be shunned. As to how the rampant homophobia in our culture thrives, the answer is simple. It feeds off of myths, misinformation, and lies.

To many, if not most, heterosexual men, the "typical male homosexual" is less good, less honest, less fair, less positive, less valuable, less stable, less intellectual, less friendly, less clean, more shallow, more unhealthy than the typical male heterosexual. Above all, he is seen as less masculine. This is not the reaction of only uncultured rednecks. In a January 1977 *Psychology Today* poll of readers' attitudes about masculinity—a group of respondents markedly more affluent and better educated than the average American—a surprising 70 percent reported believing that "homosexual men are not masculine," a decidedly damning view in a society that so admires masculinity. To me that reinforces my suspicion that the homosexual is our culture's bad boy: the very model of what the "teachings" say you are not supposed to be.

In one study demonstrating attitudes of heterosexuals toward homosexuals, participants placed stick figures representing themselves at varying distances from a variety of categories of people. They found that participants placed themselves significantly farther from marijuana users, drug addicts, obese people, present homosexuals, and past homosexuals—in that order. Former homosexuals, it was found, were thought to be even less trustworthy than current homosexuals. In another study, the same man was rated as among the most preferred when no one knew his sexual orientation but among the least preferred when labeled homosexual.

In that same study, another facet about attitudes toward gays was revealed. In the experimental situation one "confederate" was labeled as a homosexual by a second "confederate," but was not labeled as such in a "neutral" situation. Participants were asked to perform a number of nonverbal communications and then asked to rate other members of their group, including the confederate, on a number of dimensions. There was clear evidence that participants perceived their groups less positively, and group problem-solving was less effective, when a homosexually labeled person was present. Moreover, the confederates who initially performed the labeling were all perceived as significantly more masculine and more sociable when they labeled someone homosexual than when they did not. In other words, men who demonstrate the ability to identify another man as a homosexual are rewarded and reinforced by other men in our culture.

The massive Alfred Kinsey Institute for Sex Research study, *Homosexualities,* cast a shadow of doubt on the popular image of the homosexual as neurotic, suicidal, depressed, drugged, and drunken. Nevertheless, the image has survived—along with the stubborn stereotypes of gays as women haters and child molesters—and for millions of active and passive "fag haters" it has justified a pattern of social abuse only now being challenged in the courts. Currently, there is no guarantee that such challenges can be won.

Our laws, our attitudes, our one-line jokes and innuendos blatantly victimize homosexuals. The heterosexual's message to his gay male counterpart is: "I am straight, correct, normal and good. You are abnormal, wrong, deviant and bad. Your demeanor nauseates me. Your behavior is immoral, sacrilegious. I don't want you teaching my children, in my armies, leading my congregation in church, joining my clubs."

For inspiration and precedent we can point to the Good Book itself: "If a man also lie with a man kind, as he lieth with a woman, both of them have committed an abomination; they surely shall be put to death, their blood is upon them" (Leviticus 20:13). It is not hard to conceive of the generations-long chain of fathers teaching sons, leading all the way back to the Bible. And in case there are not enough God-fearing folks around, there is plenty of good old Judeo-Christian legislation around to institutionalize the hatred of gays. Homosexual activity, even between consenting adults, is considered a criminal offense in thirty-one of these United States. The United States has the most severe antihomosexual laws in the Western world. Napoleon made consensual homosexuality legal in France in the early nineteenth century; antihomosexual laws were repealed a century ago in Belgium and Holland, a few decades ago in Denmark, Switzerland, and Sweden and in the 1960s in Czechoslovakia and England.

In the United States, whether it is Idaho's "infamous crime against nature" or New Hampshire's rubric "lascivious acts," we find a way to punish homosexuals. In Georgia the life sentence is mandatory for sodomy unless clemency is recommended. And when there is no punishment to fit the crime, or no way to prove the crime, we go beyond the law. We harass. We exclude. We prohibit. We entrap. We raid. We beat up.

At the very least, we enforce deceit. I know a gay couple who separate their single beds and put a dresser between them when relatives visit, and then push the beds back together when the guests leave. Not only are they dealing with knowing what kind of terrible things their relatives would think about them if their homosexuality were revealed, but they also have to face living a lie.

Far from being exempt from the homophobic pressures in the society, gays themselves too often—typically, in fact—buy the whole cloth. Only in them the gay-hating teachings yield not intimacy-shunning, competitive masculinity, but something more straightforwardly destructive: self-hatred.

If you are told long enough and in enough different ways that you are no good, it will only take time before some of that criticism penetrates. You can build mile-high walls to block the onslaught of epithets until those walls themselves become part of your personality. But eventually some of that judgment will seep in, and it too will become part of you. You will look in the mirror and say out loud, "My feelings are true, I'm good, I'm handsome," but another voice will be insidiously and relentlessly at work, whispering between your thoughts: "You're a freak, you're disgusting, you're repugnant, you're bad."

"There's an awful lot of self-hatred among gays," confirmed Dr. Steve Morin, a gay San Francisco psychologist I interviewed, whose clients are primarily gay:

A lot of people simply don't feel good about gay men. One gay man, who had been in one of my therapy groups, started coming to see me in private therapy. He'd walk three blocks out of his way to avoid Castro Street (a predominantly gay neighborhood) because he was "so disgusted by the sight of all those faggots." He'd broken up with his lover, who he asserted emphatically wasn't like "them"—not like those "faggots."

We do a little exercise in my gay male groups. I ask them "What are faggots like?" People come up with things like: "They aren't dependable." "They're hard to relate to." "They're promiscuous." The men have internalized many of the stereotypes the public holds to be true—whether they *are* true or not. They constitute a big barrier in getting gay men to work with gay men because they see themselves— and "their kind"—in society's light. In other words, as bad people, people to avoid.

Thus besides functioning to reinforce traditional masculine values in the fiercely heterosexual population, a less obvious result of homophobia is to instill in gays themselves a crippling self-loathing that makes their lives harder.

FATHERS OF GAYS

An organization called POG—Parents of Gays—was meeting at a Methodist church in a grungy section of New York's Lower West Side. There were about two dozen couples seated on metal chairs spaced in a circle in a dank linoleum-floored church basement. Some of these parents had been members of this group since its inception seven years earlier. Some were first-timers. I could easily tell one from the other: The new parents were sitting quietly clutching their purses and nervously fingering the creases in their hats, avoiding eye contact with anyone else and barely even talking to their mates.

It was a support group, an information-exchange center, an arena for working out guilt, shame, anger, disappointment, and a sense of failure. It quickly became apparent that most of the people doing the talking were women, the mothers of gays. The men—the fathers—sat soberly, silently, barely turning their heads toward the discussion. Two new men finally spoke out. One admitted what really bothered him about his son's homosexuality was that "he's breaking my line of immortality.'' Another—a psychiatrist who, I would have thought, should have known better—allowed that ''homosexuality is sick.'' In response to a woman who countered that the American Psychiatric Association had issued a decision that it is not a sickness, he shouted angrily, ''We got clubbed by those gays into making that announcement. They're a bunch of political barnstormers.''

Afterward people mingled. A woman approached me and said she saw me taking notes and thought I might be ''someone who knew a little more about all this.'' I told her about the book I was working on and she broke into a long lament about how terrible her husband felt. ''He feels so guilty that he did something wrong, or that he wasn't there enough, and that's why our eighteen-year-old son is gay.'' I observed her husband in a far corner eyeing us intently. I tried to reassure her—and more importantly her husband—by telling her that most of the men I interviewed told me they too felt their fathers were not around enough and that not all of those men were gay.

''Wait a second,'' she interrupted. ''I'll be right back.''

In a moment she came back with her husband in tow. After an awkward silence he introduced himself. His name was Tony; he was a general contractor from Brooklyn. He came close to me and I could smell his cigarette breath. His eyes were sad and bloodshot; he was truly shaken. I felt pain for him—not for what he was going through, but for how he was going through it.

''I don't know,'' he started, lighting another cigarette, looking left and right around the room, down at his feet, over my shoulder, at my chest—anywhere but in my eyes:

I thought I was doing things with him. I was a Boy Scout father. I just don't understand. He's confused. He's not like me. I'm aggressive. He never follows through on things. He's very immature for his age. I guess I had to grow up fast when I was a kid. My wife says the problem is I compare him too much with me when I was his age.

This could be my father talking about me when I was eighteen, I thought. This could have been any father complaining about any son.

I asked him if he could tell me something positive about his son. Tony shrugged his shoulders and raised his eyebrows, finally looking into my eyes with hope. "We've been to a professional psychologist, and he says my son isn't necessarily a confirmed homosexual yet and we could still cure him."

Looking into Tony's desperate eyes I saw the implications to this father. He did what he could to train the boy to the ways of men and masculinity, and he "failed." If a father sees his son as a reflection of himself, having a homosexual son reflects rather poorly to a man invested with the belief of the rightness of heterosexuality.

"He's not like me," Tony had told me, but I think what he wanted to assure me—and himself—was that *he* was not like his *son*. Tony wanted me to tell him his son's homosexuality was not his fault.

I could not do that, of course. The causes of homosexuality have been debated throughout history and no single answer is in sight. True, most theories center on a family psychodynamic involving both parents, with doting, seductive, and domineering mothers taking most of the "blame." In recent studies, however, passive and hostile fathers share the blame as well. Given the key role the father plays in training his son in "masculine" behavior, I wondered what happens between the two when that training creates such antithetical results. My assumption was there is a crippling sense of failure on both sides, which turns to hostility as a method of self-protection. The look in the eyes of Tony, the father of a gay man, reinforced my hypothesis. And a talk I had with Francis, who works as an office temporary while studying therapy, running men's groups, and undergoing therapy himself, went a good way toward confirming my hunch. He told me:

> I always saw my father as the object of my love, at least in the beginning. My sweetest, warmest memories of him are at

Christmas. He's showing me how this little flip-flop airplane works. And I remember feeling so happy and it wasn't so much about the toy as about *him*. The significant feeling was of strength and security and energy coming from him directly to me. I knew that everything in the world was o.k. because he was there.

"You have to be a man." That's the phrase I remember him saying most. We were taught to shake hands "like a man." He used to point to his brother who was very effeminate in behavior—he studied to be a priest, definitely didn't make it in the world of macho Italian men I grew up in—and my father'd use my uncle as an example of how not to act. "That's like a woman and you don't want to be a woman."

Francis first told both his parents of his homosexual feelings when he was twelve. He had already been having an affair for three years with a man five years older. Almost everyone in the neighborhood knew about Francis. It had gotten to the point where it was not uncommon for strangers to approach him and threaten to beat him up or tell on him if he did not give them a blow-job. After the "umpteenth" time, out of self-defense, Francis finally went to his mother and told her, but he made her promise not to tell his father until he had gotten his courage up. But over dinner one night, she told Francis' father, who maintained his cool despite an obvious internal raging fury. After dinner he brought his son down to the basement and exploded: "You put that *thing* in your mouth, that *thing* you piss out of? You're a fag, that's what you are!"

Every gay man I interviewed told me it was much harder to tell his father he was gay than to tell his mother. Many never did tell their fathers, even after they had told their mothers. Some assumed their fathers knew by inference. Others lied, describing "girlfriends" who were really boyfriends. Many of those who did tell their fathers suffered the consequence of being cut off entirely, as though they were dead. And for a few others the reason for telling was to inflict the painful sting of the truth on the man who caused them so much pain.

The difficulty lies in admitting one's failure to one's teacher, in this case one's father: "I couldn't be the man you thought you were making of me." But the other side of this admission of failure is a sharp rejection of the father as a masculine role model.

"My mission in life was to be as unlike my father as I could," a gay man of thirty-one from Los Angeles told me. "In doing that I denied a lot of my maleness. I disassociated from the qualities of strength and competence. I was a sissy, the very thing my father warned me I should never be."

The final slap in a father's face is the long-term implication of his son's sexual preference. The reason many men say they want sons in the first place—immortality, to "carry on the family name"—is ripped out of their grasp. No grandchildren! Straight men who have announced to their fathers that they are going to have vasectomies have experienced similar responses from their fathers, as have married men who have made a conscious choice not to have children.

In effect, then, the boy's homosexuality is a blanket rejection of the father, as model, teacher, standard-bearer of the male culture—as a man. Seen in this context, it is no wonder that homophobia is so pervasive in our society. The homophobic wall blocks all that is "antimale" and "antigenerational." To the fathers and mentors who take seriously their roles as trainers of the next generation of men, homosexuality is a major threat to their authority as teachers, and the validity of their teachings.

THE INTIMATE MALE: A DEAD END

If fear of homosexuality is one of the major barriers between men, and if it functions, as it seemed to, to reinforce the traditional male values, then we might safely assume that gay men, freed of that nearly inpenetrable barrier, would have the sort of intimate and supportive relationships hetero men lack.

It sounded good and many gay men would have you believe it is true—until, that is, you inquire a little further. Far from living together in a rivalry-free atmosphere in which competition, power struggles, and emotional inexpressiveness are unheard of, gay relationships contain the same obstacles as other male-male dyads. If intimate male-female relationships run into problems owing to differences in the psychology of genders, intimate male-male relationships face the dilemma of similarity. Competition becomes an integral part of the gay lifestyle.

The YMCAs and the body-building gyms of this country are filled with gay men working on their physiques only partly for the benefit of their health; they know how all-important their bods are out there on the meat market called "cruising." It is a tough contest, highly competitive. And if more enlightened gays are less concerned about another man's "lats," they may not be immune to the even keener competition over economic status, intellectual brilliance, incisive and fast-tongued wit.

Far from transcending the eternal and exhausting power struggle, gay men are totally immersed in it. And if straight men think *they've* got troubles in their sexual relationships, relating to and reacting to the iron-clad code of male values to which they were conditioned, listen to what gay men have to contend with in their personal lives. In my interview with him about his gay psychotherapy practice, Dr. Morin told me:

> You see so clearly how being two men interferes with intimacy. *The competition issue:* The competition of finances, of who's got more money, who's got a bigger cock, who's more attractive to another man, who's more loving and giving, who's got more friends—it's constant competition. *The power issue:* When you put two men together and then define them as lovers, you have hooked them into a power struggle. It can be very ugly. In order to get through it, they have to step out of their male roles. They've got to be able to compromise, and show a valuing of the relationship—attitudes that aren't particularly typical of men. Based on characteristics that best

describe males from various researches—they're very independent, almost always hiding emotions, very dominant, very competitive, almost always acting as leaders, very rough, not talkative, very sloppy in habits, having little need for security, can't express tender feelings easily—two people with these qualities could hardly be expected to have much in the way of an intimate relationship. Each one of those traits is a specific interference, in fact, to intimacy.

Gay men are commonly believed to be more promiscuous than straight men. But gay men are first males, and being male means being more sexually aggressive, whether that trait is innate or trained. The truth is, the sexual "promiscuity" of gay men reflects the male approach, unimpeded. One study on initiating sexual activity defined about fifteen steps in a man's courting and seduction of a woman, from initial eye contact to smiling to first physical contact to intercourse. The study showed that at each step the man makes the gesture but the woman, trained traditionally to be passive and receptive, either encourages or discourages the man. Women have built into their social sign language various red lights and stop signs: "Yield," "Detour," "Do Not Pass." With men, it is green lights all the way. There are no checks or balances to the sexual advancement and seduction. Ironically, the unimpeded sexuality wreaks havoc on the chance to establish intimacy—to express affection, fantasies, vulnerabilities.

Among homosexuals, then, the male style—of competitive toughness, nonintimacy, and fierce independence—contains within it the same impediments to love that heterosexuals experience. The irony is that, although culture—via fathers and other male teachers—holds them up as the very model of the Bad Boy, gay men suffer the same blocks to intimacy and growth-promoting relationships as men who tow the all-masculine, heterosexual party line.

Said Morin:

Two men come home from a day in which they have been powerful, independent, decision-making people at work and what they really need is to be able to crawl into bed with another person, their lover, in a near fetal position, and give vent to the dependency needs they've frustrated all day. But it's impossible to do that without contradicting most of what we are brought up to believe. If men are almost always hiding emotions, that doesn't leave much room for intimacy. Breaking through that barrier to express emotions is the hardest thing for men. A lot of men I see have never cried—not since they were children.

ENLIGHTENMENT THROUGH EDUCATION

To sum up, then, the problems gays and straights share are not much different from those described in earlier chapters as typically male—those that arise logically from a system of values that discourages emotional honesty and nearly deifies independence and self-reliance. Nor is the solution all that exotic: It is education, exposure to the feared "other," shattering of myths and lies. If we make no commitment to truth, homophobia will continue to pit father against son, friend against friend, gays against straights, and each man against himself.

Change comes slowly, as does new information. Only twenty years ago did the psychological research community push aside centuries of ignorance when Masters and Johnson undertook a study on homosexuality. Fifteen years later the same researchers published their 450-page tome *Homosexuality in Perspective*. The book concentrates solely—and apparently for the first time—on the simple mechanics of gay sex. The language is appropriately technical and removed. By the end we learn there are *no differences* between heterosexuals and homosexuals in the physical processes of lubrication, erection, ejaculation, and orgasm. Masters and Johnson believe that their demonstration will eventually lead to more public acceptance of homosexuality, and, at a basic level, better medical care. In the past, for example, some doctors refused to give gays rectal examinations for fear of arousing them—which, as a *Time* magazine survey of gay awareness noted, is a "concern that has never been shown by gynecologists conducting vaginal examinations."

Another landmark event, occurring three years after Masters and Johnson began their study of gays, was the convening of the National Institute of Mental Health Task Force on Homosexuality in 1967. Its chairperson was psychologist Evelyn Hooker, who had been proposing studies of the "normal" overt male homosexual and the social structure of the gay community since 1954. In 1978 she was lauding the Society for the Psychological Study of Social Issues, a division of the American Psychological Association, for dedicating an entire issue of its *Journal of Social Issues* exclusively to theory and research on social concerns of gay people. "What is notable or perhaps even historic about this issue?" she asked rhetorically in the epilogue of the issue. "This is a first in publishing in the social and behavioral sciences." When she chaired the NIMH Task Force, she said, "there was literally no published research on any of the topics covered here."

Knowledge yields to action slowly. It was not until December 1973 that the psychiatric community, in the form of the American Psychiatric Association, removed homosexuality from the association's list of mental disorders. Psychiatrist Judd Marmor's was one of the voices of reason at that time:

> Surely the time has come for psychiatry to give up the archaic practice of classifying the millions of men and women who accept or prefer homosexual object choices as being, by virtue of that fact alone, mentally ill. The fact that their alternative life-style happens to be out of favor with current cultural conventions must not be the basis in itself for a diagnosis of pathology.

It took the governing body of the American Psychological Association yet another year to follow suit and adopt the following resolution:

> Homosexuality per se implies no impairment in judgment, stability, reliability, or general social or vocational capacities.

Further, the American Psychological Association urges all mental health professionals to take the lead in removing the stigma of mental illness that has long been associated with homosexual orientation.

Over time, we as a society are coming to realize that there is not much difference between gay men and straight in how they relate to their fathers, how they relate to their brothers, how they relate (sex included) to other men. What makes some men homosexual and others heterosexual may remain one of those unsolvable mysteries of the human psyche. But the more I think about it, the less etiologies seem to matter. "A man's a man for a' that," wrote Scottish lyricist Robert Burns. We are men first, men last, men always and in all ways. Race, creed, color—even sexual preference—all take second place to the primary instinct of gender:

> For a' that and a' that,
> It's coming yet, for a' that,
> That man to man the world over
> Shall brothers be for a' that.

Conclusion:
No Man Is an Island

> I did not find the world desolate when I entered it.
> My fathers planted for me before I was born. So
> do I plant for those who will come after me.
> —*The Talmud*

Men—from any generation, from any culture—have a legacy to live up to and a legacy to live down. As our grandfathers did for our fathers, so did our fathers do for us, and so do we do for our sons. The torch of masculinity gets passed down through the ages through the lineage of men.

That is both the good news and the bad news. For there are values and behavior patterns we learn from our fathers, mentors, brothers, friends, and other men—that we cannot learn from the women in our lives—to be cherished forever. But we also inherit some negative elements of the man-to-man interaction and they too become part of every man's burden.

To ignore or to deny one or the other is to negate both. We cannot appreciate the positive without acknowledging the negative. Men, I have noticed, tend to cast things as either black or white; an indecisive man is considered less of a man. That tendency may come from being conditioned to always have an answer, right or wrong. Or it may be in reaction to dealing with the ambivalence and ambiguity of relationships with other men—the ambivalence and ambiguity that come from not having clear models on which to base one's own values. In either case, it is a dangerous tendency. But, for many men, it may be even more dangerous to admit to both sides of a man's world—for it admits to a degree of fault, of vulnerability or at the very least an unsureness.

I have reported here on men's feelings and experiences related to the men in their lives and in so doing have illustrated what and how we teach each other about how to be men, and how to *be* with men: both the good and the bad, the push and the pull, the approach and the avoidance, the love and support, the resentment and competition, the bonds and the barriers. But if this book purports to illustrate anything, it is that men *are* important to each other.

There would appear nothing profound about that statement and yet it would also appear to be a fact of life that many men ignore. I say that after having heard so many men recognize so few men whom they consider important teachers, which leaves us pilgrims without a candle. But, as I have argued, we are each other's teachers through the ages and stages of our lives, and by cutting ourselves off from our fathers, by keeping all men at arm's length, we deny ourselves the most important lessons of our lives.

Men should talk to each other. Not the proverbial "shoptalk," but the deeper feelings about work, about love, about themselves, *about their feelings for each other.*

Keeping it all to oneself—being the strong, silent type—does not anymore seem to be an appropriate answer. In fact, it is quite literally killing us. Sidney Jourard in *The Transparent Self* points out that the shorter life expectancy of men, as compared to women, may be due in part to the increased stress men's bodies undergo by internalizing feelings, pressure, pain. Men who function that way are like pipes ready to burst from too much pressure. Expressiveness is the safety valve that reduces the pressure and allows our systems to work so much more productively. That has been corroborated, as Daniel Goleman noted in the Foreword to this book, by more recent research at Southern Methodist University showing a strong relationship between the failure to unburden oneself and poorer health.

The structure for such man-to-man dialogue is already in

place and has been, Lionel Tiger might suggest, since the first men's clubs were established for the purpose of hunting, gathering, and making war. Today's Kiwanis Club or Wednesday night bowling league or Saturday night poker gang may be a quantum anthropological leap forward, but then again there is a consistent and identifiable energy generated by all-male groups that spans all time. There are, as well, the so-called good ol' boys networks—a cross-social, cross-professional communications system that rivals AT&T. No, the problem is not structure. The problem is content. How will we fill that time together?

I found a glimmer of hope in the patterns that emerged from my own research—specifically the stages of reverence, revolt, and reconciliation that men go through with their fathers. That phase of reconciliation is a recognition of the importance of that man in particular—and it is, therefore, a reunion with all men in general. It is an acceptance and acknowledgment of how much we want and need that connection.

And, more encouragingly, I see a broad-scale reconciliation on a societal level for American men in the 1980s. I see it in the increasing awareness by many new and some old fathers of the vital and pivotal roles they play in their sons' development. I see it in the earnest efforts by men to reestablish (or, in many cases, to establish for the first time) ongoing relationships with male peers—relationships based on something more substantive emotionally than sports, stereos, and stock prices; relationships whose primary and conscious purpose is for the sake of mutual support and respect. I see it in the national men's movement, albeit diminutive compared to the women's movement, which makes itself worthy by posing the question, "How can we work it out with the opposite sex until we've worked it out with our own?"

And I see it in the reawakening of interest in men's groups which, like women's consciousness-raising groups, have allowed men to explore their own masculine dimensions in safe structured contexts. One I attended in Berkeley in the fall of

1984 focused on what its leaders, three psychologists, called "male empowerment." Male power seemed to me to be the very thing we had set out to disarm ourselves of when the issues of sex roles came to the fore in the early 1970s. But then, I realized, was not reconciliation with fathers and friends in effect an issue of empowerment—self-empowerment?

Finally, I see the patterns I have discussed here embodied in the latest work of poet Robert Bly, who has deemed the '80s as the decade of men and himself as a sort of Johnny Appleseed, planting seeds of old myths into the unconscious of men, connecting present and future generations with their own past. Bly has also been encouraging men in men-only workshops to come back to their power, to "show their swords," as he puts it, alluding to the tale in the *Odyssey* in which Hermes instructs Odysseus to draw his sword on Circe as a show of strength.

But mostly I look for and see change in the microcosm—in myself. In my own journey through the last several years researching and writing this book, I have felt, in the imagery of Bly's "wildman," like Daniel Boone on a hoary and hairy adventure in the uncharted wilderness of male psychology, in search of my own Holy Grail. I have come through that wilderness—not necessarily unscathed, but by necessity a better man for it. And for that I have many men to thank.

Appendix

Although I've finished this book, my interest continues—in fact deepens. That is one reason I have included the following questionnaire, the same I used when interviewing subjects. I would like some additional feedback. If this book affected you at all, it will have raised some questions in your mind—and quite possibly some answers. Are there questions I did not ask here? Answers I never heard? I would like to continue the exploration in a man's world. Perhaps you would like to do a little introspective exploration yourself. Send me your responses and reactions for your own sake and for mine, as my writing and research continue to focus on men's issues. I invite both men and women to join an open dialogue. My mailing address follows this questionnaire.

You could also use this questionnaire as a springboard for further discussion—and intimacy—with your own friends. You are bound to discover things about each other, and how you relate to each other, that will doubtless bring you closer.

ABOUT GRANDFATHERS

What do you recall about your relationship with your grandfather? What kind of man was he? What did you two do together that gave you a special feeling? What did you learn from him? How did he show his love to you—or did he?

How did your father and grandfather get along? Did you see them fight or embrace? Did you talk with your father about his relationship with his father? In what ways do you see them as alike? How are you and your grandfather alike?

ABOUT FATHERS

What is your earliest memory of your father? When you think of him then, how do you picture him? And now?

How much time did you spend alone with him when you were younger? Or ever? What did you do together?

Did your father hug or kiss you? Or you him? Now?

Did you or do you have private "man-to-man" talks with him? On what kinds of occasions? Did he ever give you the birds-and-bees rap?

Have you ever seen your father cry? How did it make you feel?

Does he express emotions to you, like anger or love?

Do you ever say "I love you" to him? Or him you?

Do you think he tried to imbue you with a special philosophy? What was his favorite saying or what phrase do you associate with him?

In what ways are you similar to your father? In what ways different from him?

Do you respect your father? And he you? How do you demonstrate it to each other?

ABOUT SONS

Did you or do you want a son more than a daughter?

How is your relationship with your son different from or similar to yours with your father?

Is your son like you? How or how not?

Do you spend time alone with your son? What is the quality of that time? Focused or distracted? Do you try to talk about what is on his mind or in his heart?

What do you want to give your son that your father did not give you?

Do you feel a special responsibility to show your son some of the ways of a man's world?

If you have two sons: Do you prefer one over the other? Do you feel differently toward the older than younger? How? Did you feel it was more important to try to mold the older than the younger? How did you encourage them to relate to each other?

ABOUT BROTHERS

What did you and your brother do alone together when you were younger? Now? How often do you see each other?

Did you fight as kids? Physically? Verbally? Do you now?

What is the age difference between you two? Did you feel you had to live up to your older brother's reputation? Or did you feel as though you had a personal mentor ushering you into the man's world? Did you resent the attention your younger brother got? Does the older/younger syndrome still exist between you?

Over what issues are you jealous or competitive?

Did you ever have a really intense confrontation with your brother? Did you have intimate talks?

Do you think the term "brotherly love" refers to you and your brother?

Did you ever work together? If not, could you imagine doing so?

How would you describe how close you are now? Is your relationship based on the past or present?

ABOUT MALE PEERS

Who was your first male friend? What did you do together? What attracted you to each other? Were you supportive of each other? Can you think of a time that you felt a special bond with him? Were you competitive—over looks, athletic prowess, intelligence, girls, economic background? How were you similar? Dissimilar? Are you still friends?

Who is your oldest continuing male friend? Describe that relationship and why it has endured.

Describe a friendship with an old buddy from elementary or high school. Can you see any similarity among your male friends?

What do you get out of your friendships with men that you do not get with women friends? What frustrates you about your friendships with men?

Did you belong to such all-male groups as Cub Scouts, boys camp, fraternity, sports team, men's club or Armed Forces? Where did you fit into the social fabric of such groups? Would you describe yourself as a leader or follower or neither?

Under what conditions do you go to male friends for "man-to-man" talks? What's hardest to talk about with men? What do you talk to men about most?

How physically affectionate are you with your men friends? When was the last time you cried in front of a man?

How many really close friends do you have right now? How often do you see them? What do you do together? How did you meet? What is the attraction? Are they of similar background, profession, prowess?

Have you ever been involved in a dramatic face-off with another man? Over what?

How do you work out your differences with men friends?

Have you and a friend both been interested in the same woman? What happened? Did your friendship survive?

If your wife or girlfriend does not like your male friends, do you see them without her, not see them at all, or not see her?

ABOUT HOMOSEXUALITY

Did you have any homosexual encounters when you were young? Later? Were you involved in group "circle jerks" or gang bangs? How did all that feel to you?

How comfortable do you feel in the company of a gay man? Have you ever talked to a gay man about his sexual preferences?

Have you at least intellectually explored the possibility of sex with a man? If you are straight, can you verbalize why you have not had sex with a man?

How would you react if you found out a man who has been a very close friend is gay? Would you discontinue the friendship? Talk about it with him? Never discuss it?

Please mail your responses to:

> Perry Garfinkel
> In A Man's World
> P.O. Box 3225
> Oakland, California 94609

Bibliography

Adams, Bert N. *Kinship in an Urban Setting*. Chicago: Markham, 1968.

Adams, Virginia. "The Sibling Bond: A Lifelong Love/Hate Dialectic." *Psychology Today*, 15:32-4, June 1981.

Adelson, Joseph and Elizabeth Douvan. *The Adolescent Experience*. New York: Wiley, 1966.

Aldrich, Nelson W., Jr., editor. "Wraparound: Family: The Blood-Red Inkblot." *Harper's*, May 1975.

Arnstein, Helene S. *Brothers and Sisters/Sisters and Brothers*. New York: Dutton, 1979.

Bank, Stephen P. *The Sibling Bond*. New York: Basic Books, 1982.

Bell, Alan P. "Role modeling of fathers in adolescence and young adulthood." *Journal of Counseling Psychology*, 16(1):30-39, 1969.

Bell, Donald. *Being A Man: The Paradox of Masculinity*. Lexington, Mass.: The Lewis Co. 1982.

Benson, Leonard. *Fatherhood: A Sociological Perspective*. New York: Random House, 1968.

Berg, A. Scott. *Max Perkins: Editor of Genius*. New York: Pocket Books, 1978.

Biller, Henry B. "Father absence, perceived maternal behavior, and masculinity of self-concept among junior high school boys." *Developmental Psychology*, pp. 178-181, 1971.

————"Father dominance and sex-role development in kindergarten-age boys. *Developmental Psychology*, pp. 87-94, 1969.

Bradley, Bill. *Life on the Run*. New York: Quadrangle, 1976.

Brain, Robert. "Business Friends," *Human Nature*, November 1978.

Carroll, Jerry. "The Despotic Father Figure is Fast Disappearing." *San Francisco Chronicle*, June 1, 1982.

Chesler, Phyllis. *About Men*. New York: Simon and Schuster, 1978.

Clark, Don. *Loving Someone Gay*. New York: New American Library (Signet), 1978.

Cohen, Albert K. *Delinquent Boys: The Culture of the Gang*. New York: The Free Press, 1955.

Corner, George W. *Attaining Manhood: A Doctor Talks to Boys About Sex*. New York: Harper and Row, 1952.

Dickey, James. *Deliverance*. Boston: Houghton Mifflin, 1970.

Eivers, Richard Warren. "Fathering in the Eighties." *New Age*, Vol. 6, No. 12, June 1981.

Erikson, Erik. *Childhood and Society*. New York: W. W. Norton, 1950.

Exley, Frederick. *A Fan's Notes*. New York: Ballantine, 1968.

Farrell, Warren. *The Liberated Man*. New York: Bantam, 1975.

Fasteau, Mark Feigen. *The Male Machine*. New York: Delta, 1975.

Firestone, Ross, editor. *A Book of Men: Visions of the Male Experience*. New York: Stonehill, 1975.

Freud, Sigmund. *Collected Papers, Volume V*. London: Hogarth Press, 1953.

Freud, Sigmund. *Totem and Taboo*. New York: Vintage, 1946.

Friday, Nancy. *My Mother, My Self*. New York: Dell, 1977.

Garfinkel, Perry. "The Not-Quite-Ready-For-Prime-Time-Movement." *The Real Paper*, January 20, 1979.

Gelb, Hal. "Sam Shepard on myths and heroes." *San Francisco*, September 1983.

Gilder, George. *Naked Nomads: Unmarried Men in America*. New York: Quadrangle, 1974.

Gold, Herbert. *Fathers*. New York: Random House, 1967.

Goldberg, Herb. *The Hazards of Being Male*. New York: New American Library (Signet), 1976.

Golding, William. *Lord of the Flies*. New York: Coward, McCann, 1954.

Goleman, Daniel. "As Sex Roles Change, Men Turn to Therapy to Cope With Stress." *New York Times*, August 21, 1984.

Gentleman's Quarterly. Vol. 48, No. 4, Summer 1978.

Greenfield, Jeff. "The Black and White Truth About Basketball." *Esquire*, Vol. 84, No. 4, October 1975.

Gross, Amy. "The New American Hero." *Mademoiselle*, July 1978.

Hall, Elizabeth. "A Conversation with Erik Erikson," *Psychology Today*, June 1983.

Hamill, Pete. "The New American Hero." *New York*, December 5, 1983.

Hamilton, Marshall. *Father's Influence on Children*. Chicago: Nelson-Hall, 1977.

Hatterer, Lawrence J. *Changing Homosexuality in the Male: Treatment for Men Troubled by Homosexuality*. New York: McGraw-Hill, 1970.

Hix, Charles. *Looking Good*. New York: Wallaby, 1977.

Hodgman, Christopher H. "Talks Between Fathers and Sons." *Human Sexuality*, April 1975.

Horowitz, Jay. "View From Beta Mountain." *Los Angeles Times*, February 25, 1979.

Janeway, Elizabeth. *Man's World, Woman's Place: A Study in Social Mythology*. New York: Dell, 1971.

Jewish Publication Society of America. *The Torah: The Five Books of Moses*. Philadelphia: Jewish Publications Society of America, 1962.

Johnson, Robert. *HE: Understanding Masculine Psychology*. New York: Perennial Library, 1977.

Johnson, Sharon. "Divorced Fathers Organizing to Bolster Role in Children's Lives." *New York Times*, August 1, 1977.

Jourard, Sidney. *The Transparent Self*. New York: Van Nostrand, 1964.

Kaplan, Peter W. "The End of the Soft Line." *Esquire*, Vol. 93, No. 4, April 1980.

Karlen, Arlo. *Sexuality and Homosexuality: A New View*. New York: W. W. Norton, 1971.

Keyes, Ralph. "The Height Report." *Esquire*, Vol. 92, No. 5, November 1979.

Kinsey, Alfred C., Wardell B. Pomeroy and Clyde E. Martin. *Sexual Behavior in the Human Male*. Philadelphia: W. B. Saunders, 1948.

Kleiman, Carol et. al. "Secrets of the New Male Sexuality." *Ms.*, Vol. VI, No. 10, April 1978.

Klemesrud, Judy. "The Year of the Lusty Woman." *Esquire*, Vol. 90, No. 13, December 19, 1978.

Lamb, Michael E., editor. *The Role of the Father in Child Development*. New York: John Wiley and Sons, 1976.

Levinson, Daniel. *The Seasons of a Man's Life*. New York: Alfred A. Knopf, 1978.

Lewis, Robert A. "Emotional Intimacy Among Men." A paper presented at the September 4, 1976 meeting of the American Sociological Society, New York.

Lorenz, Konrad. *On Aggression*. New York: Bantam, 1977.

Malinowski, Bronislaw. *The Father in Primitive Psychology*. New York: W.W. Norton, 1927.

Markus, H. "Sibling Personalities: The Luck of the Draw." *Psychology Today*, June 1981.

McCabe, Bruce. "Taming macho man: A more sensitive male comes to the screen." *Boston Globe*, January 27, 1980.

McGuire, William, editor. *The Freud-Jung Letters*. Princeton: Princeton University Press, 1974.

McWilliams, Wilson Carey. *The Idea of Fraternity in America*. Berkeley: University of California Press, 1973.

Mellen, Joan. *Big Bad Wolves: Masculinity in the American Film*. New York: Pantheon, 1977.

Merton, Andy. "Hanging On (By A Jockstrap) To Tradition At Dartmouth." *Esquire*, June 10, 1979.

Miller, Stuart. *Men and Friendship*. Boston: Houghton Mifflin, 1983.

Montagu, Ashley. *The Anatomy of Swearing*. New York: Collier, 1973.

Morin, Stephen F. "Educational Programs as a Means of Changing Attitudes Toward Gay People." *Homosexual Counseling Journal*, Vol. 1, No. 4, October 1974.

————."Heterosexual Bias in Psychological Research on Lesbianism and Male Homosexuality," *American Psychologist*, Vol. 32, No. 8, August 1977.

————, and Garfinkle, Ellen M. "Male Homophobia," *Journal of Social Issues*, Vol. 34, No. 1, 1978.

————, and Riddle, Dorothy I., editors. "Psychology and the Gay Community," *Journal of Social Issues*, Vol. 34, No. 3, 1978.

Morris, Desmond. *The Naked Ape*. New York: Dell, 1969.

Newsweek. "How Men Are Changing." January 16, 1978.

Nietzsche, Friedrich. *The Philosophy of Nietzsche*. New York: Modern Library, 1954.

Paige, Karen Ericksen. "The Ritual of Circumcision." *Human Nature*, May 1978.

Parlee, Mary Brown and the editors of *Psychology Today*. "The Friendship Bond." *Psychology Today*, October 1979.

Pfouts, J.H. "Sibling Relationship: A Forgotten Dimension," *Social Work*, May 1976, pp. 200-204.

Pietropinto, Anthony and Jacqueline Simenauer. *Beyond the Male Myth: What Women Want to Know about Men's Sexuality*. New York: New American Library (Signet), 1978.

Playboy. "Playboy Interview: Burt Reynolds." *Playboy*, October, 1979.

Pleck, Joseph H., "Man To Man: Is Brotherhood Possible?" In *Old Family/New Family: Interpersonal Relationships*. New York: Van Nostrand, 1975.

————"The Male Sex Role: Definitions, Problems, and Sources of Change," *Journal of Social Issues*, Vol. 32, No. 3, 1976.

————"The Psychology of Sex Roles: Traditional and New Views," In *Women and Men: Changing Roles, Relationships and Perceptions*. New York: Aspen Institute for Humanistic Studies, 1976.

————"Men's Power with Women, Other Men and Society: A Men's Movement Analysis." In *Women and Men: The Consequences of Power*. Cincinnati: Office of Women's Studies, University of Cincinnati, 1977.

Pleck, Jose and Jack Sawyer. *Men and Masculinity*. Englewood Cliffs, N.J.: Prentice-Hall, 1974.

Post, Henry. *The Ultimate Man*. New York: Berkley Windover, 1978.

Price, Richard. *Bloodbrothers*. New York: Bantam, 1977.

Robison, Mary. "The Brothers: Memories of being buried alive in boys." *Esquire*, January 1983.

Rogers, Michael, editor, et al. "Men on the Ropes." *Rolling Stone*, No. 197, October 9, 1975.

Ross, John Munder. "Fathering: A Review of Some Psychoanalytic Contributions to Paternity." *International Journal of Psychoanalysis*. No. 60, 1979.

Roszak, Betty and Theodore. *Masculine/Feminine: Readings in Sexual Mythology and the Liberation of Women*. New York: Harper Colophon, 1969.

Roth, Philip. *My Life As A Man*. New York: Bantam, 1975.

Rubin, Zick. "The Search for Reunion." *Psychology Today*, June, 1982.

Schacht, Richard. *Alienation*. New York: Anchor, 1970.

San Francisco Chronicle. "Eastwood Shoots His Way to the Top." Janaury 13, 1984.

Shaw, George Bernard. *Man and Superman*. New York: Bantam, 1959.

Sheehy, Gail. *Passages*. New York: E.P. Dutton, 1976.

———"Introducing the Postponing Generation." *Esquire*, October 1979.

Shepard, Sam. *Seven Plays*. New York: Bantam, 1981.

Silverstein, Charles. *A Family Matter: A Parents' Guide to Homosexuality*. New York: McGraw-Hill, 1977.

Sullivan, S. Adams. *The Father's Almanac*. New York: Dolphin, 1980.

Sweeney, Joan. "Divorce—What Role for Fathers." *Los Angeles Times*, December 23, 1982.

Talese, Gay. *Thy Neighbor's Wife*. New York: Doubleday, 1980.

Tavris, Carol. "Men and Women Report Their Views on Masculinity." *Psychology Today*, Vol. 10, No. 8, January 1977.

Thompson, Keith. "What Men Really Want: A New Age Interview with Robert Bly." *New Age*. Vol. 7, No. 12, May 1982.

Tiger, Lionel. *Men in Groups*. New York: Vintage, 1970.

Time. "Football as Erotic Ritual," November 13, 1978.

———"How Gay is Gay?" April 23, 1979.

Tripp, C.A. *The Homosexual Matrix*. New York: New American Library (Signet), 1976.

Turgenev, Ivan. *Fathers and Sons*. New York: Bantam, 1959.

Valliant, George. *Adaptations to Life*. Boston: Little Brown, 1977.

Vallely, Jean. "Dean Martin's Closest Friend is Frank Sinatra (He Sees Him Twice A Year)," *Esquire*, July 4, 1978.

Vincent, Stephen. *White Lights & Whale Hearts*. Trumansburg, N.Y.: The Crossing Press, 1971.

Wagenvoord, James, editor. *Men: A Book for Women*. New York: Avon, 1978.

Wallerstein, Edward. *Circumcision: An American Health Fallacy*. New York: Springer, 1980.

Williams, Heathcote. "The Foreskin File." *CoEvolution Quarterly*, No. 28, Winter 1980.

Weinberg, Martin and Colin Williams. *Male Homosexuals: Their Problems and Adaptations*. New York: Penguin, 1975.

Woolf, Bob. *Behind Closed Doors*. New York: New American Library (Signet), 1977.

Zilbergeld, Bernie. *Male Sexuality: A Guide to Sexual Fulfillment*. Boston: Little Brown, 1978

Notes

Foreword

xiii. "In the 1950s the secret was." N.Y. Times, Aug. 21, 1984.
xiv. "They fear that they will." N.Y. Times, Aug. 21, 1984.

Introduction

4. "It was not, and still is not." Tiger, xix.

Chapter 1

8. Men breaking down the walls. See Carroll in *S.F. Chronicle*, Garfinkel in *The Real Paper*, Goleman in *N.Y. Times*, Johnson in *N.Y. Times*, Eivers in *New Age*, *Newsweek* Jan. 16, 1978.
9. "The relation of a boy." Freud, in "Dostoevsky and Partricide" in *Collected Papers*, p. 229.
10. Fathers' influence on sons. Biller, in "Father dominance," *Developmental Psychology*, p. 87-94.
11. "Dad tiptoed into my room." Gold, *Fathers*, p. 26
12. "Boys identify with father." Benson, p. 15
13. "Men . . . instrumental . . . women . . . 'expressive.' " Benson, p. 30
15. The natives are "quite ignorant." Malinowski, p. 14.
15. "Natives affirm without doubt." Ibid, p. 12.
15. The father as "indispensable socially." Ibid, p. 85.
15. "until recently the father." Ross, p. 317.
15. "not only is it a household." Malinowski, p. 88.
16. "the ignorance of paternity." Ibid, p. 95.
16. "I didn't know what was up." Anderson, in *A Book of Men*, pp. 30-39.
17. Pile of sociological surveys. In Biller: Lefkowitz (1962), Altucher

(1957), Distler (1964), Stears (1951), Stoltz (1954), Tiller (1958), Lynn (1959), Hetherington (1966), Miller (1958), Pope (1953), Mischel (1958), Todd, Brannigan and Murphy (1970), Meerlo (1956), Douvan and Adelson (1966), Gray (1959), Deutch (1960). Also see Men's Studies section of Human Studies Collection at MIT's Humanities Library.

17. Gang cultures, Cohen, p. 78.
18. Time spent alone with fathers. Brown (1961), in Hamilton, p. 154.
20. "The father is not so constant." Ross, p. 322.
22. Couvade. Lamb, p. 58.
23. "It has been a recurring problem." Pleck, "Men's Power with Women, Other Men, and Society," p. 18.
25. See the Old Testament, Genesis XVII, verses 10-13, 23-27 and XXI, verse 4.
25. "a variety of reasons." Paige, *Human Nature*, p. 40-48.
25. Medical fallacies of circumcision. Wallerstein, throughout.
26. "I am a man." Williams in CoEvolution Quarterly, p. 69-77.
26. "The common pattern is for a village." Paige, p. 46.
27. "For me you took on the enigmatic." Kafka, *Diaries 1910–13*, p. 78
28. Third- and fourth-grade boys. Lefkowitz (1962) in Benson.
29. Limit-setting and decision-making. Biller, "A multiaspect investigation of masculine development in kindergarten-age boys." *Genetic Psychology Monographs*. 1968. p. 89-138. Also Biller, in "Father dominance and sex-role development in kindergarten-age boys." *Developmental Psychology*, 1969, p. 87-94.
29. Seventh and eighth grade boys. Distler (1964) in Benson.
29. High-achieving boys. Hamilton, P. 215.
31. "Although Hugh Hefner's father." Talese, p. 30.
32. "The law for father and son." Shaw, p. 79.
33. "Greatness of name in the father." Johnson, *Timber*, p. 18.
35. "Parricide is the principle and primal crime" Freud in *Collected Papers*, vol. V, pg. 229.
35. "This violent primal father." Freud, *Totem and Taboo*, p. 183.
36. "The truth of Freud's notion." Ross, p. 319.
38. "In spite of everything." Freud, in *Collected Papers*, *Vol. V*, p. 184-185.
38. "zealous proprietor." Turgenev, p. 200.
41. "The death of my father." From interview with Merle Haggard in WET magazine, winter 1981.

Chapter 2

47. "My father has never spoken." Gold, p. 1.

54. "And we waited, talking and thinking." In *Phaedo*, Plato, in *The Dialogues of Plato*, translated by B. Jowett, 4th edition revised (Oxford, The Clarenden Press, 1967)

54. "One of the most complex. "Levinson, p. 97.

54. "He may act as a teacher." Levinson, p. 98.

58. "The mentor he formerly loved." Levinson, p. 101.

63. Erickson's theories on generativity are contained in *Childhood and Society*. See also Hall's interview with Erikson in *Psychology Today*, June 1983, pp. 22-30.

64. The influential editor was T. George Harris, founding editor of *Psychology Today* and *American Health*.

66. "I can't tell you how glad." Berg, p. 163.

67. "One year ago." Ibid, p. 201.

67. "I'm mightly glad." Ibid, p. 201.

68. "Had always thought a good story." Ibid, p. 173.

68. "We create the figure." Ibid, p. 207.

68. "I am a brave man." Ibid, p. 214.

69. "The only standard." Ibid, p. 231.

69. "I, who thought Tom." Ibid, p. 297.

70. "I can't express certain kinds of feelings." Ibid, p. 395.

70. "Are you the man I trusted." Ibid, p. 397.

70. "For fear that it may be killed." Ibid, p. 398.

70. "Tell me what there is." Ibid, p. 398.

71. "I can easily imagine a biography." Ibid, p. 423.

71. "This letter is a sad farewell." p. 422.

71. "I've made a long voyage." p. 441.

72. "You have inspired me," McGuire, p. 27

72. "I only fear that you." Ibid, p. 30

73. "I hope you will gain recognition." Ibid, p. 48

73. "My veneration for you." Ibid, p. 51

73. "Let me enjoy your friendship." Ibid, p. 122

73. "That evening freed me." Ibid, p. 217

73. "One accords a charming." Ibid, p. 220

73. "Rest easy, dear son." Ibid, p. 250

74. "One repays a teacher." Ibid, p. 491

74. "How different I am." Ibid, p. 522

74. Freud "underestimates my work." Ibid, p. 525

74. "Look at your bit of neurosis. Ibid, p. 526

74. "Your technique of treating." Ibid, p. 534

74. "I propose we abandon." Ibid, p. 539

Chapter 3

77. "When people speak of their siblings." Pfouts, p. 200.
77. "If you till the soil." Genesis 4: 12–16
77. "May God give you." Genesis 27: 28–30
78. "By your sword." Genesis 27: 40
78. "But when you grow restive." Genesis 27: 40
78. "Let but the morning." Genesis 27: 41
78. "Now Israel loved Joseph." Genesis 37: 3–4
78. Manual workers are more satisifed. Psychologists Form and Geschwender in Adams, p. 116.
79. "Siblings are in fact." Bert Adams, p. 117.
79. "In this case it appears that." Adams, p. 117.
79. "Little in common." Ibid, p. 117.
80. Comparative IQ studies. Pfouts, p. 200-203.
83. "Keeping a distance." From *True West* by Sam Shepard, in *Seven Plays*, p. 59.
83. Mondavi et al. in *S.F. Chronicle* article by Milton Moskowitz, "Sibling Rivalry in the Air," April 25, 1981.
83. Ross and Milgram research reported in *Psychology Today* article by Virginia Adams, pp. 38-40. June 1981
84. Brother-sister comparison. Burt Adams, p. 122.
86. The brother horde. Freud, *Totem and Taboo*, p. 183.
86. "In thus ensuring." Ibid, p. 188.
89. Markus's report in *Psychology Today*, June 1981, p.35-37.
90. NIMH, Maccoby and Miller-Maruyama research reported in *Psychology Today* article by Markus.
91. "Later borns see themselves." Markus, p. 36.
91. Reliable birth-order research. Adams, p. 120.
93. Ross and Milgram, *Psychology Today*, p. 41.
94. Cicirelli's study in *Journal of Marriage and the Family*, 1980. Reported in *Psychology Today*, June 1981.
95. "Siblings are more and more dependent." *Psycholgy Today*, June 1981, p. 47.

Chapter 4

97. "Our strongest descriptions." McWilliams, p. 1.
97. "Of all the terms of kinship." Ibid, p. 18.
98. "Produces self-contempt." Ibid, p. 47.

99. The Dartmouth College episode was reported by Andy Merton in *Esquire*, June 19, 1979.

102. Initiation as part of male ritual. Tiger, p. 185.

104. The Cornell incident was reported by Tiger, pp. 187-188.

105. "Secret Societies." Tiger, p. 167.

Chapter 5

111. Ad samples from *GQ* and *Esquire* between June 1979 and August 1983.

111. "Every change in men's fashions." Post, p. 120.

111. "The Ultimate Man." Post, p. vii.

112. "What is 'the look'?" Hix, p. xiv.

113. "In the end it's you." Ibid, p. 164.

113. "The way you look." Post, p. 56-57.

113. "Men on the Ropes," *Rolling Stone*, October 9, 1975, No. 197.

114. "Everybody's got buddies." Ibid, p. 39.

114. "The macho frontiersman." From Carol Tavris's intro to survey, *Psychology Today*, Vol. 10, No. 8, p. 35.

114. "The Year of the Lusty Woman," *Esquire*, Vol. 90, No. 13, Dec. 19, 1978.

114. "The hard-line culture," *Esquire*, Vol. 93, No. 4, April 1980.

115. "The male machine is a special kind." Fasteau, p. 1.

115. "From Daniel Boone." Ibid, p. 205.

116. "Hollywood knows well." Mellen, p. 5.

117. "American Films." Ibid, p. 5.

118. "The silence of the male hero." Ibid, p. 13.

118. Quotes from *My Life East and West* by William S. Hart in Mellen, p. 35.

119. Eastwood top box-office attraction reported in *S.F. Chronicle*, Jan. 13, 1984.

120. "The kind of thing I do." Mellen, p. 269.

120. "With consummate inexpressiveness." Ibid, p. 267.

121. "When those men get together." Ibid, p. 17.

122. "Masculinity declawed." In "The New American Hero," by Amy Gross in *Mademoiselle*, July 1978.

123. "People are tired." *Playboy*, October 1979, p. 70.

Chapter 6

127. "If one would have a friend." Nietzsche, p. 63–64.

130. "In our interviews friendship was largely." Levinson, p. 335.

131. "Boys put greater spatial distance." Carol Guardo, "Personal Space in Children," in *Child Development*. 40 (1969) 143–51.

131. "Boys show less stability." John Horrocks and George Thompson, "A study of the friendship fluctuations of rural boys and girls," *Journal of Genetic Psychology*, 70 (1947) 53–63.

132. Male-male friendship less intimate. Douvan and Adelson, pp. 174–202.

132. "Males generally disclose less." Jourard, p. 166.

132. "Men's friendships . . . less close and spontaneous." Alan Booth, "Sex and Social participation," *American Sociological Review*, 37 (1972): 183–192.

132. "Relationships with men as a negative quality. Thomas Shipley and Joseph Veroff, "A Projective Measure of the Need for Affiliation," *Journal of Experimental Psychology*. 43 (1952) 349–356.

132. "To a disquieting degree." Douvan and Adelson, p. 178.

139. "Men are extremely secretive." Zilbergeld, p. 4.

141. "Almost everyone appears." Montagu, p. 65.

142. Height studies reported by Ralph Keyes in *Esquire*, November 1979.

146. "Deception is crucial to success." Greenfield, in *Esquire*, October 1975.

148. "I came to view our competition." Bradley, p. 100–101.

149. "Why did football bring me so to life." Exley, p. 7.

150. "Value homophily." McWilliams, p. 44.

Chapter 7

162. "The seemingly shameful." Clark, p. 6.

164. Kinsey, p. 120.

165. *Psychology Today*, January 1977, Vol. 10, No. 8, p. 42.

166. Study of stick figures conducted by Wolfgang and Wolfgang (1971) in *Journal of Clinical Psychology* 27, 510-512.

166. Perceived and unperceived homosexual studies conducted by Karr, unpublished doctoral dissertation, University of Washington, 1975.

177. Time, April 23, 1979, Vol. 113, No. 17. pp. 72-78.

177. "What is notable." Evelyn Hooker's epilogue in *Journal of Social Issues*, 1978, Vol. 34, No. 3.

Conclusion

179. "I did not find the world desolate." The Talmud, Ta'anit, 23A.
180. The SMU study was conducted by James Pennebaker, and will be reported in the *Journal of Personality and Social Psychology*, in press for 1986.

Index

THIS BOOK
BELONGS TO

. . . .

For Great Aunty Betty and Harold.
Both inspiring in their own special way.

———⟨◈⟩———

Creative Directors Hannah Read-Baldrey & Christine Leech
Art Director & Designer Christine Leech
Stylist & Illustrator Hannah Read-Baldrey
Photographer Tiffany Mumford

For Quadrille Publishing
Editorial Director Jane O'Shea
Creative Director Helen Lewis
Project Editor Lisa Pendreigh
Production Director Vincent Smith
Production Controller James Finan

Published in the United States by
North Light Books
a division of F+W Media, Inc.
4700 East Galbraith Road
Cincinnati, Ohio 45236
(800) 289-0963
First Edition.
15 14 13 12 11   5 4 3 2 1

media
www.fwmedia.com

ISBN: 978-1-4403-1440-7

Printed in China

Everything
Alice

NORTH LIGHT BOOKS

Cincinnati, Ohio
www.CreateMixedMedia.com

contents

Welcome

to the wonderful world of Alice, where all is not what it seems

This book began as a little idea, a little idea hatched within an ordinary conversation over a cup of tea. We were having a chat—stood at the bottom of a staircase in a location house, which was dressed as Christmas day even though it was July—and simultaneously we both exclaimed how we would love to make a craft book with the theme of Alice in Wonderland. Years later you are now holding our first book in your hands... and we couldn't be prouder!

To create *Everything Alice* we spent the summer months preparing all the projects: we sketched out ideas on napkins in pubs and cafés; we got dirty collecting old bits of furniture from dumpsters to revamp into stunning Fabric-Covered Furniture (see pages 66–67); we rummaged through London's finest charity shops to buy tea sets for our Vintage Cake Stand (see pages 92–93); we selected beautiful fabrics for all of our fantastic sewn projects, including The Dandy White Rabbit (see pages 14–17); and we delved into craft shops for everything in between. Our partner-in-crime, Tiffany Mumford, took the beautiful photographs in this book. We all worked hard to get each image just right: it was great fun setting up the larger scenes, such as the Shadow Puppet Theater (see pages 58–61), which was a truly magical experience.

Most of the photographs were shot at Hannah's parents' stunning home, for which we have to give special thanks. After visiting Christ Church, Oxford and the gardens Alice herself played in, we couldn't have found a better alternative! While photographing we were lucky with the weather, except the day of the croquet game. That day the August heavens opened causing sodden playing cards, damp fabric hedgehogs, and the paint to run on the flamingos that took Christine's father and us hours to make, never a good look...

Once the photographs were taken, Hannah returned to her kitchen table to create the intricate paper-cut illustrations dotted throughout this book while Christine began the mammoth task of designing the book so that every page is perfectly Alice.

Everything Alice is the creative must-have for any Alice lover and an enticement for those who are yet to fall down the rabbit hole. We do hope you love this book as much as we do!

~ ON THE ~
TRAIL OF ALICE

One November morning we wrapped up warm and caught a train to Oxford for a trip to Christ Church, part of the town's renowned University, and to take a look around the home of Charles Dodgson, aka Lewis Carroll.

At 11a.m. we were announced by the tinkle of the bell on the heavy wooden door of Alice's Shop, an old building on St. Aldate's. This shop would have been known to Carroll and, as it is situated opposite the University, he is sure to have visited. We battled our way through the extraordinary collection of Alice-related trinkets, from plastic rulers to handmade chessboards, and both bought something; it was hard to resist.

It was here local historian Mark Davies kindly took us on a tour that brought Carroll's Victorian Oxford back to life. In 1851 Carroll read Maths and Classics at the University before staying on to become a reverend. He met and befriended the Dean's three daughters, Lorna, Edith, and Alice Lidell, and they often spent time punting along Oxford's waterways. During these outings Carroll created wondrous stories; one such tale was Alice Underground, which the real Alice persuaded him to write down. This became the story we know and love today!

Do you know many of the characters from the tales were based on real people and places? Familiar references are still scattered around the University: reflections of the Cheshire Cat can be found in the chapel where there are a selection of gruesome gargoyles carved into the stone arches, one of which appears to be a smiling cat. Within the wooden paneled Great Hall are two central fireplaces, both appointed with golden firedogs with comical elongated necks; one can't help but assume these were the inspiration for Alice's neck to grow.

Even Alice's Shop is mentioned in *Through the Looking Glass* when the story tells of a room suddenly filling with water. On first glance this seems pure fantasy, however in the December of 1852 the flooding of the low-lying ground near the waterways was so bad that this parade of shops could only be accessed by boat via the first-floor windows.

Carroll was inspired by the people he met everyday. It is thought the Queen of Hearts was based on Alice's governess, Mary Prickett: "The very essence of all Governesses." The White Rabbit may have been Alice's father, Henry; at that time Oxford worked on its own time that was five minutes later than GMT; that's why the White Rabbit was always late. A recent theory suggests the Mad Hatter was fashioned on Mr. Randell, a local tailor and mayor. His house sits oddly on arches over the river with chimney pots that look like a pair of March Hare's ears! Even the famous croquet game was a reference to when the Royal Family came to visit.

Our trip to Oxford gave us a fantastic insight into the world of Alice; if you get the chance, go!

"'The time has come,' the Walrus said, 'To talk of many things: Of shoes and ships and sealing-wax Of cabbages and kings And why the sea is boiling hot And whether pigs have wings.'"

CRAFT KIT

A good craft kit is like a magpie's nest; full of little scraps of fabric, paper, and sparkly things that may be useful one day.

Scissors: *Never use scissors for cutting both paper and fabric; they will stay sharper longer if they only do one job. Small embroidery scissors are useful for snipping stray threads, while pinking shears create decorative edges.*

Glues: *White craft glue is useful for many projects as an adhesive and a sealant. A glue gun is great for fixing things fast, while specific glues for fabric, paper, and ceramic are also useful. Glue dots come in all shapes and sizes and are a clean and easy way to fix things.*

Tapes: *Cellophane, invisible, masking, and duct tape.*

Craft knife

Wire cutters

Staple gun

Stapler

Paper fasteners

Wallpaper paste

Mosaic grout

Sewing machine

Sewing needles: *A good selection of needles with various size holes and thicknesses, including ones for embroidery. A big blunt needle with a large eye is very useful for threading ribbon or elastic through hems.*

Pins

Threads: *Various cotton and silk threads for sewing and embroidery.*

Buttons & beads: *Of all shapes and all sizes.*

Scraps of ribbon & fabric: *For decoration.*

Silver garden wire

Tailor's chalk or disappearing-ink pen

Tape measure

Steel ruler

Assorted paint brushes

COOKERY KIT

Quality cookery utensils will not only last you years but will help you achieve perfect results.

Kitchen scales & measuring spoons

Wooden spoons

Measuring cups

Sifter

Whisks: *Electric, balloon, or food processor.*

Rubber spatula: *Perfect for cleaning bowls.*

Rolling pin

Mixing bowls: *Big ones for cakes and small ones for frosting.*

Baking sheet: *Best with turned-up edges, for extra grip when removing from a hot oven.*

Cupcake baking pan

Foil, plastic wrap & baking paper

Cooling rack

Candy thermometer

Cocktail sticks

Cupcake liners

Piping bags: *Disposable ones are best to reduce mess.*

Piping ends: *A ⅜" nozzle for macaroons and a selection of smaller star and writing ends for decoration.*

Knives: *Bread knife and other sharp knives.*

Selection of cutlery

TIME FOR TEA JEWELRY

The miniature furniture and accessories designed for dollhouses
make great charms for this most curious jewelry.

For the bracelet
medium-weight gold chain
   wire cutters
medium and large gold
   jump rings
1 toggle clasp
dollhouse tea set or other
   miniature items and charms
an assortment of glass and
   crystal beads
head pins
glass seed beads
2 pairs of round-nose pliers

The beauty of this jewelry is that each piece is unique: it's a great way to use up all those odd beads and little charms that are bought on a whim or are left over from other projects. Tiny buttons, sequins, and bells look lovely interspersed with beads and a miniature tea set—pretty much anything with a hole in it can be hung on a chain!

Bracelet

Using the wire cutters, cut a 7½" length of gold chain. Next, using jump rings, attach one part of the toggle clasp to each end of the gold chain.

To plan your design, lay the chain out in a line and arrange your beads and charms along it until you are happy with the order. We suggest placing a large charm, such as a teapot, in the center of the bracelet and then adding approximately two beads between each medium-size charm, such as a teacup.

For beads with a hole through their middle, thread a seed bead onto a head pin followed by the bead and another seed or smaller bead. Using round-nose pliers, make a wrapped loop (see page 12). For the tea set, buttons, and any beads with a hole through the top, attach them to a jump ring.

Using jump rings and following your design, attach the beads and charms to every other link of the chain. The more beads and charms you add, the more jangly the bracelet but also the heavier!

~ Time For Tea Bracelet ~

continued

~ Time For Tea Earrings ~

Earrings

For the earrings
lightweight gold chain
wire cutters
1 pair earring wires
head pins
2 small jump rings
various glass and crystal beads
2 pairs of round-nose pliers
dollhouse tea set

~ Using the wire cutters, cut two 1" lengths of gold chain. Attach an earring wire to the last link of each chain.

~ For each earring you will need about five small beads plus little crystals to provide some extra sparkle. Attach the beads to the chain by hooking the loop of the head pin through a link of the chain before completing a wrapped loop (see below). Attach the beads to alternate sides of the chain links.

~ Finally, attach a teacup or milk jug to the bottom link of the chain using a small jump ring.

HOW TO MAKE WRAPPED LOOPS

1 Thread the beads onto the head pin. Using round-nosed pliers, form a loop leaving a small stem of head pin above the beads.

2 Grip the loop with the pliers and then, using the second pair, wrap the head pin around the wire stem down to the bead. Cut off any excess wire.

~ Time For Tea Necklace ~

Necklace

For the necklace
5mm gold jump rings
head pins
32" lightweight gold chain
a selection of beads
glass seed beads
2 pairs of round-nose pliers
wire cutters
dollhouse tea set

~ Join the two end links of the chain with a jump ring. Attach your teapot to this ring. Hang a variety of beads and charms on either side of the teapot. You may prefer the teapot and just one other bead on your necklace, or you could fill the entire chain.

"Alas for poor Alice! when she got to the door, she found she had forgotten the little golden key, and when she went back to the table for it, she found she could not possibly reach it: she could see it quite plainly through the glass, and she tried her best to climb up one of the legs of the table, but it was too slippery; and when she had tired herself out with trying, the poor little thing sat down and cried."

DRINK ME

THE DANDY WHITE RABBIT

Lovingly create your own handsome White Rabbit toy. He looks super-dashing in his suit, accessorized with a bow tie and pocket watch; perfect for the rabbit about town!

For the White Rabbit

1 ⅛ yd white velvet fabric
8" medium-weight cotton floral
  print fabric, for ears
matching sewing thread
large bag of toy stuffing
2 black buttons, for eyes
pink embroidery thread,
  for whiskers

For his suit

20" blue cotton print fabric
12" pink cotton print fabric,
  for jacket lining
matching sewing thread
2 floral buttons, for jacket
30" length of 1"-wide pink
  grosgrain ribbon, for bow
  tie (optional)

For his pocket watch

8" square white felt
blue embroidery thread
6" narrow blue ribbon

Note: The seam allowance is
⅜" throughout.

Warning: Do not use small
parts, such as buttons, if you
are making this toy for a
small child as they can be a
choking hazard.

To make the White Rabbit

✎ Using the templates on page 134, cut two of each of the following from the white velvet: head, ears, and body. Cut four of each of the following from the white velvet: arms and legs. From the floral print cotton cut two more ears for the inners. Transfer any markings from the templates to the fabric.

✎ To join the arms and legs, place together two of the velvet pieces with right sides facing. Pin and baste. Stitch around the sides using a ⅜" seam allowance and leaving the top edge open. Clip the curved seams. Turn right side out (if it helps, use the handle of a wooden spoon). Press flat. Fill firmly with toy stuffing, packing evenly from the hands and feet upward.

~ stuff the arms & legs ~

~ attach the ears ~

✎ To make the ears, place together one white velvet piece and one floral print cotton piece with right sides facing. Stitch around the sides, leaving the bottom edge open. Turn right side out. Press flat. Fold each of the sewn ears in half along their length so only the white velvet is showing. Pin together on the fold in the same direction.

✎ To attach the ears to the head, lay out one of the head pieces flat with the right side facing upward. Place the folded ears on the point marked "A," aligning the raw edges. Place the second head piece on top with the right side facing downward. Pin and baste. Stitch around the sides, leaving the neck edge open. Turn right side out. Press flat. Fill the head firmly with toy stuffing.

continued ☞

~ attach the arms & legs ~

To make his suit

⌇ Using the templates on page 135, from the blue print cotton cut two trousers (on the fold), two jacket fronts, and one jacket back (also on the fold). From the pink print cotton cut two jacket linings. Remember to flip the jacket front and lining templates to cut one left side and one right side.

~ make the suit jacket ~

⌇ To attach the arms to the body, lay out one of the body pieces flat with the right side facing upward. Place one stuffed arm on the point marked "B" and the other on the point marked "C," aligning the raw edges. Place the second body piece on top with the right side facing downward. Pin and baste. Stitch along the sides only. Turn right side out.

⌇ To attach the head, press under a ³/₈" hem along the body's top edge. With the central front seam lined up with point "D," place the head into the pressed seam on the body. Pin and baste. Topstitch along the shoulder line. Fill the body with toy stuffing.

⌇ To attach the legs, press under a ³/₈" hem along the body's lower edge. With the central front seams facing forward, place a leg at either side of the body's bottom edge. Topstitch all along the bottom line.

⌇ Add two black buttons for eyes. Add whiskers to his nose by knotting and fraying a length of pink embroidery thread.

⌇ Place together the two trouser pieces with right sides facing. Pin and baste. Stitch along the outer and inner sides, leaving the top and bottom leg edges open. Turn right side out. Press flat. Press under a ³/₈" hem around the waistband and topstitch down. Stitch a ³/₈" double hem on each trouser leg, ensuring the raw edges are not visible.

⌇ Place together the jacket linings and fronts with right sides facing. Pin and baste. Stitch along the shoulder, front and lower edges only. Turn right side out. Press flat.

⌇ Press under and stitch a ³/₈" hem along the neck and lower edges of the jacket back. Place together the lined front jackets and the jacket back with right sides facing. Pin, baste, and stitch. Turn right side out. Press back the lapels to reveal the lining. Dress your Dandy White Rabbit in his suit and stitch on two jacket buttons.

~ embroider the pocket watch ~

To make his pocket watch

⌒ Using the template on page 134, cut two pocket watch pieces from the white felt. With blue embroidery thread, hand sew blanket stitches just over half way around the watchface (see page 24). Lightly fill the watch with a small amount of toy stuffing. Continue stitching around the watchface until it is completely closed. With pink embroidery thread, add the fast and slow hands.

⌒ Attach a length of blue ribbon to the back of the watch. Stitch the top of this ribbon to his suit jacket, just under the lapel.

And there you are, your Dandy White Rabbit is complete. Give him a kiss!

"Oh my ears and whiskers, how late it's getting!"

HEART LETTER HOLDER

Cherish your precious postcards and letters with love.

You will need

2 sheets mounting board,
 each 17" x 17"
40" x 20" of 1¼"-thick batting
stapler and staples
24" x 24" toile de jouy or other
 medium-weight cotton
hot glue gun
5½ yd of ³⁄₈"-wide ribbon
12 brass paper fasteners
12 fabric-covered buttons,
 ½" in diameter
16" length of stiff jewelry wire

Draw a heart template about 16" wide by 16" tall, and use it to cut two heart shapes from the mounting board.

Fold the batting in half so it is double thickness. Using one of the heart-shaped boards as a template, trace the heart outline on the batting. Draw a second heart outline 1¼" all around outside the first. Cut out the larger heart. Lay out the cut batting flat and place one heart-shaped board on top. Fold the edges of the batting over the heart-shaped board and staple in place, pulling it taut. Trim any excess batting.

Lay out the cotton print fabric flat, with the wrong side facing upward. Trace the heart outline on the fabric, then draw a second outline 4" all around outside the first. Cut out the larger heart. Place the batting-covered board on top of the fabric heart, with the batting side down. Using a hot glue gun, adhere the fabric to the reverse of the board, pulling it taut. Start with the straightest sides, then clip and notch the fabric so it lays neatly around the curves.

Lay lengths of ribbon across the heart board, equally spaced at about 4" intervals. Place four in left-slanting diagonals and four in right-slanting diagonals to make a lattice pattern. Leave an extra 4" of ribbon at each end. Where the ribbons cross, use a craft knite to pierce a small hole through the

cover the board

fix the ribbons

board. Push a brass paper fastener through each hole and secure at the back. Take the excess ribbon ends over to the reverse of the board and glue in place, pulling taut. Using a hot glue gun, cover each fastener head with a fabric-covered button.

To make a hanging hook, pierce two holes in the second heart-shaped board in the upper center, about 6" apart and level horizontally. Feed a length of wire through these holes and wrap the ends around themselves to secure.

Line up both of the heart-shaped boards, with reverse sides facing. Using a hot glue gun, adhere the boards together, tucking any raw fabric edges neatly inside.

DRESS-ME ALICE
& WHITE RABBIT

Have splendid fun dressing up Alice and the White Rabbit in outfits fit for the Royal Court, a tea party, or even a boating trip down the river.

You will need
thin cardboard
white craft glue
scissors

Color photocopy these pages. Glue the copy onto thin cardboard. Carefully cut around both characters, their clothes, and their accessories.

Fold the cardboard backward along each dotted line on the characters' stands and the tabs on their clothing.

Stand up and dress.

LAVENDER DORMICE

These sleepy dormice are scented with dried lavender, which is a natural moth repellent.
Hang them by their tails in your wardrobe or nestle them in your underwear drawer.

You will need

small amount of fabric, such
  as velveteen, for mouse's
  body, tail, and outer ears
small amount of contrasting
  print fabric, for mouse's
  bottom and inner ears
matching sewing thread
tailor's chalk
toy stuffing
dried lavender (about
  1 tablespoon per mouse)
ribbon, for decoration
small button, for decoration
dark embroidery thread,
  for eyes

~ attach the bottom ~

Note: The seam allowance is
$^3/_{16}$" throughout.

Warning: Do not use small
parts, such as buttons, if you
are making this toy for a
small child as they can be a
choking hazard.

Trace and cut out the templates on page 128. Fold a 8" x 8¾" piece of the mouse's body fabric in half widthwise with right sides facing. Place the body template on the fabric and draw around it with tailor's chalk. Pin both sides of the fabric together. Stitch from points "A" to "B," via the nose. Trim the excess fabric close to the line of stitching and up to the chalk mark on the open edge.

Using the bottom template, cut one bottom piece from the contrasting print fabric. Align point "B" of the body with point "C" of the bottom and points "D" on both the body and bottom. Pin and baste. Stitch down both sides, leaving the lower edge open.

Turn the body right side out and fill with a mixture of toy stuffing and lavender. As the body is stuffed, the fabric around the hole turns in on itself creating a neat edge. When plump, hand sew to close the opening.

There are two ways of making the mouse's tail. If you are using a fabric with a bit of stretch, like fleece or velveteen, cut a 12" x 1½" rectangle. Fold the fabric in half lengthwise with right sides facing. Starting at one corner, stitch diagonally across to the opposite corner. Trim the excess fabric close to the line of stitching. Turn right side out. This can be tricky with such a small tube, so use a pencil to poke the fabric out. If you are using a stiffer fabric, like cotton or linen, follow the same method but stitch the tail fabric together with the wrong sides facing. Trim the excess fabric with pinking shears. Hand sew the tail to the mouse's bottom using a small button for decoration.

Place a 4" x 2¾" piece of each of the velveteen and contrasting print fabric together with right sides facing. Using the ear template, draw two ears on the wrong side of the print fabric. Pin and baste. Stitch around the curved sides, leaving the lower edge open. Trim the excess fabric closely around the stitching line. Turn right side out. Turn the inside raw edges and press. Pinch each ear together at the base to create a mini dart. Secure with a couple of stitches. Hand sew the ears to the body. Finally embroider onto the mouse's head sleepy eyes in dark embroidery thread using a few backstitches (see page 24). Decorate your mouse with ribbons.

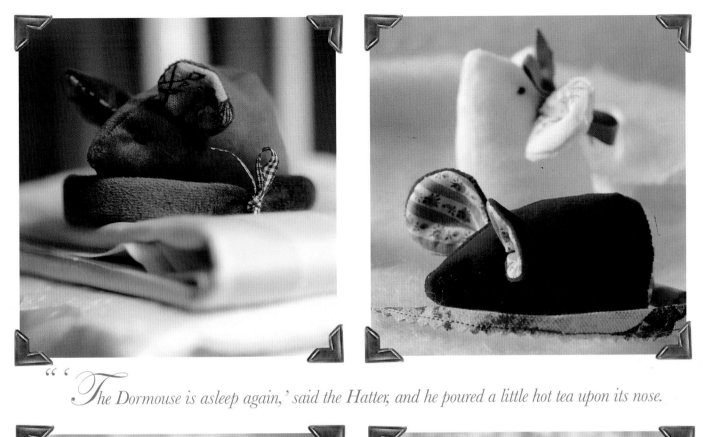

" ' *The Dormouse is asleep again,' said the Hatter, and he poured a little hot tea upon its nose.*

'I wasn't asleep,' he said in a hoarse, feeble voice: 'I heard every word you fellows were saying.' "

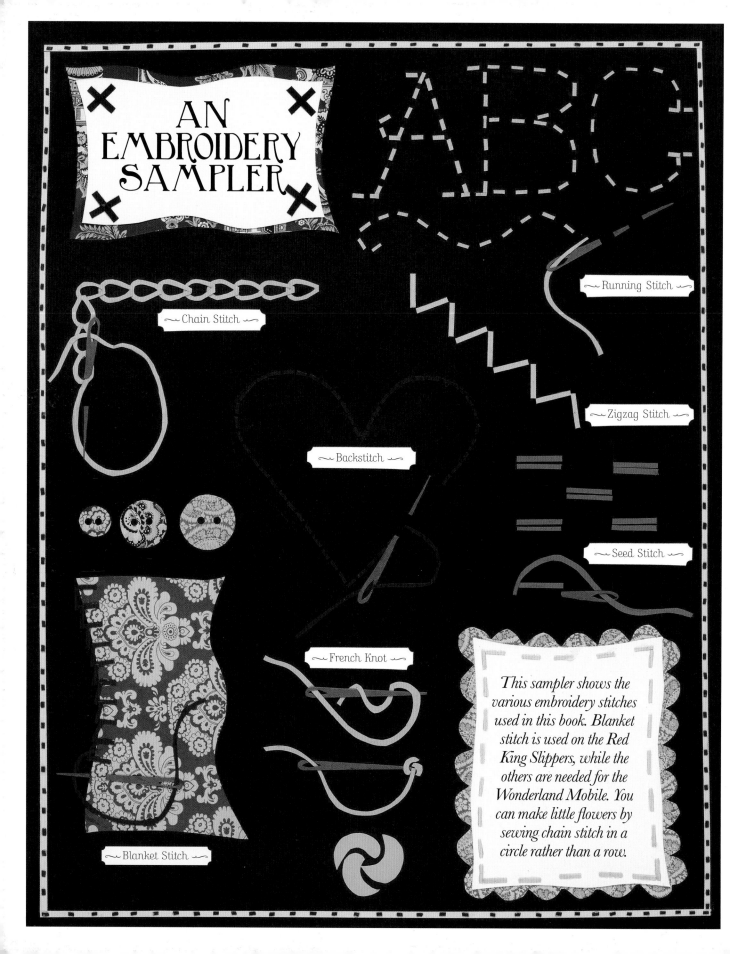

AN EMBROIDERY SAMPLER

ABC

~ Chain Stitch ~

~ Running Stitch ~

~ Zigzag Stitch ~

~ Backstitch ~

~ Seed Stitch ~

~ French Knot ~

~ Blanket Stitch ~

This sampler shows the various embroidery stitches used in this book. Blanket stitch is used on the Red King Slippers, while the others are needed for the Wonderland Mobile. You can make little flowers by sewing chain stitch in a circle rather than a row.

INVITATION PILLOW

This pillow is a real invitation to have a sit down and a bit of a rest. It can be personalized with a name or a full address. By adjusting the size and type of fabric used, you can turn the case into a purse, make-up bag, or even an elegant clutch.

For the pillow
36" x 18" oatmeal linen
36" x 18" cotton print fabric, for the lining
matching sewing thread
pillow form to fit cover

For the decoration
pink embroidery thread
4" x 3" white felt
4" x 3¼" pink velvet
16" length of small pompom trimming
scrap of narrow pink satin ribbon
small decorative button
black embroidery thread
multicolored sequins
12" length of gold rickrack
8" length of 1½"-wide striped grosgrain ribbon
large gold button

Note: The seam allowance is ³/₈" throughout.

~ make the basic envelopes ~

❧ Using the template on page 136, cut two envelope shapes; one from the linen outer fabric and one from the cotton lining fabric.

❧ Fold the cotton lining envelope where marked with right sides facing. Pin and baste. Starting at the lower edge, stitch up each side, finishing ¼" from the top edge. Repeat with linen outer envelope. Turn the linen outer envelope right side out.

❧ Slip the outer envelope inside the lining envelope, with right sides facing. Pin and baste around the lower curved envelope opening (1) and the envelope flap (2).

~ 1 ~

~ 2 ~

❧ Stitch around the opening and flap, leaving 4" unstitched along one straight edge—this is the turning hole.

❧ With sharp scissors, clip the corners and notch the curved seams so that the envelope lays neatly when pressed.

❧ Turn the envelope right side out through the turning hole, then ease the lining down into the outer envelope.

❧ Press all the seams, easing the fabric at each curve to give a nice rounded shape.

~ turn the cover right side out ~

continued 🖙

To decorate

✒ Embroider onto the front panel your chosen name and, if preferred, address in pink embroidery thread using backstitches.

✒ Using the template on page 136, cut out a Queen's head silhouette from the white felt. Adhere the felt Queen's head to the small rectangle of pink velvet with fabric glue.

✒ Place the pompom trimming around the edges of the velvet, covering the raw edges. Pin and baste. Stitch in place.

✒ Decorate the Queen's head by adding a ribbon bow for her sash, a small button for her earring, and embroidering a small French knot (see page 24) in black embroidery thread for her eye.

✒ Using a fine brush, paint the shape of a crown in fabric glue on the Queen's head. Sprinkle sequins onto the glue crown, then press so they stay in place. Shake gently so any loose sequins fall off. Alternatively, if the pillow is going to be frequently laundered, use a length of sequinned ribbon or hand sew individual sequins in place for the crown.

✒ Place the stamp on the front panel of the pillow in the top right-hand corner. Pin and baste. Stitch around all sides. Cut three lengths of gold rickrack. Stitch or glue the rickrack over the stamp for the postage mark.

✒ Machine stitch or hand sew onto the lower back panel a diagonal line from both outside corners to the center of the opening.

✒ In the center of the flap, machine stitch or hand sew a buttonhole. Fold the length of striped ribbon in half at a slight angle. Snip diagonally across both ends. Place the gold button with the folded ribbon beneath to align with the buttonhole. Sew in place to make the Royal seal. Finally, insert a pillow form and deliver to a worthy recipient.

"The Fish-Footman began saying, in a solemn tone, 'For the Duchess. An invitation from the Queen to play croquet.' The Frog-Footman repeated, in the same solemn tone, 'From the Queen. An invitation for the Duchess to play croquet.'"

WANT TO BECOME A QUEEN?

Can you believe as many as six impossible things before breakfast? If so you might have what it takes to become a queen. With instruction from REAL QUEENS (Red & White) you can learn the correct etiquette, deportment and manners. Packed full of hints, tips, and useful lessons, this postal course proves ANYONE can become a Queen!

A LESSON IN DEPORTMENT
by the Red Queen

1 "Look up, speak nicely, and don't twiddle your fingers all the time."

2 "Curtsey while you're thinking what to say, it saves time."

3 "Open your mouth a little wider when you speak, and always say 'your Majesty.' "

4 "Always speak the truth – think before you speak – and write it down afterward."

5 "Speak in French when you can't think of the English for a thing – turn out your toes as you walk – AND REMEMBER WHO YOU ARE!"

THE WHITE QUEEN'S PATENTED EXERCISE TO PREVENT CRYING

"Consider what a great girl you are. Consider what a long way you've come to-day. Consider what o'clock it is. Consider anything, only don't cry!"

" 'That's the way it's done,' says the Queen 'nobody can do two things at once, you know.' "

COULD *YOU* BE A QUEEN?
take our test to find out

Addition
Q. What's one and one and one and one and one and one and one and one and one and one?

Subtraction
Q. Take nine from eight.

Q. Take a bone from a dog: what remains?

Division
Q. Divide a loaf by a knife – what's the answer to that?

Languages
Q. What's the French for fiddle-de-dee?

ANSWERS **Addition** 10, unless you lose count. **Subtraction** Trick question, it's not possible. The dog's temper would remain. The dog would lose its temper. Then if the dog went away, its temper would remain! **Division** Bread-and-butter. **Languages** Fiddle-de-dee is not English, find out what language "fiddle-de-dee" is, then find the French for it!

A satisfied customer says:

" *WELL, this is grand! I never expected I should be a Queen so soon. I was afraid the crown might come off, but I shall be able to manage it quite well in time.* "

Alice Liddell, 7 and a half exactly

SEND NO MONEY NOW
PAYMENT ONLY ON CORONATION

QUEEN ALICE BAG

*This bag is the perfect size for carrying a sandwich and your favorite
"Alice In Wonderland" tales down to the river for a little adventure...*

For the bag

36" x 18" oatmeal linen
36" x 18" cotton print fabric
matching sewing thread
36" length of 1½"-wide striped
  grosgrain ribbon, for the strap
strong sewing thread

Note: The seam allowance is
³⁄₈" throughout.

For the decoration

8" x 6" white felt
8¾" x 7¼" pink velvet
33" length of medium-size
  pompom trimming
decorative button
black embroidery thread
multicolored sequins
³⁄₈"-wide gold rickrack
8" length of 1½"-wide striped
  grosgrain ribbon
scraps of ribbons

☞ Using the template on page 137, follow
the instructions on page 26 for the Invitation
Pillow to make the basic envelope.

☞ Place one end of the shoulder strap
ribbon on the inside flap of the bag, just
above the opening. Pin and hand sew the end
in place using a strong thread. To reinforce
the stitching, sew a rectangle, then sew
diagonal lines between the corners. Take
care not to sew through to the linen outer
envelope. Repeat with the other end.

To decorate

☞ Using the template on page 136, cut out
a Queen's head silhouette from the white felt.
Place the head in the center of the rectangle
of pink velvet. Pin and either machine stitch
or hand sew with blanket stitches around the
Queen's head.

☞ Follow the instructions on page 28 for
adding the pompom trimming, button
earring, embroidered eye, and sequin crown.
Use a wider brush to apply the fabric glue for
the crown for more sequins. Stitch the stamp
on the front panel of the bag, add the postage
mark to the stamp, and embroider the extra
lines on the envelope back in the same way.

☞ Follow the instructions on page 28 to
add the buttonhole, button, and ribbon.

☞ If the bag gets dirty, sponge clean with a
little warm water.

WHITE RABBIT & CHESHIRE CAT MASKS

These masks are great fun for parties and masquerade balls.

You will need
white craft glue
white mosaic grout
tile clippers
hot glue gun

For the White Rabbit:
1 sheet of white mounting
  board, 22" x 17"
³/₈" square mosaic tiles:
  230 white, 110 cream, 90
  pink (approximate quantities)
14" length of ¹/₄" wood
  doweling rod, for the handle
white acrylic paint

For the Cheshire Cat:
1 sheet of black mounting
  board, 12" x 17"
³/₈" square mosaic tiles:
  120 black, 50 gray
  (approximate quantities)
14" length of ¹/₄" wood
  doweling rod, for the handle
black acrylic paint

Using the templates on page 137, cut two of your selected mask shape from the mounting board. Paint your doweling rod the corresponding mask color—white for the rabbit and black for the cat—and leave to dry.

Cover your work surface with a protective sheet as mosaic work can be messy! Apply a dab of white craft glue to the back of each mosaic tile and adhere to one mask shape, leaving a ¹/₁₆" space between tiles. Get creative and make up your own pattern. Trim away overhanging tiles with the tile clippers. Leave to dry thoroughly for at least two hours.

As an alternative to ready-made ³/₈" mosaic tiles, make your own small tiles from old pots and crockery in your required colors. Wrap the crockery in a few sheets of newspaper, then place into a thick plastic bag. Make sure you put the bag on a durable surfaces before smashing the crockery into small pieces with a hammer. Remove the pieces carefully from the wrapping as they will be sharp.

Mix the white mosaic grout to the manufacturer's instructions in a jar or plastic container. Keep a bowl of water and a sponge nearby. Spread the grout over the mosaic, working it into the spaces between each tile. Try to keep the surface of the grout as smooth as possible. Leave the mask on a flat surface and allow the grout to dry fully. It's best to leave it overnight.

Once dry, wipe down the mosaic with a damp cloth to remove any excess grout. Leave to dry for a few hours more, then give it a final polish with a soft cloth.

With a hot glue gun, stick the second mask shape onto the back of the tiled one, sandwiching the doweling rod in between (on whichever side of the mask you prefer).

HOW TO RUN A CAUCUS RACE
by the Dodo

1 A Caucus race is the best thing for getting oneself dry after a soaking, or to warm oneself on a winter's day. It can be run indoors or outside, by however many people are present.

2 Mark out a sort of circle around trees or furniture, the exact shape does not really matter. Each participant can start the race wherever they choose around the course.

3 The pleasure of a Caucus race is that there is no "One, two, three, and away." Everyone can begin running when they like and let off when they like (good for smaller creatures). Some critics say it is not easy to know when the race is over.

4 After half an hour or so someone must call out "the race is over" and then there will be prizes.

5 The joy of this race is that everyone is a winner. Suitable prizes are comfits and thimbles.

SUGAR & SPICE COMFITS

The Victorian comfit was a nut, seed or piece of spice covered in hard sugar, rather like the sugared almonds of today. Often they were used as a breath freshner. These comfits are less laborious to make than the Victorian version, but just as tasty.

It's the caraway, fennel, and coriander seeds that give these comfits their unique flavor, so it's up to you what other nuts and dried fruit you use. Apricots, pistachios, and ginger each have a lovely jewel-like color that make the comfits look delightful.

9 oz mixed nuts
1³/₄ oz sunflower seeds
1 tablespoon coriander seeds
1 tablespoon fennel seeds
1 tablespoon caraway seeds
3¹/₂ oz dried fruit
superfine sugar

≈ Place a thin layer of the nuts and seeds on a baking sheet and toast under a broiler at medium heat, shaking continually, until they are just browning on all sides. Remove from the broiler and leave to cool.

≈ Add the dried fruit to the nuts and seeds, chopping any large fruits into smaller pieces.

≈ Now for a bit of magic. When we first heard of this method, we really didn't believe it would work—it's real kitchen alchemy. Sprinkle a layer of superfine sugar into a skillet, just deep enough so that it covers the base of the pan. Place over a low heat, watching carefully for the magical moment the sugar simply disappears and turns into a syrup. Remove from the heat right away and immediately stir in the fruit and nuts, making sure they are all evenly covered by the sugar syrup. Be careful as the syrup will be extremely hot.

≈ Cover a baking sheet with parchment paper and spread the caramelized comfits over the sheet to cool. The sugar syrup will have stuck the fruit and nuts together in clumps; if any are particularly large, gently break them up into daintier morsels.

≈ These comfits are a great snack to take on walks and tasty sprinkled over ice cream. Store in an airtight container for up to a week (but they don't last that long in our house).

"The next thing was to eat the comfits: this caused some noise and confusion, as the large birds complained that they could not taste theirs, and the small ones choked and had to be patted on the back."

DRINK-ME CORDIALS

These cordials are easy to make, but to an extent they rely on personal tastebuds!
When mixing the final drink, you may want to add extra sugar and dilute to taste.

"Tied round the neck of the bottle was a paper label, with the words 'DRINK ME' beautifully printed on it in large letters. It was all very well to say 'Drink me,' but the wise little Alice was not going to do that in a hurry.
'No, I'll look first,' she said, 'and see whether it's marked "poison" or not'… She had never forgotten that, if you drink much from a bottle marked 'poison,' it is almost certain to disagree with you, sooner or later. However, this bottle was not marked 'poison,' so Alice ventured to taste it, and, finding it very nice (it had, in fact, a sort of mixed flavour of cherry-tart, custard, pine-apple, roast turkey, toffy, and hot buttered toast), she very soon finished it off."

Lavender Lemonade

The addition of lavender to this lemonade brings a modern twist to a perennial favorite.

1 cup and 2 tbsp sugar
1¼ cups lemon juice
14 stems fresh lavender

☙ Add the sugar to 2¼ cups of water and boil until disolved. Add the lavender and remove from the heat. Cover the pan and leave to infuse the sugar syrup.
☙ When cool, add 2 cups water and the lemon juice. Strain to remove the lavender.
☙ Serve with crushed ice and garnished with lavender flowers.

Strawberry & Raspberry Refresher

For an adult drink, adding a shot of vodka to this juice makes a refreshing summer cocktail.

10½ oz frozen raspberries   1¼ cups sugar
7 oz fresh strawberries   3 tbsp lemon juice

☙ Place the fruit and sugar into a pan. Simmer gently over a medium heat for 20–25 minutes, stirring occasionally, until the sugar is dissolved and the fruit is pulpy.
☙ Mash the fruit, then strain the mixture. Do not push the fruit through the strainer as that will give a cloudy juice. Be patient!
☙ Discard the pulp. Add the lemon juice to the fruit syrup. Add 4¼ cups of boiling water. Leave to cool, then refrigerate.
☙ Serve with crushed ice and garnished with mint leaves.

Pear & Ginger Cordial

This cordial is deliciously warming on a winter's day when served hot.

1¼ cups sugar   1 tsp cream of tartar
1 large ginger root   ½ cup and 2 tbsp lime juice
1 piece lime rind   2 pears

☙ Add the sugar, chopped ginger, lime rind and cream of tartar to 1¾ cups of water and boil for 5 minutes. Add the lime juice.
☙ Return to the boil, then add the peeled, chopped pears. Simmer until softened. Mash the pears to a pulp then strain.
☙ Store in a sterilized bottle and keep refrigerated. Serve diluted to taste.

Elderflower & Rhubarb Cordial

Pick fresh elderflowers in early summer. For the rest of the year, use store-bought cordial.

2¼ cups sugar   1 sliced lemon
20 elderflower heads   3 sticks rhubarb

☙ Add the sugar to 4¼ cups of water and boil until dissolved. Remove from the heat.
☙ Place the elderflowers (shaken to remove any bugs) and sliced lemon into a container. When cool, pour over the sugar syrup.
☙ Cover with a cloth and leave to infuse the sugar syrup for at least two days, or longer for a stronger flavor. Stir regularly.
☙ Place the chopped rhubarb into a pan and strain over the elderflower cordial. Bring to the boil, then simmer until the rhubarb is soft. Leave to cool, then strain.
☙ Store in a sterilized bottle and keep refrigerated. Serve diluted to taste.

"*Tied round the neck of the bottle was a paper label, with the words*

DRINK ME

beautifully printed on it in large letters."

HUMPTY DUMPTY DOORSTOP

*K*eep your door open *in style with this sleepy Humpty, a perfect gift for an Un-birthday present.**

For Humpty Dumpty

40" square medium-weight or heavyweight white cotton

40" square medium-weight or heavyweight striped cotton duck cloth

matching sewing thread

toy stuffing

1 large plastic sandwich bag

approximately 1 1/2 lb split peas or rice, for filling

4" x 4" red fabric, for cheeks

red and black embroidery thread

3 buttons (optional)

1 3/4 yd length of 2"-wide velvet ribbon (optional)

For his hat

1 sheet of medium-weight black cardboard, 8 1/2" x 12"

20" x 20" black cotton

8" length of 3/8"-wide red ribbon, for bow

Note: The seam allowance is 3/8" throughout.

Warning: Do not use small parts, such as buttons, if you are making this toy for a small child as they can be a choking hazard.

~ prepare the pajamas ~

~ 2 ~

☞ Using the templates on page 132, cut one tab on the fold and then four of each of the following from the white cotton: body, arm, and leg. Cut four of each of the following from the cotton duck: pajama body, arm, and leg. Snip each body piece at points "T," "B," "A," and "L."

☞ Turn up a 3/8" double hem on all the pajama pieces at the waist, wrists, and ankles. Pin and stitch. Lay out the white pieces flat with the right sides facing upward. Place the hemmed pajama pieces on top with the right sides facing upward. Pin and stitch. To join the arms and legs, place together two of the pieces with right sides facing. Pin and stitch around the sides with a 3/8" seam allowance,

leaving the top edge open. Turn right side out (if it helps, use the handle of a wooden spoon). Press flat. Fill firmly with toy stuffing, packing evenly from the hands and feet upward.

☞ To attach the arms and legs to the body, lay out one of the body pieces flat with the right side facing upward. Place one stuffed arm and leg on each of the points marked "A" and "L," aligning the raw edges and making sure the hands and toes point upward. Pin and stitch. Join the other body pieces together. Pin one body piece to a second along one side only with right sides facing; line up points "T" and "B" and the waistband of the pajamas. Stitch. Attach the third body piece in the same way.

~ 1 ~

~ stitch together the body ~

continued ☞

*Un-birthday present: a gift received on any of the 364 days when it is not your birthday.

"'*Must a name mean something?*' Alice asked doubtfully
'*Of course it must,*' Humpty Dumpty said with a short laugh:
'*my name means the shape I am —
and a good handsome shape it is, too.
With a name like yours, you might be any shape, almost.*'"

~ join the body ~

~ fill with split peas or rice ~

~ To join all the body pieces, pin the one with arms and legs attached to the sewn three with right sides facing and positioning the limbs inside the body. Join as before, lining up points "T" and "B," but this time stitch along both sides.

~ Turn the body right side out, poking the arms and legs through the turning hole at the top. Place the plastic bag over your fist and push your hand through the hole inside the body. This forms the lining so the split pea or rice filling will not get damp. Using a jug, carefully pour the filling into the plastic bag. Once the body is nicely full, tie the bag into a firm knot.

~ To make the tab, turn under a ³/₈" hem on both long sides and press. Fold in half lengthwise, aligning hemmed edges, and topstitch. Fold the tab in half to make a loop then place in the opening at the top of the body, tucking the edges of the opening under. Pin and stitch across the tab to close the opening.

~ Embroider the face with whatever expression you prefer—our Humpty has sleepy eyes embroidered in black thread. We added small red disks of fabric edged in blanket stitch for his cheeks and a chain stitch mouth. Add other finishing touches of your choice—we gave our Humpty some pajama buttons, velvet ribbon trims, and a simple rosette.

To make his hat

~ Using the templates on page 132, cut from the black cardboard one of each of the following: hat top, side, and brim. Lay out the black fabric flat with right side facing downward on a sheet of newspaper. Apply white craft glue to one side of the cardboard pieces then adhere to the fabric, leaving a ¹/₂" margin around each shape. Allow to dry. Cut out the shapes plus the ¹/₂" margin. Clip the excess fabric, then pull taut over to the reverse of the cardboard and glue in place. For the hat's side, trim the excess fabric from one short side. Roll the hat into a tube, overlapping the remaining excess fabric over the other short side and glue in place. Fold the long sides over and glue taut. Leave to dry (use a paperclip to hold the tube together until dry). Join this tube to the hat's top and brim with a glue gun. Tie a length of red satin ribbon into a bow around the brim. Glue gun the finished hat to Humpty's head.

"*Humpty Dumpty sat on a wall:*
Humpty Dumpty had a great fall.
All the King's horses and all the King's men
Couldn't put Humpty Dumpty in his place again.

⟨────⊱⊰────⟩

'*That last line is much too long for the poetry,*'
Alice added, almost out loud, forgetting that
Humpty Dumpty would hear her."

CHESHIRE CAT HAND WARMER

Keep snuggled with a cute microwaveable lavender-scented hand warmer.

~ stitch the head ~

You will need

10" x 10" medium-weight cotton print
 pieces 10" x 10" cotton jersey
tailor's chalk or soft pencil
matching sewing thread
4" x 4" of $^3/_8$"-thick cotton batting
about 18 oz rice, for filling
4 dried lavender heads (optional)
2 nonmetallic buttons, for eyes
nonmetallic embroidery thread

Warning: As you will be heating this in
the microwave, do not use any metallic
buttons or threads.

Lay out one square of cotton
jersey flat, place the second on top with
the right side facing upward then place
the cotton print on top of them both
with the right side facing downward.
Pin together and press flat. Using the
template on page 131, trace the outline
of the cat's head onto the reverse of the
cotton print. Stitch all the way around
the outline, leaving a 1¼" opening at
the lower edge for the turning hole.
Trim any excess fabric after it has been
sewn (otherwise the jersey has a
tendency to move about), leaving a
seam allowance of $^3/_8$".

Turn the head right side out
through the turning hole, ensuring the
two jersey layers are to the back and the
print cotton to the front. Press flat.

~ quilt the ears ~

~ fill with rice ~

~ embroider the face ~

☛ Using the template on page 131, cut two ear shapes from the cotton batting. Insert them into the cat's head through the opening and maneuver the batting pieces so one sits snugly in each ear. Machine stitch or hand sew along the quilting lines as marked to create a padded effect.

☛ Place the rice in a jug. If you wish to use lavender, take the dried lavender heads and run two fingers down each stalk to remove the flowers. Stir the rice and lavender mixture together, then pour carefully into the cat's head through the opening between the cotton and jersey layers. Place a bowl underneath to catch any stray grains of rice.

☛ Hand sew the opening closed then, following the guide on page 131, add the cat's nose, mouth, and whiskers in black embroidery thread using small backstitches. Add two mis-matched, nonmetallic buttons for eyes.

☛ You can now heat up your cute cat. Place it in microwave at a medium-high heat for 2 to 3 minutes.

CUPCAKE EMBROIDERY BOX

The charm of this box is that it works at many different sizes. A small cupcake makes a perfect gift box for something special while larger ones are great embroidery or jewelry cases—the soft frosting top is perfect for storing either pins or brooches.

For the case

1 sheet $^1/_8$"-thick buff or white
   cardboard, 12" x 17"
masking tape
14" x 6" cotton print
scrap of felt, for base
14" x 8" fabric, for lining
thin double-sided tape
white craft glue, watered down
$3^1/_4$" length of $1^1/_2$"-wide ribbon

For the lid

$16^1/_2$" x $5^1/_4$" white stretch
   cotton jersey or fleece
white embroidery thread
polyester toy stuffing
ribbons and beads, for
   decoration
3" length of narrow ribbon and
   small button, for fastening

For the cherry

8" x 4" red fabric
5" x $2^1/_2$" green fabric
4" x 2" brown felt
pipe cleaner
embroidery thread
polyester toy stuffing

To make the case

☞ Using the templates on page 127, cut one of each of the base and sides from $^1/_8$"-thick buff or white cardboard. If you are using pale fabrics to cover the case, a darker shade of cardboard may show through.

☞ Roll the sides piece into a conical shape, overlapping the short edges by approximately 1". Fix the join securely with masking tape. If necessary, reinforce this join with another narrow piece of cardboard.

☞ Slip the base piece into the sides so that it sits snugly at the bottom. Fix the base piece to the sides using masking tape. Keep this neat so there are no bumps to show through.

~ reinforce the side join ~

B fabric fixed in place with tape

A Neatly hemmed edge plus strip of tape

To cover the case

☞ Using the template on page 127, cut out one sides piece from the print cotton adding a $^3/_8$" seam allowance all the way around.

☞ Turn under a $^3/_8$" hem at one short edge of the sides fabric (see A). Fix in place with double-sided tape. Starting at one side of the join, fix the unhemmed short edge of the sides fabric to the cardboard case with more tape (see B). Wrap the length of the sides fabric around the case, aligning top and lower edges and overlapping the raw edge with the hemmed edge. Fix in place with more tape.

☞ Clip the $^3/_8$" seam allowance all the way around both the top and lower edges, spacing each cut approximately $^3/_8$" apart.

continued

~ cover the case ~

~ glue the lid base ~

~ gather the lid ~

~ line the case ~

To make the lid

✑ Using the template on page 127, cut an inner and outer lid from white cardboard.

✑ Turn under a ³/₄" hem along one long side of the white jersey fabric. Press and stitch. To join the tube, fold the fabric in half widthwise with right sides facing and stitch along the short edges, stopping ¹/₄" before hemmed edge. Pass a length of embroidery thread through the gap in the hem, leaving an extra 4" of thread at each end.

✑ Slip the larger cardboard disk into the fabric tube and position it 1¹/₄" in from the unhemmed lower edge. The stretch of the fabric holds the disk in place. Take this 1¹/₄" over to the base of the disk and glue in place.

✑ Place the lid on a flat surface. Fill the fabric tube with a large handful of toy stuffing, adjusting the amount until it looks right. To gather the lid, draw up the lengths of embroidery thread as tightly as possible. Do not worry about the small hole left in the "frosting" as this will be covered by the cherry. Decorate with ribbons and beads.

✑ Cut the disk of lining fabric using the template. Snip ¹/₄" cuts around the circumference. Spread a thin layer of glue onto the smaller cardboard disk and cover with the lining fabric, taking the excess fabric to the reverse side.

✑ Run a strip of tape around the inside rim of the case, very close to the top. Fold the fabric to the inside and stick it to the tape—the cuts in the fabric allow it to overlap giving a smooth finish. Repeat at the base.

✑ To prevent the box from slipping, cut a disk of felt the same size as the base using pinking shears. Glue in place.

To line the case

✑ Using the template on page 127, cut one disk from the lining fabric. Snip ¹/₄" cuts around the circumference. Spread a thin layer of glue onto the inside base of the case and a little way up the sides. Place the fabric disk inside the case and press. Leave to dry.

✑ For the hinge, cut one 3¹/₄" length of 1¹/₂"-wide ribbon. Glue the first 1¹/₄" of ribbon to the inside of the case at the join.

✑ Using the template on page 127, cut one sides piece from the lining fabric using pinking shears. Spread a thin layer of glue onto the inside of the case. Place the fabric inside the case and press. Leave to dry.

"Soon Alice's eye fell on a little glass box that was lying under the table: she opened it, and found in it a very small cake, on which the words '**EAT ME**' *were beautifully marked in currants."*

~ attach the cherry ~

To make the cherry

Trace and cut out the templates on page 127. Fold the red fabric in half widthwise with right sides facing. Place the cherry template on the fabric and draw around it with tailor's chalk. Pin both sides of the fabric together. Stitch along the curved sides, leaving the top open for a turning hole. Trim the excess fabric close to the line of stitching and up to the chalk mark on the open edge. Turn right side out and press. Turn under the open edges and press. Repeat with the green fabric and leaf template.

To make the stalk, fold the brown felt in half. Place the straight edge of the template along the fold. Stitch along two sides. Trim the excess fabric close to the line of stitching. Insert the pipecleaner and twist into shape.

Hand sew a line of running stitches around the opening of the cherry. Fill with toy stuffing and then pull the stitches up tight. Before the hole closes completely, stitch the leaf and stalk to the inside of the cherry. Tie the gathered threads tight. Pull the leaf down and hold in place with a few stitches. Sew the cherry to the lid covering the center hole.

~ join the lid ~

To join the lid and case

Align the seam of the lid with the join of the case. Place the lined lid disk in the center of the lid, covering any untidy edges and sandwiching the ribbon hinge between the lid and the disk. Glue in place. If you want to add a button and ribbon fastening to the front of the case, sandwich a 3" loop of narrow ribbon between the lid and disk, then hand sew a button to the case to match.

WONDERLAND MOBILE

You will need

2 small tree branches, one
slightly larger than the other
a selection of felt squares in
various colors (we've used
mainly white, red, pink, beige,
purple, yellow, blue, and
brown, but it's useful to have
scraps of several other colors
for the smaller details)
fabric glue
a selection of embroidery floss
in contrasting colors
a selection of small buttons
and tiny seed beads
polyester toy stuffing
gold embroidery thread,
for hanging cords, cut into
20" lengths

Note: When gluing the felt
pieces in place, use a thin
layer so you can still push the
needle through the glued felt.

*The bold shapes and intricate embroidery of this
mobile will delight and entertain a young baby for
hours. Each motif is so special that you could easily
make just one or two of your favorites either to stuff
with batting and use as pincushions or fill with
lavender to make into scented sachets.*

*Unless otherwise stated, each motif is identical on
both sides, so whatever you do on one side be sure to
do on the other. When attaching a hanging cord,
sew it in the center of the motif so it hangs straight
from the twig.*

TO CONSTRUCT THE MOBILE
*Making a mobile that is balanced and hangs evenly
involves a bit of trial and error. Often it is easiesr
to construct the mobile in the place where it will
hang. Fix a small hook in the ceiling. Tie the larger
of the two tree branches to this hook with a length
of strong thread—start by tying the branch in its
middle, but this may need adjusting to get the
branch to hang level. Tie the smaller branch from
the larger branch. Attach a hanging cord to the
center of each motif. Hang the White Rabbit from
the center of the smaller branch, then add the other
motifs. You'll need to adjust each motif to keep
them balanced. To attach the Cheshire Cat to the
larger branch, either use strong adhesive and glue
him in place or attach a cord and wrap the thread
around the branch to secure.*

White Rabbit

Using the templates on page 125, cut
two each of "A," "C," and "E" from white
felt. Cut two "B" from blue felt. Cut one "D"
from yellow felt. Glue the inner ears "B" in
place. Following the guide on page 126,
embroider the inner ears, flowers, and eyes on
both "C" pieces, but embroider the pocket
watch on just one. Embroider the flowers on
both "E" pieces. Sandwich piece "D" between
the two "E" pieces. Secure with a small stitch.

Place the larger tail piece only in
between the two body pieces and sew the
rabbit pieces together with running stitches,
starting above the tail and stitching around
the outer edge. At the ears, attach one of the
outer ears "A." Continue stitching to just
before the tail, leaving a small opening.
Fill with toy stuffing. Sew the opening closed.
Sew the second ear piece "A" in place.

> "*All in the golden afternoon
> Full leisurely we glide;
> For both our oars, with little skill,
> By little arms are plied,
> While little hands make vain pretence
> Our wanderings to guide.*"

Mushroom

⬤ Using the templates on page 124, cut two "A" from red felt. Cut two "B" from beige felt. Cut two "C" from white felt. Glue a flesh "B" and stalk "C" to each "A." Following the guide on page 126, embroider and add the buttons to both sides.

⬤ Sew the mushroom pieces together with running stitches around the outer edge, leaving a small opening. Fill with toy stuffing. Sew the opening closed.

Cupcake

⬤ Using the templates on page 124, cut two "E" from white felt. Cut two "D" from pink felt. Cut two "C" from green felt. Cut two "B" from red felt. Cut one "A" from purple felt. Glue the icing "D" to each case "E." Following the guide on page 126, embroider both sides. Embroider both "B" pieces. Sandwich piece "A" between the two "B" pieces. Secure with a button on each side.

⬤ Place the larger cherry piece only in between the two "D" pieces. Sew the cupcake pieces together with running stitches around the outer edge, leaving a small opening. Fill

with toy stuffing. Sew the opening closed. Embroider and sew together the leaf "C" pieces, then sew in place.

Crown

⬤ Using the templates on page 124, cut two "C" from orange felt; two "B" and four "D" from red felt; two "E" from white felt; and one "A" from purple felt. Glue two "D" pieces and a brim "E" to each "C." Following the guide on page 126, embroider both sides. Sandwich "A" between the two embroidered "B" pieces. Secure with a small stitch.

⬤ Place the larger heart piece only in between the two crown pieces. Sew together the crown pieces with running stitches around the outer edge, leaving a small opening. Fill with toy stuffing. Sew the opening closed.

Heart

⬤ Using the templates on page 125, cut two "A" from purple felt. Cut two "B" from pink felt using pinking shears. Glue the smaller hearts "A" in place. Following the guide on page 126, embroider both sides.

⬤ Starting on a straight side, sew the heart pieces together with running stitches around the outer edge, leaving a small opening. Fill with toy stuffing. Sew the opening closed.

Cheshire Cat

⬤ Using the templates on page 125, cut two each of "A," "B," "C," and "F" from brown felt; two of "E" and one of "H" from pink; two of "D" from green; and two of "G" from orange. Glue "E," then "G" to each ear "F." Glue a head and tail and to each "A," and the flower and leaves to one "A." Following the guide on page 126, embroider the body and tail on both sides, but the face and ears on only one side.

⬤ Sew the cat pieces together with running stitches around the outer edge, leaving a small opening and catching in the ears between two head pieces. Fill with toy stuffing. Sew the opening closed.

"*Thus grew the tale of Wonderland; Thus slowly, one by one
It's quaint events were hammered out, And now the tale is done,
And home we steer, a merry crew, Beneath the setting sun.*"

HOW TO DECORATE AN EGG

1.

Empty your egg by making small pinholes in the top and bottom of the shell and then blowing gently into one hole until the contents of the egg come out of the other hole. Using red and blue acrylics, paint on Humpty's stripey pajamas.

2.

Using a fine brush carefully paint on Humpty's face.

3.

Enlarge the accessories below to 150% on a color photocopier and glue to thin cardboard. Cut out the shapes and stick to your egg Humpty using small glue dots.

GIANT ROSE LIGHTS

*W*in first prize this year for the best roses with this spectacular display of easy-to-make lights. If you cannot find a string of large bulbs, you can easily make smaller roses for a string of smaller lights.

You will need

1 string of 10 outdoor LED globe lights

5 sheets of thin red cardboard, each 22" x 17"

5 sheets of thin white cardboard, each 22" x 17"

Warning: To avoid any fire risk, use only outdoor LED lights with these light shades. As they are made from cardboard, these rose lights are suitable for outdoor use only in good weather but can be used indoors.

~ trim the brim ~

~ start the rose ~

☞ Cut a 16½" disk from each sheet of cardboard. Find the center point. With paper scissors, cut a rough spiral shape starting at the outer edge and working into the middle. Keep the lines of the spiral between 4" and 5½" apart, but it is fine if the edges are slightly wavy.

☞ Cut a small hole in the very center of the spiral. Feed your light bulb through this central hole in the cardboard spiral. With the first section of the spiral, form a cone around the bulb and staple to secure, avoiding all wires.

~ staple in place ~

~ repeat for each shade ~

☞ Continue spiraling the cardboard around the bulb and stapling to secure. Twist and tighten as you proceed.

☞ Repeat for each rose, alternating between red and white. For greater impact, make more than one string of lights.

SHADOW PUPPETS

You will need

2 sheets, 9" x 12", of thin black
  cardboard; and 1 sheet, 22" x 17",
  of thin white cardboard
10 wooden kebab skewers
4 brass paper fasteners
an old pillowcase
a flashlight

To make the puppets

Trace the templates here onto
black cardboard and cut out. For the
Alice puppet, attach the hands and
arms to the shoulders using paper
fasteners at the marked holes. Glue
the wooden skewers to Alice's arms
and legs so they face side out. Glue
wooden skewers to the other shapes
to use for manipulating them.

To make the theater

Photocopy the curtains here,
glue to the white cardboard, and
cut out. Cut a rectangle to the
size of the theater from the
pillowcase and glue between
the curtains. Cut two 4"-tall
cardboard triangles and glue
to the theater's reverse
side for support. Place the
flashlight behind the
theater, turn the lights off,
and it's showtime!

TEACUP CANDLES

Curiouser and curiouser as Alice once said... These candles make a lovely and unusual gift or table center for your Mad Hatter's Tea Party. Fine bone china teacups work best as the thinness of the china lets the light shine through as the candle burns.

You will need

old teacups

candle wax (approximately 9 oz of wax will fill four average-size teacups)

tacky wax (for attaching the wicks to the base of the teacups)

wire-filled wicks with metal clip bases

candle thermometer

old saucepan

old food cans

wax fragrance and colors (optional)

➽ Fill your teacup with hot water to warm it, so it won't crack when you pour in the hot wax. Choose a length of a wick that is at least ³⁄₄" greater than the height of your teacup. Add a blob of tacky wax to the metal base of the wick and fix it to the base of the teacup.

➽ Make a simple water bath in which to melt the wax. Place an old food can inside an old medium-sized saucepan; if you squeeze one side of the can slightly to create a spout the wax will pour more easily. If your wax has come as a block, chop it into small chunks. Place the wax chips in the can. Fill the saucepan with 2" of water. Place the pan over a medium heat and bring the water to a boil, making sure the water doesn't enter the can. If you wish to add fragrance or color to the wax, do it now following the manufacturer's instructions. Heat the wax, checking the thermometer and making sure it never boils. Once the wax has reached the required temperature, remove from the heat.

➽ Pour the wax carefully into the teacup. Use an oven mitt to hold the can and pour slowly, holding the cup at a slight angle to prevent any air bubbles from forming. Make sure the wick remains as upright as possible.

➽ As the wax cools, it may sink a little around the wick. If this happens, fill the dip with a little more wax as the candle sets for a level finish. Leave the candle to harden overnight, then light, enjoy, and daydream.

HOW TO MAKE A WATER BATH

old food can

wax

old saucepan

water

heat

FABRIC-COVERED TEAPOTS

Create a colorful home for your blooms! These eccentric teapot planters brighten up any windowsill.

You will need

teapot—any size or color
white craft glue
20" x 20" cotton print
waterproof matte varnish
potting mix
bedding plants

~ *cut the fabric into strips* ~

~ Clean your teapot and remove the lid. Cut some of your fabric into a few small strips around 2" wide and 4" long. In a plastic cup mix your white craft glue; one part glue to one part water.

~ *start with the spout* ~

~ Beginning with the spout and handle, paint the glue directly onto the teapot, then onto the fabric strips. Wrap your fabric carefully around the teapot, trimming any excess pieces as you proceed.

~ *cover the teapot's body* ~

~ Now work on the body, using longer strips about ³/₈" wide. Once the body is fully covered, leave it to dry. A good tip is to place your teapot on a kitchen cooling rack so the air can get to the bottom.

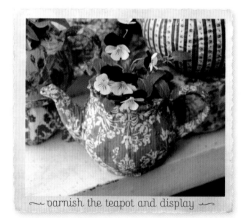

~ *varnish the teapot and display* ~

~ Once dry, paint the fabric-covered teapot with a layer of waterproof matte varnish. Fill the teapot with potting mix and plant.

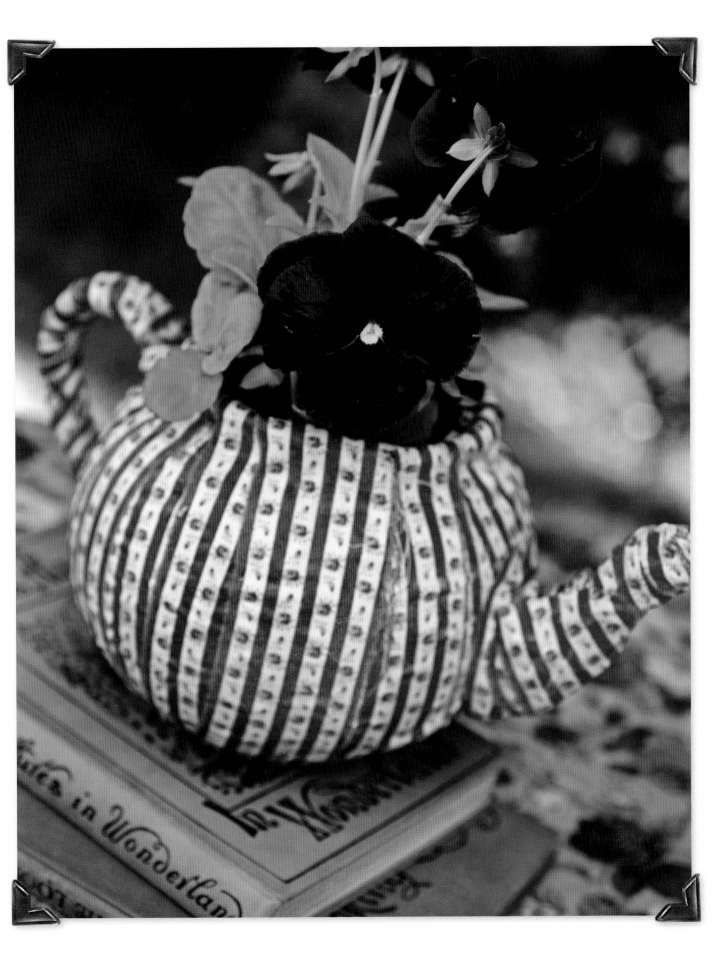

FABRIC-COVERED FURNITURE

There is nothing more fabulous than transforming an old boring piece of furniture into a masterpiece by covering it in a bright fabric. Believe it or not, all of this stunning furniture was taken from dumpsters or donated by people who were throwing it away. Also it's a great opportunity to use up old bedspreads, duvet covers, and other colorful scraps of material. We brought it all back to life with this very simple—slightly messy— but ultimately very effective method. One of our favorite sayings when doing this project was "everything looks better with a pompom trim!"

You will need
an old piece of furniture
brightly colored patterned fabric
wallpaper paste
pompom trimmings and tassels
waterproof varnish

❧ Clean your item of furniture, ensuring there is no dust, dirt, loose nails, or sharp edges.

❧ Mix up wallpaper paste in an old bucket and cut fabric into long strips. Dip the fabric strips into the paste and squeeze away the excess. Wrap the strips around the legs and other tubular parts. For flat areas cut the material roughly to shape, dip in paste and stick down. Use a painter's brush to smooth the material down and remove excess paste.

❧ Leave to dry. If you are planning on leaving any of the furniture outside, then apply a couple of coats of waterproof varnish.

❧ When dry, go to town with your pompom trimmings and tassels.

"Alice thought she had never seen such a curious croquet-ground in her life; it was all ridges and furrows; the balls were live hedgehogs, the mallets live flamingoes, and the soldiers had to double themselves up and to stand on their hands and feet, to make the arches."

HOW TO PLAY CROQUET
by the Red Queen

1 In the absence of flamingos and hedgehogs a traditional croquet set can be used. To begin, appoint one person the Queen and one person in charge of hoops.

2 The Queen must decree "Off With Their Heads" at least once a minute as and when she sees fit. The chosen person then leaves the game immedietly. The hooper can change the hoop positions when ever they please.

3 This is a very fast paced version of croquet. Everyone begins at once and can use any ball available. The aim of the game is to get through all the hoops before being beheaded.

TOPIARY CUPCAKES

These unusual cupcakes are a great show piece for any celebration.

You will need
12 store-bought chocolate cupcakes
7 oz powdered fondant icing sugar
14 oz royal icing sugar mix
12 round candy lollipops
edible green glitter
green food coloring
red food coloring
1 large orange cut in half

Makes 12 cupcakes

Lay out your 12 cupcakes on a tray. To make the grass, mix up the fondant icing sugar by adding water, following the manufacturer's instructions. Add a few drops of the green food coloring. Lightly dust your work surface with the powdered sugar and roll out. With a cookie cutter, cut 12 circles, approximately 1½" in diameter. Brush the backs with water and stick to the top of the cupcakes.

For the topiary, sift 10½ oz of the royal icing sugar into a bowl; only add a little water as the mixture should be thick but workable. Add a few drops of the green food coloring. With the back of a fork, smooth the icing onto the lollipops, completely covering them and twisting as you proceed to make a textured surface. Sprinkle with edible glitter and leave to dry at room temperature, using orange halves as a stand by piercing the skin with the lollipop sticks. Once hard, mix up the remaining royal icing, split into halves and add red food coloring to one. Pipe each tree with either red or white roses.

To finish, pierce the topiary lollipop sticks into the centers of the cupcakes.

MAD HATTER CUPCAKE BOX

The Mad Hatter's top hat makes an ideal traveling box for delicate cupcakes, ensuring they get to the recipient looking pristine. If you don't get peckish on the journey, that is.

You will need

medium-weight cardboard
assortment of patterned papers
white craft glue
craft knife
metal ruler
scissors
double-sided tape
assortment of feathers, buttons, and ribbons, for decoration

~ trim the brim ~

~ score the paper ~

To make the base of the box, cut a 5¼"-diameter disk from the cardboard. Using white craft glue, cover the cardboard disk completely with patterned paper. Trim the edges neatly using a craft knife.

Cut a 9" x 1½" rectangle of patterned paper. Using a metal ruler and the blunt end of a pair of scissors or craft knife, score a fold line on the wrong side of the paper, ⅜" in from one long edge.

~ fold the tabs ~

~ fix to the brim ~

To make the tabs, cut a series of small snips, approximately ¼" apart, along the top edge of the paper up to—but not over—the fold line. Overlap the two short ends to make a tube and secure with double-sided tape. Fold the cut tabs inward.

Using white craft glue, fix the tabs to the brim, making sure the tube is centrally positioned. Cut a 3"-diameter disk from the same patterned paper used to cover the brim. Glue this small paper disk inside the tube to cover up the messy tabs.

continued ☞

~ glue the crown ~

~ decorate and hide! ~

🖙 To make the crown, cut a 10¼" x 3¼" rectangle from patterned paper. Following the same method, make a tube with fold-over tabs as before.

🖙 Cut an 3¼"-diameter disk from patterned paper. Glue to the tabs on the crown of the hat. Trim away any excess paper from the disk.

🖙 To make the hat band, cut a 10¼" x 1½" strip from a contrasting paper. Wrap it around the crown, fix with glue at the back, and decorate with feathers, buttons, and any trimmings you have spare. Leave to dry.

🖙 Once the glue is dry, carefully place a cupcake inside the brim of the hat and cover with the crown.

"'*Take off your hat,*'
the King said to the Hatter.

'*It isn't mine,*' *said the Hatter.*

'*Stolen!*' *the King exclaimed, turning
to the jury, who instantly made a
memorandum of the fact.*

'*I keep them to sell,*' *the Hatter
added as an explanation; 'I've none
of my own. I'm a hatter.*' "

"'"Will you walk a little faster?" said a whiting to a snail.
'There's a porpoise close behind us, and he's treading on my tail.
See how eagerly the lobsters and the turtles all advance!
They are waiting on the shingle — will you come and join the dance?
Will you, won't you, will you, won't you, will you join the dance?
Will you, won't you, will you, won't you,
won't you join the dance?""

RED VELVET CUPCAKES

For the cakes

1 cup plus 2 tbsp. self-
  raising flour
1/2 tsp. baking powder
pinch of salt
2 heaped tbsp. unsweetened
  powdered cocoa
2 tbsp. natural red food coloring
1/4 cup unsalted butter
3/4 cup superfine sugar
1 extra-large egg, beaten
1 tsp. vanilla extract
1/2 cup sour cream or buttermilk
1/2 tsp. white vinegar
1/2 tsp. baking soda

For the frosting

1/4 cup butter
1/2 cup full-fat cream cheese
1 1/2 cups confectioners' sugar
1 tsp. vanilla extract

Preheat the oven to 350° F. Place 12 paper liners in a cupcake pan. (Makes 12 cupcakes.)

Sift the flour, baking powder, and salt into a bowl and set aside. In a small bowl, combine the cocoa powder and food coloring; blend until thick and shiny with no lumps. Cream the butter and sugar together in a large bowl until light and fluffy. Slowly add the egg, then the cocoa paste and vanilla extract; mix until smooth. Add the sifted flour and the sour cream or buttermilk, stirring in alternate spoonfuls until the mixture is well blended. In a cup, mix the vinegar and baking soda; it will fizz! Combine this with the cake mixture.

Spoon the cake mixture into the paper liners, dividing it equally, and bake for 20 minutes. Leave the cakes to cool fully before adding the frosting.

To decorate: Combine the butter and cream cheese; blend until smooth. Sift in the confectioner's sugar and add the vanilla extract. Using a large star-shaped nozzle, ice the cupcakes. Add crowns cut from gold paper using the template on page 136. If desired, make the crown strip longer, then cut hearts from the crown and glue to the crown tips.

"Then followed the Knave of Hearts, carrying the King's crown on a crimson velvet cushion; and, last of all this grand procession, came the King and Queen of Hearts."

RED KING SLIPPERS

The Red King was a sleepy kind of fellow; his loud snores were often mistaken for thunder. These warm slippers are ideal for all the family, from babies to grannies, and they'll make you smile every time you look at their curly toes.

You will need

thick felt—the amount varies depending on the shoe size; to fit an average-size child's foot, you will need 3 pieces of felt, each 8½" x 12"

embroidery thread in contrasting color

40" length of pompom trimming (optional)

other pompoms or scraps of felt for trimmings

Note: If possible, try to get natural wool felt as it is much thicker and warmer than polyester felt.

~ join the heel ~

~ stitch the toe ~

> Using the templates on pages 128–129, cut the four uppers and two soles from felt. Hand sew the heel seam with blanket stitch.

> Again with blanket stitch, sew the uppers together at the front from the top, around the toe curl, down to the point marked "A."

~ attach the sole ~

~ add some decoration ~

> To attach the sole, line up point "B" with the heel seam. Sew the sole in place with blanket stitch.

> Decorate the slippers by adding felt shapes, pompom trimming around the opening, or large pompoms to the toes.

"'It's only the Red King snoring,' said Tweedledee. 'Isn't he a lovely sight?' said Tweedledum.

Alice couldn't say honestly that he was. He had a tall red night-cap on, with a tassel, and he was lying crumpled up into a sort of untidy heap, and snoring loud – 'fit to snore his head off!'"

TWEEDLEDUM & TWEEDLEDEE SHOEBAGS

These drawstring bags do a great job protecting your shoes. They are almost the same but slightly different, just like their namesakes.

You will need per bag

scraps of fabric, such as heavyweight cotton, denim, and linen, for front panel

$12^1/_2$" x $10^1/_4$" heavyweight fabric, for back panel

2 pieces, each $14^1/_4$" x $10^1/_4$", of lightweight cotton, for lining

matching sewing thread

tailor's chalk or disappearing-ink pen

2 lengths of cord or ribbon, each 32" long

9" x 5" fabric, for drawstring hearts

ribbons, lightweight cotton print scraps, braids, and buttons, for decoration

Note: The seam allowance is $^3/_8$" throughout.

✎ To make the patchwork bag front, machine stitch together pieces of contrasting pattern fabrics to make a panel $12^1/_2$" tall x $10^1/_4$" wide. For Dum's bag (top left) we joined eight 4" tall x $5^1/_2$" wide patches. For Dee's bag (bottom right) we pieced together four $6^5/_8$" tall x $5^1/_2$" wide patches.

✎ Press open the seams, then, if necessary, trim the panel down to $12^1/_2$" x $10^1/_4$".

✎ To join the front panel and lining, place together the patchwork panel and one lining piece with right sides facing. Pin and baste. Stitch along one short edge with a $^3/_8$" seam allowance. Repeat with the back panel and the remaining lining. Press open the seams.

✎ Place together the front and back panels and the lining pieces with right sides facing, aligning the main seams between the outer panels and the linings. Pin and baste.

✎ With either tailor's chalk or a disappearing-ink pen, on the lining mark parallel lines at $^3/_4$" and $1^1/_2$" down from the main seam. This is the drawstring channel.

✎ Machine stitch the panels together, starting at the base of the lining, up to the first drawstring channel mark. Start stitching again after the other mark. Repeat on the other side. Leave a 4" opening in the lining for the turning hole.

✎ Turn the bag right sides out through the turning hole and press. Turn under the edges and hand sew the turning hole closed.

✎ Ease the lining down into the outer bag until the bases touch. Approximately $^3/_4$" of the lining will be visible above the top edge of the outer bag. Press along this edge to make a firm crease in the lining.

✎ To make a border, turn down the lining until the drawstring channels can be seen. Press. Topstitch along the border's lower edge.

drawstring channel

outer

lining

turning hole

drawstring channel

drawstring channel

drawstring channel

seam

turned down lining

continued 🖝

SHOEBAGS {CONT}

☞ Attach a safety pin that is small enough to pass through the drawstring channel to one end of an 32" length of ribbon or cord. Pass the safety pin and cord into the left-hand channel hole and thread it around the channel and back out of the same hole. Repeat with the other length of ribbon or cord and the right-hand hole.

To decorate

☞ Using the 2¼" apron heart template on page 139, cut eight hearts with pinking shears from a print fabric. Sandwich one end of a drawstring between two hearts and stitch the hearts together around the edge. Repeat on the three other drawstring ends.

☞ Add any other decoration, such as lines of gold braid or letters and shapes made from narrow gold cord.

To make the rosette

☞ Tear or cut four 5½" x ¾" strips of lightweight cotton. Fold each strip into a loop. Place the loops one on top of each other in a star formation with raw ends together. Secure with a few stitches in the center.

☞ Tear or cut a 16" x 2¼" strip of lightweight cotton. Sew a line of gathering

stitches along one long edge. Pull the thread ends to gather the strip into a circle. Gently flatten the gathers to create even pleats. Press. Sew the two short edges of the strip together.

☞ Place the fabric star in the center of the pleated circle. Secure with a few stitches in the center. Use a large button to cover the center.

☞ Fold in half a 12" length of 1¼"-wide ribbon. Cut the ends into neat diagonal slants. Sew to the underside of the rosette. Secure the rosette to the shoebag with a few stitches.

"Tweedledum and Tweedledee agreed to have a battle!
For Tweedledum said Tweedledee had spoiled his nice new rattle.
Just then flew down a monstrous crow, as black as a tar-barrel!
Which frightened both the heroes so, they quite forgot their quarrel."

– FAMILY LAWYERS –
TWEEDLES
– Est. 1871 –

WE SPECIALISE IN:

FAMILY INTRODUCTIONS

CASE STUDY 1:

Tweedledum is a firm believer in correct manners. "The first thing in a visit is to say 'How d'ye do' and shake hands." If meeting two people at once to save hurting anyones feelings take one hand of each person at the same time. This may lead to a short dance round in a ring (Four times round is usually enough). This dance is a great icebreaker as to say 'How d'ye do' after the dance is slightly belated and you will find that you know the people very well by then."

CONFLICT RESOLVEMENT

CASE STUDY 2:

Last year Tweedledee stole Tweedledum's nice new rattle. Dum wouldn't have minded so much but it was a new one. To bring peace and harmony back to the family, the Tweedles planned a civilised battle between half four and six then stopping for dinner. Ever safety conscious, the brothers protected themselves with bolsters, blankets, hearth-rugs, coal-scuttles and used saucepans for helmets. Dum tends to hit everything he sees and Dee hits everything within reach, whether he sees it or not. By pre-planning the battle the brothers were able to manage all aspects of the fight and resolved their issues with as little fuss as possible.

THE BROTHERS HAVE LEARNED FROM PERSONAL EXPERIENCE HOW TO MANAGE ALL ASPECTS OF FAMILY LIFE AND NOW WISH TO OFFER YOU THEIR KNOWLEDGE

WONDERLAND APRONS

*Create one of these stunning aprons to keep you neat and tidy in the kitchen
while cooking a storm with our "Eat Me" recipes.*

Alice's Apron

You will need

2 3/4 yd of 51"-wide (minimum)
  toile de jouy fabric
2 1/4 yd x 4" lightweight
  white cotton
matching sewing thread
3 1/4-yd length of 3/8"-wide
  navy velvet ribbon
39" length of 3/8"-wide
  white lace

Note: The seam allowance is
3/8" throughout.

☙ Using the template on page 138, cut two bib and skirt pieces from the toile de jouy. Transfer any markings from the template to the fabric.

☙ To make the apron, place the pieces together with right sides facing. Pin, baste, and stitch around the edges with a 3/8" seam allowance, leaving between points "A" and "B" open. If necessary, clip the curved seams. Turn right side out. Press. Turn under a 3/8" hem along the open edge and topstitch closed.

☙ For the neck strap, cut a strip of toile measuring 44" x 4 3/4". Press under a 3/8" hem on all edges, keeping them straight. Fold the strip in half lengthwise with right sides facing out. Topstitch along all four sides.

☙ To make the strap frill, fold the white cotton in half lengthwise with right sides facing out. Press. Pin the strip along the neck strap in evenly spaced box pleats. One way to do this is to pin the middle and ends of the strip to the corresponding points on the strap, then work the pleats within these sections. Baste, then topstitch. Pin the neck strap to the top of the waistband at the marked points "X" and "Y." Pin and sew the strap to the apron with the frill on the outside edge.

☙ For the waistband tie, cut a strip of toile measuring 95" x 6 3/4". Make as for the neck strap. Fold the tie in half and mark the center with a pin. Align this pin with marked point "C" on the apron. Pin in place across the waist and over the neck strap ends. Topstitch in place.

☙ For the skirt frill, cut a strip of toile de jouy measuring 59" x 6 1/4". Turn under a 3/8" hem along both sides and the bottom edge. Trim with velvet ribbon. To make evenly spaced box pleats, pin the raw edge of the frill to the marked line "3" on the apron. Pin and baste, then topstitch. Cover the raw edge with a length of lace and velvet ribbon.

☙ To finish, trim the bib of the apron with lace and velvet ribbon as shown.

HOW TO BOX PLEAT

Fold the fabric so the two upper folds of the pleat face in opposite directions, while the two under folds are laid toward each other.

Queen of Hearts' Apron

You will need

2 ³/₄ yd of 51"-wide (minimum)
   red polka dot cotton
matching sewing thread
4¹/₂-yd length of 2"-wide cream lace

Note: The seam allowance
is ³/₈" throughout.

⟞ Using the template on page 138, cut two bib and skirt pieces from the cotton following the heart neckline. Transfer any markings.

⟞ To make the apron, place the pieces together with right sides facing. Pin and baste. Stitch around the edges with a ³/₈" seam allowance, leaving between points "A" and "B" open. Clip the corners and notch any curved seams. Turn right side out. Press. Turn under a ³/₈" hem along the open V-shaped neckline and press.

⟞ For the neck strap, cut a strip of cotton measuring 44" x 4³/₄". Make as for the method given for Alice's Apron on page 82. Sandwich one end of the neck strap between the apron at point "A." Pin in place. Repeat with the other end at point "B," making sure the strap is not twisted. Topstitch along the neckline between points "A" and "B" to secure the strap and close the opening. Trim the outside edge of the apron with lace.

⟞ For the waistband tie, cut a strip of cotton measuring 95" x 6³/₄". Make as for the neck strap. Fold the tie in half and mark the center with a pin. Align this pin with point "C" on the apron skirt. Pin the tie in place across the waist. Topstitch in place and trim the upper and lower edges with lace.

⟞ For the waistband tie ends, cut four small hearts from the cotton using the template on page 139. For each end, pin two hearts

together with right sides facing. Stitch together, leaving the top edge open for inserting the tie end. Clip the corners and notch any curved seams. Turn right side out. Turn under a ³/₈" hem along the open edge and press. Insert one end of the tie into the heart. Pin in place. Repeat with the other end and the second heart. Topstitch to secure the hearts and close the opening. Trim the hearts with lace on both sides.

⟞ To make the pockets, cut four large hearts from the cotton using the template on page 139. For each pocket, pin two hearts together with right sides facing. Stitch together, leaving one side edge open. Clip the corners and notch any curved seams. Turn right side out. Turn under a ³/₈" hem along the open edges and press. Topstitch to close the opening. Trim the hearts with lace on one side. Topstitch the pockets to the skirt of the apron, leaving the top open.

~ Queen of Hearts' pocket ~

Cheshire Cat Apron

You will need

3⅓ yd of 51"-wide (minimum) striped
  cotton duck cloth
matching sewing thread
9" square of red felt
6¼-yd length of ¾"-wide black hemming
  tape (can be iron-on for ease)

Note: The seam allowance
is ⅜" throughout.

❧ Using the template on page 138, cut
two bib and skirt pieces from the cotton duck
cloth. Transfer any markings.

❧ To make the apron, place the pieces
together with right sides facing. Pin and
baste. Stitch around the edges with a ⅜"
seam allowance, leaving between points "A"
and "B" open. Clip the corners and notch
any curved seams. Turn right side out. Press.
Turn under a ⅜" hem along the neck edge
and press.

❧ For the neck strap, cut a strip of fabric
measuring 44" x 4¾". Make as for Alice's
Apron on page 82. Sandwich one end of the
neck strap between the apron at point "A."
Pin in place. Repeat with the other end at
point "B," making sure the strap is not
twisted. Topstitch along the neckline

between points "A" and "B" to secure the
strap and close the opening.

❧ To make the frills, cut three strips of
fabric measuring 59" x 6¼". Turn under a
⅜" hem on the sides and lower edges of the
frills. Trim with black tape. Pin the raw edge
of one frill to the apron along the marked
line "3," making evenly spaced box pleats.
Baste, then topstitch in place. Repeat along
lines "2" and "1," making sure each frill
overlaps the one below by ⅜".

❧ For the waistband tie, cut a strip of
ticking measuring 95" x 6¾". Make as for
the neck strap. To attach the tie, follow the
method given for the Queen of Hearts'
Apron opposite, making sure the frills are
fully tucked beneath the waistband. Baste,
then topstitch in place.

❧ To make the Cheshire Cat appliqué,
using the template on page 139, cut the cat
shape from red felt. Pin and baste the felt
shape to the upper right of the bib. Topstitch
in place, leaving the tail unstitched and free.

" 'I want a clean cup,' said the Hatter. 'Let's all move one place on.'

He moved on as he spoke, and the Dormouse followed him: the March Hare moved into the Dormouse's place, and Alice rather unwillingly took the place of the March Hare. The Hatter was the only one who got any advantage from the change: and Alice was a good deal worse off, as the March Hare had just upset the milk jug into his plate."

MUSICAL CHAIRS: AN INSTRUCTION
by the Mad Hatter

1 Place a number of chairs in a line. You must have one less chair than participants.

2 All participants must stand in a row in front of the chairs. When the music starts everyone must move around the chairs in a clockwise direction.

3 When the music stops all participants must try to sit on the chair closest to them. The player left without a chair is eliminated and one chair is also removed from the game.

4 Start and stop the music at varying intervals of time. Eliminate one participant and one chair each time.

5 Award a prize to the last remaining participant, that being the person sitting on the last chair.

TEA SET INVITATIONS

Every party needs invitations so why not make these simple and effective cards.
You could always try your hand at Looking-Glass writing for secret messages.

You will need per invitation
4 sheets of thin patterned
  cardboard, each 33" x 23½"
white craft glue
1 mini luggage tag (optional)
alphabet rubber stamps
  or pen

For the envelope
watercolor paper
heart-shaped hole-punch

☞ Using the templates on page 130 and the patterned cardboard, cut one teapot and the two teapot-base disks (small and medium); then cut one teacup, two saucer disks (small for the center and large for the base), and a saucer rim piece. Cut one small connecting tab and one label per invitation.

☞ Glue the saucer rim and center to the saucer base, and the teapot-base center to the base. Fold the connecting tab in half. Glue half of the tab to the lower edge of the back of the teapot or teacup and the other half to the center of the teapot base or saucer.

☞ Either by hand or with a small rubber stamp, write the type of celebration on the label (or luggage tag)—for example, birthday party, anniversary party, wedding—and your message on the back of the invitation.

☞ For the envelope, cut a square of watercolor paper big enough for your invite (test size with scrap paper first) and fold each corner to the center. Hole-punch a heart in the point of the bottom envelope flap. Cut a small scrap of patterned cardboard and glue it behind the heart-shaped hole so the pattern shows through. Glue the envelope's bottom flap to the side flaps. Leave the top flap open so you can place the invitation card inside. When the invite is ready to mail, glue down the top flap of the envelope or use a sticker to secure.

CROWN PLACE CARDS

These crowns make delightful place cards, but they work equally well as quirky little party favors and unusual napkin holders.

*M*ake these crowns in sophisticated creams and gold to add a touch of elegance to your dining table or use brightly patterned cardboard for a children's fun party. You could just make the basic crown and then let your guests decorate them as a party activity; they make great going-home presents.

You will need per place card
1 sheet of thin cardboard,
   8¼" x 12"
ribbons, scraps of paper,
   and stick-on gemstones or
   sequins, for decoration
1 sheet of patterned paper,
   8¼" x 12"
alphabet rubber stamps
   or pen
double-sided tape
14" length of thin elasticated
   cord, to hold crown on head
1 paper napkin

☞ Using the templates on page 129, trace your chosen crown outline onto the reverse of the thin cardboard. Use a hard pencil so no marks are left (although you can easily remove any marks with an eraser).

☞ Cut out the crown shape carefully with either a pair of scissors or a craft knife and cutting mat.

☞ Using a thick needle, pierce two holes in the crown where marked on the template.

☞ Now it's time to get creative! Decorate the crown with sequins, stick-on gemstones and ribbons. Personalize each crown to suit your individual guests.

☞ To make the nameplate, cut the shape from contrasting paper and adhere to the center of the crown with glue or double-sided tape. Add the name of your guest to the the nameplate either with rubber stamps or in pen in your finest handwriting.

☞ Fix a thin strip of double-sided tape to the overlap edges of the crown. Join the edges and fix in place. Make sure the points of the crown line up.

☞ Tie a knot in one end of the elasticated cord. Thread the cord through one of the holes. Thread the other end of the cord through the second hole and tie another knot. If you want to fix the cord more firmly in place, use a square of tape.

☞ To use the crown as a napkin holder, simply push a napkin inside the crown from beneath so it sits neatly inside.

*" To the Looking-Glass world it was Alice that said
'I've a sceptre in hand, I've a crown on my head.
Let the Looking-Glass creatures, whatever they be
Come and dine with the Red Queen, the White Queen, and me!' "*

VINTAGE CAKE STAND

"I love shopping for vintage tea sets; you can pick up some bargains from charity shops, yard sales, and internet auctions sites. My favorite vintage brands are Shelly, Foley, and Tuscan China." Hannah

You will need
4 plates in consecutively smaller sizes
4 small teacups, glasses, or candlesticks
pen
ceramic glue or superglue

➤ Play around with the layout of your cake stand before committing to glue the crockery together.

➤ Find the central point on the base of each piece and mark the spot in pen. For each level, glue the corresponding plate to its connecting teacup, glass, or candlestick, aligning the marks. Allow the glue to set. Working from the bottom up, join the glued sections together layer by layer.

➤ To clean, always wash the cake stand gently by hand.

THE PERFECT AFTERNOON TEA

Afternoon tea is a perfect time for friends to get together for a good gossip and some tasty treats.

Setting the scene

Freshly ironed linens, sparkling silver and fine china are a must for a nicely turned out tea party. Make the centerpiece of the table a well-laden cake stand, while posies of fresh flowers add interest—but nothing too scented that will mask the smell of home-baked cakes and brewing tea. Keep flowers small and low so your guest's view is unobstructed. Lighting is all important at elegant soirees; candlelight or peach-colored light bulbs cast a flattering glow.

Filling the cake stand

On the first tier, place dainty finger sandwiches. On the second tier, small scones with cream and jams served in seperate bowls. An array of bite-size petit fours and pastries will complete your tea. Enjoy!

CHESHIRE CAT SANDWICHES

Watch your very own Cheshire Cat disappear before your eyes as your guests delve into these delicious stripy sandwiches!

You will need
1 loaf of medium-sliced white bread
1 loaf of medium sliced wholewheat bread
butter
sandwich filling of your choice

➤ Butter the white and brown loaves. To make the striped bread, place alternate white and brown slices on top of each other. We layered four slices in a block; each of these blocks makes two sandwiches made up of three-layers.

➤ Push the slices of bread down gently and evenly, then wrap tightly in plastic wrap and freeze for a few hours.

➤ Remove the bread from the freezer and leave to defrost for approximately 30 minutes. Slice downward with a sharp breadknife—much like a normal loaf—through the layers in $^3/_8$" slices to reveal your stripy bread. Neaten the slices at each end by trimming the crusts. Add your favorite sandwich filling.

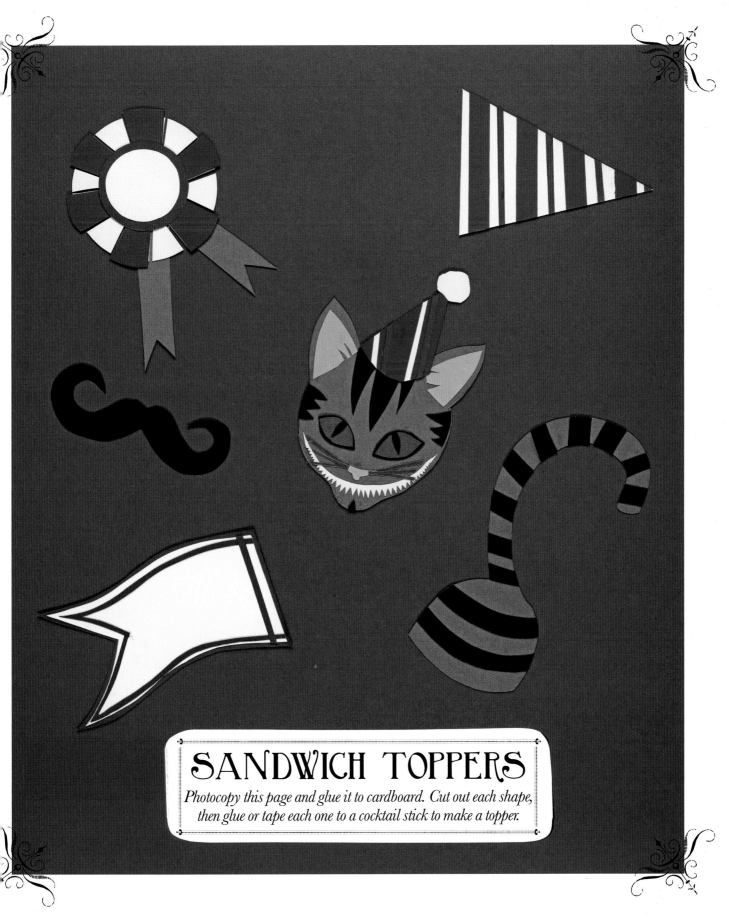

SANDWICH TOPPERS

*Photocopy this page and glue it to cardboard. Cut out each shape,
then glue or tape each one to a cocktail stick to make a topper.*

WONDERLAND COOKIE CUTTERS

Although there are plenty of interesting shaped cookie cutters available, it's always good to be able to make something completely unique for a special occasion. With this method, cutters are simple to make and in almost any shape imaginable.

You will need

disposable aluminum baking pans
(ones with long straight edges are best)
metal ruler
old scissors or tin snips
protective gloves

~ remove the straight sides ~

~ score the overlapped sides ~

↪ Wearing gloves to protect your hands, cut the straight sides from the baking pan. Flatten them out as much as possible. To make a 4" diameter heart cutter you need approximately a 16" length of these straight sides.

↪ Lay all the flat aluminum pieces together in a long line, overlapping each end by approximately ³⁄₈". Using the metal ruler and scissors, score a straight line along the long edge approximately ³⁄₈" in from the rim.

~ press the rim down flat ~

~ shape the cookie cutter ~

~ the finished cutters ~

↪ Fold the rim inward along the scored line and, using closed scissors, press the aluminum down as flat as possible. This locks the strip together.

↪ Gently bend the aluminum strip into your required shape. Join the cutter by slotting one end of the strip into the other. Press together firmly.

↪ Using your fingers and thumbs, smooth out any bends and corners in the cutters to perfect the shape—teacup, mushroom, or pocket watch!

HOW TO "FLOOD" ICE

Flood icing gives a lovely smooth surface to a cookie. It is a very satisfying way of decorating cookies and achieving a professional finish.

You will need
royal icing sugar mix
small amount of water
selection of food colorings
piping bags with small round nozzles
squeezy condiment bottles

1 Mix a small amount of the royal icing sugar with a few drops of water to make a smooth consistency that forms soft peaks. The icing needs to be just stiff enough to keep its shape when piped. Divide the icing into small bowls—one for each color you wish to use—then add the food coloring and mix well.

2 Using a piping bag with a small round nozzle, pipe the outline of each seperate colored area onto your cookies. Leave to dry for a few minutes.

3 Mix a little more royal icing sugar with a few more drops of water to create a runny icing that drips off your spoon. Mix in the food coloring then place in a piping bag (or if you can find them, a plastic condiment bottle as they are less messy and easier to clean). Fill each outlined area with the color to match in zigzags. It's okay to ice three or four cookies at a time as the icing takes a while to dry.

4 Using a cocktail stick, move the icing around to fill any little holes and create a flat surface. Leave to dry (ideally overnight) in a cool place. If you wish to add any extra details or further flourishes to your decoration, use soft-peak icing and a fine nozzle or the excellent ready-made decorating tubes.

WONDERLAND COOKIES

Too many of these magical mushroom cookies might possibly make you grow bigger.

You will need

- 1 cup and 2 tbsp. unsalted butter
- 1 cup and 2 tbsp. superfine sugar
- 1 teaspoon vanilla extract
- 1 extra-large egg, lightly beaten
- 4⅓ cups plain flour

Cream together the butter, sugar, and vanilla extract in a bowl until light and fluffy. Don't overmix, though, or your cookies may spread in the oven.

Add the egg and gently mix. Add the flour gradually and mix well. The dough is ready when it forms a single lump in the bottom of the bowl and no crumbs are left.

Wrap the dough in plastic wrap and chill in the refrigerator for at least 1 hour. (Alternatively, you can freeze the dough for up to one month.) Preheat the oven to 350° F.

Place the dough on a floured surface. Roll out the dough to an even thickness of approximately ¼". Using your cookie cutters, press out the cookie shapes. With a spatula, transfer to a parchment-paper-lined baking sheet. Chill for 30 minutes more.

Bake for 10–12 minutes until the cookies are golden brown. Leave to cool completely on a wire rack.

How long your cookies last will depend on the appetite of who you've made them for! But un-iced, they should last for up to one month in an airtight box.

JAM JAR TOPPERS

You will need

oddments of fabric,
   twice the diameter of
   the lids on your jam jars
elastic bands
a selection of ribbons
   and other trims
stick-on labels

❧ Cut a disk of fabric twice the diameter of your jam-jar lid—ie. for a 3" lid, cut a 6" disk. Trim the circumference with lace or bias binding, or cut a zigzag edge with pinking shears.

❧ Place the disk centrally over the lid and secure with an elastic band. Tie a ribbon over the elastic band to hide it. Write the date and jam flavor on a stick-on label.

PRETTY PRESERVES

Red Rose Petal Jam

This jam has a distinct floral flavor, combining notes of strawberry with citrus.

You will need
8 oz edible red rose petals
2 cups superfine sugar
juice of 2 lemons
few drops of rosewater

Makes 5 medium jars

Place the petals in a colander and rinse them under the faucet. Remove the stems and any discolored petals. Place in a large bowl and cover with water. Place a smaller plate on top of the petals to push them down.

Soak at room temperature for at least 1 hour (this can be done for up to 3 days).

Drain the petals and pat dry with kitchen towel or whiz in a salad spinner. Bruise the petals slightly with your hands and place them back into a bowl. Add a few drops of rosewater to taste. Sprinkle the petals with one third of the sugar and lightly toss to coat evenly. Cover the bowl with plastic wrap and leave overnight to infuse.

In a deep saucepan, bring 4^1/$_4$ cups of water to a boil. Add the lemon juice and remaining two thirds of the sugar. Stir in the petals with a wooden spoon and simmer for 30 minutes.

Bring the mixture back to a boil and simmer for 15–20 minutes, until the jam has thickened. Remove any froth as it boils. To test if the jam has set, spoon a small amount onto a plate and place in the refrigerator for

one minute. If it forms a skin, the jam is ready. If it is still runny, boil the jam and test it every 3 minutes. Leave the jam to cool in the pan for 10 minutes.

To sterilize the jam jars, boil them in water. Pour the jam into the jars, seal, and leave to cool. Take care as the jars will be very hot.

Spread onto some crusty white bread or a croissant with some unsalted butter. Yum!

Merry King Marmalade

Why not spread this fragrant citrus treat on top of some hot toast? Perfect for breakfast.

You will need
6–8 small oranges
juice of 1 lemon
4^3/$_4$ cups granulated sugar

Makes 5 medium jars

Slice the oranges in half and squeeze out their juice. Scoop out any remaining flesh from the oranges and whiz in a blender. Sieve into

a deep saucepan along with the juice. Remove any pith from the orange halves. Slice the rind into thin matchsticks.

Add the lemon juice, rind matchsticks, and 6 cups of water to the orange juice in the pan. Bring to a boil, then simmer for 1^1/$_2$ hours. Remove any froth as it boils. At this stage, for a clear

marmalade, remove the pieces of rind.

Add the sugar and stir well until dissolved. Simmer for 10–15 minutes more or until thickened; remove any more froth as necessary. To test if the marmalade has set, spoon a small amount onto a plate and place in the refrigerator for one minute.

If it forms a skin, the marmalade is ready. If it is still runny, boil and test it every 3 minutes. Leave the marmalade to cool in the pan for 10 minutes.

To sterilize the jam jars, boil them in water. Pour the jam into the jars, seal, and leave to cool. Take care as the jars will be very hot.

"*She took down a jar from one of the shelves as she passed; it was labelled*

ORANGE MARMALADE

but to her great disappointment it was empty."

MARCH HARE'S TEAPOT COZY

Make teatime extra special with this spin on the classic "house" teapot cozy.
Be careful not to gossip too much over your tea as he is listening!

You will need

40" x 40" beige cotton twill

20" x 20" of ³/₄"-thick cotton batting

20" x 8" cotton floral print

20" x 8" white felt

small 4"-square scraps of contrasting cotton floral prints for windows, doors, and curtains

12" length of pompom trimming

32" length of lace

Note: The seam allowance is ³/₈" throughout.

Using the templates on page 133, cut two basic house pieces for the front and back of the cozy from cotton twill. Cut two roof pieces from the floral print. Cut four window pieces from the scraps of contrasting floral prints. Cut one door piece, one door arch, and one heart all from the scraps of contrasting floral prints.

Stitch one roof piece to each of the basic house pieces. Using zigzag stitch, stitch two window pieces to the each of the house pieces, then stitch the door, arch, and heart pieces to the front only. Zigzag stitch across the windows in both directions for the window panes. Zigzag stitch "cake slice" sections on the door arch for the window panes. Sew a length of pompom trimming along the top of each window and a length of lace along the lower edge of the roof.

Using the templates on page 133, cut two basic house pieces from cotton batting. Cut two inner cozy pieces from the cotton twill. To each inner cozy piece pin the decorated front and back of the house with right sides facing. Stitch around the curve leaving the straight lower edge free. Turn the right side out and stuff each with batting. Turn over a double hem on the inner cozy lining so that it sits on the outer side. Pin in place then topstitch to hem.

Using the templates on page 133, cut two outer ears from white felt and two inner ears from scrap floral print cotton. Zigzag stitch the inner ears onto the outer ears. Pinch at the bottom so inner ear is facing inward and pin upside down to front of house (so that the ends are facing upward).

To finish, baste both front and back together along the curve with right sides facing, making sure the roof lines align. Stitch together. Turn right side out and your teapot cozy is ready for its first pot of tea!

"She came in sight of the house of the March Hare: she thought it must be the right house, because the chimneys were shaped like ears and the roof was thatched with fur."

AFTERNOON TEAS

There is nothing more relaxing than a cup of tea, but why not spice your tea up a little with these aromatic combinations.

Each mix makes around 3½ oz of tea, providing you use heaped tablespoons. Simply throw all the ingredients into a bowl and mix. Store in an airtight container or decant into pretty presentation bags and tie with ribbon. Photocopy "The Perfect Cup of Tea" instructional and present it with the tea as a gift.

Black & Blue Tea

5 tablespoons dried cornflower petals
2 tablespoons dried lemon rind
8 tablespoons loose-leaf Earl Grey tea

Cornflower is not only aesthetically stunning with its bright blue petals, but it also holds great health benefits: it is an anti-inflammatory and it improves digestion.

English Rose Tea

5 tablespoons dried red rosebuds
2 tablespoons dried orange rind
8 tablespoons loose-leaf part black tea

This soothing aromatic tea has many traditional medicinal benefits; it is full of antioxidants and vitamin C, which cleanse the body and help with natural defenses.

Sunflower Petal Tea

5 tablespoons dried sunflower petals
10 tablespoons loose-leaf part black tea
1 cinnamon stick

Reminiscent of summer on a chilly day, the rich, sweet honey aroma of sunflower petals with spicy cinnamon adds a sumptuous note to any black tea.

A SERIES OF INSTRUCTIONALS no. 2

THE PERFECT CUP OF TEA

It is traditional to use a teapot while making tea; it allows the tea time to infuse thus giving a fuller flavor.

You will need
Teapot • Tea Strainer
Teapot Cozy (optional)
Cups & Saucers

Fill the kettle with cold fresh water and boil. It is important not to re-boil water as it decreases its oxygen content making the tea less flavorful.

Warm the teapot with a splash of the boiled water and swirl around.

It is usual to add two teaspoons of tea per cup plus one for the pot.

Add boiling water and leave to steep for 3–4 minutes.

Strain into a cup and enjoy!

BEADED NAPKIN RINGS

Making an initial napkin ring for each of your guests gives your tea party a truly personal touch, and they also double as delightful party favors.

You will need

2 pairs round nose pliers
wire cutters
¼" glass or plastic beads
15 gauge silver-plated wire
20 gauge silver-plated wire
22 gauge silver-plated wire
cardboard tube, such as a toilet
    paper tube

For the napkin ring

☞ Cut a 32" length of 15 gauge wire. Wrap the wire around a cardboard tube approximately four times to form a loosely wound coil. Slip the wire coil off of the cardboard tube. Pull the two ends of the wire toward each other to tighten the coil.

☞ Separate one end of the wire slightly from the coil; wrap this separated end around the entire coil to secure, making sure the other end is enclosed. You may find it easier to use round nose pliers to pull the wrapped wire end tight. Gently shape the coil in one hand to form an oval.

~ back of the ring ~

For the decoration

☞ To make the beaded decoration, cut a 14" length of 20 gauge wire. Depending on the intricacy of your chosen initial letter, you may need a slightly longer length of wire.

☞ Using two pairs of round nose pliers, form a small loop at one end of the wire— hold the wire with one pair of pliers and form a loop with the other—to stop the beads from falling off. Thread the wire with your chosen beads. When the wire is fully threaded with beads, make another small loop in the same way. A little space between the beads for movement is preferable.

☞ Referring to the templates on page 131 for inspiration, bend the beaded wire into your chosen shape. If you prefer to form a heart rather than an initial, bend the beaded wire in the middle so that the two halves overlap then gently form each end into a heart. Continue molding the wire until you find a shape that pleases you.

☞ To fix the beaded decoration to the napkin ring, cut a 10" length of 22 gauge wire. With the coil join to the back, wind the wire neatly around the front of the napkin ring and then once over the decoration (between two beads) and back around the napkin ring. Repeat wherever the decoration comes into contact with the napkin ring. Trim all the wire ends and tuck them in for safety.

DUCHESS MACAROONS

*These exquisite rosewater and crushed lavender crème macaroons
are so scrumptious they are good enough for any royal!*

For the rose macaroons

1½ cups confectioners' sugar
4½ oz ground almonds
1 tsp. cream of tartar
3 extra-large egg whites,
   at room temperature
a pinch of salt
¼ cup and 1 tbsp. superfine
   sugar
a few drops of pink food
   coloring
2 tsp. rosewater

For the lavender crème

2 tbsp. unsalted butter
5 tbsp. cream cheese
¾ cup confectioners' sugar
4 heads of fresh edible
   lavender flowers

To decorate

edible crystalized flowers

Makes 20+ macaroons

Preheat the oven to 320° F. Line two baking sheets with baking parchment paper.

In a food processor, grind the contectioners' sugar, almonds, and cream of tartar to a fine dust—this will take at least 3 minutes.

In a large bowl, whisk the egg whites with a pinch of salt until they thicken and form soft peaks—or until you are able to hold the bowl upside down above your head without them falling! Sift the superfine sugar into the egg whites a spoonful at a time. With each addition, slowly whisk the sugar in until the mixture is thick and glossy. Add 2 or 3 drops of pink food coloring along with the rosewater and stir to combine.

Sift half the confectioners' sugar mixture into the egg whites. Using a spatula, gently fold the two together until smooth. Repeat with the remaining confectioners' sugar mixture, but avoid overworking it. The resulting macaroon mixture should have a ribbon-like consistency.

Spoon the mixture into a piping bag and pipe small rounds—each about ¾" wide—onto your prepared baking sheets. It is best to use a plain ⅜"-wide nozzle and, when piping, simply squeeze the bag while holding the nozzle still. Make sure you leave a 1¼" space between each macaroon as they will expand slightly in the oven.

Leave your macaroons to set at room temperature for 15 minutes before baking:

it is very important that they form a skin before going into the oven. Bake for 10–12 minutes, then remove from the oven.

Leave to cool on the baking sheet for 10–15 minutes. The macaroons are ready to move only when the hard outer shell has formed. Remove the macaroons from the baking parchment paper—they will be sticky underneath so be careful; you may find it easier to use a frosting spatula—and place flat side down onto a cooling rack.

To make the lavender crème: Mix the butter with the cream cheese in a bowl, making sure it is well mixed. Sift the confectioners' sugar into the mixture and blend well.

Using a pestle and mortar, gently crush the small lavender flowers and then fold them into the crème. Cover the bowl and leave the mixture to infuse for 1 or 2 hours (for a stronger flavor, leave the mixture overnight).

To assemble: Dollop a teaspoon of the lavender-infused crème onto half of the cooled macaroon shells and then sandwich each together with a second shell. Add the finishing touch by decorating each macaroon with an edible crystalized flower.

Sit back with a cup of tea and enjoy a little piece of macaroon heaven!

PLAYING CARD BUNTING

This wonderful bunting is easy to make and it is very effective. The textured paint surface
on the motifs gives a wooden effect as well as waterproofing—perfect for outdoors.

You will need

2 sheets of white mounting
   board, each 22" x 17"
black, white, and red
   acrylic paint
white craft glue
wide paintbrush
1 sheet of thin cardboard,
   8" x 12", for stencil
hole-punch
11-yd length of 2"-wide
   red ribbon

Makes 4⅓ yards of bunting

✎ Using the templates on page 139, cut four hearts, diamonds, clubs, spades, and playing-card shapes.

✎ In three separate pots—one for each color—mix one part acrylic paint to one part white craft glue. The red paint is for the hearts and diamonds, the black paint is for the clubs and spades, and the white paint is for the playing cards. Lay the card shapes out on sheets of newspaper. With a wide paintbrush, dab paint on one side of the card shape so it has a raised effect. Leave to dry. Repeat this process on other side. For even more texture, repeat this process.

✎ Using the templates on page 139, make the two stencils from the thin cardboard. With contrasting color paint and using the stencils, dab the paint onto the diamonds and playing-card shapes. Leave to dry.

✎ With a hole-punch, make a hole in the center of each club, diamond, and spade card shape, approximately ¾" from the top. Make two holes in each heart and playing-card shape, one on either side.

✎ Cut a 4⅓-yard length of ribbon and hang this where you want the bunting, such as outdoors for a garden party. Cut a shorter length of ribbon for each card shape. Thread each shape onto ribbon and tie them securely to the longer ribbon in a bow.

"'Who cares for you?' said Alice,
'You're nothing but a pack of cards!'"

CURIOUS TEAPOT CAKE

Create this fabulous centerpiece for your tea party; it makes a great talking point and is almost too good to eat! The teapot shape is formed from a microwave sponge cake cooked in a bowl.

For the cake
1 pre-cooked small microwave sponge
   cake made in a 2-quart bowl

For the icing
1 pack of ready-rolled marzipan
1 pack of ready-made rolled fondant icing
apricot jam
4 cups confectioners' sugar, sifted
pink, green, and blue food coloring
disposable piping bags and nozzles
fine paintbrush

For the decoration
2 blocks of white polymer modeling clay
1 box of toothpicks

~ mold the clay handle ~

~ mold the clay spout ~

☞ Warm the clay in your hands so it is workable. To make the teapot handle, roll the clay into a 6"-long sausage approximately ³/₈" wide. Flatten the sausage, then roll each end inward to form a spiral. Mold into a handle shape with the spirals facing inward. Pierce each spiral end with a toothpick.

☞ To make the teapot spout, work the clay into a slight cone shape approximately 4" long. Mold into an "S" shape. With a sharp knife, cut across the top to form the spout hole and along the lower edge that will connect to the teapot. Pierce the lower flat edge with two toothpicks.

~ insert the cocktail sticks ~

~ bake the clay shapes ~

☞ To make the teapot lid bobble, roll a ball approximately ³/₄" in diameter. Pierce with a toothpick.

☞ Place on a tray and bake in the oven following the manufacturer's instructions. Once hardened, leave to cool.

continued

~ cover the teapot cake ~

~ cut out the teapot lid ~

~ assemble the teapot ~

☞ To decorate the cake, place the pre-cooked sponge onto a flat serving plate or board. Using a pastry brush, coat the surface of the cake with apricot jam. Smooth the ready-rolled marzipan onto the cake, covering it completely. Trim any excess from the lower edge to neaten. Repeat with the ready-rolled icing. Keep all the trimmings of icing for the next step.

☞ To make the teapot lid, roll the remaining icing out to approximately ³/₄" thick on a surface lightly dusted with confectioners' sugar. Cut a 2¹/₂" disk from the icing—if you don't have a pastry cutter the correct size, use the rim of a teacup or glass.

☞ Coat one side of the teapot lid with apricot jam and place on top of iced teapot cake. Next, attach the baked clay teapot handle, spout, and lid bobble by pushing the toothpicks into the cake.

~ pipe the iced flowers ~

~ blend the icing ~

~ taa-daaah! ~

☞ Mix up the icing in a bowl following the packet instructions. Divide the icing equally into four small bowls and add food coloring to three, leaving one white. With a piping bag and a 2mm round nozzle, pipe the flower and leaf decoration onto the teapot.

☞ For a more professional look, wet a fine paintbrush and blend the different icing colors into one another.

☞ Serve the finished teapot cake on the plate or board or, alternatively, transfer it carefully to a small cake stand. The perfect centerpiece for any Mad Tea Party!

CHOCOLATE TEASPOONS

The only thing as pointless as a chocolate teapot is a chocolate teaspoon!

You will need
milk or plain chocolate, glass bowl, saucepan which the bowl is slightly too big to fit into, a selection of teaspoons, edible silver, coins

🍂 Break the chocolate into small pieces and place in the glass bowl.

🍂 Fill the saucepan with a small amount water and balance the glass bowl on the rim of the pan. Place over a low heat and stir until the chocolate is melted. Do not allow the chocolate to boil or come into contact with the water.

🍂 To ensure the chocolate sets flat in the spoon bowls, prop the handles up on stacks of coins until level. Carefully fill the spoons with chocolate. Leave to set and then decorate with the edible silver. Stir into coffee, hot milk, or hot chocolate for an indulgent treat.

MAD HATTER HATS

If you've a wedding, garden, mad, or costume party to attend, one of these hats is sure to get you noticed.

For a Mad Hatter's tea party, one must be modeling the very latest head gear! Why not try your hand at making one of our designs?

We used contemporary materials mixed with the traditional—such as poly mesh, a brightly colored starched gauze, which comes in

pliable strips and hat bases. The wonderful thing about millinery is that anything goes. Especially when you are a Mad Hatter!

Flamingo Headpiece

You will need

1¾-yd length of 1¼"-wide poly mesh
bias binding
invisible thread
teardrop base poly mesh headpiece in pink
30-piece fan of flamingo feathers

☞ To make the loops, bend the first
4" of the poly mesh bias binding into an
elongated loop. Stitch securely with
invisible thread. Do not cut. Repeat
with the next 8" of the binding for the
concertina effect. Repeat three times
more, each time adding another 4" to
the loop length.

☞ Sew the loops to the headpiece
with a line of stitches along the lower
edge of the longest loop. Stitch securely
in place at the front.

☞ Split the fan of feathers into
groups of five. Place them between
each loop, then sew in place.

Cup & Saucer Hat

You will need

4"–4¾" plastic plant pot
20" x 20" toile de jouy fabric
white craft glue
1 sheet of stiff cardboard, 8" x 11"
gold spray paint
old teaspoon
39" length of ⅛" gold rope trimming
round base poly mesh headpiece in cream

☞ To cover the plant pot, place a pen
mark on the inside rim of the pot. Make
a snip in the fabric and lie the pot
on its side so the pen mark
lines up with the snip. Roll the
pot along the fabric until it has
done a full rotation. Make
another snip. Adding a ¾" seam
allowance on all sides, cut out the
slightly curved rectangle between
snips. Clip and notch the seam
allowance at ⅜" intervals.

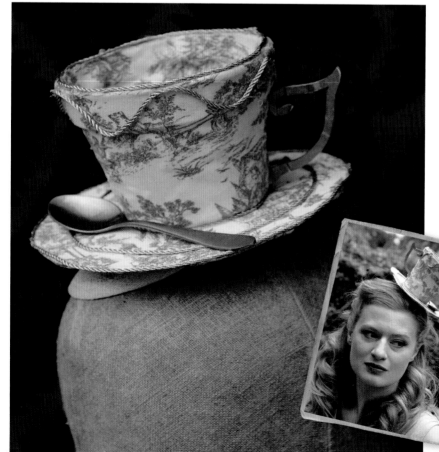

Pour a little white craft glue into a pot and soften with a dash of water. Paint the glue onto the wrong side of the fabric rectangle and smooth onto the plant pot. Trim the overlapping side seam to neaten. Turn the seam allowances over at the rim and base.

To cover the inside of the pot, cut small strips of fabric to the height of the pot. Glue the strips neatly to the inside of the pot. For the inner base lining, trace around the pot's base and cut out a fabric disk. Glue the fabric disk to the inside base for a neat finish.

For the saucer, cut a 6¹/₂" disk from the cardboard. Cut a 8" disk from the fabric. Glue the cardboard to the center of the fabric. Clip and notch the ³/₄" seam allowance and take over to the back of the disk. Glue in place. Leave to dry thoroughly.

Cut a teacup handle from the cardboard and spray with gold paint. Spray the teaspoon with gold paint. Leave to dry.

With a hot glue gun, glue the saucer to the teacup, then glue on the handle. Glue the spoon to the saucer. Decorate with the gold rope trim. Glue the cup and saucer at an angle to the headpiece.

White Rabbit Ears

You will need
2¹/₄-yd length of silver stiff jewelry wire
40" x 20" white satin
³/₄" pearlescent beads
wide poly mesh headband in pink

To make the frame, twist together the ends of the wire to form one large loop. Trim any sharp ends. Keeping the wire flat, pinch the middle together. Mold each side into an ear, forming two petal shapes in a figure eight.

Fold the fabric in half with wrong sides facing. Sandwich the wire frame in between the fabric. Pin in place. Trim any excess fabric along the open edges, leaving a 1¹/₄" seam allowance. Tuck in the seam allowance and pin—stretch the fabric taut but do not pull the frame out of shape. Machine stitch around the outer edges.

To attach the ears to the headband, fold the ears in half at the central point so both are facing foward. Feed the headband in between and wrap the back ear around the front ear to make a knot. Check that the ears are securely fixed and will not move around when worn. Curve the ear tips inward.

For the pearl decoration, cut an 8" length of wire and thread on the pearlescent beads. Tuck into the ear knot and twist the ends of the wire together. Trim any sharp ends.

Playing Card Hat

You will need
thick wool felt: 8" square in each of red and
    white, and 8" x 12" piece in black
wide black hairband
11" length of stiff jewelry wire

✒ Cut out the felt shapes in varying
sizes ($1^1/2$"–$2^1/2$"). Cut two hearts and
two diamonds in red felt; two spades
and one small and one large club in
black; and one card shape in white.

✒ Glue the small club to the card
shape. Mold a semi-circle shape out of
the wire and glue the ends slightly to
one side of the hairband using a hot
glue-gun. Attach the shapes with a
slight overlap onto the wire. To finish,
cut a $^3/8$" x 12" strip of black felt and
glue to the back of the wire, gluing $^1/2$"
at each end to the hairband.

White Rose Hat

You will need
clear plastic haircomb
20 circles $9^1/2$" in diameter and 25 circles
    $7^3/4$" in diameter, all cut from various
    white and cream fabrics (such as stiff
    netting, silk, gauze, and satins)
$3^1/4$" felt disk
spray starch

✒ Fold each of the small and large
circles into quarters and trim the
curved edges into heart shapes. Unfold
and place the large circles one on top of
another in sets of five, alternating the
fabrics and colors. Don't worry about
lining them up too neatly. Repeat with

the small circles. You will now have five
sets of small circles and four sets of
large circles.

✒ Fold each set of five into quarters
and sew a few stitches at the point to
secure the circles together.

✒ Take the disk of felt and sew the
four larger petal quarters to its center,
creating a circle. On top of this sew
four of the five smaller petal quarters,
staggering the first quarter so the top
and bottom set don't line up.

✒ Sew the fifth petal quarter into the
center of the rose. To plump up the rose,
separate each set of petals by pulling
individual petals away from each other.
For extra stiffness spray the rose with
the starch and iron individual tips.

✒ Stitch the haircomb in place on the
felt disk and wear with pride.

" 'Curiouser and curiouser,'
cried Alice
(she was so much
surprised, that for the
moment she quite
forgot how to speak
good English).' "

A
B
C
D   D
E

CROWN
Cut one of A and four of D
Cut two of B, C and E

A
B
C
D
E

CUPCAKE
Cut one of A
Cut two of B, C, D, and E

A
B
C

MUSHROOM
Cut two of A, B and C

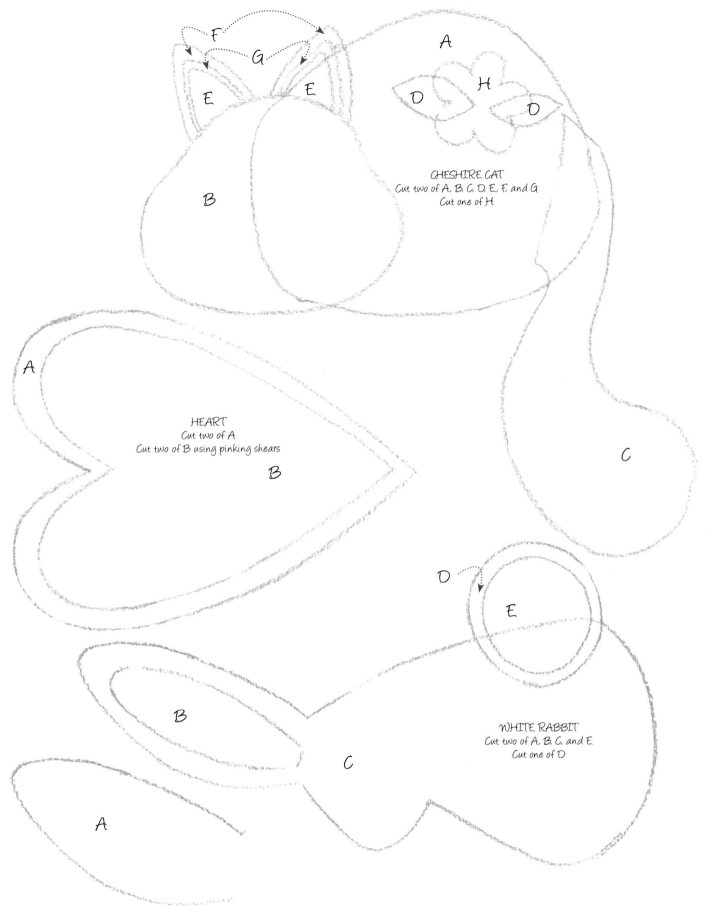

CHESHIRE CAT
Cut two of A, B, C, D, E, F, and G
Cut one of H

F

G

E   E

A

D   H   D

B

A

HEART
Cut two of A
Cut two of B using pinking shears

B

C

D

E

B

WHITE RABBIT
Cut two of A, B, C, and E
Cut one of D

C

A

KEY

Seed stitch   Chain stitch

French knot   Running stitch

Add a bead   Backstitch

This stitch guide shows you what stitch
to use where. The color indicates the
type of stitch and not the color of the
thread, that decision is up to you.
For help on how to do the stitches, see
the embroidery sampler on page 24.

Enlarge cupcake case, base and lid by 140%

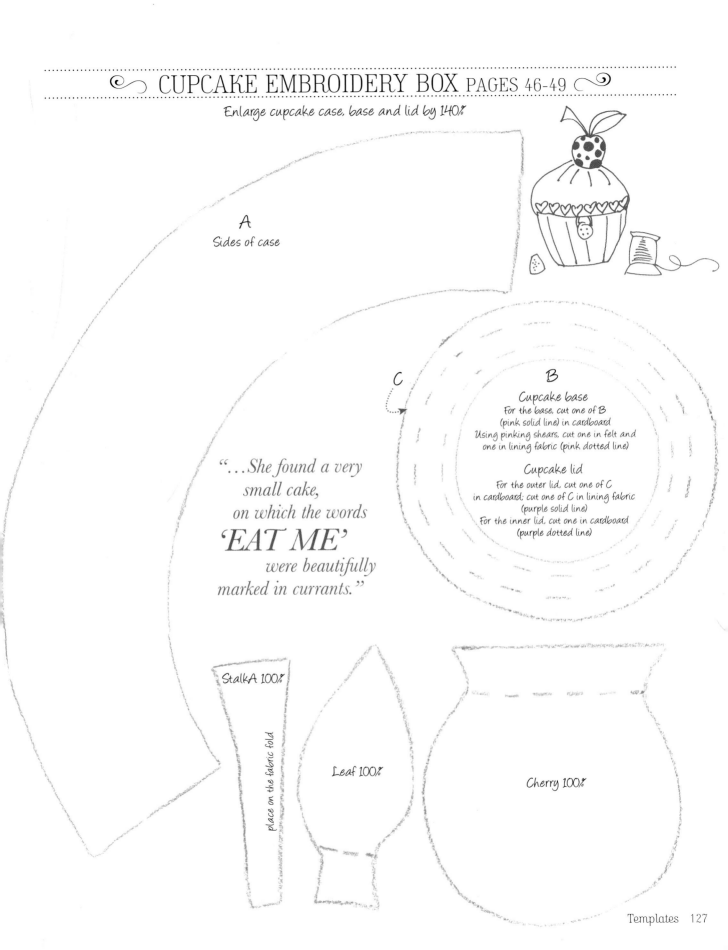

A

Sides of case

C

B

Cupcake base
For the base, cut one of B
(pink solid line) in cardboard
Using pinking shears, cut one in felt and
one in lining fabric (pink dotted line)

Cupcake lid
For the outer lid, cut one of C
in cardboard; cut one of C in lining fabric
(purple solid line)
For the inner lid, cut one in cardboard
(purple dotted line)

*"…She found a very
small cake,
on which the words
'EAT ME'
were beautifully
marked in currants."*

Stalk A 100%

place on the fabric fold

Leaf 100%

Cherry 100%

❧ LAVENDER DORMICE PAGES 22-23 ❧

Mouse pattern pieces are actual size

EARS

B

BODY

ear placement

eye

C

BOTTOM

D

UNDERBELLY

D   tail placement   D

A

❧ RED KING SLIPPERS PAGES 76-77 ❧

For a baby's feet, use at 100%. For a child's size 11½, enlarge by 130%. For a woman's size 7, enlarge by 200%. The percentages given for enlargements are a rough guide only: for a more accurate fit, draw around the foot of the slipper wearer and enlarge the templates so the sole matches your foot outline.

A

UPPER
For one pair of slippers,
cut four uppers

CROWN PLACE CARDS PAGE 90-91

Enlarge each crown shape by 140%

hole

hole

overlap area

overlap area

hole

hole

B

SOLE
For one pair of slippers,
cut two soles

"It's only the Red King snoring."

Enlarge templates by 130%

"*It's always tea-time,*
and we've no time to wash
the things between whiles,'
said the Hatter with a sigh."

SAUCER

LABEL

TEACUP

TEAPOT

TEAPOT
BASE

CHESHIRE CAT HAND WARMER PAGES 44-45

Enlarge template by 120%

quilting guide

quilting guide

embroidery guide

turning hole

NAPKIN RING ALPHABET PAGES 108-109

Use as a guide for the initial letters

A B C D E F G H I J K L M
N O P Q R S T U V W X Y Z

Each square of the graph paper is equivalent to ¾"

T   T

BODY

L

pajama fabric

place on the fabric fold

ARM

A   A

pajama fabric

pajama fabric

TAB

A

L   L

B

LEG

HAT TOP   HAT BRIM

HAT SIDE

Each square of the graph paper is equivalent to 3/4"

INNER TEAPOT COZY

8¼"

13½"

OUTER EARS

11"

INNER EARS

7½"

THE DANDY WHITE RABBIT PAGES 14-17

Each square of the graph paper is equivalent to ¾" or enlarge by 200%

A

HEAD
Cut two

EAR
Cut two in
plain fabric
and two in
patterned

ARM
Cut four

LEG
Cut four

D

BODY
Cut two

B

C

WATCH
Cut two

"The Duchess!
    Oh my dear paws!
Oh my fur and whiskers!
She'll get me executed,
        as sure as ferrets
    are ferrets!"

JACKET BACK
Cut one

place on fold of fabric

place on fold of fabric

TROUSERS
Cut two

JACKET FRONT
Cut two

JACKET LINING
Cut two

"*Oh my ears and whiskers, how late it's getting!*"

INVITATION PILLOW PAGES 26-28

Each square of the graph paper is equivalent to 1½"

Use head at 100%
for the stamp on
the pillow

Enlarge head by 150%
for the stamp on
Alice's bag

Alice

CROWN PAGE 75

Each square of the graph paper is equivalent to 1½"

Each square of the graph paper is equivalent to 1½"

Each square of the graph paper is equivalent to 1½"

A   B

Queen of Hearts'
Apron neckline

X   Y

C

1

2

Cheshire Cat
Apron ruffles

3

Enlarge templates by 160%

CHESHIRE CAT
APRON MOTIF
Enlarge cat by 150%

QUEEN OF HEARTS'
APRON POCKET
Enlarge by 170%

WAISTBAND TIES
Enlarge by 170%

Directory

While making and baking the projects and recipes in this book we found many inspiring people and places for supplies and ideas. Here are some of our favorites.

SUPPLIERS

ANTIQUE CHINA
Look for antique china in your local flea markets, thrift stores or online auction sites, such as eBay:

eBay
Shopping on eBay is a brilliant way to snap up bargains on vintage china. Remember to look for pretty brands such as Shelly, Tuscan China, Foley, and Wedgwood.
www.ebay.com

BAKING SUPPLIES
Inspired by the Wonderland tales, our Alice recipes are typically English ones. If you have difficulty finding any of the ingredients, look online at the following sites:

Wilton
A specialty cake store that stocks a huge array of baking and decorating supplies, including ready-to-use decorators' icing and rolled fondant icing in several colors.
www.wilton.com

Ultimate Baker
For bakeware, including a large range of cookie cutters, and cake decorating ingredients such as rolled fondant icing.
www.cooksdream.com

SEWING SUPPLIES
For general and specialty fabrics, felt, ribbons and trims, sewing notions and tools, try these online suppliers:

Aetna Felt Corporation
Manufacturers of top quality craft felts. They also stock Eco-fi, a felt made from 100% Certified Recycled PET bottles, which is availabled in over 30 colors.
www.aetnafelt.com

American Ribbon
One of the oldest manufacturers of high quality ribbons in the USA, including satin and grosgrain in over 20 colors.
www.americanribbon.com

DMC
Producers of superior quality embroidery floss and other needlework essentials.
www.dmc-usa.com

Free Spirit Fine Quilting Fabric
Producers of a wide range of cotton fabrics for patchwork and quilting, from designers including Amy Butler and Kaffe Fassett.
www.freespiritfabric.com

Riley Blake Designs
Brightly printed cotton fabrics available in bundles and jellyrolls. Also ribbons and trims, including pompoms and ric-rac.
www.rileyblakedesigns.com

JEWELRY MAKING SUPPLIES
For jewelry wire, beads, charms, and other gems, try your local craft store or these online suppliers:

Fire Mountain Gems
Suppliers of an inexhaustible variety of charms, beads, crystals, rhinestones and all other jewelry making supplies, including tools, wire, and sculpting clay.
www.firemountaingems.com

Malin Co.
Manufacturers of wire products, including craft wire for jewelry making in a range of gauges.
www.malinco.com

MILLINERY SUPPLIES
Try your local craft store for millinery supplies or hunt online:

California Millinery Supply Company
Manufacturer of a number of useful items for making your own headware, including hat frames and millinery wire.
www.californiamillinery.net

From the Neck Up
This website has a good list of millinery suppliers.
www.hatbook.com

INSPIRATION

Alice's Shop

This is the actual shop featured in Carroll's Through the Looking Glass as depicted by Tenniel in two illustrations. It is also where the real Alice Liddel shopped for sweets. It is full of Alice treasures.
83 St. Aldates
Oxford OX1 1RA
+44 (0)1865 723793
www.aliceinwonderlandshop.co.uk

Alice Sculptures

These unique brass sculptures were commissioned by George Delacorte in honor of his wife, Margarita and are a wonderful place to visit if you are ever in town.
East Side
Central Park
NYC
www.centralpark.com

Alice's Tea Cup

A whimsical tea shop with Alice in Wonderland themed murals and an enticing menu of teas from around the world.
220 East 81st Street
NYC 10028
212 734-4TEA
www.alicesteacup.com

Alice Tour

Bring Victorian England and the world of Lewis Carroll back to life on a walking tour of Oxford with local historian Mark Davies, author of Alice In Waterland.
+44 (0)1865 798254
www.oxfordwaterwalks.co.uk

Bailey Tomlin Hats

Designer Bridget Tomlin truly is The Mad Hatter; her fantastical headware designs are the perfect accessory for any tea party.
Clockwork Studios
38 Southwell Road
London SE4 9PG
+44 (0)20 7274 9588
www.baileytomlin.com

Beatrix Ong

Designer Beatrix Ong's London shoe shop has taken inspiration from the Alice tales with her giant knitted clock, stack of playing cards, and even a Cheshire Cat on the back wall.
8 Newburgh Street
(just off Carnaby Street)
London W1F 7RJ
+44 (0)20 3463 7369
www.beatrixong.com

Bridport Old Bookshop

Possibly the most wonderful old bookshop in the world: this hidden gem is full of vintage books. specializing in children's stories.
11 South Street
Bridport
Dorset DT6 3NR
+44 (0)1308 425698

Christ Church College, Oxford

This is where Lewis Carroll studied and lived, you can visit the university and its Great Hall.
St. Aldates
Oxford OX1 1DP
www.chch.ox.ac.uk

Laduree

Simply the best macaroons in the world! A taste of heaven in every morsel.
87–135 Brompton Road
London SW1X 7XL
www.laduree.fr

Les Trois Garçons

As soon as you walk through the door of this restaurant you feel like you have entered into another world, surrounded by theatrical stuffed animals dressed in crowns and jewels. The food is also out of this world!
1 Club Row
London E1 6JX
+44 (0)20 7613 1924
www.loungelover.co.uk

The Lewis Carroll Society

Founded in 1969 to bring together people with an interest in Charles Dodgson, to promote his life and works.
50 Lauderdale Mansions
Lauderdale Road
London W9 1NE
www.lewiscarrollsociety.org.uk

Thelermont Hupton

The place for surreal homeware design injecting humor into every piece, such as the Stuck On You hooks. Well worth a look.
Station Approach
London Road
Great Chesterford CB10 1NY
+44 (0)1799 531986
www.thelermonthupton.com

Hannah Read-Baldrey

To see what Hannah's been up to when not book-bound, log on to
www.couturecraft.blogspot.com

Sylvie Fleury

www.sylviefleury.com

Tim Walker

An inspiring photographer who loves fairytales and grand scales.
www.timwalkerphotography.com

Tiffany Mumford

An equally inspiring photographer, who we worked with to create this book.
www.tiffanymumford.com

" *A large rose-tree stood near the entrance of the garden: the roses growing on it were white, but there were three gardeners at it, busily painting them red. Alice thought this a very curious thing* "

Index

Hannah & Christine

With thanks

To Jane, Lisa & Helen at Quadrille for their guidance, encouragement and belief in us and our mad ideas. To Tiffany for her amazing photography and for reining us in when our ideas went that little too crazy.

Hannah I have to thank my amazing parents, Matthew and Stephanie, for allowing us to take over their house for two weeks. My wonderful husband, Brendan, for (constantly) living in our mad house with my crazy things coming and going. And to our family cat, Harold, who will be very much missed.

Christine Thank you so much to my remarkable parents for all their support and belief in me and my endeavors. To mum for her roadtesting and research, to dad for his wooden flamingos and problem-solving and to both of them for giving me my skills and knowledge of all things craft. To my wonderful sister Jo, Ian, Oliver, and Elliot for their support and slipper-trying-on. To Jake, Kirsty, Laura, Stuart, Matt, Hannah, Cath, and Lottie, I promise I'll talk about something else from now on!